NIGH

DEN PATRICK is the author o
published in 2014, and was nominated for the British Fantasy
Society Award for Best Newcomer in 2015. *Nightfall* follows
Witchsign and *Stormtide* as the final title in the acclaimed The
Ashen Torment series. He lives in Chelmsford with his wife
and their two cats.

You can find Den on Twitter at @Den_Patrick

Also by Den Patrick

NIGHTFALL

DEN PATRICK

Book Three of The Ashen Torment

HARPER
Voyager

Harper*Voyager*
An imprint of HarperCollins*Publishers*
1 London Bridge Street
London SE1 9GF

www.harpercollins.co.uk

HarperCollins*Publishers*
1st Floor, Watermarque Building, Ringsend Road
Dublin 4, Ireland

First published by HarperCollins*Publishers* 2020

This paperback edition 2021
1

A catalogue record for this book is available from the British Library

ISBN: 978-0-00-822824-8

Set in Meridien by Palimpsest Book Production Limited, Falkirk, Stirlingshire

Printed and bound in the UK by CPI Group (UK) Ltd, Croydon CR0 4YY

MIX
Paper from
responsible sources
FSC **FSC™ C007454**
www.fsc.org

This book is produced from independently certified FSC™ paper
to ensure responsible forest management.

For more information visit: www.harpercollins.co.uk/green

For Simon and Heather

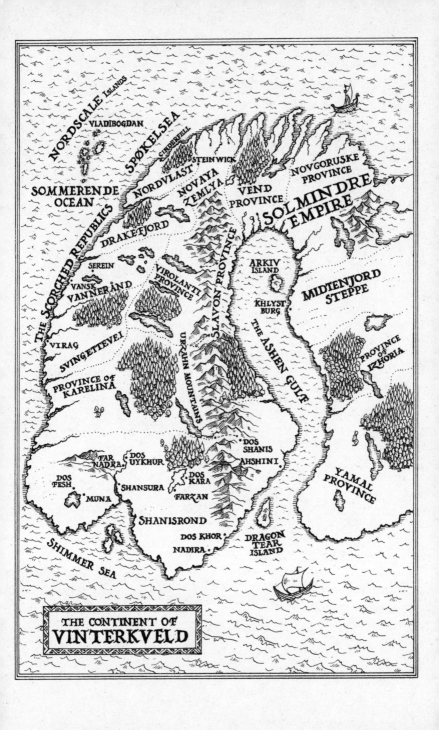

THE CONTINENT OF
VINTERKVELD

CHAPTER ONE

Kjellrunn

Word of the Solmindre Empire's defeat at Dos Khor spread across the continent in a thousand conspiratorial whispers. As ever, when the Vartiainens are involved, it was difficult to discern truth from hyperbole. With hindsight, I came to realize that even the most outlandish exaggeration was a pale shadow compared to the Stormtide Prophet.

– From the memoir of Drakina Tveit,
Lead Librarian of Midtenjord Province

Kjellrunn stood at one end of the altar with her head bowed, willing herself not cry. She was attired in the vestments of a priestess of Frejna, her hair plaited into an elegant crown around her head. Trine stood in a similar pose at the opposite end of the altar and was careful to avoid catching Kjellrunn's gaze. Sundra greeted the townsfolk with Maxim at the temple door as they entered. The sun had begun to set and a fragile calm descended on Dos Khor after the shocking events of the previous day. Novices and crew members from the *Watcher's Wait* stood quietly at the back of the temple watching the small benches fill with local worshippers. All the seats were taken and yet more people came through the doors, uncertainty written on their faces. Soon the congregation stood three deep at the sides of the circular temple. Kjellrunn imagined she could feel a breathless need. These people had come to hear something that made sense of all they had seen. The leviathan had been shocking in size and fury, more shocking still for the simple truth that a girl such as Kjellrunn could summon it from the sea to destroy two Imperial galleons.

'Are you sure you're up to this?' said Romola as she emerged from the shadows. A serious expression crossed the pirate's face, replacing the usual look of wry amusement. 'Where I come from we give people a few days to get used to the loss before we say goodbye.'

Kjellrunn leaned forward and whispered, 'We can't delay in this heat. The bodies will go bad . . . It has to be now.' Romola nodded and made to turn away but Kjellrunn took her by the hand. The pirate raised an eyebrow. 'But I agree with you,' added Kjellrunn. 'For what's it worth, I think we could all use some time to catch our breath.'

The service was especially long. The names and ages of the children who had died defending Dos Khor were read out, prompting tears from the townsfolk. Sundra moved on to the pirates next, though she had the good grace to call them sailors, and praised their courage in the face of such intimidating odds. Kjellrunn listened to the high priestess's words and a moment later Maxim would translate what Sundra had said for the sake of the local congregation. The novices and the pirates hugged one another, numb with shock and hollow-eyed. And then the high priestess spoke warmly of the renegade Vigilant who had served as a mother and a mentor to the novices. Kjellrunn squeezed her eyes shut and forced herself not to cry. She would grieve Mistress Kamalov in private, she promised herself.

Finally, when Kjellrunn could bear no more, Sundra brought the mass funeral to a close and the townsfolk patiently queued before the altar. Each person kissed the fingertips of their left hand and touched it to the stone as they bowed, before setting down one coin and one piece of fruit. All of the worshippers shot glances of awe at Kjellrunn, who bowed to each of them and forced a smile as best she could.

'What are they doing?' said Kjellrunn quietly when she caught Sundra's eye.

'Perhaps it is the custom here?' Sundra smiled as another person left a coin and piece of fruit on the altar. 'Or perhaps they are merely giving their thanks.'

The custom took half as long as the ceremony itself and Maxim appeared through the last of the worshippers. Kjellrunn had not had a chance to speak to the boy since the previous day. He had been busy preparing the temple while Romola had insisted Kjellrunn rest alone in her room.

'It's nice to see you back in a black dress again,' said Maxim.

'I think it's called a vestment.' Kjellrunn plucked at the linen fabric.

Maxim shrugged. 'Still looks like a dress no matter the name.'

Kjellrunn held her arms out to him and they hugged. For a fleeting second she thought of Steiner, wondering what it would have been like to be the older sibling.

'You know they have a fancy name for you now?' said Maxim. 'The Stormtide Prophet. Seems to me you didn't really need that book about Frejna's wrathful aspect.'

'I suppose not. The answers were inside me the whole time. They just took a while to find.' Maxim took her hand in his and tugged. 'What are you doing?' she asked.

'Leading you outside.'

'It's been a long day, Maxim. I'm not sure I feel like meeting anyone right now. So much has happened—'

'And a lot of the townspeople are still here. They want to thank the Stormtide Prophet personally.' The boy grinned.

'Come on, it'll take your mind off things, just for a moment.' He began to lead her away as Sundra called after them.

'Tread carefully,' said the old woman. 'Nothing like this has happened for a very long time. There's no telling how people will react.'

Trine remained standing by the altar, her gaze sliding between Sundra and Kjellrunn.

'Hoy there,' said Kjellrunn. Trine's eyes widened, clearly surprised that she was being addressed. The girl, who was about the same age as Kjellrunn and just as scrawny, had been a constant thorn of irritation since they first come into contact with each other.

'I think there's been more than enough fighting lately,' continued Kjellrunn.

'Too much,' replied Trine.

'There's no good reason you and I have to be at odds with each other. Agreed?'

'Of course.'

'And we'll need to find a way to cremate bodies without you using your powers. You'll get sick if you keep using the arcane so regularly. Mistress Kamalov was right. I should never have suggested it. It was wrong of me.'

A small smile crept across Sundra's face and Kjellrunn took it as one of approval.

'How did you do it?' Trine cleared her throat, her expression wary, barely able to maintain eye contact. 'How did you summon the leviathan?'

'I don't know.' Kjellrunn rubbed her forehead wearily. 'Not really. I just know I was angry and that I wanted to protect everyone.'

'I feel the same way. You know, when the fire comes.' Trine forced a wary smile. 'We have that in common at least.'

'I think we have more in common that either of us would like to admit,' replied Kjellrunn. 'That's what Mistress Kamalov said, before she—' But Kjellrunn couldn't finish the sentence. An image of the renegade Vigilant flashed before her eyes. One moment she had been on the beach, directing the flow of battle; the next she had died, cruelly burned by arcane fire. Burned by the very Empire she had fled.

'You should go,' said Trine. 'There are a lot of people who want to meet you. We'll speak later, I hope.'

'We will,' replied Kjellrunn, surprised to find that not only was she telling the truth, but perhaps she was looking forward to it. She followed Maxim into the street, where knots of people waited, sipping from clay mugs and sharing flatbreads. There was a hushed, fragile quality to the conversations and people spoke in reverent tones. Smiles appeared on the faces of the townspeople as they caught sight of Kjellrunn and many bowed on instinct.

'This is all very strange,' she whispered.

'One day you're running away from the temple' – Maxim shrugged – 'the next you're destroying Imperial galleons. It's never not strange with a Vartiainen around.'

'We all serve in our own way,' said Kjellrunn, hearing Mistress Kamalov's wisdom in her words. She almost smiled and wondered where Steiner and her father were, but didn't have the chance to linger on her thoughts for long. The people of Dos Khor approached, keen to know more of the Stormtide Prophet.

'Kjellrunn, wake up.'

She opened her eyes and squinted at her bedroom door with bleary irritation. The townspeople had kept her busy late into the night until Sundra had insisted she go to bed and get some rest.

'What is it?' she called out, her voice a dull croak. Maxim's head peeked around the edge of the door. There was a frantic cast to his eyes that caused her pulse to race a little faster.

'You know how Frejna has her two crows?'

'Of course. Se and Venter.' Kjellrunn swung her legs out of bed, bemused why Maxim should arrive so early with such questions about the goddesses.

'And how Frøya has her two cats?'

'Diplo and Lelse.' Kjellrunn frowned. 'Maxim, these are folk tales that even small children know.'

'You're wrong. A lot of children don't know the old tales because the Empire didn't like anyone talking about the goddesses.'

'What's got into you this morning?' asked Kjellrunn, crossing the room to the door.

'Get dressed and come downstairs.' Maxim hurried down the tower's stone steps. 'And be quick!' he called over his shoulder.

Kjellrunn pulled on her vestments and straightened them as best she could; then she pulled a comb through her hair, thinking of all the times Steiner had teased her for the unruly tangle.

'I'm a priestess now,' she reminded herself. 'I need to look like a priestess.'

She descended the stairs to the temple proper, hearing low voices and the occasional peal of laughter. The novices were arrayed around the altar in a semicircle; many were kneeling and attending to something on the floor.

'What's going on?' whispered Kjellrunn to herself. Sundra stood by the altar with a look of cheerful confusion and Kjellrunn understood why. 'Where did all of these cats come from? There are so many of them. Are they strays?'

'They were in here this morning, first thing.' Sundra shrugged. 'Sleeping on the altar or curled up on the benches. Strange that they should only come to the temple now; we've been here for weeks.'

One by one, all of the cats turned to stare at Kjellrunn.

Tortoiseshell and long-haired gazed at her with unblinking eyes. Black and white, tabbies, and those the colours of rust and gold looked in her direction. All began to purr with a sound that was alarming in its intensity. Sundra began a long, helpless, wheezy laugh.

'This isn't funny,' said Kjellrunn, feeling uncomfortable under the watchful gazes of so many creatures.

'It seems Frøya has sent a sign, as if more were needed, that you are her chosen one.'

'But Frøya only has two cats,' replied Kjellrunn.

'Frøya has been known to overdo it,' admitted Sundra.

The rest of the day proved to be equally strange. Kjellrunn headed to the beach where they had fought against the Empire. The many felines followed like an entourage. The novices followed in turn, fascinated by Kjellrunn and the cats in equal measure. Romola's crew were already stripping the Imperial ships for timbers they could use to repair the *Watcher's Wait*. The dull sound of industry was carried on the breeze as the men and women sweated and grunted, toiling on the wrecks as best they could.

'Did I really snap that in two?' Kjellrunn nodded to the sculpture of a hand. Once it had stood some twenty feet tall, but now it was missing its fingers.

'You broke off the top section and flung it at the Imperial galleons,' replied Maxim. 'I'd be completely terrified of you if I didn't know you were on our side.'

Kjellrunn though the boy was merely gaming with her, but she caught the look in his eye and the truth of his words: she was wielding powers that others could barely comprehend. Even novices trained at Vladibogdan struggled to understand the raw strength of her abilities.

'You know I'd never hurt you. I'll do anything to keep you safe.' She spoke the words to Maxim, but her thoughts had drifted across the Ashen Gulf to Steiner and Marek.

Arcane fire had blackened the pale sand, but the winds had erased the scorch marks. Kjellrunn looked for the place where Mistress Kamalov had breathed her last obdurate breath, and was frustrated when she couldn't find the spot her mentor had fallen.

'Why come back here?' said Maxim, his tone quiet. Kjellrunn looked up from her musing to see the boy had a sullen expression in his eyes.

'I don't know really,' admitted Kjellrunn. 'I just wanted . . .'

'A lot of people died here. It's a wretched place.' And with that the boy slunk away, heading towards the town with rounded shoulders, his head hung low. Kjellrunn took a few moments to thank the dead for their sacrifice before her thoughts turned to the sea. She sent her awareness out over the waves and down into the cool depths. Something brushed against her senses, a smell of salt, a vast pressure at her brow; sound became muted in that moment.

'So you're still here,' breathed Kjellrunn to the presence in the water. 'You're still here,' she repeated with a slow smile.

It didn't take long to find Maxim, though the trail of cats and novices was an unwelcome impediment to someone who enjoyed wandering alone as much as Kjellrunn did. The town square of Dos Khor was crowded with carts and wagons of a visiting caravan. Traders were setting up stalls and the townsfolk were already milling about in anticipation of hard-to-find foods and spices.

Maxim was talking to an older boy who was peeling an orange and gesturing in a lazy fashion. Kjellrunn felt a spike of irritation . . . no, she realized, jealousy. The older boy was dark-skinned, with a wide face and strong cheekbones. He was perhaps Steiner's age; he certainly seemed to have Steiner's confidence.

'North?' said Maxim.

'Yes, across the desert from Ahshini.' He cast a look over his shoulder at the caravan. 'We travel down here three times a year to trade and get the news, but this time I'm here for something more special.'

'Who's this, Maxim?' said Kjellrunn, stepping closer and drawing herself up to her full height. She hoped she looked imposing in her black vestments.

'I'm Xen-wa.' He grinned and proffered Kjellrunn a segment of orange. For some reason she found his easygoing nature galling. This was the site of a battle, after all.

'I don't want your fruit,' she said, trying to imitate Sundra at her most stern. 'What is it you're seeking?' Maxim frowned at her in confusion.

'Unless I'm wrong,' said Xen-wa, 'I think I'm seeking you.' He tossed the orange segment in the air and caught in his mouth.

'Are you an Imperial spy?' blurted Kjellrunn before she'd really thought what she wanted to say.

'I wouldn't be a very good one if I admitted it to you, would I?'

Maxim laughed and Kjellrunn felt herself blush. She'd never had much cause to speak to boys her own age in Nordvlast. The experience was nothing like she had imagined.

'I'm a storyweaver,' said Xen-wa. 'I'm not dangerous. Well, mostly not. I come seeking the Stormtide Prophet. The air is alive with whispers on the wind, whispers that speak of Frøya's disciples returning, the Lovers' uprising, and the death of Veles, father of gholes.'

'Who are the Lovers?' said Kjellrunn, turning up her nose.

'Steiner Vartiainen and his wise woman, Kristofine. That's what they're calling them. The Lovers.'

'You know about Steiner?' Kjellrunn took a step closer. 'He's still alive?'

'I know only what I've heard,' said the storyweaver. 'And I'll trade you a tale for a tale.'

'What do you want to know?' said Kjellrunn. She was desperate for word of her brother and father.

'I want to know how you destroyed two Imperial galleons.' Xen-wa flashed his irritating smile. 'You're her, aren't you? The Stormtide Prophet, Chosen of Frøya.'

Kjellrunn was about to answer but looked over her shoulder, where the novices all gazed at her with wary reverence. Any number of cats wove in between her ankles or watched the unfolding conversation as if they understood every word. It seemed ridiculous to even attempt denying it.

'My name is Kjellrunn,' she replied. 'Come to the temple and I'll tell you what you want to know.' She held up one finger. 'And in return you'll tell me of my brother.'

The self-assured smile slipped from Xen-wa's face and Kjellrunn felt a chill pass through her. The storyweaver performed a small bow.

'It will be as you say, prophet.'

CHAPTER TWO

Steiner

Until that point I had been consumed with the quiet and subtle work of gathering information for Felgenhauer, who had disguised herself as another Vigilant. I confess, I felt adrift and without purpose after the Matriarch-Commissar departed with her nephew.

> – From the memoir of Drakina Tveit,
> Lead Librarian of Midtenjord Province

It was just before dawn; a prelude to the sun lay across the horizon like the dull steel of a battered blade. Dark grey clouds crowded the sky as the *Morskoy Volk* sailed the Ashen Gulf, the dark green waters turbulent beneath the hull. Steiner stood at the prow of the ship pondering the fate of his father.

All winter they had travelled across the continent together, often freezing, often hungry, always fearful of discovery by Imperial soldiers. The spring promised only a chill rain, the turmoil of revolution, and perhaps his father's execution at the hands of the Emperor himself. Steiner glowered at the distant coastline, cursing the time it took to travel each league. He wanted nothing more than to make port at Khlystburg.

'How much longer?' said a woman's voice behind him.

Steiner forced a brave smile and turned to Kristofine, reaching out on instinct to slip an arm around her waist.

'I'm not sure. The captain told me to stop asking him. It seems the winds have been on the change.' Kristofine glanced over her shoulder to the stern of the ship, where Captain Sedey tended the wheel and pretended not to notice the young lovers. Sedey was a heavyset man in his fifties, missing the lobe of one ear along with one of his eye teeth. His long and lank black hair had been pulled back into a ponytail beneath a greasy hat. 'I think he regrets bringing us aboard.'

'I'm sure he'll feel differently once Felgenhauer pays him.' Kristofine pressed her head against his shoulder. 'Did you get any sleep?'

'Not much.' Steiner rubbed at his eyes. 'All I could think of was Silverdust being eaten alive by Bittervinge. I came up on deck to clear my thoughts but . . .' His mouth twisted in a grimace of upset and his shoulders slumped as his gaze fell on the eastern horizon.

'You're worried for your father.'

He nodded and sighed. There was nothing Kristofine could say, no promise she could make that Marek would be returned to them unharmed, but he was glad of her company all the same.

'We lose two people for every one who joins our cause,' Steiner said after a time.

'That's not true,' Kristofine remonstrated gently. 'You have no idea how many people are out there' – she gestured towards Slavon and all the provinces and republics to the west – 'that have been inspired by what we've done.'

'But Silverdust. All those soldiers.'

'They knew what they were getting themselves into. We have to keep fighting for that. We have to keep fighting for them. Besides, you're the dragon rider, remember?'

'Steiner the Unbroken,' he replied, his tone laced with sarcasm. 'I don't feel very unbroken lately.'

'But together, we're the Lovers, bringing hope and rebellion to Vinterkveld.' She said all of this with a wry smile and Steiner felt himself grin in response. 'It will do no good for Steiner the Unbroken to be maudlin, will it?'

Steiner nodded. 'Where would I be without you?'

Kristofine's answer was interrupted as the former Matriarch-Commissar of Vladibogdan arrived on deck. Felgenhauer, Steiner's aunt, stared at both of them and for a fleeting moment a look of irritation crossed her face. She was flanked by Sergeant Tomasz and Lieutenant Reka.

'I wasn't sure if you'd made it out of the library,' said Steiner to Reka. He grinned and grasped the soldier's forearm.

'I wasn't sure myself,' replied the lieutenant. 'I was out cold when they dragged me from the library. I only woke this morning. You fought well.'

'It was chaos.' Steiner's expression darkened. 'Not sure if I was fighting so much as staying alive.'

'Well, I'm glad you did,' replied Tomasz. 'Your aunt would skin us alive if we let anything happen to you.' Another look of irritation troubled Felgenhauer's face and Steiner felt his own annoyance rise in response.

'On the subject of fighting,' said the former Matriarch-Commissar, 'Kristofine nearly died in the library. No civilian should be caught up in such harrowing circumstances.'

'Civilian?' said Kristofine, her voice quiet and firm. 'There was nothing civil about my sword when I thrust it into Bittervinge's throat.'

'Kristofine recruited a gang of bandits to our cause,' said Steiner. 'We would never have made it without her. She's hardly a civilian.'

'The fact that you survived is a miracle,' continued

Felgenhauer, ignoring her nephew. 'Steiner spent more time keeping you safe than actually fighting.'

'That's not true,' said Steiner, annoyance giving way to anger.

'What are you saying?' added Kristofine.

'I think it best' – Felgenhauer narrowed her eyes – 'for your safety and Steiner's, that you remain with the ship when we go ashore at Khlystburg.'

'My place is at Steiner's side.' Kristofine said it loud enough that even the sailors at the stern of the boat looked up from their chores.

'And I'm ordering you to stay behind.'

'Ordering?' Steiner snorted an incredulous laugh. 'You're not a Matriarch-Commissar any more, and we were never soldiers.'

'Steiner.' Felgenhauer shook her head. 'You've already lost your father—'

'I didn't lose Marek,' snarled Steiner. 'He was taken from me. And I will get him back.'

Felgenhauer held up her hands with a placating gesture. 'I'm just trying to make sure you don't lose anyone else, and fight a rebellion at the same time. Prisoners don't last very long in the Emperor's presence. You should prepare yourself for the worst.'

No one had much to say after that and the knot of people unravelled. Tomasz and Felgenhauer headed to the stern to speak with Captain Sedey. His aunt glared over her shoulder as she walked away.

'You know I've trained a few soldiers in my time,' said Reka quietly as he looked out to sea. 'I've never taught a woman, mind.'

'Woman are just like men,' said Kristofine. 'Just more adaptable.'

'Adaptable?' replied Reka, looking at her from the corner of his eye with curiosity. 'How's that?'

'We have to be adaptable to put up the changing whims of you menfolk.'

Reka let out a gruff laugh. 'Do you still have your sword?' Kristofine nodded. 'Good. You can adapt to my lessons. They start in an hour.'

'Are you serious?' Steiner could barely believe what he was hearing.

'Do I look serious?' replied Reka.

'You do look fairly serious, now you mention it,' replied Kristofine.

Steiner smiled and clapped the man on the shoulder. 'Thank you for this.'

'Don't get too comfortable, dragon rider. You're getting lessons too. I saw you swinging that hammer around. It's a wonder you haven't hurt yourself.'

'What?'

'Lessons!' replied Reka. 'For both of you. You're going to have to fight like legends if you want to be remembered as legends.'

'I just want to get my father back,' muttered Steiner.

'That's all well and good,' said Reka, sounding neither well nor good, 'but there's a rebellion on, if you hadn't noticed.'

'I'll get my sword,' said Kristofine.

'I'll get my sledgehammer,' said Steiner, feeling a touch of chagrin as he went below decks.

Reka was patient, tough and fair in equal measure and Steiner found himself thinking of his father often during the lesson. The men had little in common other than that they had both been soldiers for the Empire at some point but Steiner drew comparisons between the two of them nonetheless.

'That's good,' said Reka as Steiner and Kristofine performed an attack with their very different weapons against imaginary opponents. 'Too many times I've seen both of you overbalance and leave yourself open. This is better. Of course, fighting on dry land will be better still, but we have to work with what we have.'

Steiner felt a small surge of pride that he was improving, and Kristofine flashed a grin at him, caught up in the same feeling no doubt. Reka had them switch their weapons for old broomsticks which were cut down to an appropriate length.

'These aren't ideal but the principles are the same.' The lieutenant sparred with them slowly, explaining as he went: parry, riposte, the placement of feet, the disposition of weight, and other soldier's secrets. Before long they were sparring with each other, though Steiner felt about as uncomfortable raising a weapon to Kristofine as he could remember, even if it was only a broom handle.

'That's good,' said Reka. 'Now repeat the sequence I taught you again, but faster.'

A few of Sedey's sailors watched the weapons practice with admiring glances, no doubt amused to have such famous passengers. Felgenhauer appeared behind them and cleared her throat. The look on her face had the sailors slinking back to their tasks.

'Reka. A word.'

'I can hear you well enough right here,' said the lieutenant with a hard look on his craggy face.

'I thought we agreed that Kristofine would stay on the ship when we reached Khlystburg. Why are you teaching her how to fight?'

'Agreed?' Reka shook his head. 'It didn't sound like Steiner agreed with you.'

'I'm quite capable of being disagreeable all on my own,' added Kristofine, performing a flourish. It might have been impressive had she not been armed with a length of old broom handle.

'I gave you an order,' said Felgenhauer to Reka, but the lieutenant, far from being cowed, shook his head and chuckled.

'I didn't leave the Empire just so I could take orders from another Vigilant. I follow *him* now.' The lieutenant gestured to Steiner. 'And it seems the lad is guided by his lady love, so there'll be no staying on board the ship for her.'

'This is foolishness,' said Felgenhauer. 'And you're encouraging it.'

'I just survived fighting a gods-damned dragon in a burning library, I saw a cinderwraith swallowed whole and I doubt that's the worst thing I'll see before all of this is over, so you'll forgive me if I've taken leave of my senses.' Reka's frown deepened but his tone was firm and even. 'But know this: I'll teach whom I please.'

Felgenhauer balled her hands into fists and made a sound somewhere between a growl and a sigh before stalking back below decks.

'I can't believe you spoke to her like that,' said Steiner.

'Well, it's true. She's one of the good ones, mind' – Reka nodded towards the departing form of Felgenhauer – 'but I'm sick of taking orders. I'll fight alongside the both of you, but my days as an obedient comrade are over.'

'You're in good company,' said Kristofine. 'Steiner has an obedience problem too.' They all laughed, as much to break the tension from the standoff with Felgenhauer as anything else.

'How are your arms?' said Reka. 'Sore yet?' Steiner shook his head. 'Good.' Reka grinned. 'More practice then!'

Steiner and Kristofine retired below decks to wash after their weapons practice, as much as anyone could stay clean aboard the crowded ship. The hold had been pressed into service as an infirmary, canteen and barracks for the soldiers that had escaped from Arkiv Island following the destruction of the

Great Library. Felgenhauer kept herself apart from the men, save Tomasz, who stood guard over her like a faithful wolfhound.

'So you've finally stopped all that racket,' said a voice from behind Steiner. Captain Sedey appeared out of the gloom, shaking his head as he drew close. 'Can't say I'm keen on fightin' on my ship, even if it's only to practice.'

'What news?' asked Kristofine. 'When do we make landfall?'

'The winds are not kind and we're not on a course I'd have chosen,' the captain sneered. 'Progress is slow but believe you me, I want you disembarked as quickly as you do.' He slunk off with an ill-humoured look in his bloodshot eyes.

'Charming as ever,' said Kristofine quietly. 'What do you want to do?'

Steiner snatched a glance at Felgenhauer, who caught him looking and glowered back. This was not how he had imagined his relationship with aunt would be.

'Best we go up on deck. I don't care for another run-in with my aunt just now.'

They made their way out of the hold and huddled together at the prow, staring out over the shifting swell of the dark blue sea, speaking of pipe dreams. Steiner talked of his wish to be reunited with his friends from Vladibogdan while Kristofine wondered if they might open a tavern one day, somewhere warm, far away from Nordvlast. The time crawled by until the sailor in the crow's nest began shouting in earnest. Steiner and Kristofine both scrabbled to their feet and searched the horizon. A plume of fire erupted in the distance and Steiner squinted until he could make out the silhouette of a ship. A dark shadow hovered above the vessel; great wings held the creature in the dark grey skies and a terrible certainty gripped Steiner.

'It's Bittervinge.'

'You don't know that,' said Kristofine softly. 'At this range

it could be . . .' Her words tailed off as the dragon released
another jet of fire. The sails suddenly caught alight, becoming
beacon bright on the choppy waters.

'This is my fault,' breathed Steiner. 'We should have finished
him in the library.'

'Don't be so hard on yourself,' replied Kristofine. 'It's not as
if we had a choice. We were lucky to escape with our lives.'

Felgenhauer and her cadre rushed up on deck with looks
of horror on their faces and a dozen questions frozen on their
lips. Captain Sedey swung hard on the ship's wheel and the
vessel came about, setting a course away from the winged
terror in the skies to the south-east.

'It's a merchant ship,' said Reka, squinting hard.

'Bittervinge will be feeding,' said Felgenhauer. 'Getting his
strength back after the battle in the library.'

'We hurt him badly,' said Tomasz. 'And that was before
Silverdust . . .' The sergeant fell silent as Steiner turned a hard
stare upon him, warning him against saying the words he could
not. Kristofine squeezed his hand to get his attention.

'What happened to Silverdust wasn't your fault either,' she
said, her voice low but firm.

'I know, but if I'd fought a little harder he might still be
here.' Steiner's thoughts turned to the men aboard the ship
in the distance. 'How do we stop him now that he's free of
the library?' he asked. 'Am I supposed to sprout wings?'

'Bittervinge will seek out the Emperor,' said Felgenhauer.
'But not before he's regained his strength. He'll attack the
city and feed. A creature like that, chained up for seventy
years' – she shook her head – 'he'll want to make a point,
remind everyone just how terrifying the dragons were. And
with every attack the Emperor's credibility will fade.'

'Surely the Emperor is powerful enough to defeat
Bittervinge?' said Steiner.

'Perhaps,' replied Felgenhauer. 'But the Emperor has always

been a man who used the right tool for the job, even during his more unhinged episodes. He'd want your black iron sledgehammer. That's the weapon which brought Bittervinge low before.'

'But what about all the people in Khlystburg?' asked Kristofine.

'We should warn them,' said Steiner.

'They'll know soon enough,' replied Felgenhauer, her words crisp and quiet and dreadful. 'I didn't want him to escape the library any more than you did.'

Steiner continued to watch the dragon attack the merchant vessel on the horizon as the others drifted away to speculate and ponder.

'It was hard enough to wound the bastard,' confided Steiner to Kristofine. 'Even with Felgenhauer and Silverdust by our side.' Another plume of fire descended on the ship in the distance. 'What hope is there now with Silverdust gone?'

'We'll think on it.' Kristofine put an arm around him. 'There has to be an answer. Bittervinge has been brought low by men before.'

'By the Emperor and my great-grandfather,' replied Steiner. 'But I've a feeling the Emperor won't give his advice freely, and my great-grandfather is dead.'

'We'll think on it,' repeated Kristofine, frowning at the horizon. 'Nothing's impossible. Even dragons.'

The merchant ship was now a fiery wreck, slipping beneath the waters of the Ashen Gulf. Bittervinge took to the skies, his vast wings speeding him north. Steiner felt a chill run through him that had nothing to do with the wind.

'I hope you're right.'

CHAPTER THREE

Kimi

My interactions with Kimi Enkhtuya during the uprising were limited, but the stories about her and the dragons are many. I am happy to say some are even true, having had time to corroborate them in the years since. No one could have foreseen that those majestic creatures, once the bane of Vinterkveld, would be instrumental in the weeks ahead.

From the memoir of Drakina Tveit,
Lead Librarian of Midtenjord Province

Kimi watched the ground pass beneath them from her vantage point at the base of the dragon's neck. She sat just in front of muscular shoulders that heaved and flapped vast wings. Her passage across Izhoria had been dizzying in so many ways.

Do not look down.

She was still getting used to Namarii dropping his words directly into her mind. The sharp teeth, long jaw and draconic tongue prevented the dragons using human speech, but their mastery of the arcane grew a little more with each day. Kimi pulled her eyes from the swamp that blurred by under her feet and fixed her gaze on the horizon.

That is much better. You are making yourself sick, though I do not understand why.

'I'm fascinated by just how fast we are moving,' she shouted above the wind that roared past with every beat of the dragon's wings. 'It's mesmerizing.'

And exhausting. I grow tired. With that simple statement, and with neither consultation nor permission, Namarii dipped his head and began to descend from the skies. Kimi was beginning to realize she was less a rider and more a passenger, a thought that brought a feeling of irritation and no small amount of powerlessness with it.

'It's only midday,' shouted Kimi as the wind whipped at her cloak and made her eyes water, but Namarii didn't reply. The dragon begin to circle around the northern edge of the Izhorian Forest. A glance over her shoulder confirmed that Flodvind and Stonvind were following Namarii's lead. Flodvind caught the sunlight, revealing stunning azure scales in a dozen shades of blue. Taiga was not so much riding as clinging to the dragon for dear life. Kimi suspected the high priestess had made the journey north with her eyes closed, praying fervently for safety. Stonvind by contrast was a dark grey silhouette in the sky and Tief rode the dragon proudly with a grin of exhilaration. Suddenly the ground was very close, lurching up to meet them much too fast. Kimi felt a surge of panic before Namarii flared his wings and landed gently.

I can sense your worry and discomfort. Is flying really so terrible?

'It's not terrible.' Kimi swung her leg over the dragon's neck and slid down to the ground, glad to have something firm beneath her feet. Her knees almost gave out and she stumbled sideways before regaining her balance. 'Ugh.' Her stomach flipped and then became still. 'Flying is not terrible,' she reiterated, though even she would admit she was trying to convince herself. 'It just takes some getting used to.'

The greatest tragedy of your race is that you are born without wings.

'Yes. It's an absolute tragedy,' muttered Kimi before sucking down a deep breath. The feeling of sickness passed and she whispered thanks to Frøya for a safe journey, her fingers going instinctively to the artefact that hung around her neck.

It was not Frøya's goodwill that kept you safe while in the air. Namarii tossed his head. *It was my skill and attention.*

'Of course,' replied Kimi, though she was beginning to think dragons might be held aloft by the sheer power of arrogance.

Flodvind and Stonvind landed a few dozen feet away, folding their wings neatly and rolling their shoulder muscles. Tief jumped down, shouting joyfully before his knees gave way and he fell face first into a pool of swamp water. He jumped up and ran over to Kimi, laughing loudly.

'It's incredible! We're dragon riders! Can you believe it?'

'Tief, we've been doing this for two days now—'

'But can you believe it?' he continued.

'Not only can I believe it,' replied Kimi, 'but I can feel it too.' She pressed her fingertips into the aching muscles of her backside and winced.

'Just wait until I see Steiner!' continued Tief. If Kimi hadn't known better she'd have assumed he was a little drunk. She glanced over her shoulder at the considerable presence of Namarii and let herself feel awe at the dragon's regal profile. Her eye drifted over scales that seemed to be brown but in truth held the myriad tones of a forest in autumn. And there were the horns, teeth and talons, all shining as if made of polished obsidian.

Tief has a point. Namarii stretched out his neck and flared his wings. *We are magnificent.*

Kimi laughed at the dragon's remark before heading over to where Taiga still clung to Flodvind's neck. The priestess was muttering calming words to herself.

This one has been sick. The azure dragon snorted a plume of smoke that Kimi interpreted as displeasure. A slick of vomit ran down the base of the dragon's cobalt neck. Taiga looked up from her perch; she was deathly pale.

'Thank the goddess. We've finally stopped.'

Kimi helped the high priestess down and set to cleaning the sick from Flodvind's scales with swamp water. Tief took his sister to one side and offered her something to drink.

'I'm very sorry about this,' said Kimi to Flodvind. 'It's very strange to us to be in the air. It does strange things to our stomachs.'

No matter. Flodvind crossed her front paws and set her head upon them, the gesture curiously cat-like. *I like her. She has a good soul. She has an odd mind yet is fiercely dedicated.* When Flodvind's words appeared in Kimi's mind they arrived softly, like the patter of rain, so different to Namarii's direct and regal tone.

'She nearly died in Izhoria,' said Kimi. 'Poisoned by a ghole's claws. We're lucky she's still with us.'

'Luck had nothing to do with it,' chided Taiga. 'The goddess brought me back whether you want to admit it or not.'

Kimi nodded but said nothing. So much had happened in Izhoria. So much so quickly. She touched the jade carving that hung from her neck, remembering the great power she had wielded over the gholes. A power seemingly bestowed by Frøya.

'Your sister is very quiet,' said Kimi to Flodvind as she continued cleaning the dragon.

What sister do you speak of?

'Oh, I thought . . . Is Stonvind male?'

Stonvind and I are not related. In truth I don't know whether Stonvind is male or female at present.

Kimi frowned. 'What do you mean, "at present"?'

The dragons of old were solitary by nature. They were not known to take mates as you humans do. Dragons can change their gender as suits their needs. We have no need of one another in order to procreate.

'I didn't know such a thing was possible.'

The one that you know as Bittervinge, father of dragons, might just as easily be the mother of dragons.

'So are you are a he' – Kimi winced – 'or a she? Presently, I mean.'

Does it bother you so very much?

Kimi opened her mouth to state that yes, it mattered a lot, but the more she thought about it less sure she was.

You can refer to me as a female if it helps. Flodvind yawned and Kimi detected a little boredom, as if such a subject was unworthy of a dragon's attention.

'And what about Stonvind?'

It seems this is very important to you.

'Well, yes. I don't want to annoy any of you.'

Stonvind will let you know if you do anything they find annoying.

'So . . . you just said "they", but I tend to use "they" to describe a group of people.'

Your language is very limited, but then I suppose humans cannot change gender at will as we dragons do. Perhaps you will unravel the mystery of it in time. You can use 'he' for Stonvind if you find it easier. Flodvind turned her head away from Kimi, signalling the conversation was at an end. Stonvind hadn't communicated anything as far as Kimi knew, but this hadn't diminished Tief's love of dragon riding at all.

'Why did we stop?' said Kimi as she returned to Namarii and fetched her gear from the dragon's back. 'We flew all day yesterday.'

We did. Namarii had a way of staring past Kimi as he communicated with her. His large amber eyes were constantly drawn to the horizon, it seemed, always watchful or distracted. Kimi couldn't decide if she found it rude or merely disconcerting. *This is the edge of Izhoria; it seemed a fitting place to rest. Besides, we are still growing, we need sustenance, and flying is vastly taxing.*

Tief had retrieved his gear from Stonvind along with his sister's gear from Flodvind. At some unspoken agreement, the three dragons launched into the air and flew over the forest. The downdraught of their wings caused the humans to cower and shield their eyes.

'What the Hel?' whispered Kimi.

'I'd say it's lunchtime,' said Tief. 'For them and for us.'

'It would be nice to be consulted,' muttered Kimi. She'd become used to giving orders since they had escaped Vladibogdan and now she felt distinctly subservient.

'I'm not sure dragons have it in them to consult with humans,' replied Tief impishly. 'But I'm sure they can learn it,' he added as Kimi's expression grew stern.

They were halfway through eating a stew that Tief had cooked, though in truth it was little more than heated water with a meagre scattering of vegetables and spices.

'We need to get to Khlystburg before we starve to death,' said Kimi.

'There's really not much of anything left to eat,' said Tief.

'You have to wonder what they've found to eat,' said Taiga, looking up from her stew towards the forest where the dragons went to hunt.

'Grave Wolves,' said Tief. 'Or gholes. I can't imagine there's anything else in Izhoria to eat. Everything else is dead.'

No one spoke much after that. Kimi forced her food down as best she could, but her appetite had fled as memories of the undead creatures of Izhoria haunted her. The dragons returned after a time, though they prowled from the forest rather than arriving by wing. Namarii closed with Kimi and she had to fight down a pang of fear.

Am I really so terrifying to your eyes?

'Honestly? Yes. You're huge. You could eat me in one bite.'

But I would not. It was you that fed us in the darkness beneath

Vladibogdan. You helped keep us alive. You conspired to set us free. You are useful. You may be useful again.

'That's all true but the terror is instinctive,' explained Kimi. 'Our whole lives, and the lives of those who came before us, dragons meant one thing.'

Death.

Kimi nodded. 'And then I was captured by Veles, who killed on a whim and made a game of death.'

And yet you slew him. You slew one of the oldest dragons in Vinterkveld. And then you took his power for yourself.

Kimi glanced at her pack. Wrapped in a cloth bound with a belt, sheathed and made safe, was the Ashen Blade. Though it appeared to be nothing more than a dagger, the weapon had the power to steal life and confer it on the owner.

You have nothing to fear, Kimi Enkhtuya. Namarii stared off into the distance. *Not from me. I would not let you ride on my shoulders if you were not also magnificent.*

'Thank you.' Kimi smiled at the compliment, but also Namarii's ever-present arrogance. 'As I said, the panic I feel is an instinctive thing, before I remember we're friends.'

Namarii snorted a plume of smoke and lay down, fixing her with one amber eye. The iris became a narrow slit of purest black. Kimi stared back, afraid she might somehow be swallowed up by the deep knowing of that golden orb.

Friends. Is this what Marozvolk was to you?

'Why are you asking me about Marozvolk?' said Kimi quietly. She looked over her shoulder but Taiga was engrossed in her own conversation with Flodvind, while Tief had settled down for a nap.

You think of her often. I can sense your sadness for her, your regret, your longing.

Kimi sat down and leaned back on her elbows, staring into Namarii's eye with a growing sense of unease. 'You see everything, don't you? Not just our actions, but the contents of our hearts.'

I had not intended to delve so deeply, but you have been seated astride me these last two days. Strong feelings have a way of making themselves known no matter how much we might wish to keep them obscured.

'I don't understand,' said Kimi, feeling irritated again. 'Veles said he couldn't read my mind the way you do.'

I am not Veles. The dragon blinked slowly. *Our relationship is different to the relationship you had with the ghole-maker. And Veles was chiefly concerned with the dead, not the living. Perhaps you trust me more than you think, or perhaps these feelings are bleeding out of you.*

'Bleeding,' repeated Kimi. 'Like a wound.'

They sat together for a while, woman and dragon, former prisoners both, feeling the spring sunshine warm them. The trees were still and the silence was deep and, for once, unthreatening. A rarity in Izhoria.

There is something else. Another sadness, but a sadness mixed with anger.

'My brother,' replied Kimi. There seemed little point in avoiding the subject. Namarii would learn of it sooner or later.

You came from the same clutch of eggs?

'Something like that.' Kimi smiled. 'He killed our father and disowned me, cast me out.' Her mouth twisted in anguish. 'He said I was an impostor. He would have killed me too had I not had help escaping.'

You are angry because he tried to kill you. Very well. We will head south after we have killed the Emperor and then we will kill your brother.

'What? No!' Kimi imagined landing in the midst of the Xhantsulgarat and Namarii biting her brother in half. It didn't horrify her as much as she thought.

You will not kill him because he is your brother?

'I don't know,' admitted Kimi. 'I feel betrayed. Can you understand that? Betrayal.'

We dragons do not trust each other. It is part of being a dragon. Earlier you used a word. Friend. You said we are friends. But is that true? I am merely a tool that helps speed you to your destination, and you in turn are useful to me. I value your insight so that we may hunt the Emperor. Is that what friends are?

'Not exactly. It's about more than simply being useful.' Kimi took a moment to absorb what the dragon had said. 'So Stonvind and Flodvind aren't your friends, just useful dragons.'

They also wish to kill the Emperor. We hunt the same enemy. They are useful to me.

'That's not the same thing as being loyal to each other.'

Every creature, great or small, is only loyal to themselves when faced with death. You know this deep in your heart, Kimi. Your own brother has tried to show you this truth. The Emperor himself reveals this truth to an entire continent every day.

Namarii's words stirred a deep unease within her. She remembered the awful moment she'd been dragged from the Xhantsulgarat as an impostor, remembered the look she'd shared with Tsen, knowing he recognized her but would maintain his lie all the same. The shame of that day swirled within her.

'Why are they so far south?' muttered Tief from behind Kimi. She looked up from her musing to see him standing atop of Stonvind, staring north from under the flat of his hand.

'What can you see?' shouted Kimi, getting to her feet and reaching for her sword.

'Looks like trouble,' shouted Tief over his shoulder. Kimi realized he was grinning and didn't much care for the manic look in his eye.

'How much trouble?'

'About a company's worth.' He slid down Stonvind's back

until he was sitting in his customary spot. 'That's about a hundred and twenty men.' Tief grinned wickedly.

Do they count any Vigilants among their number? Namarii rose to his feet and stretched his wings.

'Hard to tell at this distance,' said Tief. 'But Vigilants are less common than you might think.'

Then we shall hunt the Emperor's servants, leaving a few to spread word of our superiority. Namarii's obsidian claws raked the earth in anticipation.

'I can't fault the way you think,' said Kimi. 'But that doesn't make you any less terrifying.'

'Looks like they'll be plenty to eat for dragons,' said Tief cheerfully, but Taiga frowned in response.

'We could just fly over them,' replied Taiga. 'The Emperor is our enemy, not those misguided fools.'

Namarii released a low growl. *We found little to sate our hunger in the forest and flying is most taxing.*

'It's decided then!' said Tief clapping his hands together. 'Lunch is served!'

CHAPTER FOUR

Ruslan

One of the lesser-known tragedies of this period was the fate of the Sokolov family, who had ruled the Vend Province since the formation of the Empire. They had always been fierce guardians of Solmindre's lands, were utterly loyal, and proud of their place both geographically and in the political hierarchy of the provinces. Vend Province could always be counted on to provide timber, wheat, fish, and taxes. The Sokolov family profited from this hugely. It was an open secret that Dimitri Sokolov was hardly the man his father had wanted to succeed him, but for Dimitri to turn away from the Empire that had suckled him from infancy was unthinkable. Just as unthinkable that the Emperor might kill the young man in the Imperial Court itself, causing a scandal on a scale heretofore unseen even in Khlystburg.

– From the memoir of Drakina Tveit,
Lead Librarian of Midtenjord Province

The journey from Vend Province had been as overcast as the skies they travelled under. Boyar Sokolov had dragged himself from his mansion with all the reluctance of an aged wolfhound. His red-rimmed eyes rarely settled on any one thing or any person. When he spoke, which was rarely, his voice was a fragile whisper, his words meandering. Ruslan had witnessed all of this with the patient watchfulness of his position. The Boyar's aide waited on the broken man as best he could, restless in the knowledge he lacked the power to improve his master's situation.

They stood together at the stern of the ship and stared across frigid waters towards the capital city. They had crossed the northern reaches of the Ashen Gulf, past Arkiv Island and onwards, down to Khlystburg. The Boyar had grown gaunt during the journey, and the crew had carefully avoided him. Neither the captain nor the first mate had spoken to the nobleman, as if his disgrace might be contagious. Ruslan couldn't shake the suspicion this would be the Boyar's last voyage.

'We'll be at Khlystburg soon,' said Ruslan, to break the silence, though their arrival was plainly evident. A smudge of smoke discoloured the horizon above the city, a thousand chimneys all coughing or defecating into the air. Khlystburg hunkered beneath the pall of smoke, promising an abundance of secrets and shadows.

'This is where my son died,' said the Boyar, though the words were almost lost in his drooping moustaches. Ruslan, who had always felt short compared to the towering, barrel-chested Boyar, wanted to wrap an arm about the old man's rounded shoulders. 'I should never have sent him to such a wretched place.'

The news of Dimitri's death had diminished the Boyar. His poise, once so upright and firm, had disappeared, leaving little more than an uncertain shadow of a once-proud man. Even his clothes, always pressed and pristine, were rumpled from the journey and spotted with food.

'You could not have foreseen what befell Dimitri,' said Ruslan. He'd said it many times before and it never helped, but what else could he say?

'This is where the Emperor killed my son like a dog before the great and the good of the Solmindre Empire,' whispered the Boyar. He locked his gaze on Ruslan, his dark eyes terrible with grief – and something worse. 'The Sokolov line will not survive this scandal. That my son, my Dimitri, would spend our taxes on whores and give money to rebels and dissidents . . .' Tears tracked down his face to be lost in the stubble on his jaw. 'It is unthinkable.'

It was not the first time the Boyar had expressed his fears for House Sokolov's survival, though he was usually the worse for drink when he did. That he should repeat these words sober gave them an added weight that chilled Ruslan to his very bones.

'But the Sokolovs have served the Emperor faithfully for four generations,' said Ruslan quietly. All true of course. The sprawling dynasty had ruled the Vend Province; they had served as officers in the army and Vigilants in the Holy Synod. They had counted an Envoy among their number not so long ago. 'Surely there has to be some mistake. Dimitri might have been fond of parties and women, but he had no passion for overthrowing the Emperor.'

'My boy,' whispered the Boyar. 'My only boy.'

'We will retrieve the body and take him home to Vend for a proper burial, my lord. We will make this right.'

The Boyar snorted a bitter laugh and shook his head. Fresh tears sprang to the corners of his eyes. 'The Emperor killed him with the Ashen Blade in the Imperial Court. How does one even begin to make such a thing right? To find justice or vengeance – or simply survival?'

Ruslan wished he had an answer for the Boyar, but his mind remained blank. This was no mere footpad mugging in a backstreet: the Emperor himself had taken Dimitri's life. The enormity was difficult to comprehend, let alone provide a solution to. The ship continued towards the docks of

Khlystburg where all manner of stinking fish, surly porters, and sneering officials awaited them. All of this was watched over by Imperial soldiers, their blunt maces ready in hand, their black armour intimidating.

'The Sokolov line will not survive this scandal,' repeated the Boyar before heading back to his cramped and lonely cabin.

Ruslan stood on the dock and directed two sailors to carry the Boyar's sea chest ashore. The men struggled under the weight, muttering to each other about the ridiculous clothing nobles insisted on wearing, but it was coin not cloth that made up the greater part of the chest's contents. Boyar Sokolov descended the boarding ramp and eyed the struggling porters.

'It will not be enough,' he said once he had drawn close to Ruslan.

'You have emptied the family coffers,' said Ruslan. 'The Emperor can ask for no more reparation than that.'

'You speak as if the Emperor were a reasonable man.'

Ruslan turned away to hide his growing frustration. The Boyar's despair was a weight greater than the sea chest and he feared it would crush them both before they reached the Emperor.

'Boyar Sokolov!' A male voice boomed out across the dock. 'Welcome to Khlystburg.' The Emperor had sent a Vigilant, of course, and Ruslan almost sneered. All these years they'd pretended to remove the taint of the arcane from the continent of Vinterkveld. Decades declaring children possessed of witchsign and abducting them to be destroyed. All these years using the very same power to further the Empire's agenda. The Vigilant was attired in the customary cream padded leather jacket of the Synod, but it was the blood-red, sleeveless, long leather coat that drew eye, with geometric designs embossed from collar to hem.

'You must be weary from the journey,' added the Vigilant. He wore a hideous mask that resembled a wolverine, while one withered arm was bound up in a black leather sling.

The Boyar grunted a reply or cleared his throat, Ruslan couldn't be sure which. His attention had settled on the six soldiers waiting patiently behind the Vigilant.

'I am Exarch Zima. I have instructions to escort you directly to the Imperial Court.'

'Is it not usual for a visiting dignitary to be taken to his quarters so they may make themselves presentable?' said Ruslan, failing to hide his irritation.

'Usual? Yes.' Ruslan thought the man might be smiling behind the mask. 'But these are unusual times. Come.'

They were led through the city on foot like petty criminals. No cart provided to give them passage, no water, no tea, no respite offered. The sailors continued to grumble and curse under the weight of the sea chest, and the city folk stopped to gawk and speculate.

'You made good time,' said the Exarch in an airy tone as if this were a meeting between friends.

'I left the moment I heard the news,' said the Boyar. His gaze was fixed on a point ten feet in front of his boots, never looking up from cobbled streets and the filth they contained.

The Exarch kept up a steady stream of platitudes and small talk, and all the while Ruslan imagined a mocking smile behind the mask, that stoked his irritation to a smouldering anger.

'It must be hard for the Synod now,' said the Boyar.

'How so?' replied Exarch Zima. There was a pause and a note of surprise in the Vigilant's voice; he had been caught off balance by the Boyar's question.

'It is common knowledge across the Empire that the Synod and her Vigilants use the arcane for their own ends.'

'It is regrettable,' agreed Exarch Zima, his tone begrudging. 'We preferred to operate with a measure of secrecy.'

'The entire Empire and all the Scorched Republics know the Synod has lied to them all this time,' said the Boyar, pressing his point past the boundaries of polite conversation. 'And that you are all hypocrites.'

'That may be true.' Exarch Zima snorted a laugh behind his bestial mask. 'But the hypocrites are running the Empire, and there is no one to stop us.'

'It seems someone nearly stopped you,' said the Boyar. 'Didn't you have the use of both arms the last time we met?'

The Exarch said nothing after that, leading them to the Emperor in furious silence.

The Imperial Court was set in acres of gardens crisscrossed by gravel paths. Statues of fallen heroes surveyed all who passed by, from atop columns and plinths. Boyar Sokolov's own father had been immortalized in stone and Ruslan reached out to touch the plinth hoping it might confer good luck on his master. The buildings themselves were dressed in pale stone and the towers were set with bulbous and tapering domes, painted in bright colours.

'I had never thought I would set foot here,' whispered Ruslan.

The Boyar flashed him an angry look. 'I had never thought I would set foot here in such disgrace.'

The Semyonovsky Guard waited by every doorway, made taller and more imposing for the spears they carried. They wore a rope of black across their chests, and the red star that all soldiers wore at their brow had been recoloured in the same black enamel as their armour.

'I have become immune to its charm,' said Exarch Zima. 'Though I confess it is magnificent compared to the low buildings of Vend. Such a shame the country is a swamp.'

'*Some* of the country is swamp,' replied the Boyar in irritation. Ruslan, who had never visited Khlystburg before, much less the Imperial Court, could only stare and try and keep his mouth closed. He had no wish to resemble the dumbstruck peasant Exarch Zima no doubt thought he was. The party drew to halt in a large antechamber and Exarch Zima conferred with the guard at the doors.

'What will happen now?' whispered Ruslan.

'I will present myself before the Emperor,' said the Boyar, his tone cold and gaze unfocused. 'I will offer the money we have and more to come.' The Boyar laid one hand on Ruslan's shoulder and gripped him tightly, then drew him closer. 'I do not expect to return from the court. You have enough money to return to Vend. I suggest you do so and forget you ever attended the Sokolov line. Do you understand me?'

'I would never renounce you, my lord.'

'Then you are a fool. What has befallen Dimitri will cost all of us, even you. Not a single soul will employ you after this. No one!'

Ruslan nodded, feeling something close to panic rise in his chest. Exarch Zima gestured to the Boyar as if he were little more than a serving wench, and the doors to the court opened. Ruslan watched his master march away, crossing the polished floor at a brisk pace so as not to trail after the Exarch. The doors closed and Ruslan stood, feeling more alone than he could remember. He'd been orphaned twenty-five years ago, and while the Sokolovs were never family to him, they were all he had. Ruslan had been jealous of Dimitri in his less charitable moments. The Boyar's son had been a spoiled layabout as a child and little had changed as he grew older.

'You should move on,' said one of the Semyonovsky guards at the vast doors. He made a shooing gesture that looked ridiculous in the heavy armour he wore, but was no less patronizing for that.

'I am aide to Augustine Sokolov, Boyar of Vend Province,'

Ruslan replied, forcing as much authority and pride into his voice as he could muster.

'You should move on,' repeated the guard, though it was sadness, not insistence that Ruslan heard in the man's words. 'It's a bad business you're wrapped up in, and no one will emerge from it well.'

Ruslan nodded, and swallowed in a throat thick with emotion. He departed the antechamber in a daze.

When Ruslan became aware of his surroundings again he found himself standing before the statue of the previous Boyar, Vladislav Vend Sokolov III, in the Imperial Gardens.

'You may well be dead,' said Ruslan in a voice like rust. 'But if you have any sway on the world of the living, I implore you to look out for your son. He needs you now more than he ever did before.'

'Are you lost?' The question came from behind him, the voice as sumptuous as a brocade gown, the accent different to the people of Vend, yet still recognisably Solska. Ruslan turned to find himself face to face with three noblewomen. One was trying hard not to giggle behind a fan; she was no older than Ruslan but he would not have been able to afford her riding boots even if he had saved all year for them. Why she should need a fan eluded Ruslan; the sun was only conspicuous for its absence.

'He's not lost; he's simple.' Another of the noblewomen looked down her nose at him with her lips pursed – in contemplation or disapproval, Ruslan wasn't sure which. He was used to nobles conversing as if he were not there, he'd grown used to the idea he was below their notice, but he'd never been the topic at hand.

'Well, I think he looks lost.' The sumptuous voice again. She was an elegant brunette woman in her forties, adorned with make-up and gold jewellery, bundled up in a handsome riding cloak of verdant green.

'I'm not lost, thank you.' Ruslan bowed his head, painfully aware he knew not whom he spoke to.

'Are you the gardener?' asked the fan-bearer, a note of mocking in her words. 'Shouldn't you have tools or a shovel?'

'Of course he's the gardener,' said the disapproving noblewoman. She brushed a speck of dirt, real or imagined, from her dark purple dress. 'Look at the state of him,' she added, not giving him a moment's notice.

'Well, gardener or not' – the elegant brunette stepped forward and smoothed Ruslan's fringe back from his forehead. Her fingers were chilly but her touch was pleasant all the same – 'he's rather handsome in a rustic sort of way.'

'Rugged even!' The fan-bearer tittered and rolled her eyes as if scandalized by her companion's forwardness.

'Oh, not again,' muttered the sour-faced noble. 'Didn't you just set aside one of your peasant playthings last week?'

The elegant noble shushed her friend before turning her attention back to Ruslan and favouring him with smile. 'I'm sure I could find a few duties for you if you grow tired of tending to the garden.'

Ruslan felt himself blush, which brought a peal of laughter from the fan-bearer. Even the sour-faced noble couldn't suppress a smirk.

'I'm not a gardener for the Emperor—'

The brunette noble pressed an index finger against his lips gently. 'Do you have any idea how tiresome it is for us at court? Our husbands constantly haunting this dour place, hoping for some favour or leverage to increase their influence, while we are left to fend for ourselves.' She removed her finger and lowered her hand until it rested on his chest, over his heart.

'I . . .'

'We might have a use for a man like you,' she purred.

'You there! Aide!' A man's voice, hard and impatient. Ruslan turned towards its source, surprised to find one of the Semyonovsky guards approaching. 'Your master requires you at once!'

'The gardener has a master,' sneered the sour-faced noble.

'What's going here?' asked the guard, his black cloak snapping in the wind behind him.

'I was just offering this young man some employment.' The brunette noble smiled and lowered her gaze submissively.

'His master isn't dead yet and has need of him,' replied the guard peevishly. 'Right now.'

'Not dead,' croaked Ruslan, hardly believing it. For the second time that day Ruslan marched towards the Imperial Court, struggling to comprehend the terrible events unfolding all around him.

CHAPTER FIVE

Streig

The Great Library of Arkiv was considered one of the treasures of the Solmindre Empire. Rumours persisted that the Emperor had a copy of every book stored on the island. It was feared the destruction of the Great Library by the father of dragons, Bittervinge, would herald a new dark age of ignorance and unknowing. So much knowledge and history had slept in neat rows on countless shelves, but Bittervinge's escape from his black iron prison had reduced everything to ashes. The fate of the Great Library was a prelude to what was to come to Vinterkveld in the following weeks.

> – From the memoir of Drakina Tveit,
> Lead Librarian of Midtenjord Province

The darkness was total. Not merely an absence of light, but the deep darkness of being underground. Had it not been for the sound of his laboured breathing Streig might have thought he was already dead. Folk tales told of a Hel that resembled an endless range of cliffs where the damned fell to their deaths, only to endure the same fate the next day and every day for all of eternity. Streig's father, ever a contrary sort, had told cautionary tales of a Hel deep underground, a series of caverns and tunnels. The dead lingered as ghosts in the lonely darkness, struggling to remember the joy of their brief lives, while the shades of dragons prowled the caverns breathing ghostly fire.

'Frøya save me,' Streig whispered in desperation. It had been many years since he'd dared to whisper the names of the goddesses. His mouth was dry save for the taste of ashes and despair. 'Silverdust?

Every breath brought a stab of pain from ribs that must surely be fractured, and with the pain came terrible memories. They returned to him, alighting like dark birds, one or two at first, then more and more details forming a flock, until there was no escape from the truth.

'Oh gods,' groaned Streig in the darkness. They had been in the Great Library searching for the renegade Felgenhauer on the Emperor's orders, though Silverdust had long followed his own agenda. Loyalties, once so steadfast in the Empire, were now fickle and changing. At the height of the fighting they'd allied themselves with former Matriarch-Commissar and her nephew, the infamous Steiner Vartiainen. Steiner the Unbroken. Steiner the dragon rider. Though in truth he bore the appearance of a heavily scarred and somewhat scrawny peasant. Somehow, along with his love, Kristofine, he'd captured the imagination of peasants with yet another title, the Lovers. Yet there was no love in the ruins of the Great Library, only pain and darkness.

'Silverdust? I'm hurt. I'm . . .' Streig thought back to the long journey from Vladibogdan where he'd befriended the enigmatic Exarch. The mirror-masked Vigilant never ate, didn't sleep, and claimed to see the dead. Their journey together had revealed him as the rarest of beings in all of Vinterkveld: a cinderwraith with arcane gifts at his disposal. But even an undead cinderwraith with the considerable arcane powers of a learned Exarch could not hope to survive being consumed by a dragon.

'You're really gone,' whispered Streig.

He cradled his bruised left hand in his right, holding it against his chest. Silverdust, his only friend, had finally gone to whatever rest awaited him, though who knew what Frejna would make of such a mortal fetching up on the shores of the dead.

'You can't be gone. I need you. Steiner needs you. And the Emperor still draws breath. Where are you?'

It had been Silverdust, in his former life as Serebryanyy Pyli, who had taught the Emperor the intricacies of the arcane. If anyone was capable of surviving the jaws of Bittervinge, the father of dragons, then surely it was the often cryptic, always powerful Silverdust.

'Please, Silverdust.' Streig didn't merely need the Exarch to be alive, he needed his help. A jagged, stumbling memory returned to him of running through the library as it collapsed around him, falling through the floor and blindly staggering to a staircase leading down. The Great Library had been the largest repository of knowledge in all Vinterkveld, save the Emperor's personal library, so people said. Bittervinge's escape had heralded fire and destruction on a scale Streig had not dared to dream possible.

'All those books,' croaked Streig as he remembered the terrible heat of the inferno. It was not the Hel of folk stories, but it had been no less terrifying for all that. Now he was lost in the rubble and ashes of that once great edifice. He would die down here, a long suffering of starvation and thirst. Streig snorted a bitter laugh. To have come so far, to have crossed the continent, to have stood before the Emperor himself and witnessed the death of Father Orlov and Envoy de Vries, only to die alone of starvation.

A glow appeared in the pitch darkness and Streig blinked in breathless excitement, worried his eyes were playing tricks. 'Silverdust?' The glow became two lights, each no larger than a Shanisrond firefly. Streig blinked eyes that threatened tears of relief and reached out with a shaking hand.

'Silverdust?'

It is I.

Silverdust had forgone speech long ago, using the arcane to communicate, for the dead had no lips to speak. The words appeared in Streig's mind, no louder than a whisper.

'I can barely see you.'

I am much reduced. Here, follow me. It is imperative you survive, Streig. You must survive.

Streig took a moment to pull himself to his feet, wincing as his ribs sang with pain. 'I wasn't sure I'd see you again after . . .'

Bittervinge. Yes, being consumed by the father of dragons was not the outcome I had hoped for.

'Your talent for understatement survived the ordeal.' Streig couldn't help the slow smile that creased his lips.

So it would seem.

As the pair of dim orange lights drifted closer Streig realized he'd lost both his shield and his mace in the fighting, but somehow gained a two-handed sword. When had that happened?

'I can't see anything,' he whispered, as if afraid to rouse the attention of the darkness itself. The orange lights performed a lazy dance, orbiting a torch held in a sconce for a handful of seconds. The torch was coaxed into life, the yellow light as bright as the midwinter sun on a clear day. Streig screwed his eyes shut a moment and winced.

Are you wounded? Hurt?

'Just my eyes. The light. I don't know how long I've been down here.'

We must get you to the surface. You need food, water, rest.

'And you? Will you recover?'

Silverdust gave no answer, drifting further along the

ash-strewn tunnels beneath the once Great Library of Arkiv Island.

Streig wasn't sure how long he dragged himself through the darkness following the dancing lights. That mere embers were all that remained of the once great Silverdust troubled him greatly. The young soldier shucked off his armour as he went, relieved as the weight lessened, but no less exhausted. His arms ached from holding up the torch with his good hand, while his bruised hand gripped the great sword, resting on his shoulder.

'Do you know where you're going?' asked Streig after what seemed like an eternity. Perhaps they were in Hel after all, doomed to wander forever.

In truth, no. Perhaps these stairs will lead us to the surface.

Streig's torch lit the way, revealing worn stone steps, with small drifts of ashes like so much grey snow.

'Let me go ahead. It may not be safe for you in your current state.'

I am much reduced. There was a tired, faintly delirious tone to Silverdust's words that Streig had not heard before. *And this was not the outcome I had wished for.*

Streig felt a pang of helplessness. A wounded soldier he could tend and feed and watch over, but a wounded cinder-wraith? Who knew how to heal the undead? Was such a thing even possible?

The staircase was long and Streig stumbled twice before reaching the top, only to be greeted by a wooden door reinforced with iron studs and a lock that prevented them from venturing further.

'Gods damn it,' said Streig, shaking the door handle in desperation. He stepped back and kicked the door in disgust, jarring his fractured ribs.

I may yet have some small trick up my incorporeal sleeves.

Silverdust, the little of him that remained, disappeared into the keyhole, the motes of light shining brightly before they disappeared from view.

'Silverdust?' Streig felt a moment of panic. 'Don't leave me here.' He dropped to his knees to look through the keyhole. Light flared brightly in the dark and the smell of scorched metal filled his senses.

Hold the torch a little closer. I need its strength.

Streig did as he was told and a tongue of fire from the torch curved into the lock. The flame joined with the cinder-wraith, who bent his will to melting the metal. Streig started to sweat.

'It's taking long enough,' he complained on aching knees.

You have somewhere else to be? Another way out of this infernal maze?

'Sorry.'

Molten iron dribbled from the keyhole like filthy candle wax.

Try it now, but mind the handle – it may be hot.

Streig did as he was told and opened the door, using his shirt to protect his fingers from the heat. The sky was pleasantly vast, pale blue and scudded with wisps of white clouds so different to the black smoke that had billowed from the Great Library the day before. Streig sucked down breaths of fresh air and released sighs of relief as the wind darted around the door frame.

'Come on,' said Streig, grinning, but when he turned around he saw that Silverdust had remained in the darkness.

I cannot. I fear the wind will dissipate me. Even now I am struggling to hold myself together.

'The wind?' Streig looked back through the doorway to the courtyard that sat behind the Great Library. There was a tower on the far side, built into a sturdy wall. 'How do I get you out of here when you're like this?'

Silverdust retreated back along the corridor and the stone stairs that led to the dark netherworld beneath the library.

I have an idea.

Streig couldn't say how long they searched, but the Great Library was home to more secrets than the ones inscribed on the many books. More moderate Vigilants had begun a fashion in decades past, a desire to have their ashes stored in the vaults beneath the library itself, so they might rest in peace with the knowledge of the Empire. The practice was frowned upon, of course, but simply being a moderate in an Empire built on fear and punishment was frowned on, and so the fashion continued. The librarians conspired with the members of the Holy Synod and secreted the urns of the Vigilants in the deep places beneath the library.

'So what do we do with the Vigilant already in here?' said Streig, gently lifting a dark grey urn from a small alcove in one of the many winding corridors.

The Great Library is nothing more than ashes. A few more will not go amiss.

'You're saying I should just . . . pour him out?'

I am saying my need is greater than his, or hers, right now. Besides, there is a good chance I knew the Vigilant in life, just as there is a good chance they owe me a favour.

Streig wrinkled his nose as he lifted the lid on the urn. He poured out the ashes, covering his nose and mouth with one sleeve.

'Sorry,' he said to the cloud of grey particulate, feeling foolish even as he said the words. Silverdust drifted into the vessel; the twin lights illuminated the inside.

Do not seal the lid too tightly. I still need air, much like a living flame.

Streig could see Silverdust more clearly in the confines of the urn. Little more than a small cloud of smoke and two amber candle flames.

'We need to find someone to make you whole again,' whispered Streig to the urn, though who such a person might be he had no idea.

The wind continued to gust across the wide expanse of the courtyard as Streig made his way towards the tower. People were searching the ruins for survivors and Streig, stripped of his armour and covered in ash, looked like one more lost soul haunting the remains of the Great Library. He headed towards the stout wall that enclosed the courtyard, hoping the many towers along its length would offer a place to shelter.

Just a little further, Streig. You have done admirably. I will not forget this.

Streig clutched the urn in his wounded hand and pressed the great sword along the line of his body so as to not draw attention to himself. The tower, much like the wall, had been dressed in pale stone, intended to be elegant more than defensive. The door to the nearest tower was painted the colour of dried blood.

'Hardly a good omen.' Streig frowned and glanced down at the urn. 'Are you still in there?'

For the moment. Are we in the tower?

'Soon.' Streig set down the sword carefully and tried the door, grateful to find it unlocked. He pushed against it with a shoulder, wincing as his ribs pained him once more.

'Hello?' he called into the gloom. The spiral staircase remained silent and Streig retrieved the great sword and closed the door with his foot, before ascending the many stairs.

You are in much pain.

'I'll heal,' replied Streig, breathless with the effort and the pain in his chest. 'I just need to get you somewhere safe first. Then I can rest.'

Streig climbed the stone steps to the very top of the tower. He entered a room with a rumpled bed that had been shoved into one corner. A desk littered with correspondence sat before the window, while a trio of bird cages stood nearby, covered in black velvet. Three chairs were drawn up in a loose semi-circle before the fireplace, though it was stone-cold and home only to white ashes.

'Not the most homely of places but it will have to do, I suppose.' Streig set the urn on the fireplace and slipped the lid so it was halfway open. 'I can barely believe we escaped from that place.' He could see the ruins of the Great Library from the tower window. Smoke and dust hung over the scene in a vast and sombre pall. Streig slumped down on the bed and his thoughts turned to the many soldiers who had died in the fighting, men who would have fought side by side in previous years. Now the Solmindre Empire was divided by rebellion and mistrust.

Do not mourn for those still loyal to the Emperor.

Streig stared at the urn. 'So you can still read minds then, even in this reduced state.'

So it would seem. Rest a while and then seek out some food. Bad enough that I have wasted away. No good will come of you doing the same.

Streig shucked off his boots and loosened his belt, too tired to remove his britches. He lay back on the bed and closed his eyes, bruised hand resting on his fractured ribs, the dull pain a now familiar companion.

CHAPTER SIX

Steiner

Accounts from the survivors of Khlystburg were harrowing. The city folk lived under the constant threat from the father of dragons. Those that didn't find themselves eaten or immolated had to contend with rising food shortages due to the blockade at the port. This was perhaps the Emperor's greatest mistake during the uprising and led to widespread misery and scores of avoidable deaths. The people, ever reliant on trade, soon found their warehouses empty of reserves. Despair reigned over the city of whips, and people who had spent decades carving out a tenuous existence were forced to withdraw, signalling one of the largest migrations of refugees in the continent's history. Ultimately the blockade was ineffective at keeping out those the Emperor feared the most: the Lovers made landfall shortly after departing Arkiv Island.

> – From the memoir of Drakina Tveit,
> Lead Librarian of Midtenjord Province

The *Morskoy Volk* cut through the waters under full canvas, though the waters were choppy now the wind was up; the ship heeled with every gust. Captain Sedey stood at the helm with a sour look on his face, stern gaze set on the horizon.

Felgenhauer and her cadre of followers remained below decks so as not risk undue attention.

'We should be down there with them,' said Kristofine, her voice firm but quiet. The city, seen from afar, looked in poor repair. A pall of grey and black smoke hung over the rooftops and the stark, bright sunshine failed to gild the city in a favour-able light. Tall buildings loomed amid the murk.

'I've never been to Khlystburg before,' replied Steiner. Behind the city lay the endless reaches of the Midtenjord Steppe, barren of anything and anyone save the scrubby grass and biting winds. 'But I'd have to say it looks to be a lonely place. Never thought I'd say that about a city.'

'Not so different to Cinderfell,' said Kristofine, 'just larger. I still think we should get below decks.'

'I just want to see it,' said Steiner. 'Get the measure of it. My father is hidden somewhere in all this . . .' He gestured, unable to find a word for the sprawling capital.

'You don't get the measure of Khlystburg,' muttered Captain Sedey as he changed course slightly. 'You pay taxes, you pay bribes, you stay out of trouble, and if you're lucky, you get to walk out again and hope you never have to come back.'

'Why come here at all?' said Kristofine.

'They pay well for just about everything.' The captain released a sigh. 'Everything is imported to Khlystburg. It's a gaping maw that will swallow up anything. Timber, meat, and grain. Vodka and mead. Taxes and people. It swallows up people most of all.' The captain shook his head and looked as if he might spit in disgust. 'And it's always hungry.'

Steiner and Kristofine looked at one another with dampened spirits. Neither said anything until a pilot and tax inspector from Khlystburg came aboard from a small boat.

'This could take a while,' warned the captain. 'And prove expensive. Best to make yourself scarce.'

*   *   *

The *Morskoy Volk* finally came to rest a short way off one of the many stone piers that reached into the sea like a giant's fingers. Theirs was not the only vessel visiting Khlystburg that day. All manner of ships were idling at anchor in the steel-grey waters. The few captains that had unfurled their sails were heading out to open water; the *Morskoy Volk* was the only arrival.

'Something's off,' said Steiner as he climbed down a rope ladder. Felgenhauer and Kristofine were waiting for him in a small boat to make the short journey to shore along with Reka.

'A blockade is coming.' Felgenhauer gestured south, where three Imperial galleons edged north against unfavourable winds. 'Just like Arkiv.'

'We only just arrived in time,' said Reka. They set off, Steiner and Reka pulling at the oars. No one said a word until they were almost ashore.

'I still say we should have left you aboard the ship,' said Felgenhauer to Kristofine, almost under her breath. Steiner heard her all the same.

'And I still say where he goes I go,' replied Kristofine.

The former Vigilant turned an annoyed glare on Reka, who chuckled as he rowed, which only served to annoy her more.

'We split up,' said Steiner once they were ashore. They all knew the plan. Best to remain in small groups of threes and fours than go marching down the street like a full squad.

'I'll see you at the inn tonight,' said Felgenhauer. 'Remember what we're here to do. Finding your father comes second.'

'Rebellion first, Marek second,' he managed through gritted teeth.

'Be careful, Steiner,' added his aunt, summoning a pang of regret for the way things were between them, but there was no time to bandage the wounds; their arrival at Khlystburg ushered in more pressing concerns.

'That woman is a pain in my arse,' muttered Kristofine once Felgenhauer was out of earshot.

'I dare say she is,' replied Reka, frowning at the retreating form of Felgenhauer. 'But she loves Steiner. That much is obvious. And she'll do anything to spare him pain.'

Steiner clasped Kristofine's hand and squeezed it. 'I won't let anything happen to you,' he said. 'Not like Father.'

'I don't need looking after,' she replied with a frown. 'I came to look after you.'

'Come on, my Lovers,' chided Reka. 'No time for sentiment.'

The docks were alive with hisses and whispers of rumour and speculation. All eyes turned south to the oncoming galleons and the blockade they promised.

'They'll be here by evening,' said Kristofine.

'Perhaps,' said Reka, 'and they almost certainly have Vigilants aboard, so let's be sure to avoid the docks in the coming days.' They set off through the city, which was busier and dirtier than both Virag and Vostochnyye Lisy. Kristofine wrinkled her nose at the filth on the cobbled streets. Steiner found his anger rising as the city folk pushed past him, hard looks on their faces as Steiner shoved back.

'Keep your head,' warned Reka. 'We don't need a street brawl just because these fools don't look where they're walking.'

'Oh no,' said Kristofine. She pointed across the street to a sorry-looking building with broken shutters.

'What?' Steiner squinted; then he saw the large sheet of parchment plastered to the side of the building. He crossed the street with a frown fixed on his face. Reka and Kristofine followed. The poster displayed a likeness of a hooded Vigilant with a blank mask. Though the artist couldn't capture the effect, Steiner knew it to be the mirrored mask of Silverdust.

'What do these words say?' said Steiner. Grief flooded through him at the sight of his old friend.

'Can't you read Solska?' replied Reka.

'Can't read any language.' Steiner shrugged. 'The words have a habit of moving around when I concentrate. Trying to read makes my head ache.'

'Well, in that case . . .' Reka turned back to the poster. 'It says he is wanted by the Synod. Perhaps they don't know that he died on Arkiv.'

'Or perhaps it's an old poster,' said Kristofine, picking at one corner of the parchment.

'We should keep moving,' said Reka. They were no more than a few minutes' walk further up the street before they came to the next poster.

'Is that . . .' Steiner struggled to keep the smile off his face. 'Is that supposed to be me?'

'Steiner! It's not funny.' Kristofine marched past the poster without a backwards look. The man in the illustration was a giant wielding a hammer as long as he was tall. Gurning, scarred, and heavily muscled, the Steiner in the poster was a far cry from the wiry youth standing before it.

'Come on, now,' said Reka. 'You well know you're famous. Let's not get snared by vanity.'

'They have posters of me,' whispered Steiner, full of incredulity.

'They have posters of your legend,' said Reka. 'Now you have to measure up. Think you've got it in you?'

'Let's find out,' replied Steiner, though in truth he knew they would play everything by ear. He was here to cast down the Emperor, but thoughts of his father were persistent and the task of rescuing him was no less than daunting.

It was almost evening as they approached the inn through rancid streets. Their breath steamed on the air as the pale blue sky began its evening alchemy, transmuting through a hundred pastel hues of scarlet and saffron. A murmur of dismay passed through the city folk and many pointed north. Some of Khlystburg's citizens gazed from tower windows and called out one word to their kin in terror.

'Dragon.'

In the distance a fleck of darkness descended, like a flake of soot drifting downwards, and where the darkness fell death would surely follow.

'Bittervinge,' said Steiner.

'It could be any of them,' said Reka. 'Frøya knows why you set them all free. I agree with you on most things, but freeing the dragons was pure folly.'

'No,' replied Steiner. 'The younger ones have a right to be free, just like anyone else. Besides, it was Kimi and Silverdust who agreed to free them.'

'Is it coming closer?' asked Kristofine. Reka led them to shelter beneath a doorway arch where they still had a good view of the dragon in the distance. Fire bloomed and there was the faintest sound of screaming, spirited to their ears by a chill wind. Steiner's sledgehammer was hidden by a length of sackcloth and he reached for it on instinct; its haft was warm to the touch. He felt a shiver of anticipation pass through him that had nothing to do with his nerves or the memories of what had befallen the Great Library.

'The sledgehammer is . . . awake, I think. It senses him.'

'Has it ever done that before?' asked Kristofine.

'No, but I imagine the Great Library was the first time it had been used against a dragon in a long time.'

'That was a fight to wake the dead,' agreed Reka. 'Come on now. It looks like he's raiding further north.'

'We should go there,' said Steiner, staring at the skies above the city. 'People will be in danger—'

'Those people are already dead.' Reka's tone was stern and

firm. 'By the time we arrived he'd have likely flown on elsewhere, or retreated back to wherever he makes his den.'

'But—'

'We stick to the plan,' continued Reka. 'Your aunt will skin me alive if I let you go running off. I know you feel responsible, but no good will come of getting yourself killed the first day we arrive.'

CHAPTER SEVEN

Ruslan

*No one had given the catacombs in the city a second thought.
They, like the dead soldiers who took their rest inside, were just
a footnote from a period of history people preferred not to think
about. The Emperor on the other hand was not one to squander
resources, in whatever form they took; even a place as decrepit
and lonely as the catacombs featured in his plans.*

— From the memoir of Drakina Tveit,
Lead Librarian of Midtenjord Province

Of all the myriad possibilities that might occur that day, of
all the winding paths and snaking, poisonous routes from
daybreak to nightfall, Ruslan would never, could never, have
foreseen where he and the Boyar Sokolov might end up. And
with whom.

'Hold the torch a little higher, Rulam,' said the Emperor,
getting his name wrong. Ruslan was too awed to correct him
and did as he was told. The Emperor was a dark-haired man
with a pale complexion and a high forehead. His voice had
a whispery quality to it, yet he enunciated every word with
cold precision, somehow sounding both bored and cruel
with every utterance. Or perhaps the cruelty merely resided

in his gaze. Certainly Ruslan had never been looked upon with eyes so utterly devoid of life. And yet there was some animating presence there, something older than human experience, more chilling that the Grave Wolves of Izhoria, more bitter than a northeasterly wind in the dead of winter.

'You're staring again,' said Boyar Sokolov, leaning close enough to whisper into Ruslan's ear without alerting the Emperor.

'Come now, this way,' replied the Emperor, leading them along unlit passages with rough-hewn walls and never a window to break the monotony. Other passages branched away to who-knew-where, leading only to more impenetrable gloom. Even the memory of sunlight struggled to exist in this place, and the Emperor was another sliver of darkness, at home in it, at one with it. Knee-length riding boots of deepest black, teamed with britches and a finely tailored jacket in a matching hue. Medals and black braid crowded his chest, contrasting with a sash of crimson at his waist, drawing attention from the sheathed dagger on his hip. Ruslan watched the ruler of the Solmindre Empire descend the cold stone steps, fascinated and horrified to be so close. There was a wiry strength about him as he moved, and when he paused the stillness was absolute.

'I have not ventured this way in so long,' said the Emperor in his quiet, unnerving voice. Ruslan wasn't sure if it was merely a comment or an invitation to ask questions, but remained silent. He was only here in order to hold up the torch for his master, and his arm ached not from the burden but the duration. How long had they been walking now? Surely they had left the Imperial Palace and were a good distance outside of the gardens.

'Not much longer,' said the Emperor, as if reading his thoughts. 'It's just a little further ahead.' The ruler of Solmindre snared Ruslan in his dead-eyed gaze, and for a moment he was convinced the Emperor knew his every thought, his every hope and weakness.

'Don't just stand there staring like some slack-jawed fool,' snarled Boyar Sokolov. He wrenched the torch from Ruslan's grip and went ahead, passing the Emperor and heading ever deeper into the dank maze.

'Are we underground?' Ruslan asked.

'A little,' replied the Emperor. 'These are the secret ways that lead from the palace to key locations around the city. A man can move about undetected if he has a sharp memory for turnings and directions.'

Ruslan wasn't convinced they were only 'a little' underground. It seemed they must be in the very bones of the world, inhabiting the quiet spaces in its soul. Was the Emperor gaming with him? Casting him as a simple fool?

'You are no fool,' said the Emperor quietly. 'Naive perhaps, an optimist, but not a fool.' He turned away and followed the Boyar, his crimson sash the only colour in the gloom.

Ruslan released an uneven breath he had not realized he'd been holding, and his exhalation steamed on the air.

No one spoke of the goddesses at the Sokolov Estate, in accordance with the Imperial doctrine of the Holy Synod. Ruslan had heard the odd serf whispering about Hel of course, and knew enough that one's spirit would end up there should a person lead a wicked life, according to the old ways at least. But the old ways were not of the Empire and so Ruslan had never thought too much about the afterlife. Until now.

They stood on a narrow causeway of flagstones, raised up from depressions either side, where sarcophagi slept beneath blankets of dust. The halo of light that played around the torch didn't reach the ceiling. Not a single sound could be heard in the tunnel and it was spitefully cold, unnaturally so given the season.

'This is not Hel,' said the Emperor, and now Ruslan was sure the man could read his thoughts. 'Though some may think otherwise.'

Ruslan couldn't tell how far the causeway ran in each direction, but he had the dire feeling the place they stood in was vast.

'You are a man of great purpose, Your Imperial Highness,' said Boyar Sokolov. 'But I am unclear why you led us here.' He looked around at the many sarcophagi and the inscriptions, though they were obscured by dust. 'To tell the truth of it, I know not where I am,' he added.

'This is the final resting place of our glorious dead,' replied the Emperor. 'All those brave souls who took up arms against the dragons over seventy-five years ago' – the Emperor cast an appraising look around – 'they reside here. Those soldiers believed in me, they believed in Solmindre, and they dared to believe we could shrug off the tyranny of dragons.'

'Their sacrifice has not been forgotten, Your Imperial Highness,' said Sokolov, though his words had the tone of a formal response rather than anything heartfelt.

Ruslan waited for an answer to the Boyar's question, feeling the creeping chill of the lonely place. Why had they been led to such a dismal setting? Did the Emperor intend to kill them down here and leave them with the dead?

'Imperial scholars theorize that when a dragon consumes a person they feed not merely on its flesh, but upon its very essence.' The Emperor stepped out of the torchlight, until he appeared as nothing more than an indistinct shade, a voice in the darkness. 'And the goddesses of old, they were more indirect but no less terrible.'

The Boyar exchanged a cautious look with Ruslan; that the Emperor himself was breaking his own taboo on discussing the goddesses was unthinkable.

'How so, Your Imperial Highness?' asked Sokolov after a pause.

'The goddesses take a portion of a person's essence when they reach the afterlife. This is how the goddesses and the dragons maintain themselves over centuries.'

Ruslan's eye fell on the knife belted at the Emperor's waist, the Ashen Blade, a weapon so wicked it could drain the life from a person and confer it on the wielder. This, after all, was how Dimitri Sokolov had met his end, and it was notable that the Emperor omitted to mention his similarity to the very beings he despised.

'The souls of the Solmindre people belong to the Empire,' said the Emperor, his voice suddenly loud in the dark confines of the catacombs. He lunged back into the torchlight, animated and flushed. 'The souls of the Solmindre Empire belong to me!' He beat his medal-laden chest with one fist. 'I will rule the people of this continent in death just as I rule them in life, and I will not tolerate filthy dragons feeding on our kin, our blood! I will not tolerate foreign goddesses seducing our noble souls for their own ends!'

The Emperor had worked himself up in a crescendo and neither Ruslan or the Boyar had the coda to fill the silence afterwards. The Emperor strode off down the causeway, seemingly unperturbed by the lack of light. Ruslan hurried after him all the same and the Boyar marched stiffly behind. Scores of sarcophagi passed by on either side until they reached a junction.

'Your Imperial Highness,' asked Boyar Sokolov, 'I came to you today in disgrace with the firm intention of making amends and restoring the good name of the Sokolov line and the Vend Province. We have always been most loyal and stalwart supporters.'

'All true,' said the Emperor, his voice once more the unsettling whisper in which he usually spoke.

'Why then lead us here and speak of things that lesser men would be punished or even killed for?'

The Emperor seemed to shiver, or perhaps it was a flinch. When he turned to Boyar Sokolov there was a different quality to those eyes; a terrible sadness lingered there. 'Because I wanted someone to know what this is all for, why I do the things I do. I will not abide goddesses and winged terrors reigning over the souls of men. For the longest time the Empire has thrived.'

'But now Steiner Vartiainen stirs up discord across the continent,' said the Boyar.

'And I hear whispers,' said the Emperor, a dreadful sneer on his pale face. 'Whispers from advisers, whispers from Envoys and Vigilants. All day the whispers come; whispers on the wind speak to me even at night when I would be at my rest.'

Ruslan looked away and shifted his weight from one foot to the other, deeply uncomfortable. The man was clearly unhinged, or close to it.

'And what do the whispers say, Your Imperial Highness?' asked Sokolov smoothy.

'They whisper that the Stormtide Prophet is coming, and that people have begun to worship Frøya and Frejna.'

'But your powers are considerable, Your Imperial Highness. Your armies vast, your influence far-reaching. Surely you have a way to stop this prophet?'

'There is one way.' The Emperor gave a chilly smile. 'I have you.' He cupped one of the Boyar's cheeks with a gentle hand.

'I . . . I am not sure I understand you, Your Imperial Highness.'

'You are to be my trap, Augustine Sokolov. You will lure Steiner Vartiainen into the open, and when I have him I will be safe. The prophet will not dare risk my wrath.'

Sokolov looked to Ruslan with confusion etched into his brow, but his pride prevented him from confessing that he did not understand. Ruslan did his best to serve his lord under the circumstances.

'We have heard rumours in Vend but little of substance, Your Imperial Highness. Is there some connection between the Stormtide Prophet and Steiner Vartiainen?'

'Connection?' The Emperor smiled. 'A connection?' He laughed, though it was as cold and bitter as the catacombs where they now stood. 'She is his sister. Once I have killed her father and the aunt the prophet will pause. She will hesitate in her grief, and then I will bargain with her, a bargain for the very soul of her brother.'

'And how do I feature in all of this, my lord?' said the Boyar with a pained expression on his face.

'You will play the part of the wronged father. You will appear to be on the verge of rebellion, or at least open to the idea of it. Word will spread of your fall from grace and that is how you will earn Steiner's trust.'

'And when all of this is over' – Boyar Sokolov took a step towards the Emperor, his voice low and dangerous – 'our name will be restored along with the fortunes of the Vend Province?'

'It will be as you say.' The Emperor held up a warning finger. 'But only after you have delivered Steiner Vartiainen to me.'

The Boyar bowed and Ruslan was caught between holding up the torch and performing a bow of his own. In the end he remained upright. He'd spent the afternoon being a glorified sconce, why change now?

'Go now.' The Emperor gestured ahead of them. 'You'll find a way out in time, just try not to make any noise.'

Ruslan and the Boyar turned to look in the direction the Emperor had indicated, but all that awaited them was darkness. When they turned back the Emperor was gone, joined with the same darkness he had led them into.

On aching feet they walked, though neither of them dared to complain or speak a single word. Finally they reached a flight of stone steps and emerged in a run-down street just as the sun was setting. The entrance to the catacombs had been hidden behind a warehouse facade. The windows were closed and green paint peeled from the shutters, chained up to prevent prying eyes. Shattered crates and forgotten barrels littered the street, unlovely and unremembered.

'What now, my lord?'

'Now we find Steiner Vartiainen,' said the Boyar. 'I wanted a way to clear our name and here it is.'

'But what of Dimitri?' asked Ruslan in a hushed voice. 'What of your son?'

'Dimitri had his chance,' said the Boyar.

CHAPTER EIGHT

Streig

Not all enchanted items were forged by dragons for malevolent ends. Sometimes, an object could become a focus for arcane power just through a long association with a particular individual, though the individual in question would need to be powerful indeed.

– From the memoir of Drakina Tveit,
Lead Librarian of Midtenjord Province

Streig had regained some of his strength, though he still woke in the dead of night convinced he was buried beneath the Great Library. He only ventured out of the tower briefly – such expeditions were exhausting – but he had to find food.

Are you not even a little curious? The disembodied voice sounded rather peevish, and Streig decided he'd be feeling peevish too if he were an undead spirit confined to an urn.

'Curious about what?'

The desk, of course.

Streig dutifully rolled out of bed, where he'd been picking at the last few crumbs of bread and cheese from a wooden plate.

'It's a desk!' he said after a brief investigation.

I am half-mad with boredom. I have been swallowed by a dragon, passed from this mortal realm, presided over the intolerable cruelty of Vladibogdan, and I demand to know what documents lie upon the desk.

'I'd say you're a bit more than half-mad,' replied Streig as he sifted through the scraps of parchment that littered the surface. None of them made much sense: single sentences of cryptic warnings, often with a symbol or dots, though he did not know what these might mean. He crossed the room and fetched the urn, then set it down on the desk.

'See for yourself.'

We are in Felgenhauer's tower.

'Felgenhauer? What makes you think she's been here?'

Because this is her handwriting and these are the ciphers we devised when we were on Vladibogdan.

'She must have left after the library . . .' Streig gestured to the window. The sun was beginning to set on Arkiv, and the many avenues and boulevards were showered in a golden light that picked out the multicoloured masonry and revealed the architecture in pleasing ways. But no matter the city's splendour, his eye was always drawn to the ruin of the Great Library. It pained him to glance at the debris, and yet there were people exploring the desolation, sullied with ash and desperation. Some pointed and called out to one another but the search continued. The evening light revealed a common motif: the red star of the Solmindre Empire, worn on the brow of every helm.

'Just what we need.' Streig began to close the curtains slowly, so as to not draw attention to himself. 'Soldiers are searching the ruins.'

Silverdust made no reply from his place on the desk. The dour grey urn sat in silence, the lid ajar. A jolt of panic stabbed Streig's gut as a trio of soldiers began to make their way towards his tower, black cloaks flaring in the evening breeze.

'Frejna's teeth.' One of the soldiers raised his head, and though Streig could not see the man's eyes on account of the helm, he felt sure he had been seen. 'They're coming. What do I say?'

In a time of incessant lies, sometimes the truth is the best course.

'You're saying I should tell them I fought Bittervinge alongside Steiner Vartiainen?'

Only if you wish to dance a short jig at the end of a rope. Tell them you served me. Tell them you are wounded. Tell them Bittervinge consumed me.

'And then?'

The soldiers hammered on the door at the base of the tower and called for Streig to open up. He headed out of the chamber door and peeked down the spiral staircase. The latch rattled as the door was opened and a low murmur of voices drifted up the steps to him.

Perhaps you play up your injury.

Streig nodded and felt his mouth go dry. He wrapped a blanket around his shoulders and sat down on the chair before the fire, stoking the nearly spent firewood though it pained him to grip the poker. Armoured footfalls sounded on the stairs, the jingle of buckles and mail becoming closer and louder.

'Hoy there!' came a voice from the other side of the door. A woman's voice.

'Come in,' replied Streig. 'It's safe.' The door opened and three hulking soldiers in black enamelled armour entered the room. It was suddenly very crowded. Streig's breathing was shallow as one of the soldiers removed her helm, revealing a pale face with lines aplenty at the corners of her eyes and a look of concern etched on her face.

'Hoy there. Seems you barely made it out alive.' The soldier nodded at Streig's hand, which lay in his lap, a bruised claw. 'I assume you were caught up in the fighting?'

'I was. Forgive me for not standing and saluting, sergeant.'

'Sergeant.' The soldier laughed and her eyes twinkled a moment. 'Be a fine thing if I ever got promoted. I'm merely a corporal and I don't stand much on ceremony.' Streig forced a smile and nodded in thanks. 'You were in the library?' Impossible to miss the note of wonder in the corporal's voice. 'When it happened?'

'I was.'

Only answer what they ask you. There is no need to be generous. Streig's eye flicked to the desk and the old corporal followed his gaze.

'Friend of yours?' she said, looking at the urn.

'He was. That's all that's left of Exarch Silverdust.'

'Blood and ashes.' The corporal raised her eyebrows and let out a long sigh. 'I had no idea. How did he . . . ?'

'Bittervinge got loose. It was terrible. The Exarch tried to defeat the dragon, to contain it, but in the end . . .' Streig shrugged and looked away to the fire.

'You've been a great help,' said the old corporal. 'My lieutenant will greatly pleased with this information. Is there anything you need?'

'Perhaps you could forget you saw me,' said Streig. He lifted his wounded hand. 'I'm not sure how much more use I can be to the Emperor.'

'I see.' The old corporal nodded; then she gestured to her comrades. The armoured men took their leave, black cloaks swirling about them as they descended the stairs. 'You know how it is for soldiers,' said the corporal quietly. 'None of us really retire.' She paused a moment and looked out of the window at the ruins, now almost shrouded in darkness. 'I'll tell my lieutenant you need a while to heal. Hopefully he'll forget you're here. That's the best I can do.'

'I fought the father of dragons and dug myself out of the rubble,' replied Streig. 'I'm not asking to retire; I'm asking to be forgotten.'

'As I said, maybe the lieutenant *will* forget about you.' The corporal gave an apologetic sort of smile and left.

We must be careful for the next few days.

Streig crossed to the window and peeked through the closed curtains. 'We're always careful,' he muttered. 'And yet trouble keeps finding its way to our door.'

Scritch, scritch.

'Do you hear that?' said Streig in a voice thick with sleep. The deep darkness of night was fading with the approaching dawn. Light lingered at the edges of the curtains, making the room's furniture ghostly.

It would seem we have a visitor. Silverdust, the two glowing orbs that remained of him, crested the lip of the urn to look across the room.

Scritch, scritch.

'There it is again,' he said. Streig lifted his head from the pillow and stared into the gloom for some clue. The sound came again.

Scritch, scritch.

He swung his legs over the bed, relieved that his ribs were paining him less. It took a moment to shake off the disorientation of waking before he approached the window.

Scritch, scritch.

He pulled back the curtain to find a great black bird perching on the ledge outside. One beady eye fixed upon him before the bird released a strident call.

'What the Hel is . . .?' Streig's gaze fell on the desk, Felgenhauer's desk, covered with tiny scraps of parchment. Scraps of parchment so small one could affix them to the leg of a bird. Streig opened the window.

'Good morning,' he said to the dark bird. 'In you come then.' The crow did just that and hopped on to the desk, staring around the room with quick motions of its head.

Silverdust watched all this from his vantage point on the mantelpiece.

I had forgotten about the messengers. Felgenhauer couldn't glean information from whispers on the wind but she had a dozen or so contacts spread around the continent. They'd send word when they thought it necessary.

Streig eyed the sharp beak and the equally sharp talons and hesitated. 'I'm not sure I want to try and take the message off him.'

He is a she. All the messengers are. Be assertive yet gentle.

Streig called to the crow and softly took the bird in one hand, his fingers slipping around the breast with one thumb atop the bird's body to stop it from wriggling away. He took a moment to unpick the knot and a moment later a small roll of parchment hit the surface of the desk.

'Not a scratch,' he said proudly, then deposited the bird in the empty cage.

A masterful first attempt.

Streig took the note and smoothed out the parchment.

And? Silverdust loaded the word with impatience.

'It says, "A new power rises in Shanisrond. A wielder of the arcane perhaps the equal of the Emperor himself. They call her the Stormtide Prophet."' Streig regarded the scrap a few moments before looking up. 'What does it mean?'

It means the Emperor has more to worry about than just Steiner Vartiainen and Felgenhauer. It means change is coming to Vinterkveld.

'I'm not sure this is a good idea,' said Streig as he stepped outside the tower. He clutched the urn and raised his eyes to the cloudy skies. Spring was coming to Vinterkveld in a procession of blustery showers and overcast days.

You've been in that room for over a week. It will do you no good to be cooped up like that. Besides, I need something; it is calling to me.

The cinderwraith had a point, and though there was the occasional snarl of pain from Streig's ribs the breeze on his face felt good.

'Not a single part of it survived,' he said quietly as they crossed the wide courtyard. Somehow the ruin of the Great Library seemed worse up close than when viewed from the tower. The smell of smoke lingered in the solemn air over the site of so much devastation. 'Where do you think Bittervinge is now?'

I would rather not think about where the father of dragons is. We have more than enough problems.

'That much is true.' Streig squinted into the distance towards the docks. A glimmer of dark green sea showed itself between the spectacular buildings. 'Food becomes more expensive every day and the blockade continues without an end in sight.'

A few rag-wrapped people moved about the ruins, picking over the remains like carrion feeders. In the main they kept to themselves, lonely figures amid the rubble. The only exception was a gang of four children who fought and squealed, their swearing and laughing a jarring contrast to the scene around them.

'People died here,' said Streig, favouring the children with a dark look. One of their number stooped and fussed for a while, earning the attention of her peers. She lifted blackened stones with bare hands and brushed away the ash until she located some relic that had survived the fire.

'It's mine. I found it!' she shouted. A larger boy shouldered his way past the other children and tried to snatch it from her.

'Give it up, or you know what you'll get,' said the surly boy. The children were so intent on their argument that they failed to notice Streig approach. The girl held a mask, and though it was covered in ash Streig had no doubts whom it belonged to.

'That belonged to a member of the Imperial Synod,' he said, his voice strong, every word carrying over the ruins. 'It belonged to an Exarch called Silverdust.' The children turned to Streig with surprise written across their dirty faces. None of them was older than thirteen and all needed feeding as much as they needed bathing. 'A lot of people died in the fire,' continued Streig. 'This place is a grave and you have my friend's mask.'

The girl blanched at this and began to offer her salvage to Streig but the large boy snatched it from her. He turned to Streig and jutted his chin, both pugnacious and stubborn.

'We found it. What're you going to give us for it?'

'Is it wrong to want to punch a child in the face?' said Streig under his breath.

Unfortunately, came the response from the urn. *But there are exceptions to every rule.*

'How much money have you got?' said the surly boy.

'What do you imagine will happen to you if you're caught with the mask of a fallen Exarch?'

'What do you mean?' The boy grasped the mask a little tighter.

'What do you imagine will happen to a snot-nosed lad who is caught with the mask of a dead Exarch?'

'We were just looking for things to sell,' said the girl. 'Food is getting pricey and we're all hungry.' Her look was apologetic and Streig didn't need the arcane to sense her shame.

'Take this,' said Streig, reaching into his money pouch. 'I don't have much, but I want the mask and doubt anyone else will buy it from you.' The surly boy dropped the offending item at his feet and stalked off, gesturing his friends to follow. The girl remained and took a handful of coins from Streig.

'Thank you.'

'Do you have any family?' he asked. The girl shook her head, not looking him in the eye. 'I'm sorry. I wish there was something I could do.'

'You just did,' replied the girl, looking at the coins in the palm of her hand. 'Thank you.' A ghost of a smile crossed her lips and then she ran off across the ruins. Streig held the mask a moment before polishing it with his sleeve.

'This is what was calling to you?' he asked as the mask began to gleam.

Yes, came the reply from the urn. *I have owned it for a great amount of time, and it is imbued with some small measure of my power.* The sun shone a little brighter before Silverdust spoke again. *You're a good person, Streig. What you did for that girl. There are not many . . .*

'Let's get you back upstairs and on the mantelpiece, shall we?' He turned back to the tower and prepared for the long climb up the spiral staircase.

CHAPTER NINE

Kjellrunn

Storyweavers occupy a strange place in the societies and cultures of Vinterkveld. Often small towns can go weeks or months without word of events occurring in the wider word. Storyweavers, sometimes known as skalds in Nordvlast, Drakefjord, and Vend, are part gossipmonger, part itinerant layabout, and part keeper of ancient tales. It's a matter of prestige for a storyweaver to know a wide selection of stories, to tell them well, and be invited back to a place. Arkiv Island was overlooked by storyweavers during my time there, but there was no denying that word of the Empire's lies and the re-emergence of dragons was disseminated by these charismatic wanderers. What the stories lacked in truth and accuracy was made up for in the enthusiastic way the storyweavers told them.

– From the memoir of Drakina Tveit,
Lead Librarian of Midtenjord Province

Xen-wa sauntered through the town towards the temple. Kjellrunn could think of no other word for it. He neither hurried nor dawdled despite the novices trailing behind, almost tripping over themselves in fascination. A dozen townsfolk also followed, curious to see what the young man had to say. Kjellrunn found the scene perplexing and decided Xen-wa was nothing more than a chancer and a charlatan with good cheekbones and mischievous eyes that served him well. That Maxim trotted along by the older boy's heels only served to irritate her further.

'So you can hear whispers on the wind?' asked Maxim. Kjellrunn's own considerable powers were rooted in earth and water and she felt a sharp pang of jealousy.

'I can.' Xen-wa shrugged as if speaking of the price of flour. 'People thought I was touched in the head at first, but then I started making sense of the messages.'

'And you can send messages?' Kjellrunn felt a moment of hope but Xen-wa shook his head.

'I never learned. It seems like a good way to end up dead. The Empire doesn't take kindly to people like me, even in Shanisrond.' He stopped a moment and looked at Kjellrunn with wariness. 'People like us, I should say.' His gaze passed over the novices as they followed behind. 'Like of all of us.'

'I have premonitions!' said Maxim brightly. 'Though I can't control them.'

Xen-wa gave Maxim a friendly smile and entered the temple. He approached the altar as if he'd lived there his whole life. Kjellrunn envied the self-assured way he strolled through life. No doubt, no second-guessing.

'What guest enters this holy place?' said Sundra, emerging from her room with a stern expression. Trine followed behind the priestess, mimicking the older woman's demeanour.

'I mean no harm.' Xen-wa gave one of his disarming smiles. 'I'm just a young storyweaver with word of the great events occurring across the continent.'

Sundra made a decidedly gruff unsatisfied noise but did not object. She looked from Kjellrunn to the storyweaver and back again, though Kjellrunn was unsure why. Xen-wa encouraged everyone to take a seat for his storytelling. A few of Romola's pirates appeared along with Romola herself, who stood at the back with her arms crossed and a cool expression on her face.

'I've heard whispers on the wind,' said Xen-wa in a strong voice that carried to the back of the room. 'And I've pieced together what has happened in the north, where even now the Empire sets its gaze on Shanisrond with evil intent.'

'Get on with it,' muttered Kjellrunn, earning herself a dark look from Maxim. Xen-wa revealed how Steiner had crossed the continent on foot, making allies of bandits before attacking a mountain pass. The tale took a darker turn when Xen-wa revealed a dozen Imperial soldiers had been burned alive in the attack. Kjellrunn put this down to exaggeration.

'Steiner would never resort to such barbaric methods,' she whispered to Maxim, but the boy shushed her, eager to hear more. The storyweaver explained how the bandits had gone on to make further attacks on the Empire from their hiding places in the forests of Karelina Province.

'But what of Steiner?' called out Maxim impatiently.

'And my father,' whispered Kjellrunn. A deep undercurrent of anxiety swirled within her.

'And just days ago Steiner appeared on the island of Arkiv with his great love, the Lady Kristofine—'

'The Lady?' whispered Maxim.

'I thought she was barmaid,' muttered Kjellrunn. Not that there was anything wrong with barmaids of course, but Kristofine was hardly nobility.

'—and took part in a mighty battle with several allies. A wounded dragon was seen fleeing from the Great Library, which burned to the ground in a terrible conflagration.'

'Frejna, please, no,' whispered Kjellrunn, feeling as if she were going to be sick. Xen-wa continued to embroider his story, building up Steiner's prowess and the terrible destruction wrought by the conflict.

'They are saying Bittervinge has returned to have his vengeance on the Empire.'

A wave of despondency rippled through the room in hushed yet urgent whispers and wary glances. But something wasn't right. Someone was missing from the story was missing.

'What of Marek Vartiainen?' called out Kjellrunn, unable to leash her curiosity any longer.

'Ah!' Xen-wa held up a finger and grinned. 'I missed a part, so many are the deeds of Steiner and Kristofine. Let us retrace his steps to shortly after the battle of the mountain pass.' The tale continued to unfold until Xen-wa reached the point where Marek had been captured by Exarch Zima in Vostochnyye Lisy.

'What?' Kjellrunn lurched from her seat, eyes wide. 'My father has been captured by the Empire and you're just telling me now?'

'I'm a storyweaver.' Xen-wa shrugged. 'I thought Steiner and Kristofine were the most important part of the . . .' His words dwindled into silence as Kjellrunn stalked up to him. For a second she was sure she would slap him across his handsome face, before she remembered she was wearing initiate's robes. Attacking people in the Temple was hardly the conduct of a priestess of Frejna.

'This is how I find out my father has been captured?' she whispered. 'This isn't simply a story to earn you coin. This is my family you're speaking of.'

'Perhaps I should have said something sooner,' admitted Xen-wa with a rueful look. He took a step back, hands held up to placate her. Kjellrunn marched out of the temple, keen to be away from anyone and everyone.

The familiar form of the *Watcher's Wait* lay quietly by a stone pier, though she was much diminished from her recent encounter with two Imperial galleons. The stout Imperial vessels had carried Vigilants in addition to their regular crew, and arcane fire had rained down on the masts and sails of Romola's ship, rendering it little more than a scorched barge. The pirates who could walk were doing what they could to salvage timber from the wrecks of the Imperial ships, though it was slow work in the Shanisrond heat. Kjellrunn stood on the beach and watched the men and women work, feeling the sand between her toes, trying to overcome the shock of Marek's fate.

'He's not bad,' said Romola from over Kjellrunn's shoulder. The captain had followed her down to the shore but Kjellrunn had not slowed her pace. She had wanted to be alone after all. Romola, being Romola, had doggedly followed her all the same. 'The storyweaver, I mean. He's not that bad.'

'He's not *that* handsome,' muttered Kjellrunn.

'I meant his storytelling, not his looks.' A slow smile crossed Romola's face.

'My father.' Tears sprang to Kjellrunn's eyes and she fell into Romola's arms. The pirate captain looked surprised for a heartbeat before wrapping her arms about the slender young woman. 'He could already be dead by now,' sobbed Kjellrunn. Romola said nothing and simply held her. 'And that stupid boy blurted it out in front of everyone.' Kjellrunn broke the embrace and wiped her tears on the back of her hand.

'I forget how young you are sometimes,' said Romola, trying to stifle a laugh behind her hand.

'What?' Kjellrunn frowned.

'He's really got under your skin, right?'

'That's ridiculous. I've barely known him an hour. I'm not sure I even like boys that way.' Kjellrunn sniffed and pressed the heels of her hands to her eyes. 'It's my father that I'm upset about.' She looked out to sea and felt the comforting presence of the leviathan, solid and patient.

'He's a thoughtless fool for not telling you about your father sooner,' admitted Romola. 'But he's very young.'

'Young and annoying.' Kjellrunn gazed towards the north-east where her family were. 'If I'd been able to hear whispers on the wind I would have gone to them—'

'Leaving everyone here undefended. They would have surely perished without you.'

'That may be true, but I have to go to Arkiv and find Steiner,' she added calmly. 'And then I'm going to find my father.'

'We're not going anywhere,' said Romola, indicating the *Watcher's Wait*. 'I want to set sail as badly as you do, but we've no masts and I'm not even sure we've enough crew to make a voyage into open seas, right? I lost a lot of people.'

'Then I'll go on foot,' said Kjellrunn, knowing full well she'd have to walk all the way to Vend Province and back down the other side of the Ashen Gulf before reaching Khlystburg. Such a journey would take months. It was a childish thing to say, but she felt childish. She wanted her father, her brother, her family, and she would do anything, go anywhere to get them back.

'It's bad enough that I never knew my mother.' She clenched her fists and looked at the wrecked hulks of the Imperial galleons. 'I refused to lose anyone else to the Empire.'

'Why don't we go back to the temple and have some tea?' replied Romola. 'I'm sure Sundra will have something helpful to say on the subject, right?'

'You cannot leave,' shouted Sundra in the temple's kitchen. 'You are an initiate of Frejna. Your place is here tending to the people of Dos Khor. You made a commitment to the goddess, and to me.'

'This was not what I had in mind,' muttered Romola, taking care to stand in the doorway away from the two priestesses.

The argument had started almost the moment Kjellrunn had returned from the beach.

'What if it was your brother out there risking his life?' shouted Kjellrunn.

'My brother *is* out there risking his life!' replied Sundra, though the heat faded from her words and an expression of pained worry crossed her face. 'I don't know where he is or even if he is still alive, or Taiga either.' Sundra drew closer to Kjellrunn and took her hand gently. 'I don't want to lose anyone else, Kjellrunn, least of all you.'

'But Father needs me. I could help. The goddesses have given me these powers and a rebellion is raging across the gulf. I should go to them.'

'Kjellrunn.' Sundra pressed a hand to her forehead. 'How are you going to get there?'

'Perhaps if I can get to Arkiv I can find Steiner and we can look for my father together.'

'We lost so many on the beach that day.' Sundra shook her head with an expression of deep sadness. 'Now I'm going to lose you too.' She sat down slowly and all her years settled about her shoulders like a great weight.

'I can't just stay here like a little girl while the men in my family are risking everything,' added Kjellrunn, her voice low and calm.

'But you are a little girl,' whispered Sundra. 'Just sixteen summers.'

'And if you were me?' asked Kjellrunn.

'If I were you' – Sundra gave a small begrudging laugh – 'I would be full of the same determined intensity. But I worry for you, Kjellrunn. The bones whisper your name. They whisper death.'

'It's not my death you see,' replied Kjellrunn. 'It's the death that follows in my wake; it is the death that goes ahead of me like a stormtide.'

'Kjellrunn, listen to yourself,' chided Sundra.

'You said yourself, sometimes a priestess must watch and wait, but there are times when we must act.'

'And now is one of those times,' said Romola softly. 'If Steiner or Kimi fail to kill the Emperor then we'll have perhaps six seasons before Shanisrond is crawling with Imperial soldiers.'

'But she's so young,' said Sundra in a small voice.

'I'll go with her,' said Romola. 'I know a thing or two about getting around Vinterkveld. I can get her as far as Khlystburg.'

'But you have no ship,' added Sundra, a look of annoyance on her face.

'Not one with masts,' said Kjellrunn. 'But perhaps we don't need them.'

Kjellrunn swept back into the temple, where Xen-wa was trading coins for gossip from the other towns.

'I hope you're going to donate some of that to the temple,' said Kjellrunn with a hard look. Xen-wa glanced from priestess to pirate.

'I always feel like I'm in trouble when I speak to you,' he said slowly. His usual veneer of confidence seemed to have worn distinctly thin.

'I need you,' began Kjellrunn. Her cheeks became warm as she blushed, suddenly aware of what she'd said. 'We need you, is what I mean. We're heading to Arkiv by ship, but I – I mean we need someone with your talent.'

'I could, but I promised my family in Nadira I'd be back in the next month.'

'You have family?' Kjellrunn found this more implausible than the fact Xen-wa had arcane gifts.

'An aunt and a cat. And someone else.' He waved his hand vaguely but Kjellrunn understood perfectly.

'The Empire could be here in as little as a year and a half

and I don't suppose your aunt, your cat, or your "someone" will enjoy that very much.'

'I am not coming to Khlystburg,' replied Xen-wa softly. 'I have to go home.' And with that he departed the temple with the same maddening saunter that he'd entered with. Kjellrunn looked at Romola, who returned the look with a shrug before rubbing her forehead with one hand.

'Men, right?'

'What about boys?' Maxim had been standing by the altar the whole time, listening to the exchange between Xen-wa and Kjellrunn. Trine hovered just behind him, looking a touch guilty for such obvious eavesdropping. 'You need someone that can hear whispers on the wind—'

'Maxim, you've only just come into your powers. I can't ask you to do this.'

'You're not asking me,' he said in a tone much older than his years. 'I'm volunteering.'

'Maxim.' Romola dropped to one knee and smiled. 'You're just a kid and Khlystburg is the most dangerous place in all of Vinterkveld.'

'Dangerous?' Maxim frowned. 'I was with Steiner at the very beginning. I met him on the ship to Vladibogdan. Your ship!' He pointed an accusing finger at Romola, who stood up and backed away.

'I needed the money.' Romola glanced at Trine with a guilty expression. 'It wasn't my finest hour, right? I've changed since then.'

'I know about danger,' continued Maxim. 'Steiner and I saved each other's lives. I'd still be on that island now if it wasn't for him.'

'Where he goes I go,' added Trine, one hand resting on the boy's shoulder.

'Seems you've got yourself a crew,' said Romola. 'So what happens now?'

'Now we buy rope,' said Kjellrunn. 'Or salvage it.'

'How much rope?' replied the captain. 'And what for?'

'All the rope we can lay our hands on.' Kjellrunn led her crew from the temple. 'Come on.'

'You haven't told us what the rope is for,' pressed Trine.

'You're right. I haven't.' Kjellrunn bit her lip, unsure how her friends would react once she'd revealed how she intended to reach Arkiv and Khlystburg without sails.

CHAPTER TEN

Ruslan

Seven decades may not seem like a terribly long time to an academic or a historian, but there are a few considerations to include when it comes to the preservation of truth and the tales that are passed down over time. Men could expect to survive to fifty if they lived in the poorer provinces of the Empire, being engaged in more manual work as men often are. Low-born women could hope to see sixty years on average, but even the nobles rarely lived beyond sixty-five. Those who saw the war with the dragons first-hand were likely enjoying their final rest, and the only people who could truthfully say they remembered the giant reptiles were the Emperor himself and Silverdust. Memories fade and stories passed from generation to generation lose something in the retelling. Many city folk thought they had succumbed to madness when the dragons returned in the skies above Khlystburg. How had these creatures from story and myth appeared in the humdrum everyday life of thankless toil and harsh taxes?

– From the memoir of Drakina Tveit,
Lead Librarian of Midtenjord Province

The north of the city was noticeably more affluent than the other districts of Khlystburg. The Boyar had given him permission to take his leave, and so with no tasks to fulfil and a little money available to him, Ruslan had explored. The streets were swept by teams of low-born men and women, while the shop fronts were in good repair and recently painted. There were fewer carts transporting food and cargo, and more carriages ferrying the nobles and officials of the Empire. The homeless and the desperate were moved on by roving pairs of black-armoured soldiers and Ruslan felt their gaze fall upon him more than once. He'd been able to avoid them in the main, but finally his luck had run dry, and the aide found himself facing two soldiers, their black helms giving nothing away, save for their loyalty. The red star of the Solmindre Empire was plain to see above the eye slot.

'What business have you in this part of the city?' said one of the soldiers. Ruslan's gaze drifted to the soldier's mace, clenched in an eager fist.

'I am exploring the city, nothing more. I'm from Vend Province.'

'Vend?' He could hear the scorn in the soldier's voice. 'Buildings and roads must be quite a shock to you.'

Ruslan forced a smile and refused to rise to the soldier's bait.

'Who are you?' said the second soldier, stepping closer. 'And why are you in Khlystburg?'

'I am Ruslan Hasanov, aide to Boyar Augustine Sokolov, who has been summoned here by the Emperor himself.' Something unsaid passed between the soldiers, but neither of them moved. 'Am I free to go on my way?'

'You can go on your way,' said the soldier clutching the mace, 'but I doubt you or your Boyar will be free for much longer after that business with his son.'

'You know about Dimitri?' Ruslan had known the scandal was the talk of the nobles; clearly he'd been naive to think the news would remain within the upper echelons of the Empire.

'Everyone and their mother knows.' The soldiers turned their backs and began to walk down the street at a leisurely pace, seeming to enjoy the intimidation caused by their presence.

'Be careful now,' said an old man guiding a handcart. A rattling cough shook him as he held up a fist to his mouth. 'They're arresting all sorts these days, rich *and* poor.' He had white hair and a beard that reached his chest. One shoulder sat higher than the other and his head was cocked to one side as if he were waiting on an answer. The man's eyes were quick and bright. Ruslan didn't doubt he'd seen plenty and had plenty to tell. The cart contained rancid bones and Ruslan hoped they had belonged to animals. 'Even the loyal aren't safe when the Okhrana knock on the door at midnight,' said the old man, casting a look over his shoulder.

'Why do they come for loyal subjects?'

'The Emperor is losing his grip; he sees danger in every shadow. And even the skies are no longer safe.'

Ruslan looked up in the pale blue spring sky; it was another bright day in Khlystburg. It was still cold enough to kill any drunks should they pass out in the street.

'Has there been an attack today?' said Ruslan quietly.

'Not yet,' replied the old man. Columns of smoke on the horizon were testament to night-time predations. Draconic fire had rained down and cost people their homes and most likely their lives.

'Devoured from within,' said the old man, looking at the soldiers. 'And devoured from without,' he added, jutting his head at the skies to the north. 'The Emperor made us all believe these were the golden days, but night has fallen, I think. It's only a matter of time until darkness consumes everything.'

An uncomfortable chill raced down Ruslan's spine at the

man's words as he made his way back to the apartments where his master brooded behind brocade drapes.

The Boyar had said little since his audience with the Emperor in the catacombs, settling into a deep melancholy upon their return. It had lasted nearly a week. Neither of them had voiced their relief that the Boyar still lived, but Ruslan felt it keenly.

'Good. You're back,' said Sokolov as Ruslan entered his master's suite. The drapes had been drawn back while an untouched breakfast waited on a tray. The bed had been made and windows left ajar, which had remedied the airless and dusty atmosphere in the chamber but introduced a spiteful chill. The Boyar remained as grey as he had during the voyage, but he was dressed at least. He stood at the window watching the comings and goings of the Imperial capital with a quiet intensity.

'I think I've explored enough,' said Ruslan. 'The streets are not the safest place for one such as I.' His master refused to be drawn into conversation, wearing his silence like armour. 'I'm not used to having time on my hands, my lord,' continued Ruslan. 'Why the endless waiting? I thought we were charged with locating Steiner Vart—'

'I don't pay you to think,' snapped the Boyar. 'We came here to make sure House Sokolov endures, nothing more.'

Ruslan settled into a chastened silence, all too aware he'd overstepped his bounds as a simple aide.

'It's good that you have explored,' said the Boyar, squinting at something in the street. 'It's good to familiarize yourself with your surroundings. One can be better prepared for surprises when one knows the lie of the land.'

Ruslan was about to ask the Boyar to clarify his rather cryptic pronouncement when a knock sounded at the door. It was a measured and polite tap of someone who waited on nobility often, Ruslan guessed. A delicate, mousy girl with large eyes entered the room. She looked pale and anxious in equal measure – and for good reason, as it turned out.

'Exarch Zima is here to see you, my lord.' She bobbed a curtsey and took her leave, disappearing into the darkness of the corridor. Moments later a bestial face appeared from the gloom, the wolverine mask of Zima leering at the Boyar. He still had one arm in a sling, yet there was little to suggest he was frail or in pain.

'I would speak to you,' said the Exarch. He inclined his head towards Ruslan just a fraction and tapped his thigh impatiently with his one good hand.

'I didn't think you were here to play cards,' said the Boyar from between gritted teeth, not looking away from the window.

'I would speak to you *privately*,' pressed the Exarch, and Ruslan felt the weight of Zima's gaze fall upon him. He couldn't be sure what foul witchery the Exarch was capable of and had no wish to find out. Perhaps he could excuse himself.

'Ruslan stays,' said the Boyar. Sokolov sat in one of the high-backed leather armchairs that dominated the centre of the room, and crossed his legs. He looked at the Exarch with a grave expression, peering over his steepled fingers.

'This concerns your recent conversation with the Emperor,' said Zima.

There was dreadful stillness about him that put Ruslan on edge. The Boyar drew a short knife from the sheath at his hip and began to sharpen it slowly with a whetstone. The sound scratched its way across every polished surface in the room, including Ruslan.

'I can't very well do the Emperor's bidding,' replied the Boyar, 'if my own aide doesn't know what I'm trying to achieve.' He curled his lip in irritation, an expression he usually reserved for incompetent servants back in Vend.

Ruslan blinked in surprise. The Boyar's anger was a welcome change to the pall of despair that had hung over him, but to talk in such a way to an Exarch was unwise in the extreme.

'Very well,' said Exarch Zima and stepped towards to the chair opposite.

'I did not give you permission to sit,' said the Boyar. Zima stiffened, paused, then took a step back and folded the fingers of his good hand into a fist.

'Do you have anything to report?' said the Exarch in a quiet voice loaded with impatience.

'I have barely had a week since with my audience with the Emperor.' The Boyar continued sharpening the knife. 'He has asked me to find a needle in a proverbial haystack, or more accurately a needle that doesn't wish to be found.'

'The Emperor doesn't care for proverbs,' replied Zima smoothly. 'Only results.'

'I am completely ostracized by the court, my contacts here refuse to return my messages—'

'The ruse of your disgrace is necessary to lure Steiner Vartiainen out of hiding.'

'And if he doesn't seek me out?' asked Boyar Sokolov with a despondent tone. He ceased sharpening the knife for a moment and his eyes lost their focus.

'Are you reneging on the scheme so kindly offered by the Emperor?'

'Perhaps the Okhrana have had more luck than I in finding the needle?' The Boyar resumed his maddening *scrape, scrape* of the whetstone on the short blade.

'The Emperor set this task before you and for good reason,' added Zima.

'The Emperor set this task before me because he killed my son, and that makes people think I might join the rebels.'

Zima tilted his head to one side as if thinking this through. 'Strange. I had thought the task some form of penance for your son's treason.' Ruslan couldn't know for sure on account of the mask, but if he had to guess he would have bet a month's wage the Exarch was smiling.

'We both know Dimitri was innocent. He wasn't clever enough to get wrapped up in such intrigue. The Emperor knew it and more to the point I know it.'

'And yet Dimitri still lies dead by the Emperor's hand,' replied Zima, not bothering to hide his gloating. Boyar Sokolov clenched his jaw and stopped sharpening the dagger, looking up from the blade with eyes full of murder. 'I wouldn't chance it if I were you,' said the Exarch calmly. 'You'd be dead before you're out of the chair.' The Boyar put away the blade and took a deep breath. The Exarch turned and made to leave before hesitating by the door. 'I don't care about your injured pride, Augustine, or your grief, or the grand storied past of the Sokolov line. Find Steiner Vartiainen and set the trap.' Exarch Zima threw open the door and was swallowed by the dark corridor beyond. Ruslan closed the door quietly and sighed with relief.

'Pompous ass,' grunted the Boyar as he stood up from the chair and approached the window.

'There could still be a chance to avenge Dimitri,' said Ruslan quietly. 'There could yet be a way to preserve the Sokolov line.'

'Do you really think the same thought hadn't occurred to me while I have been rattling around this gilded cage?' The Boyar looked at him but there was no hatred in his eyes, just the heavy look of sadness that had haunted him all week. 'To double-cross the Emperor with his own scheme. Now that would be something for the history books,' he said, forcing a smile Ruslan was sure he didn't feel. 'Shall we venture out into the city?'

'You want to start searching for Steiner today?'

'You heard the Exarch. He wants results. I don't doubt I

am being watched.' Sokolov sighed. 'I must do something. And soon.'

'Yes, my lord,' replied Ruslan on instinct. The Boyar led the way into the street that he had been so fascinated by and shielded his eyes with the flat of his hand. Ruslan wasn't surprised. His master hadn't set foot outside the suite in almost a week; no doubt the light was hurting his eyes.

'Do you see that?' asked the Boyar. Ruslan followed the direction of his gaze.

'Is it the dragon?' Ruslan tried to make out the form that glided above the distant horizon of the city. 'I heard a rumour that Bittervinge, father of dragons, has returned from death itself to wreak his vengeance on the Empire.'

'Or perhaps the Emperor never killed Bittervinge in the first place,' muttered the Boyar. 'Another lie in a series of lies that has helped hold the Empire together these seven decades.'

'We should return inside, my lord. It's not safe.' But the Boyar didn't move.

'If that's Bittervinge,' he said, pointing at a dark winged shadow in the skies to the north, 'then who or what are those?' Three other dragons flew up from the south, powering towards the father of dragons on majestic wings, each a different hue to their kin, each appearing to bear a rider on its shoulders.

'We should return inside, my lord,' said Ruslan, unable to think of anything else to say at such a sight. 'This is madness.'

CHAPTER ELEVEN

Kimi

The appearance of dragons over Khlystburg both confused and terrified people, but more confusing still was the simple truth that three of the smaller dragons carried riders. None knew who these mysterious individuals were at first. Speculation was rife regarding what they wanted and why they fought the father of dragons. Word spread over the coming weeks that none other than a Yamal princess was leading the defence of Khlystburg, which captured people's imagination then, just as it does now. Few could predict then the fate that awaited Kimi Enkhtuya, or the tale of her exile and subsequent journey across the dead lands of Izhoria.
– From the memoir of Drakina Tveit,
Lead Librarian of Midtenjord Province

'The size of that bastard,' muttered Kimi as she leaned closer to Namarii's neck. Ahead of them, on the horizon above Khlystburg, was a dark silhouette that filled her with dread. The wind whipped at her and made a flag of her cloak as Namarii surged through the skies. The buildings rushed past, perhaps fifty feet below her boots, and screams sounded everywhere. The people of Khlystburg ran along the streets, desperate to reach the outskirts of the city.

'This was not how I had envisaged today would go,' she shouted. Stonvind and Flodvind flew either side of Namarii, almost wingtip to wingtip. Tief and Taiga nodded gravely. The plan had been simple: they were testing the defences at the Imperial Palace, trying to get a feel for how many Vigilants were protecting the Emperor. Soldiers they could deal with, but Vigilants were a different issue. However, what awaited them in the skies above the capital defied belief.

'Is it . . .' She could barely believe she was asking the question. Bittervinge was an old terror born from myth, a memory from nightmare, a tale from legend.

The so-called father of dragons. Namarii snorted a plume of smoke that Kimi had come to recognize as a sign of displeasure or dismissal. Tief scowled at the people below.

'They're going to get eaten!' he bellowed above the wind.

'Let's provide a distraction,' shouted Kimi.

We are here to kill the Emperor. Kimi could feel the displeasure radiating out of Namarii, or perhaps it was just the heat.

'These people need our help!' shouted Taiga, and Kimi couldn't disagree.

Bittervinge dived upon the fraught and teeming city streets, snatching a pair of people into his mouth. He had swooped into the sky again before anyone could react. One person slipped from his fanged maw just heartbeats later, only to fall to her death. The other disappeared down the dragon's throat. Flodvind released a roar, though Kimi couldn't tell if it was in irritation or challenge.

'How are we going to do this?' yelled Kimi as Namarii drew ever closer to the jet-black dragon glittering in the afternoon sun.

I have questions. Kimi could feel the tension in Namarii's shoulders. The motion of the dragon's flight was different, not the sinuous grace she had known during the last week.

'Well, I don't have any questions,' replied Kimi. 'Can we just kill him?'

Bittervinge caught sight of the three young dragons and perched on the side of a stone sentry tower, which shook and groaned under the creature's weight.

'What's he doing?' shouted Kimi.

Who can tell? But I intend to ask.

The sentry tower overlooked a market square which emptied itself in a panicked stampede. Bittervinge extended his long neck and snatched up a straggler as if they were no more than a sweetmeat. The person had time for one last scream before three savage bites ended their life. Namarii circled while Stonvind and Flodvind settled on rooftops across the market square from the father of dragons. There was a great deal of snorting dark smoke and flexing of claws from the younger dragons, while Bittervinge chewed slowly on the human he'd snared just moments before.

'My conversations with Veles always ended poorly,' said Kimi, noting how much larger Bittervinge was compared to Stonvind and Flodvind. Namarii swooped in and landed cat-like on a townhouse that overlooked the market square. The tiled roof groaned under the weight but the building stayed firm, much to Kimi's relief.

I have questions. I will have answers. Namarii folded his wings with a quick snapping motion. Bittervinge turned his gaze on Stonvind first, who flared his wings in response and raised his chin. Deep gouges appeared on the rooftop as Stonvind growled and made clear his intentions.

'What's he doing?' whispered Kimi.

Bittervinge is trying to dominate us with the force of his personality. Stonvind is letting him know he will not be cowed or make a show of subservience.

'And your mother too!' shouted Tief, dropping his trousers and baring his arse for good measure.

'Goddess help me,' muttered Kimi as she pressed one hand to her eyes.

Bittervinge turned his dark gaze on Flodvind next, seemingly rebuffed by Stonvind. The azure dragon looked to Stonvind, then to Namarii, snubbing the father of dragons with casual indifference. Bittervinge climbed to the very top of the sentry tower and flared his wings, then released a gout of fire into the sky with a terrible sound like thousand scrolls being torn apart. Flodvind responded by tapping one scythe-like talon against the rooftop, a curiously human gesture signalling her boredom. Bittervinge turned to Namarii last and long silent moments crawled by. Kimi was sure some message was being passed between them.

'What's he saying?' she whispered as the two dragons locked gazes.

He is not using words; rather he is trying to intimidate us with his size and his presence. But I have something more powerful than both of things.

'What?' whispered Kimi, unable to drag her eyes away from Bittervinge.

My anger.

Bittervinge flapped his wings, which Kimi took for petulance or irritation.

Are you such dumb beasts that you make no effort to offer me fealty or even greet me? Are you such callow and timid creatures that these humans ride you like cattle? The father of dragons projected his words into the minds of all present and Kimi gripped on to Namarii a little tighter and gritted her teeth. The words were akin to the chiming of a great bell in their quiet minds. Taiga had clapped her hands over her ears on instinct, though it would do her no good. Stonvind, Flodvind, and Namarii stared down the black dragon on the sentry tower with unflinching gazes.

Answer me! thundered Bittervinge, casting his words with such force that Tief flinched in his saddle.

We owe you neither answers nor fealty nor greeting. We owe you nothing. It was Namarii's words sounding in Kimi's mind now, measured and even. *It is you who will answer to us. You who left us to rot in the dark place beneath Vladibogdan. It was once your nest. I detected a scent on the island, but never the dragon who had made it their home. Now I see you, I smell you. You have been alive this whole time and you never came for us. Now you will tell us why.*

Namarii finished his demand with a low growl that caused Kimi's legs to vibrate and a surge of alarm run up her spine. Bittervinge responded with a terrible grinding sound, and though he cast no words using the arcane, Kimi knew it to be laughter.

Dragons are their own masters. A dragon is not to be rescued. I would never dream to swoop so low as to rescue a dragon, any more than I would expect to be rescued myself.

It was then that Kimi understood why Namarii had such trouble with the concept of loyalty or friendship.

'Not much of a father, is he?' she whispered to Namarii.

You and I have much in common in that respect. Kimi blinked in surprise at Namarii's reply, then wondered just how deeply he had listened to her thoughts while they had flown together. Flodvind and Stonvind cast furtive looks at one another but said nothing.

You did not know of my incarceration on the island of Arkiv. Bittervinge had toned down the power of his projection, so the words were the soft peals of wind chimes. *How could you? Trapped beneath Vladibogdan as you were. I suspect there is much you do not know, that you do not understand. Very well.* Bittervinge flared his jet-black wings until they were fully outstretched, casting a dark shadow over the market square below. *I will be your teacher. Throw off these weak humans and join me. We will dine on the fat continent and make every last human endure a life of suffering.*

Now it was Namarii's turn to make that awful grinding laughter, and Bittervinge startled at the mockery of it.

These weak humans slew Veles, replied Namarii.

These weak humans fed us in the darkness below the island, replied Flodvind. *They showed us kindness in a place of despair.*

These weak humans have borne their own incarceration, added Stonvind, his words sounding like rocks sliding down a mountainside in Kimi's mind.

Bittervinge shook his head and folded his wings. *And you had it in mind to come here, to Khlystburg, and tear down the Emperor who did this to you?*

'I seek vengeance!' shouted Kimi. 'For what was done to me and my people. I will face the Emperor and end his eternal rule.'

Brave words for one so young, but what do you know of vengeance? For seventy-five years I have waited in the Great Library of Arkiv. Every day was a torment to me, and now I am free I will sate myself on the souls of Vinterkveld's people. I will devour them completely, and then, when I have decimated the population and regained my strength, I will face the Emperor.

'We can't let him do that,' whispered Kimi to Namarii. 'We'd simply be swapping one tyrant for another.'

A winged tyrant, no less.

Namarii beat down with his wings and sprang into the air. Stonvind and Flodvind followed his lead a heartbeat later. Bittervinge launched himself from the sentry tower. The building sagged and collapsed in a cloud of stone dust as the father of dragons took to the sky. Tattered and ancient black wings beat the air as the younger dragons flew higher still.

This may hurt. The sound of rocks on mountainside again. Stonvind closed his wings against his sides and dived at Bittervinge. Tief made a noise that was somewhere between a battle cry and a drawn-out yell of alarm. The father of dragons responded with a gout of bright orange fire and Stonvind banked and turned, catching the blast on his breast. The dark grey dragon raked at Bittervinge with all four claws before speeding away, leaving bright gouges and shredded scales in his wake.

'Attack!' said Kimi, frustrated by Namarii's caution.

In time.

No sooner had Stonvind departed than Flodvind pounced, landing on the father of dragons in mid-air, her claws seizing the black dragon's shoulders as she clamped her maw around the dragon's head.

Fools! Witless fools! raged Bittervinge. Flodvind released a blast of fiery breath, scorching the father of dragon's obsidian scales. Bittervinge struggled to stay aloft, writhing to be free of the azure dragon's claws. Kimi could almost sense the black dragon's surprise as Flodvind released him and flew away, but not before Taiga swiped at him with her sickle, opening a cruel wound in his wing.

Now we strike, Your Highness.

The father of dragons turned to pursue Flodvind and failed to see Namarii closing in. Kimi held on with all her strength and instinctively closed her eyes. She was almost shaken loose as the two draconic bodies slammed into one another. Bittervinge spiralled downward and Kimi wondered if he might crash into the city like a downed kite. Flodvind and Taiga, Stonvind and Tief all stared, daring to hope the father of dragons had met his end, but his black wings spread wide and Bittervinge pulled out of the dizzying dive. He glided low over the city, speeding over the rooftops, heading north to the plains.

'We should go after him,' yelled Tief.

No. Namarii hovered above the city for a moment. *We have driven him off, denied him a source of food. He will remain weak for a while longer.*

'But he's wounded!' replied Tief.

As is Stonvind. And you were fortunate not to be immolated. Namarii descended once again.

*   *   *

The sight of three dragons descending from the skies caused another mass panic in the west of the city. One by one the great beasts landed in a wide square and chased off any soldiers foolish enough to stand their ground. Kimi had suggested they land nearer the docks and Namarii had seen the sense in her suggestion.

'We should have gone after him,' shouted Tief the moment all three of the dragons and their riders had their feet on the ground. He was red-faced with anger and exhilaration and Namarii stared the man down with a stillness that Kimi found disconcerting.

I was not ready. Namarii shook his head and rolled his shoulders.

Nor I. The sound of stone scraping on stone. Kimi was startled to hear Stonvind speak again. Flodvind yawned and looked away to the horizon.

'What?' Tief turned to his dragon. 'Not ready? You led the charge. I saw you claw him to ribbons! You can bet your boots he's going to be licking those wounds a good long while.'

Stonvind lowered his head so his eye was close to Tief. *And while he does so we shall eat, and grow, and gather our strength.*

'They're still very young' – Kimi crossed the square to where Tief stood, still glaring at Namarii – 'and this isn't just any dragon we're ganging up on, this is Bittervinge. Did you see the size of him?'

'You saw how it went.' Tief gestured to Flodvind and Stonvind. 'They carved him up. Flodvind alone looked like she could take him one on one.'

Tief. The word floated into their minds calmly. *My attack was successful because Stonvind created a distraction. I had good fortune, but now I am tired. It takes huge reserves to move these bones, these muscles, these wings. We must eat.*

'Hel's teeth.' Tief's shoulders sagged as the fire went out of him and he accepted the azure dragon's words. 'So what happens now?'

'We find dinner,' replied Taiga, stroking Flodvind's neck. 'And hope to the goddesses there's plenty of it.'

'I think I saw some warehouses nearby as we came in to land,' said Kimi. 'Perhaps we'll find something there.'

In his turn, Namarii lowered his head until one large amber eye was level with Kimi's face.

And then we can discuss the artefacts you are carrying.

'Oh. That.' The mere thought of the Ashen Blade made her blood run cold. Suddenly she was trapped in Veles' cave, watching him raise gholes from the bodies of dead Okhrana.

Yes. That. I felt them stir. I assume Bittervinge created them?

'Bittervinge crafted the Ashen Blades,' replied Kimi. 'But the Ashen Torment has been remade by the goddess Frøya.'

I see. Namarii rose up to his full height and huffed a great breath of irritation.

'It's likely that the Ashen Blade is the only thing that can really kill the Emperor.'

Namarii let out a long low growl that perfectly summed up how everyone felt.

'Nothing is ever straightforward, is it?' said Taiga in that relentlessly cheerful manner that Kimi found infuriating.

We will think on this more later. Flodvind approached Namarii and gave him a gentle headbutt, hard enough to move him in the direction of the docks. *For now we eat.*

CHAPTER TWELVE

Streig

All things fade in time: loyalty, enchantment, youth, enthusiasm, even duty. Sometimes, if we are fortunate, we are inspired by some other animus; new passions replace the old. But only if we are fortunate.

— From the memoir of Drakina Tveit,
Lead Librarian of Midtenjord Province

Streig returned from the shops, which were almost all bare. Those stores that still had stock were selling it for grossly inflated prices. He'd taken to carrying the urn with him on such errands, unwilling to leave Silverdust in the tower alone, defenceless.

We must a find a way to leave Arkiv or you will surely starve to death.

Streig opened his mouth to reply and his steps faltered. He was sure he could see a figure in the window.

You are anxious. Someone waits for us in the tower.

Streig's expression turned to one of dismay. 'Surely they can't have returned already?'

We shall find out soon enough, replied Silverdust.

The climb up the spiral stairs was arduous and Streig

doubted that he'd find anything good once he'd reached the top.

'Do you have any sense who it is?' he said, glancing upwards, tension written in the lines of his face.

It is the corporal. She has returned and is waiting for you.

And wait she did as Streig struggled up the many tower steps, climbing the spiral staircase one painful step at a time.

The corporal was standing next to the bird cage when they finally entered the room. She spoke quietly to the recently arrived crow, her tender manner at odds with her black enamelled armour and the mace that hung from her belt. The soldier straightened up as Streig entered; she forced a tight smile but there was little cheer in it. Her gaze drifted to the urn he clutched, but she kept any questions to herself.

'You look better,' said the corporal. 'Stronger.'

'Stronger.' Streig gave a weary smile. 'I barely made it up the stairs. Still, my ribs are better.' The corporal looked out of the window and Streig wondered if the rest of her comrades were close by. 'Are you here to tell me I'm a deserter?' he asked. 'Or are you going to order me to join your troop?'

'For once in my life I get to be the bearer of good news.' The corporal relaxed a little. 'Not often that happens for people in our line of work.'

'I'll put the kettle on,' said Streig.

'No need,' replied the corporal. 'I can't stop long but I wanted you to know this: there's a ship that's been given special dispensation to leave Arkiv. It's taking a number of loyal Imperial dignitaries back to Khlystburg along with several wounded soldiers. Perhaps if one more wounded soldier found his way to the docks he might find a way aboard.'

Streig sat down on one of the chairs and caught his breath. 'When does it leave?'

'Tonight.' The corporal's expression turned to one of regret.

'I'm afraid I can't put a word in for you. I don't have that sort of influence.'

'Tonight. So soon. Frejna's teeth.' The idea of returning to Khlystburg filled him dread but his wish to see Silverdust restored would not be silenced.

'I'll pretend I didn't hear that,' said the corporal, her eyes narrowed. 'Did Silverdust fill your head with talk of the goddesses?'

Streig held up one hand and frowned, half amused, half incredulous. 'Is now really the time to start accusing people of treason? I mean, he is dead. Very dead.' He raised the urn to make his point. 'No one has filled my head with anything.' As it turned out, the truth of that statement was short-lived.

We must go. Silverdust's words echoed in Streig's mind like the faint chime of a bell. *I am sorry, Streig, but we must take this chance.*

'The choice is yours,' said the corporal. 'I can't tarry any longer; my men are already suspicious.' She crossed the room and opened the door.

'Why?' asked Streig. 'Why do this for me if you're still loyal to the Emperor.'

The corporal looked at him for a moment and a look of pain clouded her face.

'My youngest brother is probably about your age,' she said to Streig. 'I never wanted him to join the Imperial Army. Now he is dead. Killed defending some lonely mountain pass between two provinces he neither knew nor cared for. I can't offer you a way out of the army but I can try and get you free of this damned island. You've served your time and you've fought your share. There's no good reason you should starve with the rest of the people here.'

The corporal turned and was gone with a swirl of her black cloak. The sounds of boots scuffed on the stairs as she descended, making the silence that followed all the louder.

Streig. If there were some other way, some way to spare you from this, you know I would.

'This is a fool's errand,' Streig said finally. He set the urn upon the mantelpiece. 'And I'm the perfect fool for it. Obedient, dutiful, useful.'

You are no fool, Streig. And I will ask no more of you once I am restored.

'We don't even know if you can be restored,' replied Streig, the words as bitter as they were quiet. 'Or by whom.'

Streig packed the few things he owned. He bundled up the urn in an old shirt hoping no one would search him. It felt strange to head off without armour, without a mace, without even a travel cloak. All of it had been taken from him by the fire. All of the things that made him who he was had been lost in the collapse of the Great Library.

You are more than just armour and a weapon.

'That may be true, but I feel naked without them.'

An old pack had been left behind when Felgenhauer had departed Arkiv, and Streig was grateful for it. He slung the bag over his shoulder and then fetched the great sword, though the weight made him groan with effort. He'd opened the bird-cage door and the window perhaps half an hour earlier, but the dark bird remained on its perch, watching him with quiet intensity.

'You're free to go where you please,' said Streig. 'No more messages for you.' The crow made a grumbling noise, neither coo or squawk, and fussed at her tail feathers. 'Be seeing you.' Streig gave a lazy salute to the crow and headed out of the door. The walk to the docks was a difficult one. Uncertainty about Khlystburg dogged his steps while doubts that he would be allowed aboard the ship gave him pause.

We will find a way.

'I wish I shared your confidence.' Streig took in the details of the city, all too aware that this might be the last time he saw it. While the architecture was grand the people were less so. The daily comings and goings of the port had ceased and all meaning had faltered for the majority of workers in Arkiv. Some townsfolk had loaded up carts and prepared to leave the city, but Streig couldn't think where they might go. It was not a large island, and the rocky ground wasn't suited to farming, or much of anything.

'This could all be for nothing if any loyal soldiers recognize me from the battle in the library.'

I am not sure any loyalists survived. In the end it was rebels versus Bittervinge.

Streig reached the docks and headed towards the only pier where any work was being carried out. A large number of Imperial soldiers formed a living barrier to stop anyone approaching the ship. The maces in their hands promised a quick end to any wanting to leave the island.

'This will be challenging,' said Streig. Many families were weeping and begging to be taken off the island. Outrageous sums of money were being offered in the hopes of passage aboard the ship.

'You there! You with the sword. What's your business?' A soldier stalked forward and the crowd dissolved around him, out of arm's reach.

'I'm Streig. I served under Lieutenant Reka and Exarch Silverdust in the library. I was told wounded soldiers are being given passage off Arkiv.'

'Shit.' The soldier wore his helm and Streig had no way of gleaning the man's expression nor his temperament, though his slip into profanity sounded more shocked than angry. The soldier looked over his shoulder.

'Can you get me out of here?' pressed Streig. 'Please? This sword is an artefact from the upper levels of the library. It should be returned to the Imperial Palace for safekeeping.'

'You were in the library when it came down?' asked the soldier.

'I was. I have the bruises to prove it.' He held up his hand. 'My ribs were broken too. Still not right, but I don't want to starve to death here if it's all the same to you.'

'Come on then.' The soldier gestured him forward. 'You and your enchanted sword.' A tense few minutes passed where Streig was passed up the chain of command from a grizzled corporal to a disbelieving sergeant and on to worried-looking lieutenant. Streig tramped up the boarding ramp of the *Eastern Star* and went below deck, finding a dark corner to hide away in.

You did well, Streig. It was very creative of you to use the sword as a reason to get back Khlystburg.

'I wasn't lying, just using the truth to my advantage.' He took a moment to regard the old blade. 'I'm not even sure what it does.'

It kills things. It is a sword.

'That's not very helpful. I meant the arcane aspect of the sword.'

A sword does a strange thing to a man's mind, gives him ideas about destiny or purpose. An enchantment more so.

'My purpose is to find a way of restoring you. My destiny . . .' Streig released an uneasy sigh that revealed just how little hope he had in any grand destiny awaiting him.

I am sorry, Streig.

'Just go to sleep, or do whatever it is you do in there. It's been a long day.' The ship's timbers creaked around them and sailors called out to one another as the *Eastern Star* cast off. The movement of the waves might have lulled him to sleep, but Streig's mind returned time and again to the hateful city of Khlystburg, with all its secrets and dangers.

CHAPTER THIRTEEN

Steiner

*The Semyonovsky Guard enjoy a particularly fearsome
reputation even in an Empire that prides itself on intimidation.
There is no doubt the regular soldiers are brutal and unflinching,
while the Okhrana are regarded as little more than highly adept
assassins. The Semyonovsky, however, are deemed incorruptible,
devoted to the Emperor with a quiet zealotry, and they train
once a week with the man they are duty-bound to protect. This
is the source of their pride, and their strength.*

– From the memoir of Drakina Tveit,
Lead Librarian of Midtenjord Province

Steiner and Kristofine had spent the week scouting the city
and trying to get a feel for the rhythms and routines of
Khlystburg. Reka had been their faithful shadow, while
Felgenhauer had conducted her own investigation separately.

'It never used to be like this,' said Reka. They were heading
along a broad avenue near the Imperial Palace. The road here
had been swept clean but there was a distinct lack of people
travelling along it. The few people Steiner saw wore hunted
expressions; clothes hung from gaunt frames. Many of the
shops selling food had closed their doors. The blockade was

well in place now, and word of marauding dragons was commonplace throughout the city.

'It's bad enough that Bittervinge is here,' muttered Steiner. 'But three other dragons ridden by Vigilants?'

'We don't know they're Vigilants,' replied Kristofine softly.

'We don't know what they are,' said Reka. 'And not knowing a thing rarely turns out well for a soldier.'

'Well, I don't know where you're leading us,' said Kristofine to Reka. 'And while I'm not a soldier I'd still like to know.'

Reka slowed his pace and inclined his head in the direction of a passage that led away from the avenue and the scattering of worried people.

'We've searched here already,' said Steiner. 'That's a dead end. It leads right up to the wall surrounding the Imperial Court.'

'We *have* searched here already,' said Reka with a slow smile. 'But I've learned something from an old braggart last night. The passage leads to a tavern.' He walked towards a building with black caulking and blacker timbers. 'A very particular tavern with very particular patrons.' A wooden sign hung over the door depicting a black mare against a pale blue background.

'Now isn't the time for drinking,' chided Kristofine. 'We could be discovered at any moment, or Bittervinge could attack, or—'

'Have I ever let you down?' replied Reka slowly. He gave a sly wink and headed into the tavern.

'You need to talk to him,' said Kristofine quietly. Steiner had come to recognize it was the voice she used before she lost her temper.

'I think we're here to listen,' replied Steiner. 'Just think about it: a tavern this close to the Imperial Court. There'll be any number of Imperial servants with tongues loosened by ale.'

'I hope you're right about this,' replied Kristofine, frowning as they stepped over the threshold and into the gloom of the Black Horse tavern.

The late morning became early noon and Steiner and Kristofine spent their time hiding away in a booth in one darkened corner. The tavern smelled of leather, horse, and stale beer. Candles had been wedged into small wine bottles on the tables and the marbled windows let in a cursory amount of light. Steiner imagined it would be very easy to lose track of time in a place like this, day or night.

'I don't know what I was expecting,' said Steiner, 'but it wasn't this.' He chanced a furtive look over his shoulder. They had avoided eye contact with anyone who happened to pass their table, while Reka had taken a more direct approach. He stood at the bar with three other men, all attired in leathers and horseman's boots. There were a fair few satchels slung over chairs or hanging from hooks around the room.

'Who are they?' said Kristofine. 'They don't look like Okhrana and they're not soldiers.'

'I don't know,' admitted Steiner. 'But Reka must have his reasons.'

The barkeeper was a large, hearty man with red cheeks and a thicket of dark hair that matched the wildness of his beard. Steiner guessed him to be around fifty; there was a touch of frost at the man's temples. He looked over and nodded amiably and Steiner returned the gesture.

'Careful now,' said Kristofine. 'He's coming over.'

'Can I get you something else?' said the owner, looking at Kristofine. He loomed over the table in a way that Steiner found threatening before he realized there was drunken gleam in the man's eye.

'Maybe another ale,' said Steiner. The barkeeper nodded cheerfully and returned a moment later with Steiner's drink.

'Not seen you in here before,' he rumbled.

'We got lost,' said Kristofine, 'and entered the friendliest-looking establishment we could find.'

'Friendliest, eh?' The barkeeper slumped down next to Steiner, who shuffled along the seat with a frown. 'I like that.' The barkeeper gazed at Kristofine in a docile, half-drunk stupor.

'What is this place?' asked Kristofine, adopting a look of wide-eyed curiosity.

'This *especial establishment* is my pension,' the barkeeper slurred. 'I managed to get out of the army and bought this place with a little help.'

'But these men aren't soldiers,' said Kristofine.

'Oh no,' mumbled the owner. 'This lot're much more refined. Hah! Messengers is what they are. Imperial messengers carrying the word of the Emperor himself – if you can imagine that.'

Kristofine smiled and leaned across the table slightly. She lowered her voice. 'I always thought it strange he's just "the Emperor". Surely he has a name?'

'Oh, he has a name all right. Though he'd rather no one knows it.' The barkeeper grinned. 'But we know it. The messengers and me, that is. We know all about the coming and goings of the Empire.'

'We've heard nothing since the blockade took effect,' said Steiner.

'Nothing!' The barkeeper grinned. 'Not that Bittervinge himself has returned from death? He started out tormenting the outlying farms to the north of the city but now he ventures to the city itself. Eaten four Vigilants so far – if palace rumours are to be believed.' He leaned forward. 'And I for one can believe it!'

'Obviously we know about Bittervinge.' She smiled at the drunken barkeeper. 'Hard to miss a giant black dragon in the sky.'

'That it is, my dear, that it is.'

'But the four Vigilants, that's very serious.' Steiner felt a pang of jealousy that Kristofine was giving the drunken old fool so much attention before he caught himself. She was merely getting information out of the man. Wasn't that what they had come for?

'Four is bad, especially after the business on Vladibogdan. And then a handful more perished at Shanisrond. Filthy savages.'

'I imagine there's a great deal happening that most folk don't know about,' added Kristofine, dropping her voice to a conspiratorial whisper. 'Something a man of your stature would know.'

'You're not wrong. The Emperor has dispatched most of his Vigilants to the north in the hopes they can drive the black-winged bastard away. Hah. Small chance of that.'

'I had noticed the absence of Vigilants in the city,' said Kristofine.

'And it seems the father of dragons has his own problems,' said the barkeeper. 'Three younger dragons took exception to him eating folks off the street and took him to task. I heard two Spriggani and a Yamal woman were seen riding them, if you can believe such a thing.'

Steiner, who had been halfway through a draught of his ale, spluttered into his tankard. He set down the drink and wiped his mouth before giving both Kristofine and the barkeeper an apologetic look.

'Sorry. I think I'm getting a cough.'

At that moment a section of wooden panelling at the back of the tavern slid aside. Another messenger emerged through the concealed door and joined his colleagues at the bar. The wooden panel slid back into place smoothly.

'I'll have to ask you to forget you saw that,' said the barkeeper, suddenly serious. 'That entrance is only open to regular patrons. I don't normally let customers like yourselves sit in this part of the tavern.'

'I understand. We can keep your little secret.' Kristofine smiled sweetly. 'So you were going to tell us the Emperor's name.'

'Hah! No, I wasn't. On account of it being illegal – unofficially, of course. There's a man that likes to keep his past firmly in the past.' The barkeeper stood up and made to return to the bar.

'But you do know it,' said Steiner with a note of challenge in his voice.

The tavern keeper turned back to them whispered, 'His name is Volkan Karlov.' He gave Kristofine a wink, performed a pitiful and ungraceful sort of bow, and then he went back to serving drinks.

'Come on,' said Steiner. 'We got what we came for, and more besides.'

'I liked the part where you pretended to choke on your drink like a small-town simpleton,' said Kristofine as they stepped outside.

'I thought it was important to play the role convincingly,' he replied with a smile and took her hand.

'Who would have thought it was Kimi, Taiga, and Tief up there riding dragons?'

Steiner didn't reply. On the one hand he was deeply grateful they had allies in the sky, but hadn't *he* earned the title dragon rider? Shouldn't *he* be hunting the father of dragons in the skies above Khlystburg?

'Does it bother you?' asked Kristofine.

'A little bit,' admitted Steiner. 'But I'm here to find my father, and I won't achieve that from the back of a dragon.'

'I thought we were here to bring down the Empire?' said Kristofine with a puzzled expression.

'Yes.' Steiner felt a pang of sickened embarrassment. 'I mean, we can do both.'

It was barely six hours later when they returned. The sunlight had faded behind ghostly grey clouds; finally it dipped below the horizon leaving only darkness and the ever-present pall of smoke. The streets of Khlystburg were swathed in mist and a few lonely souls hurried home, reminding Steiner of the cinderwraiths on Vladibogdan. Felgenhauer had assembled her cadre and Reka had been forced to sober up.

'Try not to hurt the owner,' said Kristofine. 'I rather took a liking to him.'

'He certainly took a liking to you,' replied Steiner. He concealed the lower half of his face with a scarf and pulled up his hood. Felgenhauer nodded to three of her cadre who stood outside the tavern. They fixed their own scarves and hoods, before pulling weapons from sacks.

'Now we find out how much mettle a simple messenger possesses,' said Tomasz as the rest of Felgenhauer's people advanced towards the tavern. The men went inside and there were a few shouts of alarm and the sound of something, or someone, being hit.

'It's not the messengers I'm worried about,' said Steiner. 'It's how many Vigilants the Emperor has at the court.' He grasped his sledgehammer in both hands as he entered the building. The patrons had pressed themselves against the walls with their hands held up. One messenger lay beside the bar with his head split open. The man gripped a short sword that he'd not drawn fast enough. Steiner pointed towards the concealed door and Felgenhauer's cadre hacked through the wooden panel with their cruel axes. The barkeeper stood behind the bar and for once his ruddy complexion abandoned him. Steiner felt a pang of regret for the old soldier before following Reka into the dark passageway.

'That could have be worse,' said Kristofine from behind Steiner.

'Much worse.'

Felgenhauer's cadre emerged in a stable. As many of the men turned to Steiner as to the former Matriarch-Commissar for orders, and it was only then he realized how he'd fallen into line under his aunt's leadership and strong presence.

'What do we do now, dragon rider?'

'This will get bloody,' said Felgenhauer, before Steiner could reply. 'The longer we tarry the more we'll have to face.' She nodded and two of her cadre opened the stable doors. As one they ran out into the Imperial Gardens, shrouded in mist and darkness. Steiner, keen to assert some authority if only for himself, led the charge across gravel paths, vaulting tended hedgerows and flowerbeds. The Imperial Court loomed ahead of them in the darkness; shuttered windows and decorative battlements gave the impression of impregnability, but Marek was in here somewhere. He had to be.

'And I will find him,' Steiner promised himself.

The two Semyonovsky guards at the tall doors barely had time to call out in alarm before Steiner had felled one. Reka and Tomasz took care of the other with muffled thumps and the brief ringing of metal on metal. The broken silence of the night resumed, though Steiner's heartbeat sounded loudly in his ears. Kristofine huddled close to him, holding her breath.

'What's the noise about?' shouted a voice from above in Solska. 'What do you see?'

'Nothing but mist,' replied Reka in Solska. 'Scared myself and walked into the wall, fool that I am.'

Rough laughter sounded from above and Steiner breathed a little more easily. Felgenhauer's cadre waited behind plants and pillars, trying their best to ignore the night's chill. A few minutes later metal scraping on metal sounded in the darkness. The bolts on the double doors were being slid open and a change of guard would be here soon. Steiner waited, pressing himself flat against the wall outside. Wood scuffed on wood as the men inside lifted the bar and set it down. The edge of the door became golden as the light inside escaped into the night. Steiner raised his sledgehammer as a sign to the soldiers.

A tide of armed bodies slammed into the doors, pressing into the antechamber beyond. Weapons sounded from armour; grunts and shocked gasps filled the air. The inevitable wet sounds of flesh and blood being hacked apart followed. Steiner charged through the doors and helped Reka dispatch a stalwart guard.

'Semyonovsky,' breathed Reka when the man lay still on the flagstones. 'Hard bastards. Well trained.'

'This way,' said Felgenhauer, entering the antechamber and gesturing to a door on their left. She made a strange gesture, half turning, half caressing. The lock clicked open and Tomasz tried the handle and pushed through.

'You couldn't have done that with the main doors?' said Steiner, only half joking. A few of her cadre chuckled.

'Difficult to know where the bar is,' replied Felgenhauer, stony-faced. 'Locks are easier on account of the metal.'

Steiner nodded as if he understood and decided he should stick to hitting things. More Semyonovsky Guard awaited them in the corridor beyond, but Steiner and Felgenhauer had the numbers. Shouts of alarm sounded through the building.

'They know we're here,' whispered Kristofine, clutching her sword at the rear of the group.

'It was only ever going to be a matter of time,' replied Felgenhauer. 'The Emperor's chambers lie this way.' She nodded towards another door and her cadre jostled against one another in the tight confines of the corridor. One moment Steiner was pressed tight against the other men, the next he was outside under the night sky. A quick look around confirmed they were in an expansive courtyard.

'Over there,' said Felgenhauer as her cadre fanned out around her, holding their weapons low. 'Those double doors lead to the tower and the Emperor's bed-chamber.'

'How do you know all of this?' asked Reka.

'He has an office just below it,' replied the former Matriarch-Commissar as if this was an adequate explanation.

They set off across the courtyard, perhaps a quarter of a mile square, decorated with the same statues and topiary they'd encountered earlier. Again Steiner led the way and his mind drifted from thoughts of killing the Emperor to finding his father. Surely the Imperial Palace would have dungeons, but would Felgenhauer know where they were located?

His worries were interrupted as the night sky flared into orange brilliance. Three pillars of fire emerged from opened windows to their left. The arcane fire illuminated the Vigilants in the building.

'Down!' shouted Felgenhauer and her cadre scattered. Kristofine froze, staring in horror at the oncoming arcane fire. Steiner grabbed her by the waist and shoved her, half stumbling behind a statue just as the fire impacted the ground nearby. Tongues of flickering red and orange devoured grass and hedge and flowers alike, while the once-white statues became blackened in a heartbeat. Someone cried out in the darkness and Kristofine groaned.

'Are you hurt?' whispered Steiner.

'No. A hard landing is all. You're heavier than you look.'

Felgenhauer floated into the air, lifting three blackened statues of Imperial heroes with the arcane.

'Go!' she roared, and with a gesture she flung the broken statues at the Vigilants standing at the windows. Steiner sprinted towards the doors to the tower with Reka running alongside him and Kristofine close behind.

'I hope these doors aren't locked,' gasped the former lieutenant.

Steiner didn't look back to see how many of the soldiers had fallen to the Vigilants' arcane fire; he focused on their destination instead. They were barely two dozen feet away when the doors opened, revealing six Semyonovsky guards bearing shields and spears.

'This is going to hurt,' whispered Steiner.

CHAPTER FOURTEEN

Kjellrunn

Accounts of the Watcher's Wait *are now so rife across Vinterkveld, so many and varied, that it is difficult to know which tall tales are real, which are false, and which are so thoroughly embroidered as to be unrecognizable. Let me start by establishing some solid truths: the captain was a woman of indeterminate age called Romola; the vessel was a fast frigate painted a dark red; the ship had at various times been involved in whatever would pay coin, from shipping children with witch-sign to Vladibogdan, transporting cargo from port to port, and small instances of piracy. Romola was an opportunist first, second, and last. She did not fight for causes or patriotism. 'I prefer not to fight at all,' she was reported to have said one night while deep in her cups, though she refuted this come the following morning.*

– From the memoir of Drakina Tveit,
Lead Librarian of Midtenjord Province

'I thought I'd be enjoying this but . . .' Romola trailed off. The *Watcher's Wait* rolled and pitched as the vessel cut through sombre green waves, heading north-east across the Ashen Gulf under a pale grey sky. The captain stood at the wheel, though in truth she was powerless to steer, powerless to give any orders.

'Trust me,' said Kjellrunn. She lay on the deck seemingly asleep, but all present knew the young woman had her eyes closed in concentration. A blanket had been provided by Trine to cover her, while Maxim had bundled his own beneath her head. Trine knelt by the priestess, holding her hand with a concerned look on her face.

'This is the first time I've been a passenger in over a decade,' replied Romola. 'And on my own ship. The wind should be at my back, not blowing in my face. This isn't right.'

'And yet we are sailing,' said Trine with a note of quiet challenge. The two black-clad priestesses had been inseparable since coming aboard, their rivalry in Dos Khor seemingly forgotten.

'I miss the sails,' said Maxim, casting his gaze to where masts had towered over the deck, promising a wealth of rigging and white sailcloth snapping taut in the breeze. 'And the crow's nest.'

'Come on.' Romola abandoned the helm and started off for the prow, glad in some small way to give rein to her restlessness.

'Where are you going?' asked Kjellrunn, opening her eyes and rising from the deck with Trine's assistance.

'It's walking or drinking,' she replied over her shoulder. 'And I've only got so much rum, right.'

The ship was still blackened in places, summoning memories of arcane fire and dying crew. They had made small repairs here and there with the time available, but Kjellrunn knew that seeing the *Wait* in such poor condition was an affront to Romola's pride and to her need for autonomy. Romola cursed under her breath.

'The ropes look like they're holding,' said Kjellrunn calmly, trying to appease the scowling captain. What the *Watcher's*

Wait lacked in rigging she made up for with the dozens of warps lashed to the bows. Those crew who had survived the encounter at Dos Khor stood at the foredeck of the ship, transfixed with awe.

'Look lively, you slack-jawed fools!' snarled Romola. 'Surely there are tasks in need of doing?'

The warps were pulled taut, reaching out ahead of the ship, disappearing beneath the water where a vast shadow moved ahead of them. 'Not in all my years at sea have I ever seen such a thing.'

'And you can bet your boots you'll never see anything like it again,' added Maxim, grinning as he performed an impression of Tief.

'It's not a permanent arrangement,' said Kjellrunn in a soothing tone. 'Just until we have a chance to repair the *Wait*.'

'I can't believe you persuaded me to lash my ship to your gods-damned leviathan,' said Romola wearily.

'I think you mean gods-blessed,' said Maxim, suddenly earnest again. 'She is the Stormtide Prophet after all.'

'Sorry,' said Romola. It was easy to forget how much Maxim idolized Kjellrunn, contrasting starkly with Romola's less-than-devout cynicism. There had been a moment, barely minutes into their voyage, when the leviathan had swum too fast and too deep. The ship had surged forward and the prow ploughed beneath the water, spume and surf washing up over the deck as all aboard cried out in terror. Kjellrunn had emerged from her trance pale-faced and apologetic before trying again more carefully.

'At least we're still afloat, right,' said Romola.

'Have some faith,' said Kjellrunn.

'Faith? I'd rather have my sails back.' Romola looked over her shoulder to the absence of masts. 'Goddesses and leviathans are all well and good but I feel like I'm missing a limb.'

*   *   *

That night the crew took their evening meal, though even Rylska, the chattiest and most cheerful of the crew, had surrendered to the subdued mood. They had spent the day in awe of both Kjellrunn and the leviathan but now were wondering why they were needed. Romola could see it in the confused frowns, the restless feet that scuffed and tapped. She could hear it in their aimless small talk and uncertain questions.

'This isn't good,' muttered Romola. 'A crew without tasks to keep them busy is just trouble waiting to happen.'

'There'll be plenty to do when we make landfall,' said Kjellrunn, finishing her broth. 'Maybe you can loot Khlystburg?'

'That should keep them loyal,' said Romola, casting an appraising eye over the crew, 'for a while at least.'

'Maybe we can buy some new masts,' replied Kjellrunn, rising to her feet. She paced the ship, passing through the decks and wandering from bow to stern. Trine followed, a faithful shadow.

'Aren't you tired?'

'I should be,' replied Kjellrunn, 'but in truth the leviathan doesn't need my constant guidance. I can still feel it' – she tapped her temple with two fingers – 'but I don't need to concentrate so hard right now.'

Prophet and priestess continued their nocturnal stroll and found Maxim sitting on a coil of rope with his back to what was left of the foremast. Kjellrunn opened her mouth to greet him but realized his eyes were closed. His head was tilted backward and every so often he would flinch or twitch as if lost to a dream. Kjellrunn slowly dropped to her knees and held the boy's hands.

'Maxim? Maxim, it's Kjellrunn. Can you speak?'

The boy smiled but his eyes remained closed. 'I can hear you fine. I'm listening. Listening for whispers on the wind.'

'What do you hear?'

'So much noise. It's hard to make sense of it. Some are

older messages I think, still drifting on the breeze even now. The newer ones are louder, mostly in Solska, but some are in Nordspråk. A few are in the Spriggani tongue.' He let out a weary sigh and opened his eyes. 'I grew up speaking Shanish with my mother and Nordspråk with my father. I don't understand a lot of what is being said.'

Kjellrunn was still holding the boy's hand and gave him an encouraging squeeze. 'I'm sure you'll get better at it over time. Try not to strain yourself. The arcane does terrible things to a person's body.'

'We may never find Steiner again if I don't listen out,' replied Maxim solemnly. 'Or worse yet we may run into trouble that I could have warned us about.'

Kjellrunn, who had never had a shred of maternal yearning in her short life, was suddenly overcome with love for this earnest, dedicated boy. 'Come on. It's time for bed.'

Maxim wrinkled his nose. 'I don't have a bed. I slept in the galley last night.'

Kjellrunn released an incredulous laugh. 'The crew often have to sleep where they can.'

'And am I crew?' he said hopefully.

'Perhaps when you're older. Why don't you come to my cabin tonight? I'm sure it'll be nicer than the galley and I can keep an eye on you.'

All night long the leviathan toiled beneath the dark waters of the Ashen Gulf. Kjellrunn drifted into wakefulness often, listening to the creaking ship and the lap of waves on the hull for want of anything better to do. Maxim rolled over in his sleep, mumbling. Kjellrunn had made a nest of blankets on the floor and lulled him to sleep with old rhymes her father had sung to her when she had been small.

Marek. Her heart ached at the thought of him, of what he must be enduring, at the prospect of not finding him.

'If I can do nothing else,' Kjellrunn whispered as she looked at Maxim, 'goddess help me to keep you safe, at least.'

Another half-hour of sleepless waiting passed by and she slipped from bed, into her clothes, taking her boots out on to the deck so as not wake Maxim. Standing at the prow, silhouetted by the first light of day, was a slender black-clad figure. Kjellrunn approached Trine and paused when she reached the remains of the foremast. Another soul she felt deeply responsible for.

'Morning,' she said to the priestess as she walked up beside her.

'Morning,' said Trine in a voice husky with the many hours of silence she had sat through. Kjellrunn smiled. The warps attached to the bow were still taut and the dark shadow beneath the waters swam, dragging the *Watcher's Wait* ever onward.

'We are close to Arkiv,' said Trine.

'And to Steiner,' whispered Kjellrunn, 'I hope.'

'How long until we make landfall?' asked Trine.

'Perhaps an hour,' replied Kjellrunn, reaching out with arcane senses to join with the leviathan. 'But there will be resistance. We must be ready.'

'I'll rouse the crew,' said Trine. 'It will give me something to do beside waiting. I've never had the patience for it.'

The crew arrived on deck not long after, listening and waiting with a quiet curiosity.

'I hope you all slept well,' said Romola cheerfully. 'Because we've a blockade to overcome and your attendance is requested by none other than the Stormtide Prophet.' A few of the crew chuckled at her forced frivolity, but a few eyed the captain warily, not used to her flippant tone.

'Untie the ropes,' said Kjellrunn, feeling a shiver of trepidation run down her spine. Trine passed on the order to the crew and they went about their work with puzzled expressions, casting looks at Romola, who could do little else but shrug and nod that they continue. The *Watcher's Wait* drifted onward for a time until its momentum was spent. The leviathan slipped deeper under the water. For a moment all was still and the dark horizon transformed itself into a welt of burning gold. Just three miles distant lay Arkiv Island, watched over by two ships, undoubtedly Imperial vessels.

'What have you done, Kjellrunn?' said Romola as an Imperial galleon unfurled its sails and set a course to intercept the *Wait*.

'It has begun,' replied Kjellrunn with her eyes closed. She could feel a faint sheen of perspiration across her brow that grew chill with the morning breeze.

'What's begun is that you've led us out here and we're adrift,' said Romola, her voice loud enough for all to hear. 'We've no sails to escape and no way to defend ourselves.'

'Have some faith,' replied Trine. Her black hair had come loose in the night and she looked wild and strange in the dawn light.

'I have faith.' Romola frowned at the oncoming galleon. 'I have faith in canvas. I believe in rigging and sails; I believe in tides and obedient crews.'

'Obedient crews need weapons,' said Kjellrunn. A few of the sailors went sprinting off across the deck to gather cutlasses and bucklers. A few short spears were handed out and everyone exchanged nervous glances. The Imperial galleon surged onward; Kjellrunn guessed its sails were given life by arcane winds. It was difficult to tell how many Vigilants were aboard, but it was safe to assume there would be a Troika of them. Graduates of the Plamya, Vozdukha, and Zemlya Academies would pool their talents for all eventualities.

'You're using us as bait,' said Romola with a dreadful bitterness. The Imperial galleon was close now, maybe a half a mile from where the *Watcher's Wait* drifted aimlessly. Romola surged forward and made to grab Kjellrunn by the throat, but the Stormtide Prophet drifted into the air, eyes still closed, a look of terrible concentration etched on to her young face. She raised her arms before her and the Imperial galleon rocked and shuddered. Screams could be heard across the water, distant and yet no less appalling for all that. Romola could only stare, startled and shocked. The galleon rolled again and the Imperial crew reacted with shouts of alarm. The panic was tangible even at this distance and the crew aboard the *Wait* watched with terrible fascination. All sailors told tales of sea monsters, but that's all they were. Tales. No one really believed in them.

'Is that it?' said Romola, her lip curling in disgust. The leviathan appeared to have given up and the galleon continued on its way, sails billowing with summoned winds. 'A couple of bumps on the hull? I don't doubt a handful of them have soiled their breeches, but I was hoping for more.'

Kjellrunn drifted down to the deck with her head bowed, hands shaking. Her hair was wet with perspiration. The prophet said nothing. How? How had she failed so thoroughly so soon?

'Prepare to repel boarders,' hollered Romola. 'They'll not give quarter freely, so there's no point in asking for it, right?'

CHAPTER FIFTEEN

Kjellrunn

The arcane powers of wind and fire are draconic in nature. When a human draws on those powers they are drawing on the strength of dragons, which pollutes the body. Dragons are magical reptiles, after all, and humans are frail by comparison. This pollution of the body manifests in many ways, and it is for this reason the Holy Synod would often speak of the taint of witchsign. They knew all too well the high cost of using the arcane.

– From the memoir of Drakina Tveit,
Lead Librarian of Midtenjord Province

The same crew who had barely survived the assault on the beaches of Dos Khor looked far from ready as the Imperial galleon came ever closer. Kjellrunn had been floating in the air just a moment ago, held aloft as the arcane surged through her. Now she stood on deck with rounded shoulders and head bowed. Her breath came fast and hard, but of the leviathan there was no trace. Her connection to that vast creature had become dull and indistinct, before fading to nothing. The ship lurched and Kjellrunn reached out for the handrail and clung on.

'Where is it?' whispered Trine, an anxious expression on her slender face. 'Where has it gone?'

'I don't know. One moment it was there. I was commanding it but now . . .' Kjellrunn frowned, fighting off dizziness and confusion in equal measure.

'You'll fight like heroes or die like dogs!' shouted Romola at her crew as the prow of the Imperial galleon cut through the murky waters, closing the gap between the two ships. The sick feeling in Kjellrunn's gut told her they'd all be dead soon enough.

'Why I trusted a deranged Nordvlast girl and her pet sea monster is beyond me,' snarled Romola in a low voice meant only for Kjellrunn and Trine. 'This whole endeavour has been pure foolishness, and it will cost us our lives.'

Kjellrunn felt a glimmer of anger and clutched the handrail a little tighter, a snarl crossing her lips to match Romola's.

'We can still win,' replied Trine. She raised her arms either side of her and splayed her fingers. Moments later her hands were wreathed in fire.

'Prepare to repel boarders,' shouted Romola. The crew wore looks of bewilderment as they brandished their weapons. The *Watcher's Wait* had survived by outrunning danger, not meeting it head on. A lance of fire raced forward from the Imperial galleon and darted overhead, landing in the waters behind Romola's ship.

'We can still win,' repeated Trine, launching her own arcane fire back at their enemy. The fiery lance crashed into the mast and the mainsail burst into flames, but the Imperial ship continued to speed towards them.

'You might want to pray to the goddess a little harder,' added Romola with a hard stare. Kjellrunn stared back, both ashamed and furious. The Imperial galleon came up beside them. So close now. Kjellrunn could see the crew, glimpse the weapons clutched in their hands, look into their eyes and witness the seething hatred.

'I should have retired,' muttered Romola.

A dull thump of thunder sounded so hard that everyone flinched. Rylska dropped her cutlass and swore while Romola looked at the clear skies above the ship.

Not thunder. Timber. The sound of breaking timber.

A heartbeat later and the galleon was listing to one side, masts leaning, sailcloth flapping. Sailors tumbled from the rigging into the churning waters below. Kjellrunn remained at the handrail, clinging on with gritted teeth as if she were caught in a gale. Her blonde hair had fallen across her face while her eyes were squeezed shut.

'I thought you said the leviathan abandoned us?' said Trine.

'Not abandoned,' replied Kjellrunn, eyes still closed. 'I lost the connection for a moment.'

Imperial sailors, who until a moment ago had been preparing to board, now clung to their ship fearing for their lives.

'This is more like it,' shouted Romola cheerfully. Trine stepped forward and a bright flare of arcane fire sped towards the Imperial vessel. Orange and yellow light hit the mizzenmast and flames consumed the canvas with a hungry intensity. A handful of Imperial sailors jumped over the side of their ship to escape the inferno. The fleeing men and women caught sight of the leviathan too late, its vast maw split wide in the sea beneath them. Kjellrunn watched four people disappear into the creature's cavernous mouth and tasted blood.

'Imperial or not, I wouldn't wish that on anyone,' muttered Romola, wrapping a hand around Maxim's eyes a moment too late. The leviathan extorted a bloody toll from the Imperial crew, smashing the gunwales and tearing through the fiery mainsail. A lone Vigilant levitated above the pitching deck of the ship but was knocked down by a falling mast, disappearing beneath the churning waters in a heartbeat.

'One less of the bastards,' replied Trine. A few of the Imperial crew leapt the distance between the two boats and clambered up the side of the *Watcher's Wait*.

'Let them surrender!' shouted Romola above the din. 'No need to be hasty!'

Four Imperial crew made it aboard and those who still had weapons gave them up willingly. They looked over their shoulders with shocked expressions writ large on their gaunt faces.

'I'd heard tales but I never believed it,' said one of the Imperial sailors.

'Get these people a tot of rum to steady their nerves,' said Romola to Rylska. 'Then find somewhere to secure them.'

For a time all anyone could do was watch the galleon sink beneath the waves. Romola dispatched a handful of her people to scavenge any flotsam that had floated free of the hold, but most likely it would all be waterlogged and useless.

'You did it,' said Trine, drawing close to Kjellrunn. The prophet had a feverish cast to her skin and her eyes remained closed. She swayed on her feet in a way that had nothing to do with the motion of the waves.

'You should get some rest,' said Romola. 'Both of you.'

'I will,' replied Kjellrunn. 'Just as soon as I've taken care of those other two galleons blockading the island.'

'Your plan of attack didn't exactly run smoothly.' Romola looked over her shoulder at her crew. 'It's too risky to attempt such a thing again so soon.

'But we must reach the island,' replied Kjellrunn. 'Steiner needs me. My father needs me.' She cast a look over her shoulder just as the Imperial galleon slipped beneath the water. 'We can do it. I know we can.'

The streets of Arkiv were lined with people. Earlier they'd cheered loud enough to be heard out in the bay, but now they had settled down to a reverent silence. The sky was a cloudless and vivid blue, and though the breeze was bitterly cold the sun shone brightly in the sky. The Stormtide Prophet, priestess of Frejna, had come to free of them of Imperial tyranny and now she was among them, clad in the black robes of her goddess. Scores of the islanders formed a long queue, desperate enough to beg the Stormtide Prophet for some small boon or favour. Many simply wanted to touch her or see her for themselves. The crew of the *Watcher's Wait* had formed a cordon in the hopes of keeping order while Maxim and Rylska had remained by the captain's side.

'Kjellrunn!' Romola called out loud enough to turn several heads, not caring that she was interrupting. A look of irritation passed over Trine's face but Kjellrunn retained her composure. The prophet finished her conversation with two islanders and excused herself.

'This could take a while,' said Romola, eyeing the queue. 'What shall we do in the meantime?'

'Ordinarily I'd suggest resupplying,' replied Kjellrunn, 'but these people have less food than we do.'

'Do we have enough time to repair my masts?' said Romola.

'I don't know how long we'll be staying. No one seems to know anything about Steiner.'

'I've never been one to stand around doing nothing.' Romola rolled her eyes and Trine stepped forward to remonstrate. It was then the cats started appearing. They came over rooftops and from winding alleys; they ran along pavements and streets. They jumped down from walls and windows, all heading towards Kjellrunn.

'It seems Frøya is pleased,' said Maxim, laughing.

'And Frejna too, right.' Romola stared up at the rooftops. Clusters of black birds looked down from their vantage points, feathers as dark as the robes of the two priestesses.

'Excuse me,' said a voice a few places back in the queue.

'I need to talk with the prophet.' The replies were quick and to the point. Heads turned and the mood soured as angry grumbling filled the air.

'Wait your turn.'

'What makes you so special?'

'Self-important librarians.'

Kjellrunn glanced along the queue and headed towards the source of the disturbance. The woman wore rumpled purple robes. She had twenty or so summers to her name and a shock of blonde hair that had been tied up in a high ponytail. Her eyes were puffy from sorrow or smoke or maybe both. Like everyone else on Arkiv, she had a hungry look about her, cheekbones just a little too sharp, complexion a touch too pale.

'The prophet will see you in a moment,' said Romola, loud enough for everyone to hear. She took a step forward and laid her hand on her cutlass to deter any thoughts of violence.

'I'm Drakina,' said the woman, eyes darting warily from the angry people in the queue to Romola. 'I think I can help you. I worked for Felgenhauer. I've seen Steiner Vartiainen. I've met him.'

It took a while longer to extract Kjellrunn from her crowd of worshippers but soon they were heading through the liberated city. Ships were already leaving port, promising to return with food as soon as the winds and tides permitted. Drakina led Kjellrunn, Trine, Romola, and Maxim to a tower that overlooked the remnants of the Great Library. The ground was blackened rubble and the ashes of thousands of books lay all around.

'Bittervinge did all of this?' asked Kjellrunn. Drakina nodded and her mouth creased with unhappiness.

'Once it started burning' – the blonde woman sighed – 'there was nothing that could be done. Nothing. They're still pulling corpses out of the rubble. Soldiers mostly.'

They headed up the stairs of the tower and Drakina shared what little food she had left.

'You said my brother was here,' said Kjellrunn. She sat on Felgenhauer's desk as if she were holding court. Trine remained close at hand, ever the faithful courtier. Drakina relayed what she knew to the Stormtide Prophet, and the brief moment she had met the dragon rider.

'I thought he'd be taller,' she admitted.

Kjellrunn smiled. 'I'd say his legend is tall enough.'

'Envoy de Vries died during the fighting,' said Drakina, resuming her tale.

'One less Envoy in the world is fine by me,' said Romola.

'And so did Silverdust,' continued Drakina.

Maxim made a small noise, loaded with shock and sorrow. Everyone turned to him and Romola put an arm around his shoulders.

'He . . .' Maxim's eyes filled with tears. 'He helped us on Vladibogdan. He helped Steiner.'

'I'm sorry,' said Drakina. 'I never met him . . .' She looked away, awkward and uncomfortable at being the bearer of such grim news.

A great wave of tiredness overcame Kjellrunn. She struggled to breathe and the edges of her vision began to darken. She was much too warm in the tower despite the chill. The floor lurched upwards and Trine caught her by one arm but struggled to slow her fall. Only Drakina's intervention prevented the Stormtide Prophet from slipping to the floor.

'Perhaps I should get some rest,' said Kjellrunn after she'd taken a moment to regain her breath. Trine and Drakina helped her onto the bed as Romola ushered everyone out of the room, even Trine.

'I'm the handmaiden of the Stormtide Prophet,' whispered Trine once everyone else had left, anger plain to see on her narrow face.

'You're a sixteen-year-old girl playing dressing up in priestesses' robes,' said Romola quietly. 'And Kjellrunn needs some rest.'

'I'm staying.'

Romola looked to Kjellrunn, who was too tired to argue or even sit up. She made a placating gesture with one hand.

'You are a pain in my arse,' said Romola, before striding out of the chamber. Trine slammed the door as the captain left and her jet-black hair fell to one side. A jagged selection of lines decorated the side of her throat like broken veins turned black. Kjellrunn's expression must have given her away as Trine pressed one hand to her throat to cover her affliction.

'Seems you have bigger problems than Romola,' said Kjellrunn.

'I'm fine,' said Trine. 'It's common for the students of Academy Plamya to have black marks on their skin.' She rearranged her hair to cover the marks.

'It's spreading, isn't it?' added Kjellrunn, her voice full of sadness and concern.

'I did what needed to be done,' said Trine; the usual fire and defiance of her tone and manner was subdued. 'The Empire took everything from me. Now it's my turn to get even.'

'Even if it costs you everything?' asked Kjellrunn.

Trine stared back, dark eyes full of pain, but had no answer for the Stormtide Prophet.

CHAPTER SIXTEEN

Steiner

Steiner's band of rebels were not the only people rising up against the Emperor at that time. Every province was fighting against a rising tide of disorder. Small acts of sabotage, assassinations, and fighting in the streets were becoming commonplace, but the fiercest fighting was always going to be at Khlystburg. How could it be otherwise?

> – From the memoir of Drakina Tveit,
> Lead Librarian of Midtenjord Province

'You took my father!' bellowed Steiner in the cold night air. Six Semyonovsky guards marched from the tower, imposing in their black enamelled armour, spear tips glittering cruelly. The Imperial Courtyard, so silent just moments before, was now full of fire and shouting. The sound of stone crunching into stone made everyone flinch; Felgenhauer was flinging statues as if they were merely toys. Someone cried out in pain and the tinkle of broken glass followed. Steel chimed on steel as loyalist met rebel, and oaths and curses were spoken in anger or desperation.

'Press on! Press on! shouted Tomasz, exhorting Felgenhauer's cadre to reach the tower where the Emperor slept.

'You took my father from me!' shouted Steiner again, working himself up into a rage. The first of the black-armoured Semyonovsky guards thrust his spear, a light jab testing Steiner's defences. He grabbed the spear shaft and forced it aside, then closed ground and smashed the guard's faceplate with a backhanded swipe from the sledgehammer. The guard stumbled in shock and Steiner delivered a staggering overhead smash that broke the man's collarbone.

Kristofine deflected a spear thrust meant for Steiner, knocking the metal point high and wide from the flat of her sword. She followed Steiner's lead and stepped in close, smashing the crosspiece of her sword into the face of the new attacker. The Semyonovsky guard stumbled back and Kristofine swiped at the man, but her blade rebounded from the plate armour, almost slashing her face. Reka hacked at the back of the guard's knees and he hit the ground screaming.

'You all right?' Kristofine took a deep yet shaky breath and nodded. 'You're doing fine, just aim for the weaker points in the armour.'

'We have to reach the office below the bed-chamber,' said Felgenhauer from behind them. She was out of breath and her temples ran with sweat. 'We have to recover the Ashen Blade. Without that we are lost.'

Felgenhauer's cadre defeated the last of the Semyonovsky Guard and Steiner raced into the tower, heading for the stairs just as a Vigilant wearing a golden wolf mask descended.

Steiner paused. 'Marozvolk?'

A second later he was flung backwards by the force of the arcane, out of the door, sailing through the air until he smashed into his comrades.

'Not Marozvolk,' he grunted as he caught his breath. Felgenhauer extended both her hands towards the golden-masked Vigilant, matching their mastery of the earth school with her own. The air shimmered with force as both tried to

crush the other with the arcane. The base of the tower began
to shake and shouts sounded in the courtyard behind them.
More Semyonovsky guards were tramping across the flowerbeds and burning hedges towards them.

'We're trapped,' said Kristofine in a panicked whisper.

Felgenhauer tensed and made a shoving gesture with clawed
hands. The golden-masked Vigilant was flung back up the
staircase of the tower.

'Inside! yelled Steiner's aunt as the first of the Semyonovsky
Guard reached them. Steiner turned to follow when a pale
man dressed in black descended the staircase. He had a high
forehead and a shrewd look about him that Steiner didn't
much care for. His right hand bore a short knife with a dull
blade that flaked with ashes as the man moved.

'Volkan Karlov,' said Steiner. His father's captor, ruler of
the Solmindre Empire, founder of the Holy Synod.

'So good of you to deliver the Vartiainen boy to me,
Felgenhauer.'

Steiner's aunt slammed a hand forward but the Emperor
stepped to the side and made a small gesture. To his left a
portion of the wall shook, dust drifted from the ceiling and
picture rattled itself off the wall to smash on the floor.

'You're making a mess, Felgenhauer,' chided Volkan Karlov
in a whispery voice. 'So unlike you.' There was something
about his eyes, black and empty of anything besides a cruel
amusement.

'Run, Steiner,' said Felgenhauer. 'Go!'

Steiner stared at what must surely be the Ashen Blade,
clutched in the Emperor's fist. Bittervinge himself had warned
them they could not defeat the Emperor without the weapon.
He gritted his teeth and stepped forward.

'We fight!' he bellowed and swung with all of his rage. The
Emperor, so self-assured, so confident, flinched backwards,
barely deflecting Steiner's sledgehammer. The enchanted

weapon met the hastily prepared force of the Emperor's arcane power. There was a flash of yellow light and a ringing sound that all but deafened Steiner. His sledgehammer careered from the Emperor's arcane shield and smashed into the wall, sending shards of stone in all directions.

'The blood runs strong,' said the Emperor. Steiner drew his sledgehammer back for another strike but Volkan Karlov batted him aside with a curt, dismissive gesture. Steiner was flung against the wall so hard he was sure a tooth must have come loose. His mouth was full of the taste of blood and chagrin. Kristofine entered the tower and lunged forward as Felgenhauer compelled a flagstone to leap up and spin towards the Emperor. The granite tile shot past Volkan Karlov's head and cracked loudly as it hit the wall behind him, exploding into heavy shards.

'Kristofine!' shouted Steiner as she slashed at the Emperor. She opened a deep cut across his shoulder before he retaliated, jerking the Ashen Blade towards her stomach. She averted the knife deftly, meeting the enchanted blade with the force of her sword and almost knocking it from his grip. But the Emperor had other weapons at his disposal. With a shimmer of arcane power, he transmuted his free hand into a fist of living stone and backhanded Kristofine across the side of her skull. Steiner was surging in to help her, but a moment too late to stop the blow connecting. He saw her eyes blink and when they reopened there was a dullness to them, her gaze unfocused.

'Damn you!' hissed Steiner, swinging the sledgehammer once more, but suddenly the weapon was intensely heavy, and he was barely able to lift it from the floor, where it scraped on the flagstones.

'We are leaving!' shouted Felgenhauer, taking Kristofine by the hand. 'Now!'

Volkan Karlov stepped forward with mocking smile on his

pale face. 'I was expecting more, Steiner.' He held the Ashen Blade before him, low and ready, his other hand gesturing to the sledgehammer, making it heavier than it had any right to be.

Felgenhauer reached up with both hands and then thrust them downward, her face contorted in pain and effort. The ceiling collapsed, burying the Emperor. Steiner dodged backwards, narrowly avoiding the same fate.

'Now, Steiner! Move!' yelled Felgenhauer. 'We can't beat him.'

They raced back into the courtyard as the Emperor emerged from the rubble, a terrible frown on his pale face. It was difficult to tell in the confusion: had he turned himself to rock to weather the collapse, or was he merely covered in stone dust? Kristofine stumbled alongside Reka, holding her head, struggling to fight off the concussion. More and more Semyonovsky guards flooded into the courtyard. A few Vigilants cast arcs of arcane fire, but there were too many of their own soldiers in the way for them to be effective.

'We're cut off,' said Steiner, swinging his hammer at the closest guard. A spear point snagged in his tunic, failing to draw blood but ripping his clothes. They hadn't moved fast enough or struck hard enough and now their own lives as well as Marek's would be forfeit.

'Form up on me!' shouted Steiner, desperate to enforce some order in the chaos. Felgenhauer's cadre began to move as a dark shadow flickered above the Imperial Court. Two of the Semyonovsky were wrenched into the air. Steiner gasped as the stars were occluded by vast winged shapes. The snatched soldiers cried out as the dragon soared higher, then released them. Another dragon swooped in, blue in colour. The great creature grabbed one soldier up in its mouth. Talons flexed and swiped, sending soldiers sprawling. Two fell to the ground missing limbs, their lives torn from them in a blink.

The carnage was brutal and sudden, but Steiner was sure he saw Taiga riding atop the creature.

The Semyonovsky Guard retreated back to the safety of the buildings surrounding the courtyard, but the Emperor was not so easily cowed. Steiner hurried away, snatching glances over his shoulder as a dark grey dragon swooped towards Volkan Karlov.

'Tief?' shouted Steiner, hardly believing what he knew to be true.

The Emperor made claws of his hands and wrenched his arms upward. A half-dozen statues floated into the air at his command, before speeding towards their target. The dragon was pelted with hunks of broken stone and turned away, swooping over the rooftop of the Imperial Court to avoid further punishment.

Kristofine grabbed Steiner's hand. 'Come on. We can't stand around watching. We have to leave.'

'But the dragons are here. Taiga, Tief, and Kimi are here.'

No sooner had he said the words than the Emperor leapt into the air and released a great gout of fire from his mouth, catching the blue dragon along one side and almost burning Taiga. Vigilants appeared on the rooftops and cast javelins of arcane flame. The searing arcane lights sped towards the dragons, who avoided them for the most part, but the dark brown dragon took a hit, and bright fire exploded across its scales.

'It's not enough,' said Felgenhauer, looking aghast. 'He's too powerful and has too many Vigilants. We have to go.'

The three dragons had evidently decided the same thing. They departed as suddenly as they had arrived, vast wings beating the night air, carrying them to safety.

With hindsight, leaving through the tavern they had entered was a mistake. It had never been part of the plan, but plans so rarely survive contact with the enemy, as Reka said later.

Tomasz led the way. He'd stolen a Semyonovsky shield during the fighting and barged through the remnants of the sliding wooden door. Felgenhauer and her remaining cadre stomped into the tavern, casting murderous looks at the few messengers who'd remained there after the initial breach. Steiner, Kristofine, and Reka brought up the rear, pulses pounding with the shock and panic of retreat.

'You filthy scum, you've finished me!' The tavern owner lunged over the bar and grabbed Kristofine's arm.

Steiner's heart stuttered as a glint of steel flashed in the gloom.

'Think you're clever for snooping around earlier, do you?' said the tavern owner, his voice seething with bitterness. 'I'll be killed for this.'

Kristofine raised her weapon, but the blade caught on the bar, and the dazed look in her eye told Steiner she was ill-prepared to defend herself. Reka was already reaching across the bar to free Kristofine's trapped arm as the tavern owner pulled back the knife. Steiner vaulted the counter top, sending half-full tankards clattering to the ground. Kristofine jerked back, but the larger man held her fast and thrust the blade forward just as Reka unleashed a solid punch that connected with the tavern owner's temple. The man spun to face Steiner, who smashed an elbow into his face, stunning him. Steiner's eyes fell on Kristofine as she rolled off the bar clutching her side. The hilt of the knife protruded from the folds of her clothes.

'Kristofine!'

'Frøya save me,' she muttered as her face paled. Felgenhauer was at her side in a heartbeat, holding her up.

'No more than she deserves,' slurred the tavern keeper. Steiner jabbed forward with the head of the sledgehammer, breaking the tavern owner's nose. The man fell to his knees with a pleading look in his eyes but Steiner kept hitting him until Reka laid a hand on his shoulder and yanked him backwards.

'He's dead! We have to go!'

Steiner looked up from his grisly work in a daze. Kristofine was hunched over, both hands forming a halo of delicate fingers about the knife hilt, afraid to touch it. Felgenhauer had an arm around her shoulders, her face full of concern.

'I thought you said the tavern keeper liked me,' said Kristofine, forcing a smile before she passed out.

Their flight through the city was fraught. They clung to every shadow and darkened back alley. Steiner couldn't help but think of a similar night in Vostochnyye Lisy. Felgenhauer's cadre cast concerned looks at Kristofine; their eyes went from the wounded peasant girl to the former Matriarch-Commissar. Steiner waited for the moment his aunt declared she had warned against this very thing, but the rebuke never came.

'She'll be fine,' said Felgenhauer, not meeting his eye. Steiner knew she was trying to be reassuring, but he didn't much believe her.

Only once did they happen upon an Imperial soldier, who had slipped away from his squad to relieve himself in a back alley. The man, seeing he was outnumbered and most certainly doomed, opened his mouth to call for his comrades; then his eyes widened in shock and he clutched at his throat. Felgenhauer stood a dozen feet from the man, immobile and full of terrible purpose. Grey veins grew across the soldier's face, petrifying his lips, his neck, his throat.

'Ggghkk!'

Tomasz had the sense to catch the man before he fell. A soldier in plate armour hitting cobblestones would attract just as much attention as a cry for help.

'What now?' whispered Steiner; Kristofine was a dead weight on his shoulder, even with help from Reka.

'We wait for the squad to move on,' replied Felgenhauer.

'Assuming they don't come looking for their friend,' muttered Tomasz, looking over his shoulder to check they hadn't been discovered.

'We don't have much time,' said Steiner. 'Kristofine is bleeding.'

Felgenhauer gave him a hard look and then continued on her way. Her cadre fell in behind her and Steiner and Reka did their best to keep up.

The inn that Felgenhauer had claimed as her barracks bore a geometric snowflake design on a teal background. To the locals it was simply 'the Novgoruske'. Lanterns shone at every window and gave the impression the inn was open, despite the lateness of the hour. The innkeeper had been waiting for them and held the door as they returned. His serious look darkened as Reka and Steiner dragged Kristofine over the threshold.

'I can't help you get rid of bodies,' said the innkeeper with a sullen look.

'She's not dead,' snarled Steiner.

'Not yet, but come the morning.'

'Bring me boiled water and vodka,' said Reka. 'I'll want a needle and thread also. And be quick about it.'

'You're him, aren't you?' replied the innkeeper. 'You're the dragon rider. You two are the Lovers.'

Steiner glared at the man. 'Just get the things my friend asked for.'

'Of course,' replied the innkeeper. 'But you should know there's a man here to see you. Some sort of noble, judging by the clothes.

It was just before dawn before Steiner emerged from his bedroom with Reka.

'And she'll live?' whispered Steiner, almost too afraid to ask.

'Now would be a good time to pray to those goddesses you're so intent on bringing back.' Reka headed to bed, shoulders curved in exhaustion, head drooping. Steiner envied the man his rest but there was still the matter of the unexpected guest to attend to. He headed downstairs still covered in the gore of Imperial soldiers. His fingernails were outlined in Kristofine's blood and he grasped the sledgehammer as if it was the only thing keeping him standing.

A dark-haired man wearing dark grey peasant attire waited for him at the base of the stairs, shifting from foot to foot with impatience.

'You're the dragon rider? Steiner the Unbroken?'

Steiner didn't feel very unbroken right then, with his love sewn back together and curled in a ball of pain and vodka in his bed. He nodded and frowned, trying not to show his worry for Kristofine.

'This way. I'm Ruslan.'

Steiner followed him to the back of the inn, where an older man stood up. Long of limb, with a chest like an ox, the clothes declared him a noble to anyone with the sense to see. His drooping moustaches were well kept and his eyes were dark shadows in the deep lines of his face. Steiner felt like a half-mad vagrant in comparison, which was at least half true, he supposed.

'I am Boyar Sokolov,' said the man. 'I understand the Empire killed your uncle.' Steiner nodded again. Not trusting himself to speak. 'We have much in common. The Emperor killed my son, Dimitri.'

'And you came all this way in the dead of night to tell me this?'

'I have information that may help you,' said the Boyar. He retook his seat and gestured to Steiner to do the same. A tankard had been set out for both of them, though Steiner had no desire to drink as he sat down.

'We lost three men tonight,' said Steiner. 'I saw dragons attack Volkan Karlov himself, and even that wasn't enough. Without the Ashen Blade this is all for nothing.'

The Boyar nodded. 'What if I could tell you how to reach the Emperor's office undetected? What if I could show you a secret way underneath the Imperial Court?' He lifted the tankard and drank, draining half the vessel before setting it down.

'You'd tell me something that important to avenge your son, would you?' Steiner tapped one blood-rimmed index finger against the side of his tankard.

'For my son, I would do far more and far worse.'

CHAPTER SEVENTEEN

Ruslan

*It is perhaps difficult for a simple member of the common folk
to imagine, as they are often too preoccupied with simple survival,
but the nobility of Vinterkveld are more obsessed with honour
and prestige than they are with money. Their histories and
victories are more precious to them any gems, their portraits
and tapestries more valuable than a vault of gold.*

– From the memoir of Drakina Tveit,
Lead Librarian of Midtenjord Province

Ruslan stood a dozen feet from the table, finding a shadow
to linger in. There were plenty to choose from and silence
lay all around, feeling as thick as fresh snow. The cooking
smells of the inn had faded, leaving only old beer and the
sour reek of working men's bodies, now gone home to their
beds. The innkeeper had extinguished the lanterns now that
Steiner and his people had returned, and the sun had yet to
rise. A lone candle provided what little illumination there
was. Boyar Sokolov sat with a grim expression, looking for
all the world like the statue of the previous Boyar, long dead
and just as stony. Ruslan stared at the man on the other side
of the table, the most wanted man in the Empire. He wasn't

much to look at: wiry rather than muscular. Every inch of his skin displayed a fine tracery of pale scars. Steiner Vartiainen was a boy in a man's world, Ruslan decided, a boy stumbling into a trap crafted by the Emperor and laid by his master. Neither of the seated men spoke as footsteps sounded on the stairs. Ruslan stifled a curse; the meeting was interrupted before it had begun.

'A little early for beer, isn't it?' A woman drifted through the inn. She was somewhere in her forties, with strong features and dark brown hair caught in a simple ponytail at the nape of neck.

'We already have drinks,' said Boyar Sokolov, his voice a deep rumble amid the silence. He shooed the woman away with a dismissive gesture.

'I'm not here to serve you,' said the woman, taking a seat beside Steiner. 'I'm his aunt, you old fool.'

Ruslan swallowed as his nerves got the better of him, unaccustomed to hearing anyone speak to the Boyar in such a way.

'I have no need to speak with you,' said Sokolov, smoothing down his moustaches. 'I came to speak to the dragon rider. Sit somewhere else.'

The woman lifted her hand and the Boyar was wrenched out of seat and slammed against the wall behind him.

'I was once Matriarch-Commissar Felgenhauer.' The Boyar's eyes widened in shock. 'You may have heard of me.' She relaxed her hand, leaving the old man gasping. 'I sit where I gods-damned please, old man.'

'Shall we try and have a conversation without killing each other?' said Steiner, irritation plain to hear. 'Usually I have Kristofine around to make negotiations go smoothly, but . . .' He clenched his jaw.

'I meant no offence,' said the Boyar.

'We're all here for the same thing,' continued Steiner. 'We

all want the Emperor dead.' He sat down and leaned towards Boyar Sokolov with a tired yet grave expression. Ruslan had thought that Steiner Vartiainen would be nothing less than a berserker barely able to speak, yet here he was appealing for calm. 'What is it you know that can help us?' asked the dragon rider quietly.

'I have learned of a secret way into the Imperial Court,' whispered the Boyar.

The former Matriarch-Commissar gave a dismissive snort and shook her head. 'We just tried a secret way into the Imperial Court,' she said.

'It wasn't so secret,' said Steiner. 'We lost three men and one more was injured. If I didn't know better I'd say they were waiting for us.'

'It is not inconceivable the Emperor had a moment of foresight,' added Felgenhauer. 'His powers in four schools of the arcane are considerable.'

'I know nothing of arrangements at the palace,' said the Boyar. 'Nor how many soldiers or Vigilants the Emperor has at his command.'

'We always knew we'd run into resistance,' said Steiner. 'Heading through the courtyard was a mistake.'

'During the war against the dragons there were a great many deaths,' said the Boyar, interrupting Steiner and Felgenhauer's reflections on the failed attack. 'It often took a hundred men to kill a single dragon. Many soldiers wanted their dead comrades to be remembered as heroes and the Emperor was keen to do anything he could to appease his men. Most of the soldiers who died were buried in war graves around the outskirts of Khlystburg, but the greatest heroes were interred in catacombs beneath the Imperial Palace itself.'

'I've never heard of any such catacombs,' said Steiner.

'It was the Emperor's intention that the people could come

to pay their respects and be inspired by such noble sacrifice,'
continued the Boyar. 'But the people, far from being inspired,
were horrified by how many corpses were transported back
to Khlystburg. The city folk began to doubt the Emperor could
ever win the war and began to despair. It was then that the
Emperor sealed off the catacombs and used them as a place
to research the arcane.' The Boyar lifted his tankard and took
a draught.

'Which is why there's a direct route from the catacombs to
the office below his bed chamber,' said Felgenhauer.

'The office where he keeps the Ashen Blade,' added Steiner.

'I know where the entrance to the catacombs is hidden,'
the Boyar went on. 'The Emperor had a warehouse built in
front of the great gates so people would forget about it, but
I did not forget. I have ancestors buried in that place.'

'And what is it you want for such a piece of information?'
said Steiner.

'Revenge,' said the Boyar, and his voice almost broke as he
said the word. 'Perhaps you have not heard, but my son,
Dimitri, was slain by the Emperor's own hand in the Imperial
Court.' The Boyar swallowed; then he cleared his throat,
struggling to get the words out. 'He was put down like a dog
on false charges, bringing our line, our good name, our entire
province into disrepute.' The Boyar leaned across the table.
'I will not tolerate it. The Sokolov line has ever been decent
and loyal. No longer. This insult cannot go unpunished.'

'Why not go yourself?' said Felgenhauer, sitting back in her
seat and crossing her arms. 'A secret route, a few trustworthy
men—'

'I am an old man,' interrupted the Boyar, sounding irritated.
'And the Emperor's powers are unfathomable to one such as
I, assuming he has arcane powers like your own.'

'He invented the Synod,' replied Felgenhauer. 'It's not just
the Vigilants that have been hiding their powers from the

common folk all this time; Volkan Karlov has too. And he's had seventy years to perfect the art.'

Outside a bell tolled with urgency and Steiner lurched to his feet. He and Ruslan approached a window together and found themselves looking at a dark shadow in the early morning.

'Bittervinge,' whispered Steiner. Ruslan felt a pang of fear pass through him. The Boyar and Felgenhauer joined them, watching the dragon attack the city, plumes of fire illuminating the pale grey and paler blue of the dawn skies.

'While the Emperor's eyes watch above for his old adversary, you may attack him from below.' The old man coughed a moment and drew in a wheezing breath. 'He will never see you coming, Steiner Vartiainen, and you can avenge your uncle, save your father, save all of us from this tyranny.'

Ruslan watched expressions chase one another across Steiner's face. Doubt, hope, willingness, then doubt once more.

'Tell us what you know,' said Steiner, his eyes darting back to the window. Bittervinge had moved on to terrorize some other part of the city. 'This had better be good. I can't end this bastard without the Ashen Blade. I need to know where he keeps it.'

'No one wants the Emperor dead more than I,' said the Boyar once more.

There was no question that Bittervinge's attacks on the city were harrowing, the plumes of smoke and the sounds of screaming were testament to that, but the terror was mercifully short. Ruslan surmised the dreadful creature was feeding where he could before fleeing north again, beyond the reaches of the Vigilants and the Emperor.

'It can only be a matter of time before he's regained his strength,' muttered Ruslan as he watched the winged monstrosity head towards the horizon.

'Perhaps he will kill both Steiner and the Emperor,' said the Boyar quietly. 'And we can return to Vend and put this dreadful business behind us.'

Ruslan said nothing, but on the long walk back to their apartments a feeling blossomed, then flourished and persisted. Steiner Vartiainen had not been the man he had expected; and more than that, Ruslan found he admired him.

'I expect that fiend Zima will be waiting for us the moment we step through the door,' growled the Boyar as they strode down the street. Ruslan could feel the impatience radiating off the man. They reached the door to the guest house just as three noblewomen dismounted from a carriage.

'Friends of yours?' asked the Boyar with a sneer. Clearly Ruslan had failed to hide his dismay.

'It's the gardener!' said the young noblewoman with a fan. The laugh that followed it was alive with a vicious glee. The dour-faced noble in the purple dress glowered at Ruslan.

'How wonderful.'

The brunette noblewoman smiled and opened her mouth to speak before remembering herself. 'My lord.' She dropped a small curtsey to the Boyar. 'I have not had the benefit of introduction. I am Lady Odessine Temmnaya.'

The Boyar took the hand that was offered and pressed it to his lips. 'I have heard of you,' he replied with a glimmer of his old wolfish charm. 'The Jewel of Virolanti Province. You have quite the reputation.'

Lady Odessine flicked a pleased look over her shoulder at her friend in the purple dress. 'And are you some great but sorely overlooked hero of the Empire, my lord?' she replied smoothly, still holding the Boyar's hand.

'Once perhaps, if only through my long association with the throne. I am Boyar Augustine Sokolov of Vend Province.'

Lady Odessine snatched her hand back as if she had been scalded. The younger noblewoman dropped her fluttering fan, while the sour-faced companion adopted a look of shock. A silence insinuated itself between the two parties, a silence loaded with surprise, disgust, and not a little curiosity.

'These three good ladies found me in the Imperial Gardens while I was waiting for you, my lord,' said Ruslan, desperate to fill the void with words.

'I will not detain you any longer,' replied Boyar Sokolov. 'Good day to you.' He slunk to the door of the guest house and slipped inside, leaving Ruslan staring at three noblewomen, uncertainty stifling thought and word.

'It seems I underestimated you,' said Lady Odessine. She cast another appraising glance at Ruslan as if he were a horse at market and stepped closer. 'Would you care to join us for tea?' Ruslan couldn't swear to it, but he was sure there was a hint of alcohol on her breath. 'Or perhaps something stronger?'

'I should attend to my lord.'

'That you should, but we will be in our rooms all afternoon should you change your mind.' She stepped closer still and whispered her room number into his ear. Ruslan shivered, then blushed, then tripped up the steps as he hurried inside.

The Boyar was in no mood to be attended. The Boyar was in no mood at all, and so he dismissed Ruslan with the strict instruction to wrestle some measure of joy from the wretched city before everything burned to the ground. Ruslan, who had never been overly burdened with an imagination, found himself knocking timidly on Lady Odessine's door.

'Just for tea,' he whispered to himself. Perhaps the Boyar's mood would improve if some gossip from court could be gleaned. The door jerked open, startling Ruslan, who had been lost in his thoughts. Before him stood the noblewoman in the purple dress, though she had forgone her usual attire for a silk robe in the same colour. She struggled to focus on him for a moment and then sighed.

'Oh. It's you. I suppose you've come to rut with my sister.'

'I'm just here for the tea, actually,' replied Ruslan. The noblewoman smiled.

'The tea is very good,' she said with a slight slur to her words. 'I'm Alena. You'd best come in.'

Ruslan dutifully followed and almost stumbled as he crossed the threshold. The suite had been surrendered to chaos. Dinner plates with half-eaten food littered a table long enough to seat eight. A decanter of wine had been emptied and lay on its side like a fallen soldier. Clothes, shoes, and cutlery were strewn across the floor, other forgotten casualties. The remains of shattered wineglasses crunched under Ruslan's boots while candles burned in lanterns of coloured glass, lending a dreamlike quality to the scene.

'Have you been ransacked?' he asked in a shocked whisper.

'Oh yes,' replied Alena. 'Very thoroughly.' She snorted an unladylike laugh behind her hand before composing herself.

'I could clear this up for you,' said Ruslan, every inch the dutiful aide.

'No, no. Come through to the bedroom.' Alena said this casually over her shoulder, as if entering a married noble-woman's chamber was of no matter. 'We're chasing the dragon.' Ruslan wondered if she too had been drinking, like her sister.

'Why would you want to chase a dragon?' asked Ruslan, although he realized he was probably missing some deeper meaning. Alena ignored him and pushed through double doors that led to a bed-chamber every bit as disordered as the suite.

'Oh! How exciting!' The young noblewoman was lying flat on her back with her head hanging off the end of the bed. Ruslan wondered why she would want to stare at the dark-ened room upside down. The odd candle penetrated the gloom here and there.

'That's Natasha,' said Alena, crossing the room to a high-backed leather armchair and slumping into it. Ruslan watched with fascination as Odessine emerged from the shadows with an elaborate pipe in one hand. She crawled up on to the bed in a nightshirt which had been ripped from hem to hip on one side.

'I'll get to you shortly,' she said in a businesslike tone, before straddling Natasha and taking a deep breath of smoke. She took a moment to set down the pipe and gently exhaled into Natasha's open mouth in a gross parody of a kiss. The two women dissolved into helpless laughter, becoming a tangle of limbs.

'Is that chasing the dragon?' asked Ruslan.

Alena looked over to the bed and raised an eyebrow. 'I'd very much say they've caught it.' Odessine and Natasha exchanged another kiss, with decidedly less smoke and more contact.

'You may have missed your chance,' said Alena. She pointed to the seat opposite. 'Sit.' Ruslan did as he was told, unable to tear his eyes from the noblewomen on the bed. He had never seen anything like it. 'So you're the aide to a disgraced Boyar, no doubt looking for employment in another household to avoid being dragged under by the scandal.'

'I've been with the Sokolovs my whole life—'

'That might be painfully true if the Emperor executes both of you.' Alena was now smoking from her own pipe, which was smaller than Odessine's.

'That won't happen,' said Ruslan, his eyes now firmly fixed on Alena. 'Reparations are under way.'

The noblewoman smoothed down her silk robe, sat forward in her chair and shook her head in disbelief. 'You're actually loyal to the old bastard. And an optimist.' She smiled. 'How charming. I thought your kind had died out with the Spriggani.'

'Some of the Spriggani still live,' said Ruslan, but it was clear Alena wasn't interested. She was loading her pipe with some sort of resin. Odessine and Natasha were focused exclusively on each other and Ruslan decided it was time to depart. He stood slowly, taking one last look around the near-ruined bed-chamber.

'How much does it cost?'

'How much does what cost?' mumbled Alena.

'All of it. The suite, the clothes, chasing the dragon . . .' He gestured around.

'Who knows? Our husbands pay for our entertainments with the taxes they claim from the peasants. It's only fair. If we have to suffer this intolerable boredom we should at least have some fun.'

'Taxes,' repeated Ruslan. He slowly made his way through the debris of the suite, and with every step he grew more certain that it would be no bad thing if the Empire failed. Would it be so terrible if Steiner succeeded and put an end to a deathless Emperor and his scores of idle and debauched underlings? Ruslan closed the door to the suite and forced the images of what he had seen from his mind.

CHAPTER EIGHTEEN

Streig

The Ashen Gulf, as it was named at the end of the war with the dragons, is an important feature of Vinterkveld. Slavon, Vend, Novgoruske, and Midtenjord Provinces all trade with each other by ship. Weather conditions in the gulf are frequently favourable so the danger to shipping is slight. The return of the dragons changed this dramatically. Many of the young dragons freed from Vladibogdan fled the continent for other lands. Some were rumoured to have taken themselves out to sea, where they lived on small rocky islands, content in their solitude. A handful of the younger dragons remained; the most famous are Namarii, Flodvind and Stonvind, of course. These dragons helped change the fate of Vinterkveld and entered into legend with their brave and daring skirmishes.

– From the memoir of Drakina Tveit,
Lead Librarian of Midtenjord Province

'Gods, I hate sailing,' said Streig. To say the ship was crowded would be an understatement. The other soldiers kept to themselves, nursing their wounds and their silence in equal measure. A few simply stared into the distance and Streig had the feeling they were reliving parts of the battle, perhaps fearing as he did that they would be buried and never make it out alive. The staring men were startled easily, and the night-times were accompanied by the sounds of sobbing. Bittervinge might not have killed these men but he had surely broken them.

Time is a great healer, Streig.

He clutched the rucksack containing the urn more tightly and looked about. He had barely moved from the cramped corner he'd settled in.

'It's not healing you though, is it?'

One needs to be alive to heal, and I have not had that privilege for a long time now.

Two dignitaries sat close by, attempting to outdo one another by demonstrating their knowledge of the Empire's predicament, or naming powerful contacts in Khlystburg, hoping to elevate themselves by association. Streig couldn't tell if it was the motion of the ship or the companions that turned his stomach.

Perhaps it would be best if you walked a few lengths of the deck to stretch your legs.

'I don't see how that will help,' replied Streig, taking a moment to steady himself. 'I'll still feel sick.'

But it will spare you from listening to these tiresome fools.

Streig rose to his feet. 'Gods damn it,' he whispered under his breath. 'Do you have to be right about everything, all the time?'

If only that were true.

The sea was choppy and the ship rolled unpleasantly. No sooner had Streig reached the deck than he overheard the captain conversing with his first mate.

'No good will come of it.' The captain was holding a telescope up to one eye and frowning. He was a tall man in his fifties with a serious demeanour. There was a good deal of white and grey in his beard, which was neatly trimmed. His jacket and boots were in good repair, much like his ship. He caught Streig's glance and nodded to him.

'Are you the soldier with huge sword I keep hearing about?'

'I am.'

'I'm Captain Hewn of the *Eastern Star*.'

'Streig.'

'They tell me you faced Bittervinge in the Great Library.' Hewn fixed him with a disbelieving look. 'That true?'

'I was there.'

'What happened?' asked Hewn.

'It was like trying to fight an earthquake,' replied Streig. 'An earthquake with teeth and talons that are large enough to eviscerate a man. We wounded him and eventually he took to wing. I suppose he decided he had a score to settle with the Emperor.' Streig gestured to the telescope. 'I overheard you talking. You said, "No good will come of it"?'

Captain Hewn pointed towards the horizon, still several miles distant but Streig knew the capital city was within reach.

'Khlystburg. They too have a blockade and I don't care much for my chances.'

'But we have special dispensation,' said Streig, thinking of the corporal's words on Arkiv. 'We're all loyal to the Empire.'

'That's well and good,' replied Hewn, 'but the Vigilants on the Imperial ships might choose to call down the arcane on us before asking any questions. Tensions are high and the Empire isn't known for its light touch.' Captain Hewn's eyes widened slightly as he remembered he was addressing a soldier. 'No offence, but you know what I mean.'

'Unfortunately I do.' Streig paused, confused at the captain's words. 'Do you mean to say the Vigilants are using their powers in public?' Streig couldn't believe what he was hearing. The carefully maintained fiction that the arcane was a taint was paramount to the Empire. If the Holy Synod were using their powers openly they would be branded liars and hypocrites.

'Rumours of people using the arcane are coming from every corner of the Empire now,' said Captain Hewn. 'And the

Scorched Republics too. I can't say I'm surprised the Synod uses that power.' The captain looked over his shoulder to check no one else was listening. 'I never trusted them, though they pay well and their coin is as good as anyone else's.' The captain took another look through the telescope and sighed. 'Damn it.'

He turned to his first mate and muttered something in a dialect Streig couldn't understand. The first mate in turn bellowed at the crew and the men and women went to work at sheets and braces. The ship swung south in response, turning away from Khlystburg.

'Wait!' said Streig. 'I have to get to the city.'

'You and everyone else aboard,' replied Captain Hewn. 'We'll put in further down the coast, somewhere we won't be turned to ashes by Vigilants. You'll have to make your own way on foot after that.'

'But it's imperative I reach the docks.' Streig clutched the bag containing the urn a little tighter.

'And it's imperative I don't take any risks that see my ship and my crew burned with arcane fire. I'm sorry. You'll be able to reach the outskirts of the city after a day's walk or so.' Captain Hewn turned away and checked in with his crew, leaving Streig alone.

Do not give up hope, Streig. I believe in you. You are nothing if not resourceful.

'Resourceful isn't the same thing as creating miracles. We've barely any food, little coin, no allies, and Khlystburg is at war.' Streig made an irritated noise in the back of his throat and stared at the horizon. 'Think I'll stay up on deck tonight,' he added. 'I can't stand being underground. I mean, below decks. I don't want to sleep down there again with all those bickering dignitaries.'

We shall rest where you are most comfortable.

* * *

Streig took up a spot at the bow and a member of the crew supplied an old cloak from a sea chest. The sun set in a swirl of bloody reds and the wind abandoned them, leaving the ship becalmed. All night Streig drifted in and out of sleep just as the ship drifted one way and then another, going nowhere. Dark dreams of falling masonry and burning books woke him, damp with cold sweat and ready to fight. Streig stood up to shake off the last of his night terrors and dragged down a shaky lungful of breath. He squinted in the early-morning light, unsure of what he was seeing.

Streig.

'I know, I can see them.' Three flecks of darkness in a dawn sky of vermilion and faded yellow. Streig wanted to call out to Captain Hewn but every muscle was locked in place. 'Not again. I can't do this. We have to get away.

But we are becalmed, and even if we were not we would fail to outrun them.

'I can't face another dragon. Not again.'

It is not Bittervinge.

'How can you tell?' whispered Streig.

Bittervinge never took allies; he only ever worked alone. There are three of them, are there not?

'Yes, three. And they're heading this way.' The silhouettes were closer now, but something was amiss. 'I know they call Steiner the dragon rider, but I never thought it possible.'

What is it?

'I think these dragons have riders,' said Streig. There was no doubt now that the three dragons were approaching, and the crew of the *Eastern Star* called out in alarm. Soon the passengers were on deck and a look of silent dread passed over everyone.

'We may not survive this if they think we're Imperial soldiers,' whispered Streig to the urn, but for once Silverdust had no words of wisdom to offer.

CHAPTER NINETEEN

Kimi

Nothing captured the imagination of the people quite like the simple act of flying a dragon. People from six years old to sixty-six wondered at it, dreamed about it, spoke about the wonder of it. It was this that helped build Kimi Enkhtuya's legend and establish Taiga as a spiritual leader during those dark days.

— From the memoir of Drakina Tveit,
Lead Librarian of Midtenjord Province

'Why are we flying south?' shouted Tief at the top of his lungs. The dragons beat their wings with a slow, steady rhythm. Kimi hunched closer to Namarii and squinted against the wind. She gripped the smaller spines at the base of Namarii's neck and tucked her boots into the grooves between the scales.

'Can you tell him that we're looking for food using the arcane,' said Kimi. 'I barely have a voice left.' They had been awake most of the night, hoping to avoid another clash with Bittervinge.

I have told them. Namarii had been quiet since the attack at the Imperial Court. His responses were short and subdued and Kimi had left him to his thoughts.

'Rest at last,' she said. 'I can't begin to imagine how tired you must be.'

It is of no concern, replied Namarii. They began to descend a few miles south of the city, a good distance from the port with its blockade and the promise of Vigilants. One by one, the dragons touched down in a cove barely big enough to contain them. Dark cliffs rose on each side and the sea whispered a hushed song on the shingle that formed the beach. Gulls shrieked in alarm at the dragons' arrival before departing at speed. The sun had risen but Kimi had no qualms about sleeping during the day.

'This is the perfect spot for smuggling,' said Tief as he dismounted Stonvind. 'You can bet your boots Romola would love it here.'

Kimi felt a pang of loss for her friend. Had they been friends, or had they merely been useful to one another? Regardless, Kimi would do anything to see the captain of the *Watcher's Wait* again. Perhaps Romola would have some method of slipping past the father of dragons to strike at the Emperor.

'I've come around to the idea that flying is spectacular,' said Taiga. She pressed her hands to her lower back and stretched. 'But it's not the most comfortable. Goddess help me. And my backside.'

As one, Namarii, Stonvind, and Flodvind took off, gliding low above the waters of the Ashen Gulf. Every so often one would open their mouth, ploughing through the sea to dredge up fish. Kimi sat on the uncomfortable stones, feeling the chill of the dawn air on her skin. Riding a dragon was not unlike working a furnace, and the drop in temperature made her shiver.

'You've got a look about you,' said Tief. Kimi didn't meet his eyes, but slung her pack behind her and lay back. Taiga rummaged around in her own pack for tea and mugs.

'He's right,' said the priestess. 'You do have a look about you. What's on your mind?'

'We faced the Emperor,' replied Kimi. 'And he was too strong for us. Too strong for them.' She nodded out to sea where the dragons hunted.

'We were testing the defences is all,' replied Tief, taking out his pipe. 'That counts for something. I dare say the dragons grow in confidence each time we engage in one of these skirmishes.'

'Could you at least make a fire before you start smoking?' chided Taiga.

'I want vengeance for my father,' said Kimi. 'And for myself. I want an end to the Solmindre Empire.'

'We'll get him,' replied Tief, his tone gruff as he took out a bundle of firewood from his pack. 'I'm here to avenge the Spriggani, remember?'

'But it's likely we will have to kill Bittervinge first,' said Taiga, sounding none too confident at the prospect. 'We can't fight the Emperor with the father of dragons snapping at our heels.'

'It's not my heels I'm worried about,' rumbled Tief.

'I'd be better off heading south,' said Kimi, 'and avenging myself on my worthless brother.'

'We came to kill the Emperor,' said Tief. 'That was always the plan.' His expression darkened. 'Besides, we just saw people in the Imperial Court carrying out their own rebellion. We're not doing this alone any more.'

'Did you see who they were?' called out Taiga as she looked for driftwood to add to the campfire.

Tief shook his head. 'It was too dark and there was too much happening,' he said. 'I think one of them was a Vigilant, a renegade Vigilant.'

'I just . . .' Kimi sighed. 'There's no question Namarii, Flodvind, and Stonvind are growing stronger all the time, but

we're up against Bittervinge, father of dragons, terror of
Vinterkveld. He was in the world before me, before my mother,
before my grandmother. What chance do we stand against
that much experience, that much power?'

'Perhaps if you used the Ashen Blade on him,' said Tief.
'A weapon like that—'

'It's evil!' replied Kimi. 'I won't sully myself by wielding it.'

'It might be your only way,' said Taiga softly. 'As distasteful
as it is.'

'I won't use that blade,' repeated Kimi. 'I won't.'

The sun was edging above the horizon now, though the
light revealed a host of grey, blurry clouds that did nothing
to lift Kimi's spirits.

'Who are they?' said Taiga, pointing at a ship far out on
the Ashen Gulf.

'Whoever they are,' replied Tief with a wicked laugh,
'they're about to be disappointed. The blockade at Khlystburg
won't let them through and there's no other port nearby.'

'You don't think it strange that all the other ships we've
seen are leaving the city and this one is arriving?' said Kimi.

'Maybe they haven't heard the Empire is falling apart.' Tief
shrugged. 'Too bad for them.'

The dragons, who had ventured further south on their
fishing expedition, returned in a great commotion of scaled
wings and grasping talons. Kimi shielded her face with her
arm as grit swirled about them. Taiga shouted incoherently
as the fire she had been trying to light was blown apart.

'What is it?' shouted Kimi. Flodvind prowled to the
shoreline once the dragons had landed.

There is something on that boat. The azure dragon was very
still, her eyes fixed on the sailing ship that was even now
changing course to avoid them.

'Could you be more specific?' asked Tief irritably, his pipe
clenched between his teeth. Flodvind let out a small snort of

sooty air that indicated exactly what she thought of his request. Tief jetted pipe smoke from his nostrils in response.

Was that it?

Tief looked at his pipe ruefully. 'I was being ridiculous, sorry.' Flodvind turned her attention back to the ship.

There is an artefact of some kind, but also something else. A cinderwraith perhaps, or something like a cinderwraith.

'Silverdust!' said Kimi. 'It's Silverdust. We have to get him.' She scrambled up on to Namarii's neck. Perhaps the Exarch would know how to defeat Bittervinge without resorting to using the Ashen Blade.

'We don't know that for sure,' said Tief with a sneer. 'Besides, why would he be this far south?'

Namarii launched into the air before Kimi could say more. The dark brown dragon's voice sounded gently in her head as they took to wing.

Your friend is not so keen to accost a ship we know nothing about.

'And you?'

I am tired. If the cinderwraith is the prisoner of Vigilants then things will become lively, but it seems important to you.

'Lively,' replied Kimi with a smirk. 'That's a nice word for it.'

This Silverdust, he is an ally of yours? A friend?

'He remained behind on Vladibogdan to buy us time. He set you free.'

He was useful. He will be useful again. Namarii's wings beat harder and he stretched out his neck in order to fly faster.

The dragons rounded up the ship in a way that reminded Kimi of three very large sheepdogs herding a lone sheep. The idea, though ridiculous, wouldn't leave her and she found her spirits improved, but not by much. Kimi directed the ship to the cove and the long process of transferring people ashore in small boats began. Flodvind continued to circle the ship, gliding over the waters, while Stonvind perched atop the cliffs, looking down on everyone with a baleful glare.

'They don't seem to have Vigilants with them,' said Kimi to Namarii.

Flodvind has the gift of sight. She assures me there is just the artefact and the cinderwraith.

Namarii touched down on the beach and Kimi slipped off his back. She drew the sword she'd used to kill Veles, more to give her confidence than out of any wish to use it. The people cowered before her and the few armed men and women among them threw down their blades. Everyone looked horrified in the presence of three dragons, not least because Stonvind could be heard growling from his perch on the cliff edge far above them. Tief had found a way down to the beach and fell in beside Kimi.

'What are we doing here, Your Highness?' he said.

'Looking for Silverdust, of course.' She turned to the people. 'Which one of you is the captain?'

An older man stepped forward, eyes darting from Namarii to Stonvind up on the cliff edge and back to Kimi and her drawn sword.

'I'm Matthias Hewn, captain of the *Eastern Star.*'

'No one is getting eaten,' she said loud enough for all to hear. The sense of relief in the small cove was like a gentle wave of cool water.

'You have a Vigilant with you?' asked Kimi. 'An Exarch?' The captain shook his head.

'We came from Arkiv,' said Hewn. 'A few wounded soldiers and dozen or so dignitaries. Who are you?'

'She is none other than Kimi Enkhtuya,' proclaimed Tief in a booming voice. 'Champion of Frøya; slayer of the dragon, Veles; a princess of Yamal. And you should be kneeling!'

As one the captives dropped to one knee and bowed their heads.

'Was that really necessary?' said Kimi under her breath.

'You seemed maudlin,' said Tief. 'I thought I'd remind you of a few things. It's impressive when you hear it like that, eh?' He grinned before starting to fuss with his pipe.

'Captain Hewn,' said Kimi. 'Please, stand up. You're sure a Vigilant didn't come aboard? He would have appeared very tall, wearing a blank curving mask with a mirrored surface.'

'I'm sorry,' said the captain, getting to his feet with a wary look in his eyes. 'All the Vigilants on Arkiv were killed when Bittervinge escaped the Great Library. That's what we heard.'

Kimi began to pace through the knots of passengers, casting her eye over the huddles of men and women. The soldiers scowled at her while the dignitaries shrank away or pretended indignant outrage to cover their fear.

'You,' said Kimi to a man in a faded blue cloak with the hood up. Kimi eyed the two-handed sword that was strapped across his back. He raised his head and pulled back the hood, revealing the face of a young man. He was handsome, she supposed, if you liked white men.

'Everyone else discarded their weapons when they came ashore.'

'I, ah, I forgot.' He set down a small pack he was clutching before reaching for the straps that held the weapon in place. Kimi knelt down so she was eye to eye with the man. He had to be a soldier, though, if she had to guess, she'd say he wasn't in the best health. He fumbled with the straps with a wounded hand.

'What's in the pack?'

'An urn,' said the soldier, setting the great sword down slowly. 'It contains the ashes of my master. He was slain on Arkiv fighting Bittervinge. I'm taking him to Khlystburg to his final rest.'

Kimi frowned. He was telling the truth as far as she could tell, but in times like these who could tell fiction from falsehood? He seemed nervous, but that might just have been a product of Stonvind's growling on the cliffs above.

'You fought at Arkiv?'

'I was in the Great Library when it fell.'

'When Bittervinge escaped?' asked Kimi. The soldier nodded. Small wonder he was so anxious.

A scattering of rocks rattled down the cliffs behind them and everyone looked up. Flodvind had ceased her gliding over the sea to take a perch above them. Stonvind had stopped growling at last.

'You found him then!' shouted Taiga cheerfully. Kimi stood up and gestured her confusion. 'Silverdust,' called Taiga.

'What are you talking about?' yelled Tief. 'This is just a soldier.'

Flodvind snorted an impatient plume of soot. *He is in the urn, you fools.*

'Of course he is,' muttered Tief. 'Where else would he be? It's so obvious.'

'Captain Hewn,' said Kimi. 'You're free to go, and your passengers along with you.' She turned to the cloaked man. 'But this one stays with me. Him, the sword, and his urn.'

'What do I call you?' said Kimi after the ship's crew and passengers had departed. Most had found a way up the cliffs and made camp just half a mile away. Tief had made a passable fish stew and Taiga was on hand with tea, as was her custom.

'My name is Streig.' The soldier looked down at the urn as if listening, then nodded. He reached forward and lifted the lid. Inside was a plume of slowly rotating smoke with two fireflies hovering inside.

'That's Silverdust?' said Kimi.

'What the Hel happened?' said Tief with a look of disbelief etched on his grizzled face. 'Where's the rest of him?'

We had to fight Bittervinge in the Great Library. Silverdust's words appeared in their minds gently, no more than a whisper. *It was hard to pierce his skin and he consumed me. I expended much of my essence burning him from the inside out. I am much reduced.*

'I'm trying to get back to Khlystburg to find someone to restore him,' said Streig. From his tone Kimi guessed he didn't hold out much hope. Tief smiled and chuckled for a moment.

'I know you hate the Empire, Tief,' said Kimi. 'But now isn't the time to crow over your enemies' misfortunes.'

Tief set down his dinner. 'I'm not laughing because the cinderwraith was eaten, I'm laughing because I know how to help him. I've done it before, on Vladibogdan. You should remember: you kicked a bucket of water over one of them. I had to coax the spirit back into being.'

'I don't remember,' admitted Kimi.

'Well, that doesn't surprise me. You'd had a big fight with Steiner.'

'You know Steiner?' said Streig.

Of course they know Steiner. Silverdust sounded impatient. *Could we progress to the part where I am restored? You can exchange war stories later.*

'I don't remember Silverdust being so surly,' said Tief, lifting the urn gently and carrying it to the fire.

'You can't blame him,' said Streig. 'He's been in there a while.'

'Are you're sure about this?' said Taiga. 'Using the arcane like this . . .' She pursed her lips. 'It comes at a cost.'

'I know,' said Tief. 'But he's one of us. He wants the Emperor dead just as much as we do. And we need all the allies we can get since we lost Marozvolk.'

That is unfortunate. I liked Marozvolk very much.

Stonvind prowled down the cliff face, huge talons gripping the stone. The dragon skidded and dropped the last dozen feet, feet crunching on the shingle. Streig flinched and looked as if he might run at any moment, but there was nowhere to go.

Tief. Stonvind's words appeared in their minds. *I will not let you harm yourself. Fire is the domain of dragons and you will poison yourself remaking the cinderwraith.*

'I said I'd do it,' replied Tief, frowning. 'I know the cost and I'm willing to pay it.'

That which Bittervinge has wounded, I will make whole.

'Far be it from me to argue with a dragon,' said Tief. 'Do you know what you're doing?'

I can sense enough of your mind to see what needs to be done.

The dark grey dragon plucked the urn from Tief's hands with the points of his talons, the gesture precise and gentle given the size of the claws. Silverdust, in his confinement, was held above the campfire and Stonvind closed his amber eyes to concentrate. A deep rumble sounded around the cove and Kimi shrank backwards on instinct. Stonvind breathed a sooty breath that mingled with the smoke from the fire. A silhouette appeared – gradually at first; an apparition of smoke. With each passing moment the form became darker, gathering every particle of soot until it was a jet-black phantom. Two golden eyes of fire blinked open as the cinderwraith was made whole.

Thank you. My name is Silverdust and I owe you a debt of gratitude.

I am Stonvind. This debt and all debts were paid the moment you freed us from Vladibogdan. The dragon climbed the cliff face to resume his perch. Streig took off his cloak and offered it to Silverdust.

'You should take this to protect you from the rain.'

The cinderwraith grasped the cloak and concealed himself as best he could.

You have done well, my friend. Thank you.

'So we have three dragons, an Exarch, a high priestess and

a dragon-slaying Yamal princess,' said Tief, counting them off
on his fingers.

Kimi laughed at Tief's persistent optimism but realized she
didn't share it. A pervading sense she was outclassed and
outnumbered remained and gnawed at her as she tried to
sleep.

CHAPTER TWENTY

Silverdust

Bravery, leadership, selflessness, a willingness to try the unthinkable. Heroes are expected to display all of these traits without question. Perhaps we have heard the tales so often that we forget the names represent real people? Fear of dying, indecision, protecting one's own needs, performing distasteful deeds to achieve one's ends. These are weaknesses real people are mired in, but they have no place in heroic tales, and that's the shame of it. The interior battles are just as hard as the exterior ones, if not more so.

– From the memoir of Drakina Tveit,
Lead Librarian of Midtenjord Province

Silverdust lifted the mirrored mask to his face and arranged the hood of the black robes. Black leather gloves were pulled on to amorphous, smoky hands. Finally the cinderwraith was covered in a way he was accustomed to, but no longer adorned in the cream and blood-red of Imperial vestments. No proclamation of his loyalty remained. He was at last his own man, in a manner of speaking.

You have done well, Streig.

They were standing in the captain's cabin of the *Eastern Star*, the ship that had brought them from Arkiv.

'Black is your colour,' said the soldier, admiring the garments he'd stolen. 'I didn't think I'd enjoy rifling through the luggage of all those dignitaries.' Streig shrugged. 'But if I'm going to be an outlaw I may well as well go all in.'

'Be sure you only steal from the Empire,' said Kimi with a note of warning in her words. She stood near the window at the back of the cabin, gazing at the rise and fall of the midnight-blue seas. Silverdust could sense the princess's feelings were as dangerous as any undertow or riptide.

'I'm going to step out and see if I can find more coin,' said Streig. 'We might have need of it for the next part of the journey.' He dared a furtive glance at Kimi, then departed, keen to be away. The soldier didn't need the foresight or sensing powers of Academy Vozdukha to know when to make himself scarce.

'I'm glad Tief and Stonvind were able to restore you,' said the Yamal princess. 'How are you?'

I am feeling more alive than I have in years, if such a thing is possible. A better question is: how are you, princess?

'I wasn't the one the one confined to an urn for days on end.'

That much is true, but I have not been disowned by my own brother. Nor has my brother allied himself with the Emperor.

'You don't know what you speak of. You have it all wrong.' Kimi took a step closer and Silverdust regarded her properly in the afternoon light. She had always been a tall, muscular woman and the last few months had only served to reinforce this. Even Veles, the most devious and deceitful of dragons, had not been able to reduce the towering physicality of Kimi Enkhtuya. But it was not the physical realm that troubled her.

Why else would your brother seek the death of your father? Why take the risk of regicide and reprisals? He could have simply waited for your father to fade away.

'Tsen is a murderous, spiteful, selfish . . .' She threw up her hands as she failed to find the right words. 'But he'd never make such a bargain with the Emperor. Never.'

Silverdust said nothing. People needed time to absorb new information, and never more so when the news concerned family. Kimi paced around the cabin, distracting herself with a dog-eared chart that had been stretched across the table. Her fingertips brushed the surface of the parchment and instinctively wandered to the lower right-hand corner where Yamal had been sketched out in the vaguest terms.

'Tsen,' she whispered before looking up with an expression somewhere between grief and rage. 'What do you know, Silverdust?'

I have heard nothing in the conventional sense, but the arcane allows me to listen in on messages that roam far and wide. The Emperor sends word to your brother. He is desperate, reckless, uncaring of who may listen in.

'What messages?'

The Emperor is under siege from all of his worst nightmares. Bittervinge attacks from above while Steiner strikes from the shadows, and the Stormtide Prophet is crossing the Ashen Gulf as we speak.

'The Emperor didn't look so desperate when we attacked him,' replied Kimi. 'He bested us easily. I couldn't take the risk of ordering the dragons to fight to the death. I couldn't risk losing them.'

And yet he sets whispers on the wind, desperate that your brother send reinforcements to Khlystburg from Yamal.

'I've no reason to disbelieve you,' replied Kimi slowly. 'But why would Tsen do such a thing?'

Only he knows the answer to that question. My guess is that the Emperor offered to stay out of Yamal if Tsen offered certain concessions. Your father's life appears to have been one of those concessions.

Kimi opened the door to the cabin and crossed the deck to the railing. She gripped it with both hands and for a moment

Silverdust was sure she would vomit over the side. Her head dipped and her shoulders shook with silent sobs.

'I don't know what's worse,' she said finally. 'That he'd kill to take the title of High Khan himself, or that he'd kill at the Emperor's bidding.'

Perhaps he merely saw a way to keep his country safe, though it cost him dearly.

'He disowned me!' shouted Kimi. She stepped closer to Silverdust, trying to use her size to cow him into subservience.

And you were allowed to escape. No one came after you.

'We escaped into Izhoria, a country full of Grave Wolves and gholes! Tsen didn't need to send anyone after us.'

Even so, it is no small thing for someone impersonating a princess to escape capture. The Emperor would have sent Okhrana after you. The Emperor would have demanded your head as proof.

Kimi looked away. The waters lapped at the hull of the ship and Silverdust could sense a weary despair settle over her.

'So you're saying I should forgive him, that he was serving his country?'

No. I am saying your thoughts linger in the south when your attention should be here, in Khlystburg. You doubt yourself, your leadership, your place in the world.

'Horseshit. I'm a dragon rider, I slew Veles in the swamps of Izhoria. Taiga gifted me with the Ashen Torment.' She reached into her shirt and pulled out the jade dragon. 'This marks me as Frøya's champion.'

You say the words easily enough, and they may well all be true, but do you believe them? Do you feel them? Do your words dispel your fears and doubts?

Kimi turned her back on the Exarch, as if an answer might be found on the horizon. In the distance a dark shadow plagued the skies above the city. Silverdust felt a moment of unease as he remembered being swallowed by the father of dragons in the Great Library.

'Get your soldier,' said Kimi, straightening up and composing herself. 'I want to get my feet back on dry land.'

It will be as you say, Highness.

The journey back to shore had a silence as stony as the shingle beach that awaited them. Captain Hewn lurked alongside Tief, desperate to know if the *Eastern Star* would remain in his ownership. Silverdust could feel the question burning in the man's mind. A few of the passengers had dared to return to the cove from the cliffs above, enquiring after their possessions on the ship. The mood was tense and sour, anger subdued by fear of the dragons.

Streig dragged the small boat on to the beach and Kimi stalked away, keen to be reunited with Namarii.

'What's got into her?' Tief asked Silverdust.

I had thought to ask you the same question.

'It's been a rough few months.' Tief tugged at one earlobe and frowned at the princess, who was doing her best to hide behind the bulk of Namarii. 'Her brother disowned her, and we thought Taiga was dead.'

'But I recovered!' said the priestess cheerfully. 'Frøya be praised!'

Frøya be praised, indeed.

'Frøya be praised.' Tief frowned at his sister as if he didn't fully approve of her enthusiasm. 'Marozvolk was killed by Veles,' continued Tief. 'That was hard on all of us. And, well . . . Kimi's never stopped worrying what would happen if the Emperor discovered she'd escaped.'

Tsen appears to have made a deal with the Emperor.

Tief took a few moments to absorb what he'd been told; then he nodded and lit his pipe. 'Hel's teeth. Makes a certain sense, I suppose. What happens now? Do you and your soldier have a plan?'

Truthfully, no. I barely hoped to be restored, but now I will venture to Khlystburg. I have my own score to settle with the Emperor. As for Streig, his part in this is over.

Streig, noticing Tief was looking in his direction, drifted over to join them from his spot by the campfire.

'Something I should know?'

You have been loyal to me many times over, my friend. The time has come for me to release you. I want you to head back to Virolanti Province. I want you to live a long, peaceful life.

'But there's still so much to do.'

There is, but I would rather have it done without your death on my conscience. We are entering a realm of dragons, Vigilants, and holy warriors.

'I'd be lying if I didn't admit to feeling outclassed,' replied Streig.

'You and me both,' grumbled Tief.

'At least you have a dragon,' said Streig, casting a look over his shoulder at Stonvind.

'There is that, I suppose.' Tief smiled and blew a smoke ring.

Go now to Captain Hewn and make the arrangements. Go while you still draw breath.

'Yes, Exarch,' replied Streig, saluting on instinct before he took off. Silverdust and Tief watched the young soldier pick his way across the shingle beach and address the captain of the *Eastern Star*.

'You're a strange one, Silverdust,' said Tief after a moment. 'One day I'll figure you out, but not anytime soon, I suspect.'

There is a reason my mask is a mirror, Tief.

'That's as maybe, but you can bet your boots it would make your allies feel a touch better if you were more transparent with us.'

Kimi approached them, but her gaze was fixed squarely on Tief. It was clear she had no interest in Silverdust or his theories about her brother's loyalties.

'Get some rest. We fly at dawn.'

'At last!' shouted Tief. 'Sounds like you've got your balls back!'

'Balls?' Kimi glowered at him and Tief coughed uncomfortably.

'I meant, you know, confidence.'

You seek to protect the city?

'Protect? No. We hunt the Emperor,' said Kimi. 'Once we've solved one problem we can turn our attention to Bittervinge.'

I also have a personal history with the Emperor, I will seek him out. I do not have the luxury of a draconic steed and I have no wish to fly. I will head to Khlystburg on foot. If fortune smiles I will find Steiner and we can bring an end to this chaos together.

'Find Steiner?' Kimi shook her head. 'In a city this big, and in so much chaos? Don't you think I'd have already tried that if it were so easy?'

I have certain advantages.

'You'd best get to the Emperor before I do,' said Kimi, her words quiet and clipped, full of murderous intent. 'He has my father's blood on his hands.'

It would be for the best if you concentrated on the father of dragons.

'And it would be better still if you remembered that I don't take orders from you.' Kimi gave the cinderwraith a hard look.

'Easy now, Kimi,' said Tief. 'He was just suggesting the most efficient way to tackle this gigantic mess.'

You have one of the Ashen Blades. I can sense it nearby. The blade that Veles stole from Bittervinge.

'Of course. I couldn't leave an artefact of such power lying on a hillside in Izhoria, no matter how much I despise it.'

Give it to me, Kimi, so that I may strike the Emperor down. Let me be your champion.

'I don't need a man to get my vengeance for me.'

Namarii unfolded his wings and stretched out his neck, his imposing presence magnified by the small cove. Silverdust knew this was for his benefit, to intimidate him, but he persisted all the same.

Kimi, I understand your anger, but I am not sure I can kill the Emperor without the knife.

'That's not my problem,' said Kimi, turning her back on Silverdust. Tief stared at her in surprise.

Even now Steiner hunts the Emperor. He will perish without the Ashen Blade.

The princess paused before looking over her shoulder. 'Steiner never ran into a fight he couldn't win or run away from. He's the Unbroken, remember?'

He will perish.

'The Ashen Blade stays with me. I'll kill the Emperor and then I'll kill Bittervinge.'

I would advise against that—

'Because I'm a woman? Because I'm a princess who's not supposed to get her hands dirty?'

Neither of those things. It is because I sense your reluctance to use the blade, which is wise. The cinderwraith moved closer and held out his hand. *Please, Your Highness. You do not understand the nature of the blade's power.*

Kimi Enkhtuya, Princess of the Red Hand Tribe, disowned sister of the High King Tsen-Baina Jet, stepped forward until her face was separated from Silverdust's mirror mask by a hand's span.

'I understand well enough, and I will have my vengeance. The Ashen Blade stays with me.'

Silverdust realized there could be no reasoning with her and lowered his hand. Kimi stalked away, boots crunching loudly on the stony beach.

'What will happen to her if she uses the blade?' asked Tief quietly.

The blade will confer the life of the victim upon the bearer. The more powerful the victim the more life the bearer gains.

'That doesn't sound so bad,' replied Tief. 'I reckon we could all use a few more years to look forward to.'

A long life brings its own complications and there are things worse than death. I hope I will see you again, Tief.

'I hope I'll see you again too,' replied Tief. 'Never thought I'd ever say that to a Vigilant.'

All things change, Tief. You must make sure she carries the knife with her. She speaks of vengeance but a reluctance remains. It will do no good if she keeps it bundled up in the bottom of her pack.

'I'll keep an eye on her,' replied Tief, watching Kimi as she tended to Namarii's minor wounds. 'I can't promise anything, mind, but then who can?'

CHAPTER TWENTY-ONE

Steiner

It is important to remember that Vinterkveld and the Solmindre Empire were never seen as safe places, even before the uprisings. There was a feeling that soldiers, Okhrana, and the Holy Synod were lurking in the shadows, ready to abduct anyone for infractions, real or imagined. Volkan Karlov encouraged this way of thinking, ruling by fear and intimidation. Sometimes the only safe place was the one within arms' reach, if only day to day and moment to moment. Perhaps this was why Steiner was so adamant that Kristofine accompany him to Khlystburg.

— From the memoir of Drakina Tveit,
Lead Librarian of Midtenjord Province

Steiner slept as much as he could but the room was thick with the smell of dried blood and old sweat. Kristofine remained asleep. Her skin had a waxy sheen to it and her eyes were haunted by dark circles. Felgenhauer had said nothing following Boyar Sokolov's departure. Steiner assumed she was angry at having lost three of her men, and angrier still that they had not heeded her warning about Kristofine.

'Gods damn it,' he whispered as he sat up. He pushed the heels of his hands against his face and released something between a sigh and a grunt. Had he ever been this tired before? Or this hopeless?

The door creaked open an inch and sliver of light fell on Reka's face in the corridor beyond. The lieutenant gestured over his shoulder with a thumb, then mimed they should drink.

'It's a little early for me,' replied Steiner as he slipped through the door, closing it behind him.

'It was early morning when we got back,' replied Reka with a smile. 'It's early evening now. Seems you and your lady had a good long sleep, dragon rider.'

'She's doing the sleeping. I've been fretting in the main.'

'Understandable,' said Reka.

The inn was half full; conversations were little more than conspiratorial whispers or a quiet grumbling. The barkeeper spent as much time eyeing the windows as his patrons, anxious in case Bittervinge returned. A couple of drinkers stared at Steiner with sideways glances.

'I'm not sure this is a good idea,' said Steiner.

'This place had a reputation for being home to more moderate thinkers back before you were taken to Vladibogdan.'

'Even so, I don't want to tempt fate by being seen in the open. Soldiers could arrive at any moment.'

Reka ordered food and beer at the bar in a loud voice. 'Are you listening to me?' pressed Steiner.

'Perhaps we should lurk around with our hoods up, speaking in hushed tones?' Reka grinned.

'Why the Hel are you so cheerful?' said Steiner.

'I'm well aware we lost three and have another wounded, but things may not be as bad it seems with this information from the Boyar.'

'Where's my aunt?' Steiner almost winced as he thought about facing her. She'd warned him that Kristofine would be wounded and now it had come to pass. That wouldn't be easy to live down and they'd problems enough.

'Up in her room with some of her cadre discussing what to do next. Some of the men have already crossed town to find the entrance to these catacombs the Boyar spoke of.' Reka nodded to the barman as the tankards were set down and a few dull coins changed hands. 'She intends to go tomorrow morning.'

'Tomorrow?' Steiner swore quietly and Reka gestured that he take a seat. 'We can't go that soon. *I* can't go that soon. Not without Kristofine.'

'Easy now.'

'Easy? None of this is easy.' Steiner scowled and looked away in disgust. The barkeeper approached and set down two shallow bowls of sausages and pulses swimming in a reddish broth.

'This is the first bit of good news your aunt has had in some time,' said Reka after the barkeeper had left them to their meal. He speared a sausage with his fork and held it up. 'It's only natural that she'd want to seize on it.'

'I can't do this without Kristofine,' said Steiner. The anger in his voice had been replaced with a more confessional tone. 'I can't go to the catacombs without her.'

Reka took a long draught from his tankard. 'You escaped from Vladibogdan without her, didn't you?'

'That was different,' replied Steiner.

'Where was Kristofine then?'

'She was back in Cinderfell. We barely knew each other before I was taken. I'd noticed her, of course. Anyone with eyes had noticed her, but the Empire took me before we had much of a chance to spend any time together. When I got free, well, it was like being given a second chance. And I wasn't so good or heroic that I didn't almost make a mess of things.'

'How so?' said Reka.

'She's good with people in a way that I'll never be, and I resented her for it. Even when it saved our lives I resented her for it.' Steiner pushed his food around the plate with a fork and clenched his jaw.

'She won't be going to the catacombs,' said Reka. 'Not in the condition she's in at the moment.'

'Then we wait and give her time to heal.'

'Time is a luxury you just don't have.' Reka shook his head 'And with the city the way it is she's best off elsewhere.'

'But she's been with me since we left Cinderfell. I don't know what I'd do without her.' Steiner realized he sounded very young, like a child trying to bargain or wheedle some concession or boon from a parent. 'I feel like I've already lost Kjellrunn, and . . .'

'And your father too.' Reka rubbed his forehead thoughtfully a moment. 'All the more reason to face the Emperor without her than risk losing her permanently.'

'I'd best get back to her,' said Steiner, unable to think of anything else to say. Reka nodded and remained to finish his beer.

Kristofine was awake when he returned to their room, though the gaze she favoured him with was heavy-lidded with sleep. Her skin was shockingly pale and there was a stillness that Steiner found unnerving. Where was his love? So vital and graceful? Where was his love with that quiet confidence and easy charm he so admired?

'I'm sorry,' he said as he sat gently on the side of the bed. He took her hand in his. 'I nearly got you killed.'

'Hush now. You know that's not true. It was just bad luck is all. Maybe your aunt is right about me. A half-dozen lessons with the sword aren't going to keep me safe during times like these.'

'She wants to go back tomorrow morning. We've learned of another way in.'

'How so?'

'A Solmindre noble switched sides, and though he's too old to be useful in a fight he knows a few things, including a secret way beneath the palace.'

Kristofine squeezed his hand and a ghost of a smile touched her lips. 'You must go with her.'

Steiner shook his head, throat thick with emotion, strangling anything useful he might have thought to say. They sat together in silence for a long time and Steiner wanted desperately to hold her, but feared any movement might cause her pain.

'I've made it this far with you,' he said finally. 'It doesn't seem right to—'

Kristofine held up a finger and pressed it to his lips. 'Remember how you envied me? How you wished you could rally people to your cause, our cause?'

'Of course. I was an arsehole and I'm sorry.'

'Well, that was my moment to do what I could. The next part is your moment, and I know you can do it. Find your father. Slay Volkan Karlov. Put an end to all this suffering.'

'I will.' Steiner nodded, full of resolve. 'For both of us.' A flicker of movement caught his eye and his gaze followed a bright flare of fire in the evening sky.

'Bittervinge,' whispered Kristofine.

Steiner nodded. 'The bastard's back.'

'The Emperor could never defeat him,' said Kristofine. 'That fell to the Vartiainen family. Now you must finish what your great-grandfather started.'

Steiner stood up and rolled his shoulders. He set his gaze on the black dragon, many miles distant, who even now was terrorizing the city.'

'You're sure?' he asked.

'Go, handsome boy.' She made a shooing gesture. 'It isn't as if we have a choice, is it?' Her hand drifted to her bandage-wrapped torso.

Steiner kissed her on the forehead and retrieved his sledge-hammer. In the space of a few heartbeats and a dozen steps he was outside his aunt's room. He didn't knock, just turned the handle and crossed the threshold. Felgenhauer had been sketching a map, surrounded by her cadre. She looked up, and for once her usually unshakable mien abandoned her.

'What are you—?'

'Just wanted to let you know I'm ready when you are.'

'I thought you'd be—'

'And I'm sorry for dragging Kristofine into this. I thought the best way to keep her safe was to keep her close. I was wrong.'

'I see.' Felgenhauer nodded to her men. 'Dismissed.' One by one they shuffled out, closing the door behind them.

'I'm sorry I was so hard on you,' she said, lacing her fingers together and looking away. 'When Akulina' – she swallowed – 'when your mother passed away I couldn't bear it. The pain was unlike anything I'd experienced before. I can't protect you from everything but I wanted to spare you that at least.'

'Grief? I already know grief. The Emperor still has Marek and I've no way of knowing if he's alive or dead.'

'We can't get distracted. We go to kill the Emperor. We'll find Marek after. Agreed?' Steiner nodded but couldn't say he felt too sure about it. 'You should know that I never approved of your mother's relationship with Marek,' continued Felgenhauer. 'There's a good chance he hates me and I wouldn't blame him.'

Steiner shrugged. 'That's the least of my worries.'

'I didn't make things easy for him or your mother.'

'You can make amends for the past once we have him back.' Steiner looked down at the crude map she'd sketched out: entrances and gateways, labyrinthine tunnels. 'Talk me through your plan. How's this going to work?'

CHAPTER TWENTY-TWO

Ruslan

Exarch Zima had long been a notable member of the Holy Synod. He graduated with honours from the academies of Vladibogdan, though it is difficult to determine when his training began and when it ended. The Vigilant was sent to work in many provinces to quell dissent, hunt down those with witchsign, and act as an investigator. Twice he was sent to work as part of a Troika with two other Vigilants, and twice the other Vigilants perished in their duty. After that Zima worked alone, though it was not Imperial custom. Any other information about the man is non-existent. He is little more than a symbol of obedience, a cipher willing to carry out Volkan Karlov's demands, no matter the price. Many Imperial records were destroyed as control over the continent began to unravel. The Empire, which had been founded on secrets, would retain them even as its grip on the population slackened.

– From the memoir of Drakina Tveit,
Lead Librarian of Midtenjord Province

Khlystburg had never enjoyed a good reputation. It was a city of extremes, much like the man who commanded the Empire. The very richest people barely saw the starved waifs that haunted the shabbier districts. One was either insulated from poverty by one's station and connections, or utterly mired in the drudgery that ensured another meal. Ruslan knew which of the two extremes he would occupy should Boyar Sokolov's reign meet an abrupt end.

In the distance he could hear screaming and bells rang out in maddening, repetitive chimes, declaring a distant part of the sprawling city was alight again. Bittervinge cared not for station or connections, it seemed; he was just as likely to feed on the wealthier people of Khlystburg as the poorer ones. Even cruelty could be even-handed sometimes.

'Much like a plague,' said Ruslan, emerging from the doorway he'd been sheltering in. A glance at the skies confirmed he was safe for now at least. He took one last glimpse at the inn across the street. Two of the upstairs windows shone with the soft gold of candlelight. Ruslan was sure Steiner and the former Matriarch-Commissar Felgenhauer were still inside. His legs ached from standing outside, not daring to take his eyes from the inn. Heavyset, broad-shouldered men had come and gone, but there had been no sign of the dragon rider or his renegade aunt.

'This doesn't feel right,' muttered Ruslan before turning his back on the place and heading back to his master. His mind raced ahead and thought of the decadence he'd seen in Lady Odessine Temmnaya's suite earlier that morning. The more he dwelt on the depravity the more he became convinced he was on the wrong side, and yet Ruslan needed the Boyar to survive. He had no wish to end his days begging in the streets of the Voronin District with those too sick or broken to find work. 'We should retreat to Vend until this sorry state of affairs has reached its final conclusion,' he confessed to the near-empty street. He had never been comfortable in his own company; an afternoon of spying alone had only encouraged him to think aloud. 'The Emperor is doomed.'

The journey back did not take long. Ruslan wondered what the city had been like before Bittervinge's return. The people he passed in the street barely looked up, afraid to meet his eyes. The entire population had been reduced to furtive scurrying, no better than rats waiting for some great bird of prey to swoop down and end their lives in a stuttering heartbeat. Ruslan kept track of Bittervinge as best he could on the horizon. The black-scaled terror never lingered for long in any one district, keen to share his fiery breath with anyone who took his fancy.

Ruslan reached the street where Boyar Sokolov had taken rooms and paused as he turned the corner, barely thirty feet from the end of his journey, feet sore, legs burning, as thirsty as he could remember. Exarch Zima alighted from a horse-drawn carriage, his crimson robes and savage mask unmistakable. The few people nearby, already preoccupied with the dark shadow that hunted the skies, now had something else to fear if only for a moment. Ruslan watched the Exarch enter the building, then slipped up to the door just as the housemaid was closing it.

'It's me. Ruslan. I'm Boyar Sokolov's aide.'

The housemaid turned her nose up. 'You'd best get in quick. Your master will have need of you now that awful Vigilant is here.'

Ruslan stared in shock. The Empire, and the Holy Synod in particular, had spent a long time ensuring the population of Vinterkveld despised those who wielded arcane powers. To speak out against a Vigilant was unthinkable, but hatred of the arcane outweighed fear of the Synod, it seemed, in some hearts at least.

'Thank you,' mumbled Ruslan as he passed the housemaid, worrying for the safety of his master. He reached the door to the Boyar's suite with his heart hammering in his chest, imagining he might be too late to stop something terrible occurring. Had Zima been sent by the Emperor to assassinate his master? Barely able to think, Ruslan turned the handle and stumbled into the room. Boyar Sokolov rose from his chair with a look of astonishment on his face. Exarch Zima snatched a glance over his shoulder.

'What is the meaning of this?' said the Boyar. 'Are you drunk?'

'I . . .' Ruslan glanced at Zima and back to his master. 'I simply wanted you to know I have returned, my lord.'

'Excuse me,' said the Boyar to the Exarch; then he marched across the room, taking Ruslan firmly by the shoulder. 'Out! Out!' The Boyar marched him down the hall until they were in the kitchens. The staff on hand departed with barely a word and the only sound was a metal lid rattling on a simmering pot of stew.

'I was worried you might be in danger,' said Ruslan, keen to avoid the Boyar's temper. 'I don't trust the Exarch.'

'And what would you, an aide, have done against the likes of that? Are you versed in the arcane now? Are you a match for the Holy Synod and their hypocrites?'

'I'm sorry, my lord.'

'What news from the inn?' said the Boyar after a pause. He smoothed down his moustaches and took a deep, calming breath.

'Nothing. Steiner and his aunt have not left the inn yet.'

'What?' Boyar Sokolov's eyes widened in disbelief.

'Some of the soldiers, Felgenhauer's men, they came and went, but Steiner himself didn't leave.'

'I had hoped they would act on the information sooner.'

'What does Exarch Zima want with you, my lord?'

'Never mind that. Get back out there. I want to know the minute they depart. And if they haven't departed I want to know why the Hel not.'

'But . . .' Ruslan swallowed. 'But Bittervinge is attacking

the city, my lord. It's very dangerous and I've barely eaten today.'

'Dangerous out there? Perhaps you have forgotten there is an Exarch in my suite, sent by the Emperor himself? If I do not allude to some sort of progress . . .' The Boyar left the consequences unspoken.

'I understand, my lord. What will you tell him?'

'I'll tell him I have found the Vartiainen boy as he wished. I'll tell him I have arranged another meeting in an attempt to persuade him to meet the Emperor for an audience.'

Ruslan nodded and hurried away. Master and servant would both meet the same fate as Dimitri if the Boyar's attempt at misdirection failed. Somehow, sneaking through a city threatened by a legendary dragon didn't seem like such a bad fate.

CHAPTER TWENTY-THREE

Kimi

Humans have expressive faces. It is a combination of expression, gesture, tone of voice, and the words themselves that help convey meaning in normal everyday conversations. Dragons by contrast can bare their teeth, snort (usually dismissively), flex their claws, extend their wings like mating birds and growl like hunting cats. The majority of their communication is geared towards intimidation, and while they enjoy many advantages over humans, I think it safe to say humans have the upper hand when communication and diplomacy are called for.

– From the memoir of Drakina Tveit,
Lead Librarian of Midtenjord Province

What are we doing? Though Namarii didn't speak the words with his lips, teeth, and tongue like a human would, he had no problem distilling a very peevish quality into his question.

'We're scouting,' shouted Kimi, struggling to be heard above the wind that whipped at them as the vast creature glided above the city. Rain clouds crowded in over the city, as dark as Kimi's mood.

Scout? A dragon does not scout. This is a task for lowly soldiers, or unproven youths. A dragon hunts.

'Do you have any soldiers to send out scouting?'

You know that I do not.

'And neither do I, so that leaves it to us.

I seek the Emperor.

'And so do I, but the simple truth of it is that we can't reach him before we defeat Bittervinge.'

I say again. I seek the Emperor. Namarii banked sharply, and the city lurched across one side of her vision. Kimi didn't want to believe he was trying to unseat her but she clung on tighter all the same.

'Damn it.' There was a single-minded simplicity to the dragons that had been refreshing at first, but had become maddening the longer they flew together.

'Why do you call off the attack each time the father of dragons flees?' asked Kimi.

I thought that was your doing. Do you not think I and my kin are capable of ending him?

'You are somewhat smaller than he is,' admitted Kimi. 'But it was you, not I who called off the attack.'

Namarii said nothing. A plume of soot was snorted into the air, which was caught by the wind and raced along the dragon's neck. The soot settled across Kimi's face and clung to her braided hair. Worst of all she could taste it.

'Let's get some rest,' said Kimi, realizing that dragons were just as susceptible to denial as humans are. Parts of the city were aflame and columns of smoke dissipated on the blustery wind. The taste of soot evoked memories of Vladibogdan and its forges. She searched the gloomy city for Bittervinge's sinister silhouette but the father of dragons was no doubt licking his many wounds, preparing for his next assault. 'Let's head back to the camp.'

You did not answer my question. Namarii banked left and headed south, back towards the cove where they had accosted the trading vessel. Kimi clung to the dragon and remained silent. Stonvind and Flodvind were returning from a fishing expedition and all three dragons alighted on the shingle beach at the same time. It was miraculous that none of the creatures collided with their kin. There was no question in Kimi's mind that they had become stronger and more graceful in the air.

You did not answer my question. Namarii flexed his claws in the shingle, making a terrible grinding sound as he did so. Kimi dismounted and stalked away, frustration gnawing on her. Had she called off the attack, or had it been Namarii? It was difficult to remember when so much was happening so quickly.

'Back so soon?' said Tief. He stared as the three dragons stood shoulder to shoulder. They stared after the Yamal princess with stern, unblinking amber gazes. 'Frejna's teeth,' he whispered. 'Just when I think I'm getting used to these creatures . . .'

You did not answer my question. Namarii craned his considerable neck until the blunt wedge of his head towered above her.

'You know why!' shouted Kimi. 'You're in my head, aren't you? When we fly, when I sleep, when I eat. You're always in my head.'

You are afraid we still lack the strength to finish the father of dragons. These words came from Flodvind, gentle and measured.

And you are correct, added Stonvind in his grinding, gravel-like tone.

Each day Bittervinge dines on a score of people, while we feed on slivers of fish. Namarii looked out to sea. *We need meat.*

'He has a point,' said Tief, tugging on one earlobe. 'They're growing in confidence. No doubt about that, but look at the size of them. They need feeding up.' He winced before saying. 'Would it really be so bad to let them eat a few Solmindre people?'

'Tief!' Taiga approached them from their campfire with a look of stony admonishment.

'Frejna knows there's enough of them and a few won't go amiss,' he added, though he sounded less sure of himself.

'I will not feed innocent people to the dragons just so we can defeat the Emperor and Bittervinge,' replied Taiga. 'I will not.' She folded her arms and frowned.

And yet there is nothing you could do to stop us. Namarii let out a low growl. The sound triggered a powerful urge in Kimi to run away, but she held her ground and glowered at the dark brown dragon. Taiga slowly drew her silver sickle and dagger – the weapons of Frøya herself, if the priestess were to be believed. She adopted a look of such unflinching fury that Kimi reached out to her.

'Taiga, I'm not sure this is the best way . . .'

'Now you listen to me!' Taiga's voice had never been loud, but there was a timbre to it that could not be ignored. 'We are here to cast down the tyranny of this continent. We're not here to add to its cruelty. We're not here to kill people just because we think there are too many of them.' The look she gave Tief could have drawn blood. 'I am a high priestess of Frøya, the way of earth and life and renewal.'

The little one bears its teeth. Namarii's words were rank with condescension. He lowered his head until his snout was just a dozen feet from Taiga. Her dagger looked pitifully small compared to Namarii's teeth.

The little one is mine. Flodvind lowered her head and moved Namarii out of the way with a motion that was more than a nudge and just slightly less than a head butt. Namarii shook himself like a dog for a moment and a brief growl escaped the dark brown dragon before he composed himself.

Then I propose a bargain be struck. Namarii's eyes flickered to the azure dragon. *Let us hunt Bittervinge, for good or ill.*

Let us dine on his corpse, added Stonvind, unmoving as the cliffside behind him. *And we will have no need for human flesh.*

And when we have picked the father of dragons' bones clean we shall turn our attentions to the Emperor. Namarii flexed his claws.

'For good or ill?' Kimi couldn't hide her disdain. 'That sounds like recklessness to me.'

You have been holding us back. Namarii retreated a few paces, but the full weight of his gaze did not leave Kimi. He flared his wings in irritation and folded them slowly.

'I was afraid Bittervinge was too strong for us. I was afraid the Emperor was too strong for us. I didn't want you to die.' Kimi stared up at the young dragon. The sun caught his brown scales, revealing all the colours of autumn once again, and Kimi was reminded how majestic the dragons could be. 'I was looking out for you,' she added. 'It's what friends do for each other.'

Friends. Namarii snorted a plume of smoke. *I have all the friends I need.* For a moment Kimi dared to hope Namarii meant the three humans standing before him, but the dragon held up one foot, the long claws shining in the sunlight. His friends, the claws he would use to kill the father of dragons if fortune smiled on them.

Kimi took a moment to rest before they took to wing again. She didn't care for the way Namarii had used his size to intimidate them, but it was what dragons did after all. Hadn't Bittervinge used the very same tactic during their first encounter?

You are displeased with me. Namarii lowered his head so Kimi could mount more easily.

'Why should that bother you? We're not friends. Now let's kill this bastard dragon once and for all.'

That word again. Friends.

Tief and Taiga shared a look, though Kimi couldn't tell if they were concerned for her attitude towards Namarii or the battle ahead. There was the familiar lurch as the dragons launched themselves into the air. Kimi was pressed against the dragon's neck and her hands gripped the reptilian scales. The ground dropped away and one by one Namarii, Stonvind, and Flodvind swooped out over the sea, gliding when they could, gaining height in lazy circles. The trading ship they had accosted lay below them, waiting at anchor. A few people could be seen on the cliffs – Silverdust, Streig, and Captain Hewn perhaps – but they were soon lost from sight as the dragons headed towards the city.

The roads heading south, if they could be called roads, were full of fleeing people made tiny by distance. Carts and wagons trundled and livestock trudged, urged onwards by those souls who had the sense to depart Khlystburg. Little did they know that Grave Wolves awaited them in Izhoria, but there was little Kimi could do to warn them.

Why do you care? Namarii's question intruded on Kimi's thoughts like rough stone on bare flesh.

'It's a human thing,' she shouted, snarling the words against the wind as the dragons' wings beat slow and strong. 'You wouldn't understand,' she added, hoping to annoy the arrogant beast. 'It's called empathy.'

A bright pinprick of fire could be seen in the distance, burning at Kimi's attention. Bittervinge was attacking the city once more.

Now we dine!

Stonvind and Flodvind, who had drifted away from their kin, closed formation and came up either side of the dark brown dragon. Taiga wore a sombre, watchful look, while Tief whooped and hollered with excitement. Kimi felt only anxiety, squeezing the air from her lungs a little more with each minute. Khlystburg rushed by underneath them, the buildings snatched away by the almost delirious speed

He remains weakened from our earlier encounters, counselled Flodvind.

His end comes, added Stonvind.

Bittervinge had landed on a row of buildings, though they had sagged under his weight and many roof tiles had slipped and smashed on the cobbled street below. The roof of one home had been torn apart and the father of dragons extended a foreleg inside, the talons questing for fresh meat. A lone voice screamed mindlessly as their doom approached, distracting Bittervinge from the young dragons speeding their way from the south. Namarii led the attack, diving low and seizing the father of dragons about the neck with all four sets of talons. Kimi was almost jolted from her seat between the dragon's shoulders and she swore in her mother tongue. She'd wanted to unsheathe her sword but it was all she could do to stay mounted. Bittervinge released a thunderous roar of pain and buffeted the younger dragon with his vast black wings. For a moment Khlystburg spun beneath them. Namarii took a moment to regain control, flaring his wings wide to stabilize himself in the air. The father of dragons surged into the sky with powerful strokes of his wings.

Pitiful! Bittervinge slashed downwards with a claw, opening three gouges on Namarii's brow, the blood bright and shocking. Kimi drew her sword, determined to score a blow against their hated enemy.

Damn you. Namarii fled and for a moment it seemed the jet-black dragon would launch himself in pursuit of his attacker, but Flodvind descended directly from above, landing cat-like on Bittervinge's back, knocking his wings askew, forcing the father of dragons back to the rooftops. The azure dragon unleashed a torrent of fire from her maw directly into Bittervinge's wounded neck. A heartbeat later and Flodvind was in the air once more, wings beating hard to give her height and distance from their enemy. Taiga met Kimi's eyes and held up a hand in greeting, a strange and kindly gesture in the chaos. Bittervinge coiled like a vast black spring, using all four legs and his tail to propel him after his sinuous attacker. Kimi felt her heart stutter as she worried for Flodvind.

'We need to help her!' she shouted at Namarii.

Stonvind, who had lined up his own attack, might have inflicted a mortal wound had Bittervinge not folded his wings and plummeted back to the rooftops a heartbeat later. Kimi would never have dreamed such a vast creature could perform a feint in combat, and the granite-grey dragon shot past his target. Stonvind folded his wings on instinct, protecting the more fragile parts of himself. Bittervinge breathed a cloud of smoky fire that engulfed both Stonvind and Tief in billowing oranges and angry reds. Kimi could hear her friend's cries even above the roaring wind and the pounding of her heart.

'Tief?'

Namarii had circled around since his opening attack and dived at the father of dragons so recklessly that Kimi almost lost her seat. The black dragon now launched himself into the air with jaws wide open and talons splayed, intent on catching the still burning Stonvind. Namarii tried to pull up from his dive but had overcommitted and had to concentrate on avoiding the street below. Kimi could only watch in dismay as Bittervinge raked his claws along Stonvind's flank. The granite-grey dragon fell from the sky and hit the rooftops with a hushed crunch, sending up a cloud of stone dust.

Of Tief there was no sign.

'May Frøya keep you close,' whispered Kimi in desperation. Namarii glided in a wide arc, circling Stonvind while keeping Bittervinge at a distance, but the father of dragons was unconcerned with anything but the downed dragon.

'We have to help them!' shouted Kimi, but Namarii kept his course, circling the danger, all sign of his earlier bravado now abandoned. Taiga and Flodvind were not so circumspect.

Again the azure dragon had gained enough height to attack from above and Taiga rode the creature with one arm raised, her sickle clutched in her fist. As Flodvind descended the heavens opened and the rains made the prospect of dragon fire unlikely. Bittervinge turned just as Flodvind ripped past him, talons rending, teeth snaring. The air was filled with a fine mist of blood. Taiga's sickle reaped its own reward, opening a bright wound in the jet-black scales.

'Attack him! For the love of Frøya, attack him!' shouted Kimi, but Namarii held his course. The father of dragons drifted across the city, moving further and further away, his wounded wings held wide. Flodvind and Taiga landed near the unmoving Stonvind.

'Tief?' Kimi could hear the panic in Taiga's voice, even at this distance, shrill and piercing. 'Tief, where are you?'

Bittervinge slipped away and finally Namarii landed by the buildings next to Stonvind.

'What happened to "Now we dine!"?' muttered Kimi as she dismounted. 'What happened to "You have been holding us back"? What happened to fucking fighting like a giant winged reptile?' she raged.

But for once Namarii had no answer for her; his amber eyes settled on the prone form of Stonvind, his head hung low, blood dripping from his deeply scored head to spatter over the street below.

CHAPTER TWENTY-FOUR

Steiner

People ask me why Steiner and Kimi didn't make more of an effort to join forces in Khlystburg, but they don't truly understand the gravity of the situation. Steiner was largely concerned with entering the palace while avoiding Imperial forces and the marauding attacks from the father of dragons. Kimi was preoccupied with many tasks, not least feeding and motivating Namarii and the younger dragons. A search of such a vast and sprawling cityscape, strewn with winding lanes and ruined towers, might have taken a solid week all by itself.

– From the memoir of Drakina Tveit,
Lead Librarian of Midtenjord Province

The sun rose over the city, fighting to be seen through dark grey clouds that haunted the sombre skies.

'At least the fires are out now,' said Steiner. They were standing at the top of the inn, where an old forgotten balcony offered a partly occluded view of Khlystburg's many domes and towers. The city was scored with dozens of wounds. Scorched and collapsed buildings marked the places Bittervinge had struck with near impunity. 'It seems Taiga brought the rain with her. I assume it was Taiga. I can't imagine Sundra up there somehow.'

'Your Spriggani friends from Vladibogdan, I take it?'

Steiner nodded. 'And Kimi. She's a Yamal princess and fierce blacksmith too. She'll be leading them, no doubt. I wish I could speak her.'

'You will in time, I'm sure of it.' Reka stared out over the city. 'But I don't think we'll see the father of dragons today.' The old soldier and the blacksmith's son shared a look and Steiner managed to say the words he'd been dreading all night.

'She's ready to go. Weak but ready. You'll keep her safe?'

'You know I will. I'll head south and find a ship to take us to Arkiv.' From anyone else this might have sounded boastful.

'I only met you a few days ago, and here I am trusting you with the most precious person in my life.'

'Have you told her that?' Reka glanced away to the horizon as he asked his question.

'That she's precious to me? Yes. Many times and a few more.'

'Good.' A fleeting look of pain crossed Reka's face. 'All too often people live their lives without saying the things that really matter, and then suddenly it's too late and they're taken from us.'

'You sound like you speak from experience,' said Steiner, not wanting to pry but feeling curious all the same. They stood in the early-morning chill a while longer; a few drops of rain fell, though it was a half-hearted affair.

'Experience is the greatest teacher,' replied Reka, still not meeting Steiner's eyes. He cleared his throat and adjusted his sword belt.

'Isn't Arkiv still blockaded?' asked Steiner, steering the conversation to more practical things.

'Word has reached us that the blockade was destroyed by the Stormtide Prophet.' Reka grinned. 'The island has just declared its independence from the Empire! All your good sister's handiwork.'

Steiner opened his mouth to speak but he found himself chuckling, softly at first, and then louder. 'Kjellrunn!' he managed to say between bouts of laughter. He carried on for a minute or so until he composed himself. 'That's the first bit of good news I've had in' – he gestured vaguely – 'much too long.'

'I hope you've said your goodbyes to Kristofine,' said Reka, 'because I don't intend on lingering too long.'

'Of course. You should go while the skies are clear.' Steiner all but winced as he said the words.

'It's the right thing to do,' said the old soldier, seeing Steiner's hesitation. 'I'll get her somewhere quiet to heal up.'

Felgenhauer's cadre took as much gear as they needed, but not everything they owned. What was the point? The looks on their faces confirmed what Steiner had not dared admit to himself: none of them expected to make it back alive. This was Volkan Karlov's palace. Hadn't they already lost three of their number trying to gain access to the tyrant and his Ashen Blade?

'How is Steiner the Unbroken this morning?' asked Tomasz, buckling his sword belt in place.

'I've been better,' he replied. Reka and Kristofine had left an hour earlier, and all of Steiner's thoughts were consumed with wondering for their safety.

'Well, whatever it is that's gnawing at you, use it. Use your anger, use your fear, use your anxiety.' Tomasz frowned. 'No mistakes today. We can ill afford them. And if you swing that hammer be sure not to miss.'

'I can promise that much,' said Steiner, hefting his great-grandfather's weapon with a small smile.

'We move now,' said Felgenhauer. 'Before I lose all patience.' She passed through the inn door without a backwards glance. Steiner joined her in the street a moment later. They walked fast, heads down and hoods up, a dozen people heavily armed and not making much effort to conceal it. The few people in the streets ahead of them decided they had other places to be and hurried away.

'I don't care for this more direct approach,' said Steiner. 'What if we're seen?'

'You mean by our friend there.' Felgenhauer nodded to the side of the street. Boyar Sokolov's man, Ruslan, was doing his best to remain unseen in the doorway of a derelict house. Steiner met the man's eyes and there was an awkward moment where Ruslan knew he had been seen.

'Why's he watching us?'

'Sokolov wants to know we're going to make the best of the information he's given us.' Felgenhauer walked faster. 'He wants Volkan Karlov dead as much as we do.'

'And we're sure the Emperor really killed his son?' Steiner cast a look over his shoulder, but Ruslan was gone, returning to his Boyar no doubt. 'This could be a trap.'

'The Emperor gutted Dimitri Sokolov with the Ashen Blade,' said Felgenhauer. 'I asked around among the locals. The story is always the same. Volkan reduced Dimitri to a husk before the very eyes of the Imperial Court.'

They turned down a backstreet and hurried on. Steiner cast furtive looks over his shoulder every so often, but no one appeared to be following them. The normal rhythms and routines of the city had slowed as Bittervinge's predations imposed chaos on Khlystburg. The bakers still went about their business; the odd building here and there had the telltale wisp of chimney smoke and the windows were lit by the orange glow of ovens. A few brave souls passed them by, taking goods to market squares that would see a brisk trade in rumours and gossip before they were forced to flee for their lives.

'I'd have imagined we'd be up to our arses in Okhrana and soldiers by now,' Steiner muttered.

'They've all pulled back to the Imperial Palace,' said Tomasz. 'And we've had word that many Okhrana have been dispatched to the provinces to keep the regional governors in line.' He grimaced. 'Hard to think about rebellion if you know assassins are prowling close.'

'Arkiv's declaration of independence has been' – Felgenhauer smiled coldly – 'inspirational. All the Emperor's resources are stretched thin. There's never been a better time to remove him.'

'This is it,' said one of the men as they turned into a dead-end street. A warehouse awaited them at the end: the facade the Emperor had used to cover the entrance to the catacombs. The windows were chained and green paint peeled from wooden shutters. Broken barrels and crates littered the ground outside, detritus of a long-disused, secret part of the city, as unremarkable as it was ramshackle.

'Let's hope the Boyar was telling the truth about these catacombs,' said Tomasz.

CHAPTER TWENTY-FIVE

Kimi

Streig still talks of the day he prayed for the first time. By this point faith had been replaced by cynicism, trust in the goddesses had soured to despair, and a generation of children had grown into adults never learning the names of Frøya and Frejna. The uprising changed Vinterkveld deeply, and the two Spriggani sisters who should have died on Vladibogdan ushered in a new age of faith and optimism.

– From the memoir of Drakina Tveit,
Lead Librarian of Midtenjord Province

'It feels like a long time since I walked anywhere,' said Kimi.

'Not since Izhoria,' agreed Taiga. They were on the southern outskirts of the city. The people cowered in their homes as the strange procession passed them by. Flodvind walked ahead of the two women, a powerful vanguard for the high priestess and princess. The azure dragon's presence ensured that every street leading south was mercifully empty.

'Strange,' said Taiga. 'You all thought I was going to die that day we fought the gholes, and now . . .' The petite Spriggani woman cast a glance over her shoulder. Stonvind limped, his painful gait matching pace with the humans ahead of him. Tief had been tied to the dragon's back, one side of his face darkened with the purple and black of deep bruising. Namarii brought up the rear. His tail was not between his legs but Kimi was in no doubt that his usual swagger was much diminished. The three deep cuts above his right eye had stopped bleeding but she couldn't bring herself to feel much sympathy for him.

'And now this,' said Kimi. The sting of defeat, wasn't that what they called this feeling? It didn't sting so much as crush the breath from her lungs; it weighed on her like a pack full of rocks. They had walked all through the night, shepherding their wounded to safety. Hard to know which was more leaden, her hopes or her legs.

'Thank the goddess, he's still alive,' added Taiga. Tears gleamed at the corners of her eyes. She sniffed hard and shook off her sadness. Tief was still breathing, that much was true, but the nature of his injuries had eluded his sister. The head wound was obvious, but what else? Would the irascible old rogue recover?

'He'll be up and about again before you know it.' Kimi tried to smile. 'He just needs a cup of that tea you make and a half an hour with that awful pipe he smokes.'

'The fool,' Taiga said cheerfully. 'He's much too old to be caught up in a revolution.'

'I'm sorry, I should never have asked you to come,' said Kimi.

'You didn't ask,' said Taiga softly. 'We volunteered. Remember? We have our own score to settle with the Emperor. Decades of imprisonment. The culling of our people.'

It was too easy to forget that her friends had two score years on her. Perhaps her companions were too old for what she asked of them? Perhaps she was too young, and perhaps neither and both were true.

They would follow you unto the ends of Vinterkveld. And beyond. Flodvind's words chimed gently in Kimi's head, and for once she was grateful for the interruption. Taiga didn't look up from her musing; the words had been for Kimi and Kimi alone, it seemed.

'I'm just glad . . .' Taiga swallowed and tried to speak again but the words were too hard to utter. Stonvind had recounted how Bittervinge had knocked Tief clear from his mount with a glancing blow from his tail. Such a fall would have most certainly killed Tief, but Stonvind had caught the man, even as the dragon fell and hit the street below.

'Stonvind is incredibly brave,' said Kimi, wishing she could do something to heal the limping dragon. Her gaze shifted and came to rest on Namarii, slinking along at the back of the procession, cloaked in shame and chagrin, she hoped. 'None of this would have happened if Namarii had shown some courage,' muttered Kimi, her voice laden with bitterness. Flodvind turned her huge, wedge-shaped head and cast a look over her shoulder at the Yamal princess.

Now is not the time to turn on one another.

Kimi looked away, feeling her cheeks burning. She'd not been chastened for a long time, and never by a dragon. 'Let's just get everyone back to the camp, shall we?' replied Kimi when she'd composed herself.

They were not alone in their trek south to the cove and its shingle beach. The buildings and streets dwindled to nothing. Columns of people were departing the city with the dawn of a new day.

'Are they following us?' asked Taiga, holding up one hand to shade her eyes from the sun.

'Hard to tell.' Kimi squinted into the distance. 'They clearly want to avoid the dragons, but there's no doubt they're headed to the cove.'

'Or the ship, more likely,' added Taiga.

A few of the refugees turned and looked back at the city.

Fingers pointed to the black-winged speck on the horizon. Bittervinge was taking his vengeance on the capital once more.

'Will he ever stop?' muttered Kimi.

'I thought he'd need a few days to recover after yesterday,' said Taiga. Flodvind paused a moment to stare at the father of dragons far behind them.

Bittervinge would rather appear relentless and suffer the pain of his wounds than give the people of Khlystburg a single day's reprieve.

'We should have stopped him,' said Kimi, more to herself than Taiga. 'It was down to us and we failed.'

We are taking a moment to rally. Is that the expression you humans use? Flodvind shook her head and blinked slowly.

'Rally?' Kimi sneered. 'It doesn't feel much like rallying.'

A leader would tell her followers they were rallying, not retreating. Flodvind snorted a plume of soot and launched herself into the air, signalling the conversation was over.

'Is she always like this?' asked Kimi.

'I don't know,' said Taiga, looking at the princess from the corner of her eye. 'We've never had to rally before.'

No one had much to say as they reached the top of the cliffs above the cove. The camp had tripled in size overnight. All manner of makeshift tents, broken-down carts, mangy pack animals, and dozens of bewildered people crowded together with desperation written on their gaunt faces. The *Eastern Star* remained at anchor, much to Kimi's surprise.

'I can't fit you all on,' shouted Captain Hewn. He was standing on a large crate and a circle of armed men provided a living fence to keep the many potential passengers at a safe distance. The mob of people quickly broke apart and retreated when it became evident the dragons had returned to camp. A few people screamed and fled, while others stood their ground and stared balefully at Kimi.

'What's got into them?' asked Taiga, unsheathing her dagger with a meaningful look.

'The old enmity,' said Kimi. 'White faces in the north, brown faces in the south, and I'm far from home which makes me fair game.' She pulled her sword from where it was slung across her back and unsheathed it slowly and deliberately.

You do not need the weapon. Flodvind, for all her great size, landed beside Kimi. The ground shook slightly. *Nothing will befall you while I draw breath. Not from these people or anyone else.*

Streig emerged from the cluster of people near Captain Hewn. He approached with a look of wariness on his face, his eyes transfixed by the wounded form of Stonvind. He still wore the two-handed sword across his back but had acquired a cutlass at his hip.

'Working for Captain Hewn now?' said Kimi.

'As a guard,' replied Streig. 'Part payment for the voyage back to Arkiv.' His gaze drifted to Stonvind, who limped past them. The dragon continued a little way until he lay down, curling his tail about himself and tucking his head beneath one vast wing. There was a long, low growl and then silence.

'What happened?' asked Streig quietly.

'Do you really need to ask?' said Kimi.

'We had a few . . .' Taiga glanced over her shoulder to Namarii. '. . . unforeseen problems.'

Flodvind lowered her head until she was eye to eye with Streig, who became very pale in the presence of the dragon. *Perhaps we could trouble you for those pack animals?* The dragon set her gaze on the small herd of mismatched animals lowing in the distance.

'The what? Of course!' Streig smiled nervously. 'I mean the refugees won't need them any more, and we can't fit them on the ship.' He was speaking very quickly. Kimi realized she now took speaking with the dragons for granted. Streig by contrast was most certainly not taking the conversation for granted and Kimi thought he did well not to flee for his life.

I cannot reimburse you for the creatures. Flodvind flexed her talons and gouged foot-deep scars into the earth. *And the loan will be somewhat permanent.*

'If you don't mind me asking,' said Streig. 'Why do dragons need pack animals? I mean you're so strong and . . .' His eyes widened as he realized the dragon's intent. 'Right. Permanent. I see.'

The herd animals were led to the cove by Streig after some negotiation with the various refugees who suddenly found their chances of passage greatly improved. The dragons slunk off and everyone present gave thanks that it was merely their faithful beast of burden that was being devoured and not a family member. The saddles were also claimed for the war effort, though they would need heavy modification to fit the dragons.

Streig returned to the campfire where Kimi and Taiga were making Tief comfortable. A kettle had been hung above the flames and food had been donated by a contingent of Yamal diplomats who couldn't believe one of their own was a dragon rider.

'It's probably for the best we don't tell them I'm a princess too,' said Kimi to Taiga. 'There's only so much a person can take in one day.' She looked around and a rising sense of panic gripped her. 'Where's Silverdust?' She stood up and searched again. 'We lost because we set off in haste. If we'd had Silverdust with us we might have stood a better chance.' She grabbed Streig by the collar and wrenched him close. 'Where is he?'

'Easy now, Your Highness.' Streig held up his hands for calm. 'You've had a bad day and a rough night. Calm down, drink some tea, get some sleep if you can.'

'He's gone, hasn't he? He's headed into Khlystburg alone.' Kimi almost ran to her pack and checked inside, her hands delving all the way to the bottom. Her fingers touched on the hilt of the Ashen Blade and she felt a pang of revulsion.

'Gods damn it,' she whispered and pulled the dagger from its place of concealment. 'At least he didn't steal it.'

'Steal what?' asked Streig.

'Never mind,' replied Kimi. 'You knew, didn't you? You knew he was going to head off on his own?'

'He told you clearly he intended to find and help Steiner – there's no great mystery to it.' Streig returned Kimi's hard stare with one of his own.

'You make a fair point.' Kimi looked towards the city and shook her head. 'Hel's teeth, Silverdust. And on his own?'

'It's been that way for him for a long time,' said Taiga. 'It makes sense he'd wander off like that.'

'What are you going to do about Tief?' asked Streig, providing a clumsy if much-needed diversion.

'Not much we can do,' said Kimi. 'We wait and hope.'

'Well, aren't you the champion of Frøya? That's what he said.' Streig smiled at Taiga. 'And you're a priestess.'

'A high priestess,' replied Taiga, correcting him gently.

'Can't you pray to her for a miraculous recovery?'

Kimi knelt down next to Tief and pulled out the jade dragon that hung around her neck.

'What's that?' asked Streig.

'This is the closest thing I have to a miracle,' replied Kimi as Taiga knelt down beside her. 'Will you pray with us?' She watched the young soldier hesitate a moment before kneeling. It was no small thing to ask an Imperial soldier to pray to a proscribed goddess, even if he was a deserter.

'What do I do?' he whispered.

'Have a little faith,' replied Kimi, though her confidence in their undertaking was far from resolute. 'The more the better, to be honest.'

'Don't worry,' said Taiga with an impish smile. 'I've faith enough for both of you.'

CHAPTER TWENTY-SIX

Kristofine

Captain Hewn became something of a friend of mine in the years that followed after. Many times, usually at the end of a function or feast, I would ask him if he had ever received his payment from Boyar Sokolov, a private joke known only to a handful of people. He would look at me with a rueful cast in his eye and reply, 'I never believed she was who she said she was for a second, but it seemed important to Streig she be aboard.'

> – From the memoir of Drakina Tveit,
> Lead Librarian of Midtenjord Province

Everything clenched tight.

Fists clenched in pain and frustration.

Stomach clenched tight from the agony of her wound.

Every ounce of energy clenched around her feelings less they flow down her face in a torrent.

Eyes squeezed shut to keep out unwelcome daylight: the dim and jumbled slowness of her thought was all she could focus on.

The city, which had been sporadically on fire ever since she had arrived, was hushed. The rain had silenced the many flickering tongues of flame during the night and even the most ardent of gossips dared not speak in anything more than a whisper. The Emperor ruled in name, yet silence reigned in Khlystburg.

'You still with me?' Reka, solid, dependable Reka, had conjured a mule out of all that silence and set his gaze south. The mule plodded beneath her and she plodded along with it. Reka had not, as far as she could tell, stopped walking since they had left the inn, leading the beast of burden by its reins.

'You tried to teach me how to fight,' she mumbled. It was hard to get her thoughts in order, harder still to say what was troubling her, but the silence troubled her more.

'I did. And I'll not hear you be hard on yourself for being laid low by a tavern keeper with a hidden knife.' The mule plodded beneath her and she plodded along with it. Kristofine lifted heavy eyelids and lifted her sagging head. Before her was the sombre, deep blue expanse of the Ashen Gulf.

'How?' was all she could say.

'I told Steiner I'd get you to safety, and that's exactly what I've a mind to do.'

'Is there's a ship down there?' she asked, afraid it was a mirage brought on by blood loss or some nameless madness.

'It is. And we're going to board it and voyage to Arkiv.'

A small settlement of refugees had sprung up at the top of the cliffs and a great deal of noise could be heard, even half a mile away as they were.

'I think they may have the same idea,' said Kristofine. 'That's a huge amount of people to fit on to one ship.'

'You're not wrong,' said Reka. Kristofine closed her eyes and surrendered to torpor once more. The wind gusted, bringing a scattering of chilly raindrops.

The noise of the crowd was both overwhelming and hard to ignore, even for someone in Kristofine's condition. The mule plodded beneath her and she plodded along with it, begrudgingly opening her eyes. They were in the midst of the camp now, surrounded on all sides by the locals of Khlystburg.

'There certainly are a lot of carts and wagons,' she said, sleepy and delirious, 'given that there are no animals.'

'I'm beginning to regret giving you that draught now,' said Reka, eyeing her warily.

'A draught?'

'Something to take the edge off. Some herbs for the pain and brandy for . . .' Reka gestured. 'Well, the brandy was for the pain too.' He took out a hip flask and medicated himself.

'You there!' came a voice above the crowd. 'I have need of your mule.'

'Here we go,' grumbled Reka. He drew steel: not a long weapon, but it was sharp in the right places and he liked the balance.

'I said I need your mule,' said a voice in the crowd. Some of the people began to stand aside and Kristofine gave a bleary smile and waved like a returning monarch.

'Lovely to meet you all,' she said.

'I can't let you go any further,' said a young man in a pale blue cloak. There was a great sword strapped to his back and a wary look in his eye. 'I need that mule.'

'I heard you,' shouted Reka. 'But I have wounded here and her needs take precedence. Now do you mind telling me how the Hel I get aboard . . .?' Reka's eyes widened as he realized who the would-be mule thief was. 'Streig? Is that you?'

'Lieutenant!'

'Streig! Smoke and ashes! I thought we lost you in the library.' The old soldier grabbed the young man in such a fierce embrace a few people cleared space, as if fighting and not a reunion were taking place.

'Streig.' Kristofine tried to sort through the jumbled mess of her memories. 'Streig in the library.' The crowd did not seem interested in whatever history existed between the two men; all eyes were fixed on Streig, or rather the two-handed blade that hung across his back. 'Didn't he used to wear armour?' added Kristofine.

'I did,' said the young man. 'Before Bittervinge buried me in books.'

'I'm so sorry.' Reka seized Streig by the shoulder. 'Everything was chaos. I didn't think we were going to make it. When the roof started coming down, well, I just . . .' Reka swallowed.

'I never blamed you,' replied Streig. 'Come on. Kimi and Taiga will want to hear what you have to say.

'The dragon riders?' asked Reka.

'The very same. Come on, now. Kimi will want to know all your news.' Streig began to lead them away when the mood of the crowd turned.

'Hoy there!' shouted an elderly man. 'I was here long before they were. I gave you my horse for your gods-damned dragons.' He took a step closer and prodded Streig in the chest with his finger 'Get. Me. On. That. Ship.'

The crowd, which until that moment had remained at a polite distance, surged forward. Reka went down first, pulled down by five people, hands reaching for his neck, seizing his arms lest he draw his blade once again. Streig fared no better; fists rose and fell and the young soldier disappeared from view as quickly as he appeared. He shouted Kristofine's name as he was dragged under. All eyes turned on her as she sat in the saddle, struggling to balance on the mule, who stood unmoving.

'Get away from them,' she shouted. Slowly at first, then in greater numbers, the crowd dispersed, leaving the bedraggled and bruised forms of Reka and Streig crawling in the mud. The city folk stared at Kristofine with expressions of terror on their pale faces.

'That's right! You run, you worthless, flea-bitten slatterns!' hollered Kristofine. 'You know who I am? I'm Kristofine of Cinderfell, Kristofine of the Lovers! My man is Steiner Vartiainen and—'

They are gone now. Do not distress yourself.

Kristofine blinked and, being unable to locate the source of the melodious voice, turned in her saddle. Sitting on the edge of the cliff was the most stunning, vibrant blue dragon.

'Oh.'

Yes. Oh.

'They weren't running way from me, were they?'

No, I am afraid they were not.

Streig and Reka had pulled themselves up and the former lieutenant stared at the dragon with unalloyed awe.

'Please tell me this one is on our side, Streig.'

The young soldier spat blood from his split lip and chuckled. 'This is my good friend Flodvind.'

Kristofine dared a look over the edge of the cliff and saw two more dragons, one a deep wood brown, the other the colour of dark grey stone.

'How?' she whispered.

'I don't know,' admitted Streig. 'I'm just glad they haven't taken up their old habits like Bittervinge has.'

The dragons did not linger for long. One by one they took to wing and headed out to sea.

'That's quite a sight,' said Reka quietly.

'It certainly is,' agreed Streig. 'Come on, we don't have long left and the city folk won't stay away for long.'

'I'm sorry, Streig. We're full to the point of going under.' Captain Hewn gave Reka and Kristofine a rueful look. They had traversed the steep and winding path down from the cliffs until they stood on the shingle beach where the sea sighed and whispered on the stones with the turn of every wave. 'I barely know where everyone will sleep as it is,' he added, rubbing his bearded chin.

'These are very important people!' said Streig.

'You've no idea how many times I've heard that today,' said the captain wearily. 'I have an entire ship full of very important people; it's practically a floating palace.' He turned to leave but Streig caught him by the arm. The captain looked down at Streig's hand with a look of growing impatience. 'I need to make ready to cast off. If you're not on board when I give the order' – the captain shrugged – 'Frøya help you.'

'We are part of Boyar Sokolov's household staff,' said Kristofine, raising her chin in what she hoped was an imperious manner. She was still somewhat giddy from Reka's draught, but at least she could keep her eyes open now. 'The Boyar will reward you handsomely for this service should you get us as far as Arkiv.'

'And who is Boyar Sokolov?' the captain sneered.

'Ruler of Vend Province,' added Reka. 'Descended from the founding families of the Solmindre Empire, and close confidant of the Emperor himself.' The former lieutenant took a step closer and Kristofine pretended not to hear what he said next. 'Please, my lady has a very delicate constitution and she is . . .' Reka laid one hand across his stomach and nodded once. Kristofine coughed behind her hand, but it was more to cover the laughter that erupted from her than to go along with Reka's ruse.

'I will demand payment from the Boyar the next time I am in Vend Province,' said Captain Hewn. 'You can be sure of that.'

'Of course,' said Reka. 'We are much obliged to you.'

They headed to the last small boat that waited on the stony shore. The crowd of those about to be left behind realized this might be their last chance. A wordless cry of rage and despair went up and blades were drawn. Streig readied the two-handed sword as the captain, his mate, and Reka dragged the boat into the shallows. The crowd came down the narrow cliff path. Falling, sliding, tumbling, heedless of the danger, desperate to be taken away from Khlystburg.

'We'll capsize if they reach us,' shouted Captain Hewn, heaving himself into the boat as waves rippled and splashed all around.

'Streig?' shouted Kristofine above the din. The people were on the beach now. 'We're leaving!'

The young soldier was holding the people back with wild swings of the great blade; they dodged out of the way to avoid the wild strikes. 'Get yourselves to Arkiv,' he shouted over his shoulder.

One of the crowd lunged forward and steel flashed brightly, but Streig stepped aside from the blow and replied with one of his own. His attacker was suddenly missing one of his forearms and screamed so loudly the crowd around him faltered.

'Frejna's teeth!' said Captain Hewn, pushing off from the beach. The mate pulled on the oars and Kristofine reached out to Streig on instinct, but it was no good. She watched him fend off the crowd, but had no idea how long he would last being so outnumbered.

'Best not to watch,' said Reka, his face twisting in despair as he placed an arm around her shoulders. 'Look away now.'

CHAPTER TWENTY-SEVEN

Kjellrunn

People forget just how young the Stormtide Prophet was during the uprising. She had barely begun to know herself, and yet the fate of an entire continent rested on her slender shoulders, and on the shoulders of her most devoted handmaiden, Trine.

– From the memoir of Drakina Tveit,
Lead Librarian of Midtenjord Province

Kjellrunn had spent an entire day in a dreamless sleep, only waking to drink water or eat what little food was left on Arkiv.

'We need to leave this place before we all starve to death,' said Romola, her anger slipping its leash. The very next morning they were at sea. Kjellrunn stood at the prow of the *Watcher's Wait*, her every sense alive. The smell of salt water, the breeze on her skin and in her hair, the vivid blue of the sky, the sound of the water as it met the hull. She could taste the salt water too, but this was the leviathan's sensation, not her own. It was easier to commune with the vast creature after resting. The colossal presence beneath the waves didn't overwhelm her in the way it had before the attack on Arkiv.

'The last week has been a blur to me,' Kjellrunn confided

to Trine. 'Sometimes I wasn't sure where the leviathan ended and I began. Does that make sense?'

'I don't know what you're going through,' admitted Trine. 'But when you first started trying to guide it, well, you couldn't even stand, let alone open your eyes.' She looked out to sea ahead of the ship and the taut ropes that disappeared under the water, warps that pulled them onward to Khlystburg.

'At first I think I summoned it with my anger, unwittingly. Then it became about control, but the idea of that was overwhelming.' Kjellrunn rubbed her forehead slowly.

'Why did you tell us, me and Romola I mean, that you could do it?'

'I said I had a plan and I was desperate enough to try it, to see it through.'

'And now?' replied Trine.

'And now it feels natural. I don't have to be angry all the time. It doesn't feel like I'm trying to assert control; it's more like an ongoing conversation.'

For a moment they stood together in silence.

'SHIP SIGHTED!' shouted Rylska from a hastily made perch amidships. Trine swore and Kjellrunn squinted into the distance.

'Never mind,' said Romola, striding down the ship from the helm. 'It's a trading vessel, and nowhere near the port. Maybe they're smuggling.'

'Smuggling what?' asked Trine.

'Who knows?' replied Romola. 'I'd rather leave them be if it's all right with you, your prophetness.' Kjellrunn smiled. Romola's irritation revealed a little more of itself with each day.

'You'll be rid of me soon enough,' Kjellrunn said softly. Romola blinked in surprise.

'I'm sorry, Kjellrunn. This is all too strange for me and I like being in control of my own ship too much.' She threw up her hands. 'Are you well? I mean really? You were practically comatose not so long ago. Now you're doing this again.' She gestured to where the vast, dark shadow moved under the waves of the Ashen Gulf.

'If I don't get to Khlystburg soon there may not be a family alive for me when I get there.'

'Steiner can handle himself,' said Romola. 'Trust me on that, right.'

'Steiner does what he thinks is right without stopping to consider if he's overextended himself,' replied Kjellrunn.

'Well, I guess it runs in the family,' said Romola. Her gaze moved to where the leviathan swam beneath the waves, before she shook her head and walked away.

The Imperial ships had arranged themselves outside the port in an arrowhead formation, the lead ship furthest out to sea. Trine gritted her teeth and sent countless arcs of arcane fire to immolate the enemy, but this time they responded in kind. Romola's crew ran from impact to impact extinguishing fires aboard the *Watcher's Wait* with buckets of bilge water. Much of the arcane fire thrown by the Vigilants had gone astray in the high winds, but two streaks of fire had found their mark.

'Gods damn it!' shouted Romola. 'There isn't that much left of my ship to burn.'

A third lance of fire crashed into the *Wait* and incinerated a crew member instantly. Another was sent overboard, alight and screaming. Romola gritted her teeth and slammed her hand against the helm.

'Frejna take you,' she hissed at the Imperial ships. 'Frejna take you all!'

The galleons blockading Arkiv had not enjoyed the luxury of having Vigilants aboard, but the ships at Khlystburg port clearly counted talented Troikas among their number.

'Hel's teeth,' complained Trine. 'There are three of them and there's only one of me.'

'Not for long,' said Kjellrunn. 'Try to hold off from using your powers.' They had not released the warps from the *Watcher's Wait*. The ship sped towards the lead galleon, led by the now surfacing leviathan. A V-shaped wave appeared in the sea before the creature and Kjellrunn could hear the screams of the Imperial sailors. A handful of them ran across the deck and flung themselves into water rather than brace for the impact that would surely end them. Kjellrunn held up a hand and Romola's crew ceased their tasks and ran to grab hold of something on deck.

'Just die!' shouted Trine, her black hair streaming in the wind. The leviathan rose up out of the water and smashed into the prow of the galleon with a deafening noise. Fragments of wood exploded upwards.

'Hold on!' shouted Kjellrunn as the leviathan sank beneath the water once more, leaving the *Watcher's Wait* to collide with the galleon. The burned bow of the red frigate ploughed into the weakened hull of the Imperial ship with a dull sound of wood grinding on broken wood.

'Weapons!' shouted Romola. Her crew sprang to their feet and raced to the prow of the ship, leaping from where the *Watcher's Wait* had embedded itself in the galleon. Trine led the way, slamming streaks of orange and yellow light with a wild-eyed intensity. Romola followed up behind and the crew let out a roar as they boarded the stricken vessel.

Only to discover it was abandoned.

'Where the fu—?' But Romola's question was soon answered. The Imperial crew had sprinted to the stern of the ship.

'She's here!' they screamed. 'The Stormtide Prophet is here!' The Imperial sailors threw themselves from the poop deck, diving into the waters to escape. The captain remained at the helm for a moment, chastising his crew for desertion.

'Return to your posts, damn you! We hold! We fight! We prevail!' A second later he was lit from head to foot in arcane fire. Trine eyed him with disgust, her hands still smoking.

'You should have run,' she whispered as the captain stumbled to the edge of the ship and threw himself overboard. It was suddenly quiet and there was no one to fight. The Vigilants on the other ships ceased casting their own fiery lances. Kjellrunn imagined they were unsure what was happening. Even the Holy Synod were reluctant to fire on their own men, it seemed.

'I was not expecting that,' admitted Romola as they turned and clambered aboard the *Wait*. 'What now?'

'There're still another two ships out there,' replied Kjellrunn. 'I don't want to risk getting that close a second time.'

The crew went about their tasks, exhilaration written for all to see on their faces. Kjellrunn gripped the guardrail of the ship tighter and closed her eyes.

'This port will be mine,' she whispered through gritted teeth. 'And I will find my family.'

The leviathan had been less than keen to return to the *Watcher's Wait* following the battle for the port. The remaining two galleons put up a fight, but the crews either mutinied or fled. The red frigate remained adrift, surrounded by the flotsam of three Imperial galleons.

'It's like we're sailing on a sea of wood,' remarked Trine, gazing at the devastation. Kjellrunn took a good look at her friend. The black sleeves of Trine's robes had been burned away until her arms were bare to the shoulders. The dark-haired girl had noticed none of this. Her haste to rain fire down on those who had imprisoned her on Vladibogdan had been paramount.

'Trine,' said Kjellrunn softly. She reached out and traced fingertips over her friend's arm. 'Look.' A tracery of fine black lines had etched themselves into the girl's alabaster skin. Soot black, the marks looked like angry broken veins.

'It's fine,' replied Trine, snatching her arm away. 'Don't touch me.' She spent a moment glowering at Kjellrunn. 'I just need to rest. That's all. I'll see you below.' And without another word she departed.

'Oh, Frejna, please help her.' Kjellrunn felt dizzy with regret and tiredness. The Stormtide Prophet leaned on the rail of the ship and stared over the side. Somehow a small expanse of water remained clear and her reflection looked back at her.

She was not alone.

On either side of her was a woman. Kjellrunn jerked upright and glanced both ways, but no one stood beside her.

'What?' She dared to look at her reflection again and sure enough the two women remained by her side. She couldn't see either of them clearly, save for the fact they were perhaps from Yamal or Shanisrond. No, that wasn't right, but neither were they Spriggani, nor were they the pale-skinned folk of the Empire or Scorched Republics.

You called me. Kjellrunn saw one of the women speak. Her words transcended speech, appearing in Kjellrunn's mind, close, quiet, intimate. One of the women was attired in green, while the other wore black vestments much like her own.

'Am I dreaming?'

Close enough. You are on the threshold of exhaustion. The fact you still stand is a miracle. What can we do for you, Kjellrunn Vartiainen?

'I'm worried for my friend. She's burning herself up.' Suddenly there were tears in her eyes. 'I think, perhaps, something similar happened to my mother.'

There is nothing we can do for your friend. She draws her strength from draconic sources. I am sorry, Kjellrunn Vartiainen.

'Will she survive?'

The women in the water did not answer.

'Will I survive?'

Seawater lapped against the hull of the *Watcher's Wait*, but still no answer.

'Why did you come if you've nothing useful to say?'

We came because you were in need, and to tell you first-hand that you have our blessing. There has not been one such as you in over a hundred years, and never has such a person been so needed.

'I could use a little bit more help than just kind words.'

Sometimes a kind word makes all the difference.

'Tell me you'll watch over my handmaiden; tell me there's a place for one who has served you.'

There is a place for everyone, Kjellrunn. There always was. There always will be for those who believe.

Kjellrunn blinked away her tears but when she looked again the women in the water were gone. Her hands were shaking and there was nothing to do but slump to the deck and curl up. Sleep pressed in on her like a heavy blanket and dreams did not find her.

CHAPTER TWENTY-EIGHT

Ruslan

Loyalty and habit make unseemly bedfellows and many loyalties that had been taken for granted were put to the test. Peasants, aides, and hirelings, who had slavishly or blindly followed their betters, now found themselves re-examining the past and its many untruths.

— From the memoir of Drakina Tveit,
Lead Librarian of Midtenjord Province

Ruslan hurried across the city to inform the Boyar that Steiner Vartiainen was on his way to the catacombs.

'It's almost done,' Ruslan chanted to himself every few steps. 'It will be over soon, and we shall be safe.'

The Boyar was waiting for him on the doorstep of their accommodation when Ruslan returned.

'They have departed the inn, my lord. They were well armed and I'm in no doubt they are on their way to the catacombs.'

'Send for a carriage at once.' The Boyar smiled, though it was a cold thing that brought no cheer.

'My lord. I have been out in the street a long time, watching. May I get something to sustain myself?'

'Yes, but you will eat on the way to court. I will not be delayed and I will not present myself to the Emperor without you."

Ruslan found himself wondering if the Boyar was a little afraid and merely needed the company to bolster his courage. 'Of course, my lord.'

'We depart at once, before that abomination Zima appears again.'

Ruslan nodded his agreement, though he had no wish to be anywhere near the Emperor or his legions of dead-eyed soldiers, much less the arcane-wielding Vigilants.

The Imperial Gardens were in disarray and a task force of sour-looking men tended the ravaged bushes. The remains of shattered statues were being carted away. Roses and vines littered the gravel paths and a dozen soldiers guarded the stables.

'What happened here?' asked Ruslan.

'You know what happened here,' snapped the Boyar. 'Steiner Vartiainen and his aunt came here.'

'They did all of this?' asked Ruslan. The Boyar gave no answer and increased his pace to reach the court. Ruslan struggled to keep up with his master, watching as one dignitary after another tried to slow the Boyar down. Sokolov flashed a metal token that bought him passage past the stern and the disapproving alike, until they were standing outside the Imperial Court itself. The way ahead remained barred by the crossed spears of the Semyonovsky Guard.

'I have orders to report to the Emperor himself.' Neither the guards or the spears moved. 'I am Boyar Augustine Sokolov of Vend Province and my news is significant.'

'I hope it is, for your sake,' said one of the armed men. The spears were raised and Ruslan had never experienced such fear in all his thirty-three years. The double doors to the court swung open, revealing a huge hall with a polished floor. Generals, Envoys, members of the Holy Synod, and a smattering of nobles and aides stood in clusters before the throne.

'Should I wait out here?' asked Ruslan. It was what he had been required to do on their last visit, after all. The Boyar, with a curt gesture and an impatient look on his lined face, motioned that he should follow. He resumed his hurried march, boot heels sounding on the polished floor, loud enough to cause a few of the courtiers to turn around.

'Hel's teeth,' whispered Ruslan as he struggled to keep up.

Standing at the right hand of the Emperor's throne was Exarch Zima. In his good hand he held a chain in much the same way a person might hold a leash for a favourite wolf-hound. Ruslan eyed the kneeling man at the end of the chain. That a collar of metal encircled his neck was bad enough, but the man was naked except for his bruises; so many bruises in various hues of violet and purple. The Imperial Court was not warm, and Ruslan felt a sympathetic chill pass over his flesh. The prisoner's hands were chained behind his back and his gaze remained lowered. 'Who is that?'

'Be quiet!' hissed Boyar Sokolov. The Emperor was pacing, as was his way, speaking with members of the Synod, who hid behind their masks. The Boyar went straight to the Emperor and dropped to one knee. 'Your Imperial Highness, it is done.'

Everyone in the room fell quiet, curiosity piqued.

'Do you hear that, Zima?' said the Emperor in his strange whisper. 'Our messenger has played his part.'

The Exarch in the wolverine mask nodded once but said nothing.

'Tell me, Augustine,' continued the Emperor, blithely ignoring the Boyar's title. 'Do you still grieve for that treacherous son of yours?'

'In truth, Your Imperial Highness, he was not my son.' The Boyar smoothed down his moustaches. Ruslan stared at his lord in confusion and realized he was not alone. The many courtiers took a step closer at this sudden revelation.

'Stand up, Augustine,' said the Emperor, taking a step closer. 'Explain yourself.'

'I raised Dimitri, it is true, but he was not blood of my blood.' The Boyar puffed out his chest and held up his head. 'He was my sister's get, a bastard that would have brought disgrace to my family had his origins been known.' Shocked whispers passed through the court like the patter of autumn rain. 'I don't see it matters now. Dimitri has brought disgrace to the Sokolov line regardless of the kindness I showed him.'

'What . . .?' Ruslan stepped towards his master. The Boyar silenced him with a look of such severity Ruslan feared he would be dismissed from his lord's service. In that moment Ruslan knew his master was not the man he thought he was, and perhaps never had been.

The Emperor thought on what he had just been told and glared at the Boyar for longer than Ruslan could bear.

'I release your line from disgrace, Boyar Sokolov of Vend Province,' said the Emperor. His smile quirked the corners of his mouth but his eyes retained that dead quality which fed the rising dread in Ruslan. 'It will be as if Dimitri had never existed. No record of him will remain. No mention of him will sully your history. The Sokolov line may hold up their heads with pride.'

'You are too kind, Your Imperial Highness,' replied the Boyar with a bow.

The Emperor took a step closer. 'And now' – he gestured to the room with an expansive sweep of his arm – 'it would please me that you tell my courtiers of the plan I had you carry out.'

'The Emperor sought to capitalize on the death of Dimitri,'

said the Boyar. 'Many might assume I would take up arms
against the Empire that killed my only son. And so the
Emperor in his wisdom tasked me with making contact with
Steiner Vartiainen, the so-called dragon rider of Cinderfell.'
The courtiers were not the only ones to react to the
name. The kneeling prisoner raised his head and set a
murderous gaze on the Boyar. Ruslan knew in his bones that
the man in chains was Steiner's father.

'I found him,' continued the Boyar. 'And directed him to
the catacombs beneath the Imperial Palace. He thinks this is
a secret way to reach the Emperor and strike at him from
inside the palace.' Ruslan shook his head in disbelief. That
the Boyar had lied to Steiner was one thing, but to lie about
Dimitri and disown his son was unthinkable.

'Steiner will find the catacombs are winding and treacherous,' said the Emperor. 'There many ways for a man to
lose himself. It is not merely the dead who haunt the lower
reaches of the palace . . .' The Emperor trailed off, and his
eyes lost some of their focus. His distraction lingered for a
moment before he said, 'Though some things are worse than
death.'

'He'll find you,' said the man in chains, breaking the silence
of the Emperor's conceited preening. 'Once Steiner sets his
mind to something—'

'Be quiet,' snarled the Emperor.

'Your catacombs won't stop him. He'll find you and strike
you down.' Steiner's father smiled through split and bruised
lips, his teeth bloody. 'And all the hateful dragon-forged trinkets in Nordvlast won't save you.'

Exarch Zima struck the man across the face and a bright
bloom of scarlet appeared as the chained man's lip split once
more. The silence that followed was awful, but it was nothing
compared to the bitter, wheezing laughter that sounded from
the prisoner kneeling by the throne.

'My name is Marek Vartiainen, and by the goddesses Frejna and Frøya I give you my word: my son will take your life!'

'I SAID BE QUIET!' roared the Emperor. He drew a dull grey blade from a sheath at his hip and advanced on Steiner's father. The courtiers shrank back, horrified expressions on their pale faces.

'He is coming for you,' said Marek Vartiainen with a savage grin. Not once did he blink, the gaze from his bloodshot eyes unwavering. The Emperor raised the dull blade just as the doors at the back of the court boomed open. Everyone turned to stare at the newcomer. A soldier marched in, sweating freely, out of breath, his black cloak tattered and his armour dull and dented.

'If this is anything less than catastrophic I will cut out your tongue,' said the Emperor into a dreadful hush. The Ashen Blade shed flecks of grey on the polished floor; some of the flakes alighted on Marek Vartiainen's matted hair.

'The Stormtide Prophet has destroyed the three galleons defending our port,' said the soldier, his eyes fixed on the arcane blade. 'She is coming ashore and we don't have the means to stop her.'

'The means to stop her?' The Emperor's words were like slivers of ice being hammered into the flesh. 'You will stop her with the armies that I have paid for with countless taxes.' The soldier flinched and, realizing he was breaching etiquette, dropped to one knee.

'She . . .' The soldier was visibly shaking as the Emperor approached him with madness in his pale eyes. 'She has a leviathan, Your Imperial Highness. I saw it with my own eyes. It is fully the size of a galleon and devoured our men.'

For a moment Ruslan thought the Emperor smiled, but soon realized the Emperor was gritting his teeth, his lips peeling back in a snarl. The soldier didn't wait to be excused, but got to his feet and backed away from the knife-wielding man before him.

'Attacked from above by Bittervinge,' said Marek Vartiainen. 'Hunted from below by my son.'

'Be quiet!' seethed the Emperor.

'And now my daughter comes for you. How will you survive, Volkan?'

'I SAID BE QUIET!' howled the Emperor, striding towards the prisoner. Marek lifted his chin, seeming to know what was coming next. Ruslan turned away, unable to watch the Emperor's savagery.

The journey back to the townhouse was a quiet one. Ruslan was too shocked to utter a sound, too sickened by what he had seen to attempt to frame it with words. The carriage clattered over the cobbled streets of Khlystburg and every beat of the horses' hooves was too loud. The city stank of decay and smoke, and Ruslan wondered if they were all dead men, simply too foolish or naive to realize their time was over. Vinterkveld was destined to be ruled by one monster or another, Volkan Karlov or Bittervinge. The carriage turned a corner just a touch too fast and Ruslan was shaken from his musing. The Boyar looked out of the window, face taut, mouth a downturned slash.

After what seemed an eternity, the carriage stopped. Ruslan opened the door and stepped down in a daze, not thinking to help his master down, not waiting to let the Boyar enter before him as etiquette demanded. He knocked on the door of their accommodation and waited.

'Ruslan.' The Boyar's voice was hushed and rusty, yet had the same effect as a knife thrust into flesh.

'You lied.' Ruslan's voice was low yet terrible. 'You lied about Dimitri.'

'It's better this way.' The Boyar cleared his throat. 'Better he never existed than to endure a shameful memory.'

'You care nothing for Dimitri's memory, only for your own

reputation. Did you know the Emperor would expunge him from all records?'

'It was a risk, but the Emperor has done it before to others, many times.' The Boyar looked away down the street, unable to meet his aide's eyes. 'Better this way,' he added, though he sounded less sure of himself.

'I didn't expect to like Steiner Vartiainen,' said Ruslan as the door opened behind him. 'But he's ten times the man you are.' The maid looked out with a nervous glance.

'You will not speak to me this way,' seethed the Boyar, trying to claw back some measure of authority, but Augustine Sokolov's hold over Ruslan had been broken.

'I am finished here,' replied Ruslan. He walked away, striding down the street, every step feeling bold and new and terrifying in equal measure.

'Ruslan! Please!' So much desperation in so few words. 'Where will you go?'

Ruslan walked onward; he knew exactly where he was headed.

CHAPTER TWENTY-NINE

Steiner

Volkan Karlov had spent decades banning all mention of the goddesses Frøya and Frejna. He had sent Vigilants, soldiers, and Okhrana to destroy the Rusalka and Spriggani, desperate that he and he alone be the most inspiring presence in Vinterkveld. The old tales were slowly erased. How fitting then that Volkan Karlov unwittingly engineered a new tale, a dark and terrible story of venturing underground and facing unknowable horrors, a tale to be retold down through the ages. The tale of Steiner Vartiainen.

–From the memoir of Drakina Tveit,
Lead Librarian of Midtenjord Province

The entrance to the catacombs had meant to inspire patriotism in the good people of Khlystburg during the Age of Fire, when man and woman had risen up against the dragons. A statue of the Emperor stood between two pairs of double doors, though the architects had not foreseen that their ruler would be dwarfed by the entrances to and from an underworld of their own making.

'I heard it said he flew into a rage upon coming here for the first time,' said Felgenhauer. Both sets of doors were twenty feet high, whereas the marble effigy of His Imperial

Highness struggled to reach twelve feet. 'Needless to say, the architects didn't get much work after the Emperor had their eyes gouged out.'

'Tell me you're not serious,' said Tomasz, mouth curving in disgust. Felgenhauer gave her sergeant a long hard look. 'All because his statue didn't reach the height of his ego?'

'That's the legend, though it happened nearly ninety years ago and you know how it goes with stories, how they get embroidered, exaggerated.' Felgenhauer stared into the face of the Emperor's statue. The sculptor had captured that patient look Volkan Karlov so often wore, but also something of the darkness beneath. 'But he's capable of anything. You of all people know that. I don't doubt the stories are true.'

Steiner listened to all of this and regarded the catacombs with growing trepidation.

'Come on, then.' He paced closer to the doors. 'This is the only way through.' The threshold to the catacombs was closed off by heavy wooden doors painted a dark and bloody red. Iron studs formed a pattern from top to bottom, black diamonds in the gloom. 'And light some torches,' he added a moment later. The men did as they were told after looking to Felgenhauer for confirmation. She nodded once and fell into step beside Steiner.

'I'm beginning to think' – Steiner rubbed his jaw – 'that the Boyar's information was—'

'A touch vague,' interrupted his aunt. She stepped forward and pushed at the door with both hands, putting her whole weight behind the effort.

Nothing happened.

Felgenhauer's cadre joined her, Steiner among them. They pushed and grunted, putting their backs to the studded wood, but the way ahead remained closed off to them.

'Is it possible the Emperor used the arcane to seal them up in some way?' asked Steiner.

'I don't know of such an enchantment,' replied his aunt.

'Perhaps it's locked,' offered Tomasz. Steiner took a step back and hefted his sledgehammer. 'What are you doing?' said the former sergeant.

'I don't have any lock picks,' replied Steiner with a grin. 'Except this one.'

'Your nephew is touched in the head,' grumbled Tomasz as the first hammer blow hit the wooden door. A cloud of splinters exploded outwards.

'Perhaps,' conceded Felgenhauer. 'But right now he's the only thing that's going to get us through those doors.'

Steiner raised the hammer again. This was going to take some work. The door shuddered on its hinges with the second strike.

'It's no good,' complained Tomasz.

'I'm just getting warmed up,' replied Steiner. The sledge-hammer hit the door again and connected with one of the iron studs, smashing it clean through the other side. It left a ragged hole. 'We will get through this,' growled Steiner, 'You have my word on it.'

There had been more statues just inside the entrance, soldiers in armour bearing shields and maces. A dozen steps took them downwards to a causeway in a wide corridor, where the glorious dead took their final rest.

'That's a lot of coffins,' said Steiner. The flickering torchlight revealed seemingly countless stone rectangles on either side of the causeway.

'They're sarcophagi,' corrected Felgenhauer. 'Coffins are made out wood.'

Steiner shrugged. 'As long as the dead stay inside them I really don't care what they're called.'

Four of Felgenhauer's cadre marched ahead, two bearing torches, the flames small and mean in the damp darkness.

The other eight soldiers followed up behind, occasionally muttering to one another, their voices low.

'Nothing feels right here,' said Steiner.

'It's just your imagination,' replied Felgenhauer. 'No one has been down here for decades.'

The corridor's ceiling was lost in the gloom above them, while the way ahead stretched on without end, or so it seemed. Every so often a statue loomed out of the darkness, sculpted in the likeness of woman wearing a sleeveless shift. They had a heavy quality to them, the carving bold, the stony expressions serious. The statues held out their strong arms, palms and fingers forming a bowl.

'Their hands would have been filled with firewood,' explained Felgenhauer in a hushed voice.

'I'm not surprised,' whispered Steiner. 'It's spiteful cold.'

'The Emperor hoped to seed a new myth, a myth that the women of the Empire would light a way home for those in the afterlife. Even back then he was trying to supplant Frøya and Frejna.'

'How do you know so much about this place? I thought it was closed to the public years ago.'

'It was,' replied Felgenhauer. 'One of my first jobs as a newly trained Vigilant was to watch over the palace. We were told not to come down here. It was understood the catacombs didn't need guarding.'

Steiner didn't much care for the direction of his aunt's conversation and glanced at the nearest sarcophagus. The lid was loose, still atop the container, but resting at an angle.

'We were told the catacombs had defences of their own since the city folk stopped visiting,' added Felgenhauer. 'But I never believed it.'

'That can't mean anything good,' replied Steiner. The soldier nearest to Steiner made to investigate the opened sarcophagus, but Steiner caught him by the arm before he could jump down from the causeway. 'Let's not make trouble for ourselves,' whispered Steiner. He held up a finger to his lips and warned the other soldiers to be quiet. Wary eyes darted from one sarcophagus lid to another. No one said a word for fear of waking the sleeping dead.

'I'm going to strangle that Boyar and take Vend Province for myself,' said Tomasz with a sullen look.

'That seems reasonable,' replied Steiner. 'I may even help you.' They headed deeper into the darkness, with only the scuff of their boots to disturb the dusty silence.

'That sarcophagus seems to have scratch marks on the outside,' said Tomasz, gripping his two-handed axe tightly.

'Easy now,' soothed Felgenhauer. 'Only the Ashen Torment can compel spirits to rise from the dead, and Steiner destroyed it.' The men relaxed a bit.

'There'll be no cinderwraiths down here,' muttered Steiner. But then he felt rather than saw a disturbance behind him and turned to see a shadow lurch away, back into the darkness. A lone torch tumbled to the causeway and rolled towards him. The men at the rear of the column turned and brandished their weapons.

'Where did this torch come from?' said one gruff voice.

'Where is Jarlen?' asked Felgenhauer. The soldiers looked from one face to another and the men at the front stopped abruptly.

'He was right here,' replied one of the soldiers near the back of the column. 'Holding the torch just behind me.' On instinct Steiner looked up just as three pale shapes descended from the blackness above them.

'Above us!' he shouted as the first of the attackers almost landed on top of him. The creature was the colour of old bone, with eight spindly legs some six feet long. A variety of jet-black eyes stared at Steiner, all in different sizes, while mandibles champed together in anticipation of the meal to

come. The sledgehammer split the creature apart with a sickening crack and Steiner hefted the weapon and struck again.

'Frejna's teeth!' The legs thrashed as the creature raged
through the pain of its wounds. Steiner stamped on the creature's head with his boot. 'Die!' he yelled, slamming his foot
down until the bone-coloured thing stopped moving. 'Just
die!'

Felgenhauer petrified her own attacker using the arcane.
The creature turned a pale grey, shaking and trembling in an
attempt to escape, but Felgenhauer's gaze reduced the living
creature to a statue in a few heartbeats. Steiner broke the
petrified form apart with a deft swing of the sledgehammer.

'Help me!' A soldier at the rear of the column cried out as
he was bitten. Three of his comrades rushed to his aid.
Two-handed axes dealt a swift death to the scuttling menace.
The sound of harsh cracks gave way to wet chopping noises
before the men stopped attacking. Steiner glanced around and
the silence of the catacombs rushed in to fill the darkness
once more.

'Is that it?' he whispered, retrieving Jarlen's torch from the
causeway.

'For now,' replied Felgenhauer.

Tomasz began to curse behind her; he flailed about in the
darkness with his torch, searching this way and that. 'They
got Breslov too. I can't see him anywhere.'

Felgenhauer knelt down beside the injured man at the rear
of the column. 'Konstantin.'

The man looked at her with wide eyes; his pale face appeared
waxy in the torchlight. 'I'm sorry, Matriarch-Commissar . . .'
He swallowed and shivered.

'Never mind that,' she said softly. 'You did your best to
protect us.'

'Thank you.' Konstantin forced a smile and nodded. 'And
to think, I might have got out of the army if I'd survived

this.' He grinned a moment and then began to shake and fit. His comrades cradled him until the tremors subsided. Felgenhauer held his hand and smiled at him, smoothing his hair back from his brow with tender fingers. Konstantin released a long sigh and then he was gone.

'Frøya save me,' whispered Steiner. 'Poison?'

Felgenhauer nodded. 'And a virulent one at that.'

'What are those things?'

'Corpse spiders,' said Felgenhauer with disgust. 'I thought they had been eradicated. I'd never even seen one before today.'

'I don't understand,' said Steiner, staring at the body of Konstantin. 'How could something so dangerous live here at the centre of the city?'

'Corpse spiders only reside under the mountains in Novgoruske Province,' said Felgenhauer. 'It's why no one dared to go digging for coal or silver until ten years ago. They abhor daylight and prefer to feed on bone marrow.'

'How the Hel did they get here?' asked Tomasz.

'And why didn't Boyar Sokolov warn us about them?' added Steiner.

'We can't think about that now,' replied Felgenhauer. 'We have to move.'

'I'm not leaving Konstantin for those things,' said Tomasz.

'We can't take him with us,' replied Felgenhauer.

'I'm *not* leaving him here as carrion for those bastards.' Tomasz looked about as stern as Steiner had ever seen. 'Bad enough they got Jarlen and Breslov.'

'As you wish,' replied Felgenhauer. She pointed at the youngest of the soldiers. 'Take Konstantin back to the catacomb gates and wait for us there.'

'But I . . .' The young soldier fell silent as Felgenhauer glowered at him.

'The rest of you, look out for each other.' She lit her own

torch and held it up. 'There're at least another two of those things out there and we can't afford to lose anyone else.'

The young soldier hefted Konstantin's corpse over his shoulder and headed back the way they had come from, though Steiner didn't envy him the lonely task. The rest of the soldiers continued on for a time and no one spoke; the shock of losing three of their number strangled the desire to say anything. The causeway began to curve off to the left but another path lay to their right.

'This is what I meant earlier,' said Steiner. 'The Boyar's information is vague to the point of being worthless.'

'How much did he tell you?' asked Tomasz, an edge of irritation in his voice.

'He said we'd need to go down before climbing up a shaft,' replied Felgenhauer.

'My guess is the way to the left just leads back to the entrance,' said Steiner. 'So we go right.' The men shared uncertain looks but nodded in agreement and followed.

'Karlin,' said Felgenhauer, 'you brought rope?'

'And a grappling hook,' replied a soldier from behind them. Ahead of them one of the soldiers swore and there was the sound of leather scuffing on stone. The soldier seemed to drop straight down rather than slip from the side of the causeway to fall among the sarcophagi.

'What is it?' Steiner pressed ahead and found that the causeway ended without warning.

'I'm all right,' called the soldier. He stood on a narrow ledge of rubble; the remains of the collapsed causeway no doubt.

'Karlin, throw him the rope,' said Felgenhauer. The soldier climbed up and brushed himself off, breathing hard.

'When I fell I dropped my torch,' he said. 'The ledge is just the start of it. There's a deeper drop beyond that. I . . . I didn't see my torch hit the bottom.'

Felgenhauer looked at Steiner and sighed.

'Damn you, Sokolov,' muttered Steiner.

'How much rope do we have?' asked Felgenhauer.

'Not enough for a drop like that,' replied Karlin.

'That's what I thought,' replied Felgenhauer. 'The rest of you head back to the catacomb gates. Steiner and I will finish this together.'

The men stood in shocked silence a moment.

'There has to be another way,' said Tomasz. 'We can't leave you now.'

'Tomasz.' Felgenhauer stepped forward and took Tomasz's head in her hands, then kissed him on each cheek. 'If I had a thousand men like you' – she smiled at her cadre – 'I could take this land and make it good.'

'Matriarch-Commissar?' said Tomasz with an expression of almost painful confusion.

'Go back to the entrance and keep yourselves safe.' Felgenhauer gave them a fierce smile. 'That's an order!'

Steiner looked over the edge and and felt his heart sink. He had a suspicion what his aunt had in mind.

'We'll see you again,' she shouted to her men.

'I don't think that's the best way to—' Steiner began to say, but before he could finish Felgenhauer took his hand and jumped over the edge, into the abyss, dragging Steiner into the depths with her.

CHAPTER THIRTY

Silverdust

The citizens of the Empire succumbed to a malaise as the old goddesses were erased from the Empire. So much of people's identity and beliefs were bound up in Frøya and Frejna, and there were rumours of other, smaller, regional deities and hearth spirits. The Holy Synod preached that a life in service to the Empire was all that mattered; but people will always search for answers to give their lives meaning. A dull cynicism remained in the absence of the divine, and nothing Volkan Karlov did could alter it.

– From the memoir of Drakina Tveit,
Lead Librarian of Midtenjord Province

The journey north through the outskirts of the city had not been without its trials. Bittervinge rarely ventured to the southern districts. Flodvind, Stonvind, and Namarii's presence were an ample deterrent even for the father of dragons, but Silverdust had not survived for so long by being reckless. The cinderwraith had hidden in doorways like a looming shade, haunting shadows until he was satisfied the way ahead was safe. Twice he had encountered looters in Khlystburg and twice they had fled. The sight of a mirror-masked Vigilant clad in black was enough to dissuade the lawless, it seemed, even in times such as these.

How pitiful that thoughts turn to greed in times of chaos.

Silverdust's ability to see the spirits of the dead had remained, even through his near destruction and subsequent confinement in the urn. Every step through the city revealed more of the lingering dead, those spirits too attached to the mortal realm to move on. They appeared to Silverdust as tongues of blue and white fire with human faces and arms contorted in expressions of mourning and grief.

Go now, gentle ones. There is nothing for you here.

But the spirits were too overcome by the horror of their passing, too confused by their sudden deaths, to be able to pass on. Silverdust moved ever onwards, a ghost among ghosts. The sometime Exarch and now restored cinderwraith had taken the secret ways through the city, down into forgotten basements, following tunnels that twisted in maddening ways, past lonely dead ends, under tumbledown archways. At last he reached his destination. To anyone else it might seem as if he stood in the aftermath of a collapsed cavern. All about him lay mounds of rubble and broken statuary, dank earth and broken bones. A halo of silver light played about Silverdust's feet, turning back the dark and illuminating the source of his lonely pilgrimage: the final resting place of Alexandr Vartiainen, Steiner's great-grandfather. The sarcophagus of the Emperor's bodyguard had been interred deep below the Imperial Palace now deeper still, due to subsidence.

It is good to see you, old friend. The cinderwraith laid a leather-gloved hand on the cold stone. Truthfully, they had never been more than comrades. In life Alexandr had been a straightforward man, both practical and loyal. He'd had little time for the Spriggani and his arcane secrets. Alexandr had warned Volkan Karlov against Serebryanyy Pyli. 'No good can come from meddling with such powers,' he'd said time and again so many decades before.

This is all my fault, Alexandr, and I have need of your counsel. Will you appear to me one last time? Will you help me set right everything I helped make wrong?

The sarcophagus lay at a steep angle, having fallen from the catacombs above. Whether it had been natural subsidence or a deliberate collapse Silverdust couldn't say, but it was a sorry resting place for someone who had helped the Emperor defeat Bittervinge.

Please, Alexandr, I have great need of you.

A flaming torch appeared from the darkness above, plummeting to the ground. It hit the rubble just a dozen feet away from where Silverdust stood. The mirror-masked cinderwraith conjured a spear of searing flame and waited. His senses warned him of a powerful presence far above, far more powerful than anything he had encountered save for Bittervinge himself. He focused his arcane senses and discovered he was mistaken. It was not a single unified power in the darkness, but three distinct and unique sources: a person and two artefacts. And they were approaching with haste.

Silverdust raised his arm to throw the arcane spear as two figures appeared from the gloom, a women and a man, joined in a fall that would surely kill them. The woman reached out with a gesture, almost caressing the air beneath her, slowing their descent. Both man and woman touched down in the rubble as if they had merely stepped from a carriage. Silverdust drew closer.

'Let's never do that again,' said the scarred man clutching a sledgehammer.

Steiner? Felgenhauer? Is that you?

The scarred man stared back with open-mouthed disbelief. 'Silverdust?' Steiner took a step closer, squinting into the darkness. The cinderwraith dispelled the flaming spear with a flick of his fingers. 'How? I saw you swallowed by Bittervinge. And you'd been wounded by an arcane blade.'

It is I, Steiner. I assure you. It was I who released the dragons after you left Vladibogdan, and it was I who was sent to hunt Felgenhauer by the Emperor. We fought side by side in the Great Library on Arkiv.

Steiner leapt forward and caught Silverdust in a fierce hug while Felgenhauer cocked her head to one side, a smile quirking the corner of her mouth.

Matriarch-Commissar. Silverdust inclined his head in respect.

'The first time we met, you were an eccentric Exarch living on Vladibogdan,' said Felgenhauer. 'Last time we met, I discovered you were a cinderwraith. Now you're back from the dead.'

Allow me to explain. Silverdust recounted his unusual journey, coming from Arkiv in the urn, and being remade with Stonvind's help.

'And they're all still alive?' asked Steiner breathlessly. 'Kimi and Taiga and Tief? We saw them recently . . .'

All alive – and riding dragons no less.

'Kimi, Tief, and Taiga. All three dragon riders.' Felgenhauer shook her head incredulously. 'Frøya save me. What strange times we live in. I'd be greatly afeared if I was Volkan Karlov.'

'Does Kimi know I'm in the city?' asked Steiner, and Silverdust could sense his excitement at being reunited with her.

Yes. She knows you hunt the Emperor. She has wanted to find you but it was impossible. Silverdust decided it was best not to mention Kimi's attachment to the Ashen Blade, lest Steiner be distracted from the task ahead.

'Why are you here?' asked Steiner. 'I mean here specifically? Do you know the way into the palace?'

In truth I do not. The catacombs are much changed since I was here last. It appears there has been a great collapse. I am here to converse with the dead. Specifically your great-grandfather, Steiner.

'That's impossible,' said Felgenhauer. 'None of the academies have ever been able to develop such powers. We have always been concerned with the elements, never the souls of the dead.'

True enough, though this is not an arcane power I draw on mindfully; rather it manifests continuously, even when I would prefer it did not.

'You can speak to dead?' asked Steiner.

I can see the dead. I saw scores of city folk, haunting the ruins of their homes, as I ventured here.

'How long have you been able to do this?' asked Felgenhauer.

I felt a change in myself following the destruction of the Ashen Torment. I assumed it was connected to that. A few weeks after you departed I found myself in the woods north of Cinderfell. That was when the power first manifested. I saw a score of dead Okhrana, shocked and lost. They were deeply confused, defeated by the hand of one supremely powerful young woman.

'Kjellrunn,' breathed Steiner.

Her powers are considerable.

'They're calling her the Stormtide Prophet,' said Steiner.

And it is right that they do. She will herald a new age of the goddesses, but only if she survives.

The temperature of the ruined catacombs, which was already chilly, became colder still. Steiner and Felgenhauer's breath steamed on the air. The arcane halo of silver light that danced around Silverdust's feet flickered, and blinked out for a moment.

He comes. Alexandr Vartiainen comes to us.

'What can you see?' whispered Steiner.

The sarcophagus is lit from within. A pale blue light, such as I have seen before. The stone container had fallen a great distance and was cracked in many places. Somehow the lid was mostly intact, though the inscription had been chipped so badly it was illegible.

'Why is my great-grandfather's sarcophagus all the way down here?' asked Steiner.

It is strangely convenient that this part of the catacombs has suffered in such a way, is it not? The Emperor has ever been fond of erasing those parts of the past he finds distasteful. The inscription was not damaged in the fall. I imagine a chisel was taken to his name, but I have found him nonetheless.

A ghostly head appeared through the sarcophagus lid, drifting higher with each moment. Silverdust could sense Steiner's disquiet and he was not alone. Felgenhauer was not such an open book, even with Silverdust's considerable powers, and yet her face betrayed her curiosity and her sadness.

'Is he here?' whispered Steiner, unable to see as Silverdust did.

More so with every moment. The spirit took a moment to gather himself, then became less transparent, an illustration of a person, grey chalk on the very fabric of the darkness.

'I can see him,' whispered Steiner.

That is not possible, replied Silverdust. The apparition now hovered above the sarcophagus, looking down at cinderwraith and mortal alike.

'I can see him too,' said Felgenhauer, her face pale in the spectral light. The spirit of Alexandr Vartiainen appeared as square-jawed as he had in life. Even his ghost wore a heavy breastplate, and he clutched a shadowy sword.

'I have seen much in this world and the next, but I never thought to see my granddaughter or my great-grandson. Who am I to thank for this blessing?'

It is I. Silverdust drifted forward. *Serebryanyy Pyli.* The cinderwraith performed a small bow.

'The Emperor's teacher. The years have not been kind to you. I do not recognize what you are. How long have I been . . . away?'

'Seventy-five years, Grandfather,' said Felgenhauer with deep reverence.

'I am sorry I never had the chance to meet you, Granddaughter.'

'We're meeting now,' replied Felgenhauer, 'that's all that matters.'

'Wait a moment,' said Steiner, a memory of Arkiv jarring something inside him. 'Bittervinge said you had the same name as me.'

'I do. Alexandr is my middle name. My father was Steiner as well, and his father before him. I used my middle name to avoid confusion. Be sure to give your own son a different name – perhaps Alexandr?'

Steiner smiled. 'It's a good name.' He paused for moment. 'Will you tell us how to defeat the Emperor?' he said.

'You seek to avenge me?'

'So the Emperor did kill you?' said Felgenhauer quietly. The ghost of Alexandr nodded.

'I was desperate to kill Bittervinge and remove the taint of dragons from Vinterkveld once and for all, but the Emperor wanted to capture it, harness it, learn from it. We disagreed. Violently.'

'How did he defeat you while you were wielding this?' asked Steiner, hefting the black iron sledgehammer.

'He lied to me and held me close, then stabbed me in the back with the Ashen Blade. I wilted and died in moments.'

'The Ashen Blade,' repeated Steiner. 'Bittervinge told me it's the only way to kill the Emperor.'

The ghost of Alexandr considered this a moment.

By now 'I imagine he has mastered all four of the arcane schools: Plamya, Voda, Vozdukha, and Zemlya. He will be largely impervious to everything and anything you can bring to bear on him.'

'Surely he knows this?' said Felgenhauer.

'He does. He is counting on it.'

'How do we get the blade?' asked Steiner.

'There is another blade, an identical one—'

'I know this,' said Steiner impatiently, 'but I can't very well go hunting through Izhoria for Veles to claim it for myself.'

The ghost of Alexandr turned to Silverdust.

'You have not told him. Why not?'

'Not told him what?' said Felgenhauer.

Silverdust would have sighed had he still had lungs. *Kimi has the other Ashen Blade. She would not release it to me. She seeks to kill the Emperor with it in order to avenge her father's death.*

They stood in the ruins of the catacombs a moment, no one knowing what to say following Alexandr's revelation. Steiner's feeling of powerlessness was almost tangible.

'You must face the Emperor, you three, and wrestle the blade from him by strength or cunning. The way ahead will not be easy. Boyar Sokolov has sold you out, but you can still make it through to the palace if you work together.'

'The bastard,' muttered Steiner. 'How do you know of the Boyar?'

'One has arrived recently from the other side. He brought news of the living.'

'Who?' asked Steiner. A moment later a second ghostly form appeared beside Alexandr, drawing a strangled sob from Steiner.

'Marek,' whispered Felgenhauer with tears in her eyes. She put an arm around Steiner's shoulders.

'No need to rescue me now, my son. I am taking my rest.'

'No,' croaked Steiner. He stumbled forward to grip the apparition of his father, but his fingers met nothing but the chill of the grave. Marke spoke.

'Concentrate on ending Volkan Karlov. He seeks to end our line – you and Kjellrunn. Do this for me. Don't let everything we have endured be in vain.'

Steiner nodded wordlessly, sinking to his knees, brought low by his grief. Felgenhauer stood behind him, a hand on his shoulder.

'I must go now, but I send all my love and all my strength to you both.' He smiled fondly at Felgenhauer and Steiner.

The apparitions smiled once more and the ghosts of Marek and Steiner Alexandr Vartiainen faded from sight, leaving them in the dank depths of the catacombs.

'We will see you again.'

Steiner covered his face with hands and let the frustration and grief course through him. 'If I'd just moved faster I might have—'

No one ever did well out of the game you are playing, Steiner. Silverdust drew near and laid a hand on Steiner's shoulder. *Now is not the time to punish yourself. Volkan Karlov has done that for you.*

They stood in silence for a time before Felgenhauer turned to Silverdust. 'Why did Alexandr call you the Emperor's teacher?'

Because it was I, in a moment of folly and hubris, who thought I knew better than my Spriggani elders. It was I who first taught Volkan Karlov the arcane. Vinterkveld has been paying the price for my mistake ever since.

'Without you there'd be no Holy Synod,' said Felgenhauer, and Silverdust felt the note of accusation in her tone keenly.

If the dragons had been exterminated as the Emperor insisted, there would be no witchsign.

'Let's not argue,' said Steiner, rising to his feet and dashing the tears from his face with the back of his hand. 'Great-grandfather said we had to work together, remember? We may not be able to count on Kimi to do right by us, but we can do right by each other.'

We should press on. Time is not on our side.

The cinderwraith, the blacksmith's son, and the former Vigilant headed deeper into the darkness, praying for a way back to the light.

CHAPTER THIRTY-ONE

Kimi

People often ask me which of the enchanted weapons or artefacts was the most powerful. Surely it was Steiner's sledgehammer? Perhaps Streig's two-handed sword? And let us not forget Kimi carrying an Ashen Blade and the Ashen Torment, or Taiga's dagger and sickle? What was most powerful during the uprising, the most influential, people ask, and I reply, 'None of them.' Willingness was what saw people through, for without willingness the first step is unthinkable.

– From the memoir of Drakina Tveit,
Lead Librarian of Midtenjord Province

Kimi and Taiga had prayed for a miracle from Frøya and tried to sleep as best they could but Tief remained unconscious. His bruises looked worse with each passing hour and the shingle beach provided a poor bed to sleep on. A cold wind swept in from the Ashen Gulf and the crash of restless waves was an unfitting lullaby. Kimi rolled on to her back to gaze up at the first stars of evening, but the skies only promised rain.

'Perhaps divine intervention isn't possible,' she said. 'Or perhaps we've fallen out of favour.'

'I suppose we had the shrine in Izhoria,' said Taiga sadly. The high priestess had also been trying to sleep, but now she propped her head up on one hand. 'And there were sacrifices.' She reached over and stroked her brother's forehead. 'We could try again, I suppose?'

It was then that the riot on the beach broke out as the last of the small boats headed back to the ship. Kimi and Taiga stood their ground, protecting Tief with weapons in hand, but none of the refugees came close to their simple camp. Neither princess or high priestess had felt like praying after the riot and night fell on the chilly cove. Later, after they'd eaten, the wind chased away the clouds, revealing an expanse of dark blue sky laden with silver stars. The crescent moon put Kimi in mind of Taiga's silver sickle, but she couldn't bring herself to hope it was a good omen.

'Maybe he'll be better tomorrow,' said Taiga, stirring up the embers of the campfire, before settling down to sleep.

The pack animals had not kept the dragons sated for long. Namarii, Stonvind, and Flodvind had set out at dawn in order to dine on fish and Kimi watched them return with a sense of awe. Stonvind's injuries still troubled him. The grey dragon landed well enough, but he walked slowly and slept often. Namarii and Flodvind had weathered their share of punishment from the father of dragons too, but neither had suffered the indignity of being slammed into the ground as their kin had.

These people are going nowhere. Namarii eyed the refugees who had returned to the top of the cliff to watch the dragons as they came in to land. *Would it really be so terrible—*

'No people!' said Taiga. 'Black, white, or brown. Believers or non-believers. It makes no difference to me. No one is being eaten!'

'Come on,' said Kimi. It was the first time she had addressed the dark brown dragon since they had fled Khlystburg. 'You want to eat? I'll find you a few scraps.'

Where are we going? Namarii released a low growl but Kimi wondered if the creature was hiding behind anger to mask his anxiety.

'To the city.' She took a repurposed saddle and slung it around Namarii's neck, making sure the buckles held fast. 'If you're not too afraid?'

Dragons do not feel fear. Namarii flapped his wings in irritation but Kimi was unperturbed.

'I suppose that was just a healthy sense of self-preservation you were displaying when we fought Bittervinge.' She let out a low mocking laugh as she climbed into the saddle.

I do not enjoy the tone you are taking with me, Your Highness.

'And Stonvind didn't enjoy being left twisting in the wind by his friend,' replied Kimi as the dragon scaled the cliff.

He did not twist in the wind. He fell from the sky.

'It was a figure of speech, you idiot reptile,' replied Kimi as she rolled her eyes.

Namarii growled again, then launched himself into the air so violently Kimi had to cling on to the saddle's cantle. The refugees from the city ran in all directions, certain their time had come, but it seemed Taiga's proscription held fast, even with a creature as arrogant as Namarii.

Namarii brought four corpses back to Stonvind at the cove and deposited them before his kin with his head held low. They hadn't needed to go far into the city to find bodies.

'I said no people!' said Taiga angrily.

'They were already dead,' replied Kimi. 'And no one is coming to bury them.'

Namarii had kept his head bowed during their exchange and Stonvind roused himself and stood up.

I am sorry, Stonvind. I failed you. Bittervinge outsmarted me in the air and I did not return fast enough to protect you in a moment of need.

Stonvind snatched up the nearest corpse with a jerk of his head. A moment later and it was gone. Kimi doubted he even chewed the body.

The humans, the ones who use the arcane, work in Troikas. Stonvind cast his words into the minds of everyone present. *And that is how it must be for us. A dragon does not have friends, you say. A dragon does not scout, you say. A dragon only keeps company with those they find useful.* Stonvind snorted a black plume of smoke that let everyone know exactly what he felt about that. *That is Bittervinge's way of thinking. We have to be better than that.*

'Well said.' Taiga was smiling broadly at the dark grey dragon. 'Now eat up the rest of these corpses before they start to spoil.' Kimi felt a little sick as Stonvind made the next three bodies disappear as quickly as the first one had.

'Would you like to say anything, Your Highness?' said Taiga. 'Now that we're all here.' All eyes turned to Kimi, and Namarii withdrew a little way.

'It seems to me,' said Kimi, 'that I've been failing you too. At first I was afraid you would get hurt, and then I was afraid we couldn't defeat Bittervinge, and I lost faith in myself and the goddess.' She rubbed her eye and told herself it was the campfire smoke. 'I lived underground for five years, working in a forge with no hope of escape. Now I find myself thrust into impossible situations, with incredible beings, but I'm just a young woman from Yamal grieving her father.'

You are the slayer of Veles, replied Namarii, lowering his head in deference.

You are the one who fed us in the darkness, replied Stonvind.

You have always been queen of your own destiny, replied Flodvind.

'That may be true but there's something else,' said Kimi.

'It's time I started using all the advantages I have available.'
She unsheathed a short dagger and a trail of ashes fluttered
to the ground. 'No matter how distasteful I find them.'

Namarii growled, *Let us defeat Bittervinge together.*

Stonvind reared up. *No more fear, no more hesitation.*

Flodvind nodded once. *With all the means at our disposal.*

Taiga held out her arms to the princess and they embraced
a moment.

'Be careful where you point that thing,' whispered Taiga,
glancing from the corner of her eye at the Ashen Blade. Kimi
sheathed the dull grey knife.

'Now let's pray to the goddess for Tief's safe return,' said
Kimi. 'And let's do it properly this time.'

CHAPTER THIRTY-TWO

Ruslan

It is impossible to fully relate just how badly the city of Khlystburg suffered during that time. The leviathan's passing caused a series of great waves that battered the docks and surrounding streets. All the while Bittervinge continued attacks across the city, setting fire to buildings and causing them to collapse. Refuse began to mount up along with the corpses of the fallen and disease became rife. Khlystburg had always been an unforgiving city, but there had been rules its people could understand. At that time there was simply chaos and uncertainty.

– From the memoir of Drakina Tveit,
Lead Librarian of Midtenjord Province

There was nothing beautiful about the docks of Khlystburg. There was nothing beautiful about any dock in any town or city as far as Ruslan could remember, though he would be the first to admit he was not well travelled.

'But this,' he said to himself as he stood on a choked street that led to the sea. 'This is carnage.' The wrecks of three Imperial galleons floated in the water, burned and smashed. Once they had represented everything noble and proud about the Solmindre Empire: masts bearing the finest canvas, stout hulls seemingly impervious to marauders or pirates. The Stormtide Prophet had reduced them to empty hulks, drifting in endless flotsam. Festering corpses floated in the water, promising a feast for the fishes and crustaceans who lingered in the depths. The piers had been abandoned, the stacked cargo left unguarded and untouched except by the water. The leviathan had thrown up vast wave after vast wave, all rushing inshore with feverish intensity.

'The prophet's leviathan,' said Ruslan, scanning the horizon for a glimpse of the colossal creature. Nothing, just the becalmed waters of the bay and a drowning silence. Ships had been left at their moorings, no longer under the watchful eyes of their first mates, given up as lost by their captains.

'Never in all my days,' whispered Ruslan, uneasy in the silence that bathed the two-mile stretch of the waterfront. Only the rats went about their business seemingly untroubled by recent events.

Ruslan, now shorn of his master, sought to make use of himself. He grinned as his eye fell on the strange form of a dark red frigate with a burned prow. The missing masts left him in no doubt it was the vessel he sought. He'd paid a good deal of coin in a handful of taverns learning and checking the rumours. This was the *Watcher's Wait*, ramshackle though she was, chosen ship of the Stormtide Prophet.

The wind gusted fitfully across the waterfront, bringing with it a snatch of music played on a stringed instrument. Ruslan headed towards it, straining to hear which direction it came from.

'Ruslan.' The voice came from behind him, as familiar as his hands or the tongue in his mouth. He turned to the Boyar with a look of disgust on his face. Sokolov was a pale, haggard shadow on a pale, haggard street. The look of pained nobility he so often wore had been replaced by one of shock and grieving.

'Ruslan, I have made a mistake. I failed Dimitri and I have failed you.'

'And now Steiner and his aunt are paying the price for it.' Ruslan clenched his hands into fists. 'Get away from here. Crawl back to Vend Province if you can.'

'What will you do now?' asked the Boyar softly.

'Why should I tell you? So you can haul yourself before the Emperor and prostrate yourself some more?'

'I want to help,' said Sokolov. 'I want to set right the wrong I have done.'

'Your conscience never troubled you before, why the change of heart?'

'I have no conscience of my own, Ruslan. Only you. I should have listened to you.'

'I'm going to seek out the Stormtide Prophet.' Ruslan glowered at the Boyar, hating himself for obeying, even after everything that had happened at court. 'I'm going to find her and tell her how much danger her brother is in. I can't save him, but she might be able to.' He took off without a moment's hesitation.

Romola's crew had holed up at an inn. The building had been abandoned when the sea had broken upon the docks. It was impossible to know how high the waves had been, but the waterfront was littered with debris and plenty of ground-floor windows were now shattered. The leviathan's passing had extracted a terrible price from Khlystburg.

Ruslan found a woman of mixed blood sitting on a chair outside the inn. She strummed an instrument and hummed softly. Ruslan stopped to listen, taking in the deerskin boots and many bangles of jet and copper about her wrists. Her black hair reached past her shoulders while her skin was neither pale nor dark brown but somewhere in between. Ruslan swallowed hard and blushed as he entertained thoughts he'd not had for many a year.

'Came for the music, right?' She smiled at him with a note of challenge or mockery, Ruslan wasn't sure which.

'I have news for the prophet, Kjellrunn.' Ruslan knew he was staring but couldn't help himself.

'That's her name: the Stormtide Prophet.' The dark-skinned woman strummed another chord on the instrument. 'You haven't seen too many people like me before, have you?'

'I'm from Vend Province,' said Ruslan, almost apologetically. 'My name is Ruslan. Steiner is in danger. I need to tell his sister.'

'Well, Ruslan from Vend Province.' The pirate, for that's surely what she was, stopped playing and stood up. 'You'd best come inside, right. And you can bring your friend with you.' She nodded to a point behind him and Ruslan realized the Boyar must have followed like a whipped dog.

'He's not with me. He's the reason Steiner is in danger. He's a worthless son of a—'

'I get the idea,' said the pirate. She beckoned with a finger. Maybe she wasn't a musician? Ruslan felt less sure of himself with each moment. He was more used to following orders than making his own.

'Who are you?' A gaunt young girl with black tattoos that spiralled over her shoulders and arms blocked the doorway. She had a shock of black hair and a sour look about her. Ruslan answered her.

'Weapons?' she asked.

'I have none,' replied Ruslan.

'Then you're more brave than you look,' replied the black-clad girl. 'Or touched in the head.'

'This is Trine,' said the pirate with a cheerful smile. 'She's only sixteen but she's killed more people than anyone else I know. Well, assuming I don't count the prophet herself.' She took a moment to consider this, then abandoned her thoughts with a shrug and pushed past the raven-haired girl with the spiral tattoos. Trine scowled at both of them and stalked to a spot near the staircase.

'We're still recovering from our first night in port,' said the pirate, waving a hand at the chaotic and waterlogged scene as Ruslan followed her inside. The main common room of the inn was littered with men and women in various states. They ran the gamut of fast asleep to wary wakefulness, and covered a continuum from merely hungover to still quite drunk.

'This is the fearsome crew of the *Watcher's Wait*?' asked Ruslan, feeling more than a touch disappointed.

'Fearsome, dreadful fearsome,' repeated the pirate. 'Every one of them a bloodthirsty killer and ne'er-do-well. I'm their captain. My friends call me Romola but you can call me sir.'

Ruslan nodded, unsure if the woman was gaming with him or not. The whole scene had the vividness and weirdness of a particularly strange dream. Boyar Sokolov entered the common room and took a seat, staring at the pirates with disbelieving eyes. It was then that Kjellrunn Vartiainen descended the stairs: enemy of the Solmindre Empire, priestess of a proscribed religion, the Stormtide Prophet herself. She was clad in black vestments and her blonde hair was tied back from her face. There was nothing ornate or special about her but Ruslan dropped to one knee on instinct.

'We have to keep this one,' said Romola. 'He is just adorable.'

'Like a puppy,' slurred a drunk pirate with deep red hair. Kjellrunn struggled not to smile and shook her head.

'Ruslan, was it?' She spoke softly and her voice was husky in a way that suggested she had been sleeping until just a few moments ago.

'Perhaps it would be best if I explained why we are here,' said the Boyar, rising from his seat and drawing himself up to his full height.

'Perhaps it would be best if you sat your old bones down,' said Romola. 'The prophet will speak to you when she's ready.'

The Boyar opened his mouth to say more but decided against it as Romola drew an expensive-looking fencing sword.

'I was at the Imperial Palace yesterday,' said Ruslan.

'You can stand up now,' said Kjellrunn. She looked exhausted, her complexion faded to the point of translucency, her blonde hair the colour of palest ashes. Ruslan did as he was told.

'I was at the Palace yesterday. I heard the Emperor has hatched a plan to cause trouble for your brother, Steiner.' Ruslan glanced at his former master, unsure of just how much he wanted to say. 'Your brother was given directions to the catacombs beneath the palace, but he was sold a lie. The catacombs hold only death.'

'And how is it' – Romola circled Ruslan – 'that a peasant like you finds himself in the presence of the Emperor?'

'I was there in service to my former master,' replied Ruslan. 'It was he that—'

The Boyar lurched from his chair and crossed the room in two quick strides. He took Ruslan by the arm but stopped suddenly as Kjellrunn lunged forward to press her knife beneath his throat.

'I've lost count of how many Imperial lackeys I've killed.' Kjellrunn's soft and husky voice had been replaced by something altogether more demanding. 'One more won't trouble my conscience so greatly.' A tense moment passed and Ruslan was sure his former master would do something to warrant a slashed throat.

'Sit. Down.' Kjellrunn's unblinking gaze brooked no refusal and Sokolov shrank backwards.

'I run a ship,' said Romola, her gaze fixed on Kjellrunn. 'We work on land and we work on water, right.' She looked around at the huddled mass of hungover crew mates. 'We don't work in catacombs. Especially catacombs beneath the Imperial Palace.'

Kjellrunn nodded; then her eyes glazed over. She took a stumbling step before Ruslan caught her. Trine darted across the room in a heartbeat, fixing him with the blackest of looks.

'I'm fine,' said Kjellrunn, and for a brief moment Ruslan saw a young girl rather than a person of legend standing before him.

'Perhaps you should sit down?' suggested Romola. Kjellrunn took the pirate captain's advice and held her head in her hands.

'I was expecting more than this,' complained the Boyar. 'Drunk pirates and peasant girl who can barely stand.'

'Have you ever brought an entire port to a standstill, my lord?' asked Kjellrunn.

'No.' Boyar Sokolov fidgeted in his chair.

'I thought not.' Kjellrunn looked up and caught the Boyar in another hard, unblinking gaze. 'It's not easy. The amount of concentration required is staggering. And so you find me staggered. You will not always find me like this.'

'We should burn him,' said Trine, and flames began to dance around her hands.

'Stop that,' said Kjellrunn softly. 'It's not good for you.'

Trine looked crestfallen but bowed her head in obedience.

'What will you do now? asked Ruslan.

'What I've always intended to do since I set out from Dos Khor,' replied Kjellrunn. 'I'm going to save my family.'

CHAPTER THIRTY-THREE

Silverdust

*The Emperor Volkan Karlov was a man of contradictions.
On the one hand he wanted all appearance of the arcane removed
from Vinterkveld, and yet there remained a part of him that
wanted to show off the enchanted artefacts of an earlier age. It
was his way of proving he had wrestled order out of chaos across
the provinces. The minor artefacts he displayed in the Great
Library at Arkiv, and even some of these were merely relics with
no noticeable arcane power. The artefacts that really mattered,
the ones with power, either cultural or arcane, he hid away.
Those artefacts he placed in a vault, so it was said, a vault with
an Impassable Gate, though few believed it really existed.*

            – From the memoir of Drakina Tveit,
            Lead Librarian of Midtenjord Province

'Now I know what it was like to live in the forges beneath
Vladibogdan,' said Felgenhauer. They had been walking for
hours, trying to make sense of the winding passages beneath
the Imperial Palace.

'This could be nothing more than tunnels and caverns that
lead nowhere,' complained Steiner. 'The way ahead could be
blocked following the subsidence and collapse.'

You have a point, but your great-grandfather assured us we could enter the Palace this way.

'I'd prefer it if he was here to show us the way,' said Felgenhauer. She sat down at the base of a statue ten feet high.

As would I. I am amazed he was able to manifest for as long as he did, and that you were both able to see him.

The torchlight flickered and the shadows danced, revealing a stone dragon leering in the gloom. Water dripped down walls of unworked stone, and a muddy slurry made footing unreliable.

'My feet hurt,' said Felgenhauer. 'We should eat.' She climbed on to the plinth of the statue, leaving muddy scuff marks on the stone.

You should rest. You are both exhausted.

'No use finally getting to the palace only to be dead on our feet,' said Steiner. 'Oh, sorry, Silverdust. I didn't mean . . .'

It is of no consequence.

'What is that?' Felgenhauer grimaced and rubbed her temples as Steiner joined her on the statue's plinth. 'It's like the pressure that builds before a storm but . . .'

There are arcane sources close by. I feel them too, though I cannot decide if they are artefacts or something else.

'We'd best reach the palace soon,' said Steiner, rooting though his pack. 'Because I didn't bring much food. I had no idea the tunnels could go on for so long.'

Steiner and Felgenhauer ate in silence. Silverdust felt the turmoil of their minds quieten before they fell asleep, huddling around the feet of the stone dragon; he hoped it wasn't an omen of things to come. If the food ran out before they found a way forward there would be nothing anyone could do to avoiding starving to death.

The silence was absolute in the depths beneath the palace and Silverdust was left with his thoughts and the presence of arcane power, close at hand yet enigmatic.

Sleep now. Rest. You will need all your strength to face Volkan Karlov.

And so aunt and nephew slept in the deep darkness beneath the palace, huddled together, muddied, bloodied, and bruised.

The halo of pale light that played around Silverdust's feet was one of the more unusual side effects of such pronounced mastery of the arcane, though he barely needed the light to see. His mind was better able to pierce the darkness and sense the minds of anyone who might venture near.

Or any*thing*.

It was the growing feeling of hunger that alerted him to the creatures' presence. Silverdust had not needed to eat in decades, and had neither the stomach nor inclination to feed on anything save the arcane itself. And yet still the feeling of hunger grew.

Steiner! Felgenhauer!

It was not his own hunger he felt; the hunger was outside of himself and it was close, so close he could almost taste it, like raw meat.

Quickly!

Steiner lurched to his feet in a daze, but months of crossing the continent and fighting had his mind working instinctively. His hand already gripped the sledgehammer and he blinked and squinted into the darkness.

'Where?'

'And what?' added Felgenhauer.

Silverdust summoned a lance of fire in his hand and threw it into the darkness. The lance followed the direction they had come from, illuminating the jagged walls, glittering from the ever-dripping water. For a heartbeat there was movement before the arcane lance crashed into the wall and extinguished itself in a shower of sparks. Bone-coloured legs were revealed briefly, and black eyes glittered before the light died out.

'Corpse spiders,' muttered Steiner. He jumped down from the plinth and pulled on his pack.

What are they?

But Felgenhauer and Steiner were already running, trying their best not to slip and fall in the muck underfoot. Silverdust threw another lance of fire, ahead of them this time, to light their way.

'They're behind us!' said Steiner.

I would prefer to avoid an ambush.

The tunnel ahead was clear and the arcane light revealed crude brickwork; an archway beckoned them from a hundred feet away, though what lay beyond remained a mystery. The arcane lance hit the wall and exploded in a dozen tongues of fire that sizzled as they died.

'Come on, Silverdust!' shouted Steiner.

The cinderwraith, who had spent decades disguising his gait as a walk, flew into the air and sped along the tunnel, passing overhead. His right hand gestured a silver beacon of light for his friends to follow, and it was with some relief the space beyond the archway was revealed to be empty and silent.

'Dammit,' wheezed Steiner as he fled from the corpse spiders. Scuttling legs scrabbled on the stony walls and splashed in the mud. Silverdust cast carefully aimed javelins of fire at the sides of the tunnel, hoping to deter the creatures, who ran on bone-coloured legs with tips like spear points.

Do not look back. Run! Run!

Felgenhauer made it through the archway first. She turned and raised her hands, then pressed inwards, as if crushing an unseen object between her palms. Steiner ran through a second later, the corpse spiders trailing him by a dozen feet, mandibles chattering, eyes like shards of jet staring with malevolence.

Dust drifted down from the archway, which began to shake and rattle. Steiner stared at his aunt in disbelief.

'Don't just stand there!' she yelled through gritted teeth. Beads of sweat appeared on her forehead.

Silverdust flung another javelin of arcane light through the archway, immolating the lead corpse spider. The hard shell crisped and split open with a popping sound, leaving the creature a blackened ruin. Two of the corpse spider's kin stopped to pick over the remains, fighting one another for the spoils, but another seven of the pale creatures surged forward.

Steiner swung his sledgehammer at the archway's column and was rewarded with a shower of stone dust that almost choked him. Felgenhauer's hands were shaking with the effort. Her lips moved silently, begging the stone to move, cajoling, threatening. Steiner swung again and the sledgehammer ricocheted from the stone, sending him stumbling backwards just as the first corpse spider made it to the archway.

Felgenhauer shouted a wordless cry and the passage was filled with falling stone, thundering down in the darkness, the sound of rock and rubble a deafening din. The passage was filled with swirling dust.

I can sense you, but I cannot see you. I can feel pain.

'I'm still here,' yelled Steiner, though Silverdust could sense his shock at surviving such a close call. 'Aunt Nika?'

Nika? Silverdust could scarcely believe someone was using the former Matriarch-Commissar's first name.

'I told you never to call me that,' came a reply somewhere close by in the cloud of dust. 'It makes me feel like I should be a hundred and two years old and wearing a headscarf like some old *kozel* at the market.'

Silverdust summoned a handful of arcane light which helped cut through the miasma, if only slightly. Sprawled on her back was Felgenhauer, holding one hand to her chest protectively. A corpse spider had managed to get through the archway, but not before the falling stone had smashed the life from it.

'It must have collided with me as it came through,' she said, wincing.

'Tell me it didn't bite you!' said Steiner. Silverdust could feel his rising panic.

'I can't say for sure.' Felgenhauer showed them her hand. A ragged gash had parted her palm from wrist to smallest finger. 'It might have been the stone.'

Silverdust had known Felgenhauer a long time on Vladibogdan. She had done her best during that time to remain a closed book to his arcane senses, and for the most part she had succeeded. Now, deep beneath the Imperial Palace, with no clear way ahead, he felt her fear and her despair, and also her desperation. She was desperate to stay alive for her nephew. Determined.

Water. Silverdust pointed at Steiner and he complied immediately. They washed the wound and the cinderwraith held up a single finger. Silver light flared brightly.

I am going to cauterize the wound in the hopes I also burn out any remaining poison. Do you understand?

Felgenhauer paled and nodded without a word.

'And may Frejna's eye not find you,' prayed Steiner.

Hold her wrist tightly. This will not be pleasant. The bright silver light edged closer to the gashed palm and Felgenhauer looked away before an agonized scream shattered the silence.

'Where is Steiner?' was the first thing Felgenhauer said when she woke from her faint. The great cloud of stone dust had subsided and any surviving corpse spiders remained silent beyond the scene of the cave-in.

He decided to scout ahead. You know how he is: impulsive and restless. Much like his mother at that age if my memory serves me correctly.

Felgenhauer forced a smile but said nothing; she held out

the wounded and burned hand as if it might suddenly shatter like glass.

He is desperate to keep you safe after losing his father, just as you are desperate to protect your nephew.

'Uh, Marek,' said Felgenhauer with a weariness that had nothing to do with her hand or her tiredness. 'Now I'll never really be able to make things right with him.'

Why would you need to? Silverdust could sense a great bitterness beneath her words.

'I never wanted Akulina to settle down with a soldier. I thought he was beneath her.'

I understood Vigilants did not take spouses. That was always my experience.

'The more enterprising individuals never really obeyed that particular doctrine.' Felgenhauer smiled. 'And some entered into marriages of sorts with other Vigilants.'

But Exarch Felgenhauer chose a soldier.

'Exarch.' Nika Felgenhauer covered her eyes with her good hand to stop Silverdust seeing her tears, but he felt them all the same. 'I forgot she was the same rank as you.' She sighed. 'She loved him so much. And in time she chose Marek over the Empire.' A tight sob escaped her. 'And over me.'

And Marek knew of your disapproval?

'Almost certainly,' replied Felgenhauer. 'Akulina had the strength to do what I failed to for years. She had the strength to leave the Synod before I did.'

But you did leave the Holy Synod.

'I was forced to defect in order to survive; it's hardly the same thing.'

And your sister returned.

'She returned so the Empire wouldn't hunt her down and find her family. Even that revealed a strength I could only wonder at.'

So your way of making amends to her is to keep Steiner safe.

'Amends.' Felgenhauer got to her feet. 'I'll never really know if she forgives me for how I was back then.'

Then allow me. I see your efforts to protect Steiner and they are nothing short of miraculous. You have put everything at risk for him. Your sister could ask nothing else of you.

Felgenhauer brushed away her tears and looked up into the mirror mask for a moment. 'Thank you, Silverdust.' She forced a brave smile. 'We should go and see what the young idiot has got himself into, or all this talk of forgiveness will be for nothing.'

As you wish.

They followed the corridor by the light that danced around Silverdust's feet. The darkness was always close at hand, and only the occasional sound of rippling water disturbed the silence. They had been walking for perhaps half an hour when a shimmering orange light appeared in the gloom ahead. The glow became rectangular, reflecting from the sides of a doorway.

'Steiner?'

They turned into a room at least fifty feet wide, and the ceiling was just as high overhead. In the centre of the room, standing before a staircase, was Steiner, who looked upon two vast double doors on the far side. The doors were the colour of a dark blue sea.

Steiner! Cover your eyes!

Silverdust turned away, though he could feel himself being drawn into the shapes and sigils that rippled and writhed across the surface of the doors. Felgenhauer stared in wonder and began to sag, almost sinking to her knees with a look of agony on her face.

Cover your eyes! But Felgenhauer was unable to move, unable to even breathe. Silverdust slipped a gloved hand over her face and she gasped in shock.

'I've closed them!' she shouted. 'What is that?'

It is the Impassable Gate. This is the vault where the Emperor discarded the artefacts of antiquity.

'I thought that was just a myth!' replied Felgenhauer. 'What is it doing to Steiner?'

I have no idea. We may already be too late.

CHAPTER THIRTY-FOUR

Kjellrunn

Not every Vigilant is a born killer, but those who survive the training at Vladibogdan are well acquainted with death. Still, the most successful Vigilants are either accomplished operators in the political field or ruthless agents of the Empire, unafraid of getting their hands dirty. There is a good reason for the Vigilant's leather coat to be dyed crimson. It makes the blood-stains harder to spot.

– From the memoir of Drakina Tveit,
Lead Librarian of Midtenjord Province

A common room full of hungover pirates, complete with a pompous but broken Boyar and his seemingly hapless aide, was not conducive to a restful environment, Kjellrunn decided. She had headed upstairs at the inn and Trine had dutifully followed. The two girls slept for a time, curled up like two cats. Kjellrunn jerked awake, her head full of half-remembered dreams and the profound sense Steiner needed her immediately. Despite the respite she remained exhausted, every limb leaden, her senses dull.

'Kjell?' Trine blinked a few times and yawned.

'We need to go.' Her eyes wandered over Trine's exposed

neck and shoulders; her tunic had drifted to one side revealing the soot-coloured marks that crawled across her pale skin. 'And I need you to stop using your powers.'

'That's ridiculous.' Trine turned away, trying to hide the hurt expression that flitted across her face.

'I'm serious,' replied Kjellrunn. 'I know you have a score to settle with the Empire, but it'll be for nothing if you don't survive the process.'

Trine scowled but said nothing.

'Now help me up, please.' A dark and fearful feeling descended on her as she slipped her feet over the side of the bed. 'Something is coming.'

'Right, you old sea dogs.' Romola gave the crew a hard look. 'You feed up and then it's all hands out on the docks looking for salvage. I want some new masts on the *Wait* by the end of the day or I'll want to know why, right?'

'The end of the day?' said Rylska, looking horrified.

'Just find me some new masts,' said Romola. 'We'll worry about fixing the ship come the morning. And no more booze!'

The crew mumbled their agreement and roused themselves as Kjellrunn and Trine descended the stairs.

'You don't look a whole lot better than you did when you went up,' said Romola to Kjellrunn softly.

'She's fine,' snapped Trine.

'And you.' Romola pointed at the black marks on Trine's neck and shoulders. 'Are you "fine"?'

The raven-haired girl stepped forward to reply but Kjellrunn raised her arm to keep them apart.

'Please. Just eat something,' she said. 'And bring me something too. I'll need my strength if we're to rescue Steiner.'

Trine skulked towards the kitchen, where Ruslan had prepared some food with limited help from the Boyar. She glared over her shoulder at Romola as she went.

'You're sure you won't come with me?' said Kjellrunn to the captain.

'This is as far as I go.' Romola looked away. 'I have a feeling I'll regret this decision, but at least I'll be alive to regret it. I've already lost half my crew and two masts. No telling what else I might lose if I venture further into Khlystburg, right?'

'I understand.' Flashes of Kjellrunn's dream came back to her, ghosts in the darkness. 'Do you think our parents wait for us in the afterlife?'

'I, uh . . .' Romola didn't have an answer for the abrupt change of subject.

'Or maybe we're all reborn as cats and crows, sent back to watch over those we love.'

'Kjellrunn.' Romola took the girl by the shoulders gently. 'You're not making much sense.'

'Or maybe we just keep coming back, over and over, born into different bodies, living different lives, dying different deaths.' Kjellrunn's gaze drifted across the room, taking in each one of the crew as if it was the last time she might see them.

'Perhaps you should sit down and have some water.' Romola gestured to Rylska, who fetched a jug and mug and brought it over.

'What body would you like to have next time?' Kjellrunn asked dreamily.

'Think I'd like to stay attached to this one, right.' Romola looked around for Trine. 'And my mind too, for that matter. Kjellrunn, you've been pushing yourself so hard. I know your powers come from the goddesses, but perhaps there's only so much this body can take.'

Kjellrunn closed her eyes and her head drooped forward though her eyes remained open. Her body was heavy and nothing happened when she tried to stand.

'Stay here,' said Romola to Rylska. 'Don't let anyone near

her.' She stood up and went to the kitchen just as Trine came through the door with a bowl of broth in each hand.

'She was asking me what happens after we die. I'm not sure she really knows what she's saying.'

'It'll be fine,' replied Trine. 'She's fine. We're both fine.'

The Boyar followed close behind the dark-haired girl; he gave the captain a pained look and continued on his way.

'Where are you going?' asked the captain, but Sokolov didn't stop, heading out into the tide-ravaged street instead.

'May Frejna's eye not find you, and may Frøya hold you close,' mumbled Kjellrunn as he passed her. She sensed a huge weight of grief and regret on the old man's shoulders.

'CAPTAIN!' Rylska used the same tone and volume she usually reserved for the crow's nest. 'We've got a Vigilant come calling,' she said, shrinking back from the doorway. She drew her blade, but they all knew how hard it was to kill a member of the Holy Synod.

And still Kjellrunn couldn't move.

'Frøya. If you're there, please help me.' Romola winced. 'I'm not sure the prophet is going to be of any use to anyone.'

Trine stood up and her hands flickered with arcane fire. 'I think I can handle a lone Vigilant,' she sneered, heading towards the door just as a wagon was thrown across the street and crashed into the front of the inn. Too large to fit through door, the wagon fractured and split. Wood and splinters exploded across the common room, and part of the axle slammed into Trine, felling her immediately.

'We're doomed,' whispered Rylska, staring at the fallen initiate of Frejna in the silence that followed.

'Be quiet!' replied Romola. She glanced out into the street, where the Vigilant approached, step following patient step. His mask was battered and chipped, styled like a snarling wolverine.

'I thought they worked in threes?' whispered Rylska.

'One is more than enough, thank you,' replied Romola, drawing her sword. 'Gods damn it,' she breathed. The chances of escaping Khlystburg were growing slimmer with every moment. The crew cowered behind benches and overturned tables, readying crossbows with worried expressions.

'Where is your prophet now?' shouted a voice from outside.

Kjellrunn trembled as she tried to force her body to do something, anything, but still she sat, helpless. The front of the inn rattled as something heavy impacted against it. The wooden walls cracked and split and the building groaned softly. Dust fluttered from the ceiling above.

'We're sailors!' shouted Romola. 'No prophets here. Just good and loyal citizens of the Empire.'

There was no reply until a large wooden crate shattered against the ruined door jamb. More broken wood showered the common room, settling on Trine's supine form.

'I am Exarch Zima and I have the sight! I know when witchsign is close by, and I know what power feels like.'

'Kjell!' Romola shook Kjellrunn's shoulders just as a shadow fell across the room and the pirates gasped. Standing in the ruined doorway was the Vigilant, terrible in dirty cream and bloody crimson.

'The Emperor will award me an entire province for this,' said Exarch Zima, barely able to keep the gloating out of his voice.

'Frøya save me,' prayed Rylska. She sprang to her feet and lunged, but her strike missed as Exarch Zima jerked backwards. Rylska retreated as Zima stumbled forward, trying to press a hand to his back. Boyar Sokolov stood behind the Exarch, clutching a short yet bloody knife.

'I always hated you,' rasped the old man, pressing his advantage with the knife held high. Zima turned and grabbed the Boyar by the throat, wounded though he was. Sokolov flailed and stabbed Zima in the chest once or twice, but the Exarch did not release his grip. Rylska and Romola lunged forward, hoping to run the Exarch through, but a well-time swipe of his arm deflected both the blades from a metal vambrace. Rylska's blade was knocked from her grip and clattered to the floorboards. The Exarch grabbed Romola's sword arm and pulled her close, slamming his masked face into hers. She fell back, blinded for a second, off balance. When she opened her eyes again she discovered Ruslan had leapt from his hiding place in the kitchen with a cleaver. The Boyar and his former servant tried their best to defeat Zima, but the Exarch was possessed of an unnatural energy. First he caught the Boyar's wrist and forced the blade back towards the man wielding it, slashing Sokolov's throat. Romola staggered to her feet but was too late to stop Ruslan from being punched across the room.

A terrible calm settled on the inn as the Boyar bled out, clutching his neck with a look of shock. Exarch Zima turned to Trine, still supine at the centre of the room.

'Now to gut this pathetic little witch' – Zima brandished Sokolov's blade – 'and put an end to this.'

'She's not the Stormtide Prophet,' said Kjellrunn. 'I am.' Romola gasped in surprise. Kjellrunn was levitating above the floor, her hair fluttering about her head as if caught in a spectral wind. Her eyes were fixed on Trine, unmoving on the floor.

'Everybody out!' yelled Romola, she snatched up Trine's limp body and fled. The pirates dived and stumbled through every doorway and window available. Exarch Zima ignored them all, closing in on the Stormtide Prophet, knife in hand. A terrible grinding sound grew louder and louder, and the building shook until it seemed it must surely collapse. Inside, the furniture was whipped up into the air, caught in a whirlwind of force. Flashes of red and cream could be seen:

shreds of the Vigilant's uniform. Zima was being torn apart in the carnage. Romola looked at Rylska and began to speak, when the very thing she was afraid of came to pass.

The inn gave one final shudder and disintegrated, raining timber across the street.

CHAPTER THIRTY-FIVE

Steiner

People often maintain that ogres and rusalka are merely old tales, told to keep unruly children in line. I find it strange that people can believe Kjellrunn summoned a leviathan, but not that creatures similar to humans might exist.

> – From the memoir of Drakina Tveit,
> Lead Librarian of Midtenjord Province

The double doors were the colour of night. Not the deep black of the skies above Cinderfell, but the darkest blue of summer at midnight. And the symbols: such shimmering, shifting symbols and words. None of them meant a single thing to Steiner, for he'd never been able to read. For him, the letters on a page had always moved, but never like this. There was an entrancing beauty to the midnight doors, and so he had stood before them and taken a moment to drink in the sight of it.

He couldn't tell how long he'd been standing there but Felgenhauer shouted something from behind him. Steiner turned on instinct and found Silverdust shielding his face with one hand and doing the same for his aunt.

'I've closed them!' shouted Felgenhauer. 'What is that?' Something passed between Silverdust and his aunt. Steiner was reminded that not all arcane speech was shared. 'I thought that was just a myth!' replied Felgenhauer. 'What is it doing to Steiner?'

'It's not doing anything to me,' he said as he crossed the room to them.

Steiner?

'Thank Frøya!' said Felgenhauer.

'What's got into you two?'

It is the Impassable Gate, Steiner. A portal inscribed with words and sigils from every language across Vinterkveld. The doors were crafted by Bittervinge himself so that no man or dragon alive could pass without dying a slow and terrible death.

Silverdust had died twice, in his own way. That he should be so agitated and so wary was baffling. 'A slow and terrible death? asked Steiner, genuinely confused. 'What do they say?'

No one knows, but my guess would be combinations of 'lie down and die' or 'stop breathing'.

Steiner looked over his shoulder. The midnight-blue doors flashed and flickered, the sigils and symbols performing their lazy dance.

'I suppose I have got a headache,' Steiner conceded.

'A headache?' asked Felgenhauer incredulously.

'But nothing bad. I've had worse hangovers, to be honest.'

Silverdust and his aunt were still cowering behind their hands, faces turned away from the source of their fear. Steiner shrugged and approached the doors. After some grunting, heaving and colourful language, the doors opened and the writhing symbols faded.

'It's safe now,' he shouted cheerfully.

Steiner! How did you overcome the Impassable Gate? This enchantment was laid down by Bittervinge himself.

'So you said.' Steiner grinned.

Now is not the time for flippancy. Every word on those doors spells death for anyone who looks upon them.

Felgenhauer began to laugh, long peals of helpless laughter that echoed off the walls and sounded down the corridor they had emerged from. Steiner continued grinning and gestured they follow him.

I do not understand.

'I can't read,' said Steiner proudly. 'Ask my aunt. She tried to teach me once. Absolutely useless! All those words, they're only meaningful if you understand them.'

Felgenhauer was still struggling to compose herself. She wrapped an arm about her nephew's shoulder. 'You magnificent illiterate fool.'

'I most certainly am,' said Steiner, entering the Emperor's vault. 'And you're welcome.'

Silverdust wandered away from them and began to light the sconces on the walls. Little by little the room revealed its many secrets to them. It was as big as the antechamber before it, and mounds of trinkets and treasures had been piled up on the flagstones.

'This is like the Great Library on Arkiv,' said Steiner. 'Except with stuff instead of books.'

'This is more than just "stuff",' replied Felgenhauer, her voice full of reverence.

Steiner stood before a glass casket at least twice his own height. Inside, stored in a murky yellow fluid, was a heavy-boned skeleton that towered over him. 'What in Frejna's name is this?'

An ogre. Silverdust approached and his mirror-mask tilted upward to take in the brutish skull of the strange creature. *Ogres lived quietly in the far eastern reaches of what is now known as the Novgoruske Province. The dragons found them great sport and their numbers were greatly reduced in the Age of Fire. It was no great effort for the Emperor to slaughter the last of them, though I begged him not to.*

'Ogres?' Steiner shook his head. 'I've never even heard of them.'

Is that not the way the Emperor works? He does not simply kill, but he erases all trace of those who displease him. Just as he erased me. I happily relinquished my old name and became Silverdust when my mortal body died on Vladibogdan. Now you would be hard pressed to find any mention of me in the histories of the nascent days of the Solmindre Empire.

'I don't suppose there's a spare Ashen Blade down here,' said Felgenhauer with a sardonic smile.

If only that were so. Had the Emperor ever troubled himself to slay Veles, then this is most certainly where he would have kept the blade.

Steiner picked his way carefully through the room, where stuffed animals he had never seen before stared back at him with glass bead eyes. Chests of money glittered, though they contained currencies that Steiner didn't recognize.

'There's a whole world down here that I never knew existed,' he said, lifting the lid on a mahogany crate. A coffin, he realized – too late. The inside contained only dust and bones, and the skull was missing all its teeth.

'I imagine they were knocked out before they died,' said Felgenhauer from over Steiner's shoulder.

'They're missing their finger bones too.' He grimaced in disgust. 'Imagine torturing someone to death and then keeping the body.'

'I can imagine it all too easily when it comes to the Emperor,' replied Felgenhauer. They took a moment to rest on a rug that had undoubtedly belonged to a now extinct tribe. Felgenhauer released a long sigh and slipped into a gentle doze.

I am not convinced I burned all of the poison from her wound. Silverdust loomed over her sleeping form. *I am sorry.*

Steiner nodded but said nothing. He didn't want to think

about a world without Felgenhauer so soon after losing his
father. He crossed the room, keen to find a distraction in
the winding paths that led between armour, paintings, furniture. Another ogre skeleton loomed in a glass casket before
he discovered a mirror almost as tall as himself and stood
before it. The edge was decorated in gold, cast in a pattern
part spiral and part roiling ocean wave.

I see you are enjoying my treasures.

Steiner looked around. The voice that had sounded in his
head was not Silverdust's, nor did it belong to anyone who
had contacted him in such a way before. The surface of the
mirror rippled and the reflection showed a pale man with a
high forehead, attired in black, with pale eyes and a piercing
gaze. There was something unwholesome about the apparition in the mirror, as if death itself had taken form and dressed
in the clothes of a man.

'Volkan Karlov,' said Steiner instinctively, his grip tightening
on the sledgehammer.

The reflection nodded once. *I am here to offer you a truce,
Steiner Vartiainen. You have proven yourself time and again and
even the best of my people do not stop you. Can we not come to some
arrangement? Must we resort to crude violence to settle this ages-old
dispute between our families?*

'You don't have a family,' replied Steiner. 'You just prey on
mine, causing misery with every passing generation.' He struggled to say the words, his throat thick with emotion. 'And
not just my family but all families across Vinterkveld, especially
those with witchsign.'

I simply wish to maintain the natural order.

'There's nothing natural about you.' To Steiner's eyes Volkan
Karlov looked no older than forty. 'It's not natural how you
last down the decades while everyone else grows old. The
way you recruit Vigilants isn't natural, and there's nothing
natural about the Ashen Blade either.'

I can see you won't be reasoned with, so let me try a different tack. You will surrender to me or the life of your father is forfeit.

'Forfeit? He's already dead.'

He is safe. There's barely a scratch on him; you have my word. Volkan Karlov smiled but there was no humour there, no warmth, nothing. Steiner couldn't say how he knew, but something glittered in the Emperor's eyes, something cold and insincere; it was as sharp as any knife and just as unfeeling.

'His shade visited me, along with the shade of my great-grandfather.' Volkan Karlov's ice-cold smile faltered and his eyes flicked away a moment. 'They told me everything.'

Lies. You have no vestiges of the arcane; you cannot commune with the dead. Volkan Karlov's expression soured to a spiteful sneer. Steiner hefted the sledgehammer and rolled his shoulders. *What are you doing?*

The head of the sledgehammer hit the mirror with a crash that startled Felgenhauer from her sleep on the other side of the room. Steiner looked down at the broken pieces of silvery glass, unable to think, unable to even breathe.

Steiner. What has happened?

'The Emperor reached out to me asking for a truce.'

'What did you see in the mirror?' asked Felgenhauer, rubbing sleep from her eyes.

'A liar and and a killer.' The overwhelming sadness for his father rose up and threatened to engulf him, but he fought it down. He would grieve later. 'We've come so far. We have to finish this.' A sound in the antechamber caught his attention. 'Quick! Close the doors.'

All three ran to the Impassable Gate and began to shove as hard as they could. Corpse spiders scuttled from the corridor beyond the antechamber, one after another rattling across the flagstones on chitinous legs.

'They must have found a way around the cave-in,' shouted Steiner as he pushed one of the doors closed, Felgenhauer and Silverdust slammed the other door just as the first of the bone-coloured horrors ventured through. Two of its spindly legs were crushed and the creature hissed in agony.

'What now?' shouted Felgenhaucr as the corpse spiders slammed against the doors.

'There must be another way out,' replied Steiner.

I can sense a breeze, a disturbance in the air. Silverdust moved to the centre of the room and looked upwards, raising his hand to better feel the source. More and more bodies crashed into the doors on the other side and Steiner's feet began to slide.

'There are too many of them!' he shouted. 'Get me something to wedge this shut.'

There! Silverdust pointed to a square of darkness in the ceiling. Steiner hadn't seen it until now, but a small viewing gallery had been built on the level above. Felgenhauer ran from the doors and levitated to the level above, gliding upwards effortlessly.

Now, Steiner. Run!

Steiner did as he was told, but the corpse spiders forced their way through the moment he moved away from the Impassable Gate. A slight gap between the doors appeared, then yawned open to let the unholy creatures into the vault. Silverdust remained at the centre of the vault, casting flaming javelins of arcane light at the breach. The spiders leapt and dodged as they advanced; some were blackened and scorched but they did not relent. Felgenhauer had landed on the level above and reached out for Steiner with both hands. Her mastery of the arcane plucked him from the floor.

'Silverdust!'

The cinderwraith cast another two javelins of fire as the corpse spiders closed with him, before wrenching the mirror mask upwards and unleashing a torrent of fiery breath.

Steiner landed on the viewing gallery with a thump, using

his hand to steady himself. A spider attacking Silverdust began to petrify under Felgenhauer's stern gaze.

'You can't fight all of them!' she shouted.

Silverdust plunged a flaming hand into the jaws of a corpse spider; then he floated up from the ground. The creatures leapt and skittered, but the cinderwraith slipped from the gouging tips of their legs and their champing mandibles. Robbed of their prey, the corpse spiders retreated from the vault, scuttling away with alarming speed.

'I really hate those things,' said Steiner.

'You're not alone,' replied Felgenhauer, looking pale. She rubbed the cauterized cut in hand, prompting a pang of concern from Steiner. 'We'd better move,' she added. 'No knowing when or where they'll next appear.

CHAPTER THIRTY-SIX

Kimi

Some call it the Battle of Khlystburg. The final reckoning between Bittervinge and Kimi's cohort was nothing short of titanic. I have recorded a dozen accounts of the battle in the skies above Khlystburg and while the stories differ many used the same expression time and again. It was as if night had fallen early on the capital city, deep shadows full of terrible purpose. Some say the sunlight was blotted out by the great commotion of dragons' wings. This is why I refer to that aerial battle as Nightfall.

– From the memoir of Drakina Tveit,
Lead Librarian of Midtenjord Province

'We can't do it here,' said Taiga, looking around the cove at the stony shingle. 'I need soil to invoke the goddess.' Rain clouds had crept back across the horizon, threatening a miserable day to anyone by the shoreline. 'Stone is fine but soil, that's where things grow. Soil is renewal.'

Soil. Stonvind prodded Tief with his great snout and gently took his collar between his lips. Slowly, Tief was lifted into the air, and Stonvind climbed up the cliff face. Kimi watched all of this with a shocked fascination.

'It was like—'

'—a mother cat,' provided Taiga with a smile. 'Yes. They continue to surprise me.' The two women gathered their things and headed up the steep cut in the cliffs. Waiting for them at the top were the three dragons, who had cleared an area of refugees.

'There are so many of them now,' said Kimi. She imagined a third of the city must have fled here, praying and pleading for a ship to come.

'Bittervinge must be reaping quite a toll on Khlystburg,' replied Taiga. She caught Kimi's wounded look and added, 'That wasn't a criticism, just speculation. We've lost time, it's true, but we will succeed.'

'The rain will make a lot of problems for these people,' said Kimi, looking towards the darkening skies. 'They don't have tents, and many don't even have a change of clothes.'

'Neither do we,' said Taiga with a wry smile. 'Something I intend to remedy when all this business is finished with.'

'All this business,' repeated Kimi. Taiga had said the words as if slaying the father of dragons and wresting power from the Emperor himself were no more than daily chores. 'I shall have a bath and purchase new dresses,' continued Taiga. It was then that Kimi realized her friend was distracting herself from the monumental task ahead. Stonvind had laid Tief on the patchy grass of the cliff top and retreated twenty feet. Namarii and Flodvind took up positions, forming a triangle around the wounded Spriggani.

'What now?' said Kimi.

'Now we see how good my memory is,' replied Taiga. She took out the silver knife, a weapon given to her by Frøya herself. 'And if those runes on the shrine actually meant anything.'

Kimi felt an awful pang of powerlessness as Taiga carved symbols into the soil around her brother. A delegation of

Yamal diplomats came to watch as the high priestess did this, whispering reverently to themselves. Taiga continued to work, often pausing to take a step back from her work. The symbols took shape at the cardinal points around Tief's slumbering form. More city folk came, intrigued by the Yamal people's interest, putting aside their fear of the dragons to venture closer and satisfy their curiosity. Kimi reached into her tunic and pulled forth the Ashen Torment, holding it between both her palms.

'I turned away from you while I was incarcerated on Vladibogdan,' she prayed quietly. 'And when Taiga and Sundra kept their faith, I did not. Nor did I ask anything from you through those long, dark years.' She pressed her hands together harder, so the hard edges of the Ashen Torment hurt her palms. 'And I'm not going to ask anything from you now, not for myself.' Taiga stood back from the last of the symbols and nodded that she was ready. 'But I'm asking you now, Frøya: return Tief to us so we may prevail against the father of dragons. Restore Stonvind so he may fight in your name.'

'Come on now, Your Highness,' said Taiga brightly, though the high priestess's smile couldn't hide her shaking hands. The rain clouds were overhead now, leaching the colour from the land. 'I barely know why we're trying to revive the truculent old fool. It would be kinder to let him sleep.'

'You don't mean a word of that,' said Kimi as she approached.

'No, I suppose I don't,' replied Taiga. Kimi knew full well how powerful the bond between siblings was. Hadn't Steiner's motivation for leaving Vladibogdan been his sister? Hadn't her own brother caused abject despair when he'd named her as an impersonator? Taiga needed Tief. She'd already had to leave Sundra behind, and that had cost her enough.

'Don't be nervous,' added Kimi. They began to kneel by Tief's feet, when the dragons did something unexpected for the second time that day.

You will all pray to the goddess Frøya! It was not Namarii's voice she heard, or Stonvind, or Flodvind, but all three, joined together in a chord of exhortation. She felt the words as much as heard them.

'But we are praying.'

We were speaking to them. Namarii raised one claw and pointed a single talon, a curiously human gesture. Hundreds of refugees had dropped to their knees, mirroring Taiga and Kimi. Many held hands and a few shared shy smiles. To pray to Frøya was forbidden to Imperial citizens, and Kimi could almost feel the thrill of excitement emanating from the crowd.

Can you feel that? Flodvind enquired of her kin.

Yes. Namarii surveyed the crowd. *A sort of anarchic glee.* No longer would the people of Khlystburg's worship be proscribed by a deathless and uncaring Emperor.

'And now we will pray to the goddess Frøya,' said Taiga, struggling to hold back grateful tears. 'We will pray to be forgiven for turning away from her; for to turn away from Frøya is to turn away from life itself. We will pray for the Emperor's downfall, and an end to Bittervinge. But most of all we will pray that Tief will be returned to us, as vital, hardworking, and cantankerous as he ever was.'

Kimi snorted a laugh and then tried to stifle it. She wasn't sure laughter was a part of prayer, but the city folk evidently saw the humour in Taiga's words and laughed too. It was no bad thing, Kimi decided; laughter was just as much a part of life as suffering and loss.

'I offer no sacrifices,' said Taiga, 'save myself and my continued service. For all of my life, however long that may be.'

'And I offer myself,' said Kimi, moved to speak by Taiga's oath. 'As a new-found servant. For all of my life, however long that may be.'

The sunlight was nothing short of blinding. Where there

had been a chill wind and the promise of rain, now there was golden light falling in diagonal columns from above. The cliff tops blazed in glorious sunshine and a gasp of surprise escaped the crowd.

'She is with us,' said Taiga, tears tracking freely down her cheeks. 'Can you feel it?' Many of the city folk cried out in joy or laughed aloud, raising their hands to catch Frøya's light. Kimi was about to reply that she felt nothing save for the warmth of the sun, but remained quiet and took a moment to search her feelings.

'I feel at peace,' she said. 'No matter my father's death, no matter Tsen's betrayal. I will trust in Frøya and see this through to the end, though it may cost me my life.' Taiga smiled and squeezed Kimi's hand. Slowly they got to their feet and Tief rolled onto his side. He covered his still-shut eyes with one arm.

'Uh. I've got a real headache,' he mumbled. After a few moments he sat up and stared at the two women standing over him. A huge shout of joy went up from the crowd of city folk, and the dragons all released plumes of fire into the air.

'What in Hel's name is going on?' said Tief, looking around in alarm though bleary eyes.

'Come and have some tea,' replied Taiga impishly. 'I'll tell you all about it.'

While Frøya had most certainly brought the light back into their lives, Tief's mood was far from sunny.

'We need to get back up there and kill that bastard.' Tief glowered at the horizon. He'd drawn his sword and was pacing back and forth.

'You've been unconscious for some time,' said Taiga. Kimi had begun to prepare a meal, more to leave the brother and sister alone than out of any need to eat. Now the stew was bubbling nicely and Kimi realized she was famished.

'I mean it, Taiga! That black-scaled bastard nearly killed me. I want—'

Stonvind, who had presided over his rider's unruly outburst for some time, reached out with one foot and pushed the small, wiry man down until he was pinned to the ground.

Pour the food into his mouth. It is the only way.

'That's not funny!' shouted Tief, wriggling under the dragon's foot. Stonvind lowered his head until the blunt tip of his snout was just feet away from Tief.

You are correct. There is nothing funny about a man who has narrowly avoided death rushing to meet the same fate.

'You don't get to tell me not to be rash!' shouted Tief. 'I've been being rash since before you were born, you oversized reptile.'

Shut up, Tief. Stonvind removed his foot from Tief's chest. *We were worried about you. At least perform the simple courtesy of sharing food with us before we rejoin battle.*

Tief brushed the dirt from his clothes and glanced at everyone with a rueful look on his lined face. A lined face that had been deeply bruised until just an hour ago.

'Food?' asked Kimi, holding out a bowl to him. He trudged over and took what was offered.

'I'm sorry for being an arse.'

'If you weren't behaving like an arse I might not believe it was you.' Kimi grinned and Tief grinned back, blushing as he did so.

'He nearly bloody killed me,' said Tief in a quiet voice.

'He nearly bloody did,' agreed Kimi. 'And it scared all of us. Not least you. But things will be different next time.'

Things will be different, agreed Namarii, nodding to Stonvind.

'I'd best eat then, eh?' said Tief.

'And smoke your pipe,' added Kimi. 'Or I really will struggle to believe it's you.'

*   *   *

One by one the dragons took off. All three now sported modified saddles, salvaged from the many pack and riding animals they had eaten. Scaled wings stretched out wide to take advantage of the thermals rising up from land itself. Namarii's ascent was smoother than it had been for days.

'I'm glad we're past the phase where you try to shake me loose,' shouted Kimi over the wind.

It is barely worth it. With the saddle you are as firmly embedded as a leech.

'Charming,' replied Kimi with an arched eyebrow.

It was an attempt at humour. Was it not amusing?

'Perhaps it's best we concentrate on killing things?'

I will take that as a no.

The three dragons flew north to the smoking and deserted city. Taiga no longer hunched down against Flodvind's neck, but sat up proudly in her saddle, shielding her eyes from the worst of the wind; her other hand grasped the silver sickle of her goddess. Tief, who had always been the more enthusiastic rider of them, now sat watchfully, neither hollering or whooping. His sword rested in its scabbard alongside the saddle. Kimi reached to the small of her back, where the Ashen Blade had been secured in a sheath.

'Every advantage available to us,' she whispered as her fingers traced the hilt of the enchanted blade.

May Frejna's eye not find you, proclaimed Namarii.

And may Frøya keep you close, replied Stonvind and Flodvind with the ritual response. They flew on, passing from bright sunlight, under dark rain clouds and back into the light once more.

They circled the city, all eyes, human and draconic, searching every shattered tower for a sign of the father of dragons. Every plume of smoke from every smouldering building offered a hiding place, but the dark majesty of Bittervinge was curiously absent from Khlystburg.

I can feel him. Flodvind stopped abruptly in the air, hovered a moment on three beats of her blue wings, before landing on a warehouse roof. The tiles cracked and groaned beneath her weight, but the building did not collapse. Stonvind and Namarii took her lead, and set down nearby.

'What do your senses tell you, Flodvind?' asked Kimi.

He is not alone. It seems even the father of dragons has need of foot soldiers, much like the Emperor.

'Foot soldiers?' asked Kimi.

Figuratively speaking. Flodvind stretched out her neck as if to get a better look at the surrounding city. *He has recruited two dragons to aid him.*

Tief swore and looked over his shoulder, expecting an attack from any quarter; his sword was in his hand.

Your friend does his best to cover his fear. Kimi guessed Namarii's words had been for her and her alone. Neither Tief or Stonvind responded.

'Can you blame him?' whispered Kimi. 'Bittervinge almost killed him last time.'

Let us hope he masters that fear. Hold on! Namarii launched into the sky a heartbeat before his kin joined him.

'What . . . ?' But Kimi didn't need to finish her question. Approaching from the west were three winged shapes, casting fearsome shadows over the docks.

So Bittervinge has persuaded some of the younger dragons to join him in his cause. Namarii released a long growl as he flew closer. *No matter. They will share his fate.* The enemy dragons were closer now, wings beating hard. Bittervinge flew at the centre of their formation, almost twice the size of the dragons either side of him.

'Nothing's changed!' shouted Kimi. 'We came to slay the father of dragons!'

Tief and Taiga nodded, heads bent against the wind that whipped past them, clutching on to their saddles tightly. The dragons reached out with talons in anticipation and Kimi could feel a growing heat, the heat of Namarii's fire. With a sound like a thousand bodies hitting the ground, the six dragons collided in the skies above Khlystburg.

CHAPTER THIRTY-SEVEN

Kjellrunn

Many people criticize the goddesses for not taking a more active role in fighting the tyranny of Volkan Karlov. I take a different stance. Many times during the uprising a friendly face might appear when it was least expected, against all odds. Perhaps it was Frejna or Frøya who rearranged the strands of chance to weave people together in times of need. Truthfully we'll never know, but I like to believe those who came into contact with the goddesses' agents became extensions of their divine will.

– From the memoir of Drakina Tveit,
Lead Librarian of Midtenjord Province

She was still floating above the ground when the crew of the *Watcher's Wait* emerged from their hiding places on the ruined waterfront. Kjellrunn looked at the devastation around her and was reminded of the woodland clearing back in Cinderfell. She had nearly killed Mistress Kamalov with her fury that day. The Stormtide Prophet descended gently, touching down on the floorboards of the inn. The building had collapsed, and each wall had split apart and fallen outwards. The point where she now stood had been the eye of storm, untouched by the objects in the room, which had leapt from the ground at her command and danced a frenzy, around and around, until Exarch Zima was nothing more than a pulped and broken smear.

'Trine?' There was no sign of the dark-haired woman. 'Trine? Oh, Frøya, what have I done?'

'She's here,' called Romola, kneeling on the docks beside the still-unconscious initiate. 'She's heavier than she looks,' the captain added as Kjellrunn approached.

'Trine?'

The girl shivered at Kjellrunn's touch and her eyes opened to narrow slits. 'Did we kill him?' she croaked from a dry throat.

'She's going to be fine,' said Romola. Kjellrunn wanted to laugh.

'He's gone,' she whispered, folding her body over the initiate and hugging her for a moment.

'Hel's teeth, Kjellrunn.' The pirate captain looked at the wreckage of the inn as best she could. 'I thought . . .' But Romola couldn't bring herself to say it. Her eyes glittered with tears and she reached on instinct for the Stormtide Prophet, holding her close.

'We're fine,' whispered Trine, rising to her feet. 'We're both fine.' But the rigid way she carried herself and the look on her face proclaimed otherwise.

The crew of the *Watcher's Wait* sifted through the remains of the inn. It was a long, sombre hour before Ruslan's body was found. He had curled up in a ball, not far from the body of his former master.

'Frøya forgive me,' said Kjellrunn as Ruslan's body was retrieved from under broken timber.

'He was already dead,' said Romola. 'Exarch Zima saw to that. I witnessed it with my own eyes.' Kjellrunn couldn't be sure whether the captain was telling the truth, or simply trying to spare her conscience. 'You saved us, Kjellrunn,' added Romola. 'All of us. The Boyar and Ruslan played their part, but they paid for it.'

'Perhaps they'd still be alive if they hadn't sold Steiner out,' sneered Trine.

'And perhaps the Emperor would have killed them both if they hadn't,' replied Kjellrunn. 'Come on.' She took Trine by the hand. 'There's something I must do.' She approached the waterfront's edge and tried not to think of Ruslan or the day she'd nearly killed Mistress Kamalov. The prophet and her initiate walked along a pier until they reached the end, as far out into the bay as she could be without getting wet.

'Kjellrunn? What's going on?' Trine's voice was rich with hushed concern. Far out to sea the leviathan breached the surface gently, so as to not cause another wave that would sweep inland.

'It's time to say goodbye.' Kjellrunn was smiling. 'He can't help us where we're going.'

'Why are you smiling?' asked Trine, looking pale and uncomfortable in the afternoon light.

'Because all things come to end.' The leviathan slipped beneath the water and Kjellrunn felt its presence becoming fainter with each passing moment. It would always be there, she realized, but for now their fates lay along different paths.

Trine looked at her arms. It was hard to ignore the spiralling soot-dark marks in the daylight; they stood out in stark contrast to her white skin.

'Dragons will be the death of me, one way or another. Either Bittervinge will snatch me up, or the taint will consume me. I can feel it, Kjell. I can feel it growing.'

'You're going to survive this,' said Kjellrunn, though in truth she was terrified of what lay ahead.

'I can't talk you out of this, can I?' Romola stood on the waterfront, overseeing the search for salvage. Maxim, who

had been under captain's orders to remain on the *Wait*, had
been summoned to where Romola could keep an eye on him.
The boy looked at Kjellrunn with wide eyes. There was awe
there, but also disbelief that she would leave him.

'I have to go. For Steiner and my father.'

Maxim nodded and turned to Romola, burying his face in
her shoulder.

'But you're so weak,' replied Romola. 'At least collect your
strength for a day.'

Kjellrunn felt the same feeling of calm she had experienced
as she released the leviathan from her control. 'I will see you
again,' she said. 'Both of you.'

No one spoke, although the air was thick with unsaid
declarations. The pirates watched her walk deeper into the
city. Some raised their hands in farewell, but most simply
bowed their heads, as if a funeral procession were passing by.
Crows flitted from rooftop to rooftop, and a score of grey cats
slunk along the streets, Frøya's familiars trailing after her
prophet. Trine walked by her side, so tired she took each step
in a daze.

The city was a place of echoes. The parts that had not burned
to the ground remained standing but shorn of purpose. No
one lingered in their home save the desperate or the mad.
The lost and the abandoned stared at Kjellrunn and Trine with
tear-streaked faces, cursing in Solska or nursing the silence to
their breast with bitter gazes.

'Do you know which direction the palace is in?' asked Trine
after they had been walking for some time.

'No. But I imagine he does.' Kjellrunn pointed at a black
fleck in the sky circling some distant district, occasionally
diving towards the surface and releasing a gout of fire. Other
winged shapes could be seen in the sky, circling one another,
like huge birds of prey.

'Bittervinge,' said Trine with such a look of unhappiness

Kjellrunn almost sent her back. She would never go, of course. Too stubborn by far. Hadn't Mistress Kamalov said they were alike?

'What are you thinking about?' asked Trine.

'Old friends,' replied Kjellrunn. 'Old and wise.'

The first group of soldiers they encountered were lingering by a junction. The battered armour made it clear they had been involved in fighting looters or insurgents, while the missing shields suggested they might not have been the victors. The men eyed the two girls with puzzled expressions, no doubt baffled by the ragged black vestments. One of their number stepped forward and hailed them in a few languages before settling on Nordvlast, though he spoke haltingly and with a heavy accent.

'No further. Danger here. Not permitted near the palace.'

'I'm sorry, but I must go on.' Kjellrunn took a step closer. 'I'm looking for my brother.'

'No brother here. Go back.' The soldier reached out to take her by the shoulder but Kjellrunn knocked his hand aside with a simple sweep of her wrist.

'I said no further.' The soldier grabbed again, but this time he went for Kjellrunn's hair. She punched upwards with the power of her legs and her whole body underneath her fist, which now shimmered as granite. A loud crack sent the man sprawling and he hit the cobbles, his armour making a din as he landed. The remaining soldiers stared at Kjellrunn, disbelief etched on their dirty faces. Their eyes drifted to her fist, made stone by the arcane.

'It's the prophet!' said one of the men, and as one they turned and fled. Trine smirked; then she released a peal of nervous laughter.

'That was far easier than it had any right to be.'

'And you didn't have to use your fire,' said Kjellrunn.

'Perhaps we'll win the war on your reputation alone?' Trine grinned again and watched the soldiers retreat. Kjellrunn looked down at her fist and noticed she still felt the abiding sense of calm from earlier.

Onwards they went. Bittervinge continued to wage his own war in the skies, but there was no way of telling where the Imperial Palace was. Kjellrunn was confident she knew the way. Khlystburg had been founded according to the Emperor's design, and all roads led to the centre. The city was abandoned here and only the sounds of vast reptiles fighting above them sundered the silence.

'It's as if Bittervinge swooped down and ate everyone,' said Trine.

'I imagine that's exactly what he's been doing,' replied Kjellrunn. 'And those that haven't been eaten have fled.'

Trine nodded towards a street that was flanked by grand buildings featuring golden domes. Ten soldiers blocked the far end.

'That has to be the palace behind them,' said Kjellrunn. A look overhead confirmed her retinue of crows maintained their vigil from the rooftops, while the cats remained on the ground. 'Let's hope these ones are as brave as the last batch.'

A crossbow bolt whipped past so close it might have snagged her hair. A shocked moment passed before Kjellrunn reached out with a flat hand. More crossbow bolts sped down the street, hitting the ward of arcane force she had conjured before her. Trine sheltered behind the prophet and swore gently as more bolts impacted the wall of force.

'Should I . . . ?'

'No,' said Kjellrunn. 'Don't use your powers unless you absolutely need to.'

Kjellrunn began to walk down the street, her features caught in a frown of concentration rather than anger. More bolts were fired to no avail and two of the soldiers panicked and ran. Kjellrunn was just thirty feet away now, causing the men to discard their crossbows and snatch up maces. She took a deep breath and her skin shimmered with a silvery white light before becoming dark granite.

'I'd rather not hurt you . . .' she began to say, but the men surged forward, as much scared as furious. They raised their weapons with wordless howls, eight armoured men determined to smash the life from the Stormtide Prophet and her initiate.

'Kjellrunn?'

'Frøya forgive me,' she whispered as a handful of cobbles wrenched themselves out of the street and sped towards the black-armoured soldiers. Some saw the danger and raised their shields in time, but two were pelted so hard they fell where they stood and moved no more.

'We won't survive this,' said Trine, looking genuinely scared before she remembered herself and began to scowl. Her hands became living tongues of flame just as the soldiers drew close and all became chaos.

Kjellrunn weathered the blows as they took their toll on her. She worried her granite skin would fracture, and she along with it, but somehow she stayed in one piece. She punched with fists of stone and one by one the men were knocked down. The smell of scorched flesh told her that Trine had not held back. Arcane fire flared brightly behind her, but Kjellrunn couldn't turn to make sure Trine was unharmed: the three soldiers in front of her were almost falling over one another in their haste to kill the Stormtide Prophet.

The first she petrified with a look, but petrification took long seconds, and another soldier smashed her in the chest with his mace, knocking her backwards. She fell and landed awkwardly, struggling to get to her feet. Trine was no longer content to merely conjure flames from her hands; she had become a living being of terrible fire. From head to toe the flames raged around her, and she raged with it, launching

herself at the soldier who had struck Kjellrunn. The man
screamed as she caught hold of him, her embrace an inferno.
Kjellrunn got to her feet and grabbed the last of them by the
throat, hands of stone choking the life out of her attacker.
His helmet was knocked loose as he resisted her, gasping for
air that would not come, and slowly, far too slowly, the life
faded from his eyes. Kjellrunn released an exhausted sigh
before she realized the arcane fire was still burning behind
her.

'Trine?'

The soldier's burnt corpse lay on the cobbled street, armour
smoking, yet Trine remained afire, a silhouette of a person
in yellow and orange.

'I can't make it stop,' sobbed the girl of the crackling flames.

'Just take a deep breath,' urged Kjellrunn. 'You're safe now.
They're all dead.' Kjellrunn thought the girl had squeezed
her eyes shut, though it was difficult to tell.

'This was always going to be my end,' replied Trine above
the sound of the fire.

'No!' shouted Kjellrunn. 'Just try and let go of your anger.
We'll make you whole again. There must be a way. Frøya
is the goddess of life!'

'But we're committed to Frejna,' said Trine. 'Our way is
death.' The flames dwindled but of the girl Kjellrunn had
known there was no sign. Every inch of Trine's skin was now
the colour of soot. A flicking crown of fire continued to dance
around her head.

'That's good,' said Kjellrunn. 'That's good.' But her heart
was heavy with the lie. Trine tried to cry, but her tears
sizzled down her face as she shed them. Slowly she sank to
her knees and the fire abandoned her. Kjellrunn slipped
to her knees at the same time, but the heat prevented
her from cradling the girl of cinders. Smoke drifted from her
blackened skin and her shoulders slumped forward.

'I'm sorry,' she whispered. 'I was always too keen to burn those Imperial bastards.'

'Always,' replied Kjellrunn, smiling through her tears.

'I hated you at first,' added Trine. 'I know I'm not the easiest person to like but we're friends now, aren't we?'

'Friends? More like sisters,' replied Kjellrunn. The soot-dark skin was turning pale now, flakes of grey drifting from Trine's shoulders and arms. Her once raven-black hair fluttered on the breeze as fine white ashes.

'I'm an initiate of Frejna,' said Trine, struggling to keep her head up. 'That has to count for something on the other side. Do you think the goddess will look after me?'

'Never mind Frejna,' Kjellrunn embraced the girl and though the heat was considerable she endured it with arms of stone. And then the heat and the tension went out of Trine's body. Kjellrunn wept, and with every tear a little more of Trine became ashes drifting on the wind. Kjellrunn couldn't say how long she knelt there in the street, holding on to the little that was left of her friend.

A tongue of fire appeared in the darkness but it was merely a torch, held aloft by a man, perhaps Steiner's age. He wore a large two-handed sword across his back and approached Kjellrunn warily.

'I'm Streig,' he said. Kjellrunn nodded and stood up, her vestments covered in Trine's ashes. Her hands, no longer granite grey, trembled with grief and tiredness.

'I'm looking for my brother.' She swallowed and thought she might start crying again. 'And my father.'

'You must be Kjellrunn,' said Streig quietly. 'Come on. Let's get you off this street. You look as if Frejna herself is perched on your shoulder.'

'She has been,' replied Kjellrunn. 'For a long time now.'

Streig helped her to stand and together they headed towards the palace.

CHAPTER THIRTY-EIGHT

Steiner

No one knows for sure how the battle in the throne room unfolded. Those who survived rarely spoke of it, and then only to the others who had been present. Everyone who emerged from that day was irrevocably changed, the living and the dead.
– From the memoir of Drakina Tveit,
Lead Librarian of Midtenjord Province

'And I thought the stairs from the forge to Academy Square were bad,' said Steiner, breathing hard. They had slept for a while on a landing between staircases, resting as best they could on cold stone blanketed with dust. The little food they'd brought had all gone along with the water. Hunger gnawed at Steiner's guts just as thoughts of what had befallen his father gnawed at his thoughts. Time and again he turned away from dire speculation, trying not to think about a world without his father in it. The stairs, like his darkest fears, were taking their toll. Had Kristofine survived? Perhaps Reka had been unable to get her back to Arkiv? Had she'd died on some goddess-forsaken beach, desperate to board a ship? Tief, Taiga, and Kimi had dragons, he reasoned, but had they been able to best Bittervinge? Might Kimi have found a faster way to reach the Emperor? Was he already too late?

Silverdust ceased the endless climb and laid a hand on Steiner's shoulder. *Your concern for your friends does you credit, but you should not torture yourself so. My prescience tells me you will see Taiga again.*

'And the others?'

That I cannot tell. Some are too far away. Others have paths that have not yet been decided, by themselves or by others. Prescience is not an exact art and I was never particularly gifted with it. I receive flashes, glimpses of possible futures. Nothing is guaranteed, Steiner. You of all people know that.

'How long do you think we've been down here?' asked Steiner, taking a moment to catch his breath.

Difficult to tell in the endless darkness.

'Something else this place has in common with the forges of Vladibogdan,' muttered Steiner.

'At least it's dry now,' replied Felgenhauer. The mud on her boots had dried and flaked off during the countless footfalls up the seemingly endless steps. Their torches had burned down to nothing, and now they relied on Silverdust, who held up a nimbus of pale arcane light around one hand. The stairs followed the five sides of a deep chute. Steiner cast a glance down, hoping the corpse spiders were far below them. At some point they'd been down there, in the darkness, on the lowest step. A look upwards confirmed nothing but more stairs and more darkness. Steiner's thighs were burning with the effort, his muscles leaden.

Not much further. Just a few more levels.

'Do you think the Emperor will let us sleep a while before we kill him?' asked Steiner, forcing a grim smile.

'We may be fighting sooner than you think,' said Felgenhauer. She stopped walking and held up a finger to her lips.

'I can't hear anything,' whispered Steiner.

There are people nearby. I sense them, their thoughts and their feelings.

'What are they feeling?' asked Steiner.

They are nervous. Come. The cinderwraith pushed on, gliding up the stairs; he had abandoned all pretence of walking like the living. The next landing featured a wooden door with a dull brass handle, dusty and discoloured. Metal rattling on metal sounded from the other side. Perhaps they were just in time to join the fight against the Emperor.

Felgenhauer tried the door but it was locked – to Steiner's frustration.

'Lock pick,' she said.

'Lock pick,' replied Steiner, lining up his sledgehammer with the handle.

I was going to suggest a stealthy approach but . . .

Steiner swung the sledgehammer and the entire mechanism broke free of the ancient wood and shot out the other side. Steiner struck the door again, splitting it down the middle.

. . . it seems we are tackling any potential adversaries head on.

'It'll be fun,' said Steiner, heading through the shattered door. In truth the very idea of fun was far from his mind. All he wanted to do was strangle the life out of Volkan Karlov, if such a thing could be done. A short dark corridor gave way to a larger room with a roaring fire. Steiner sprinted forward, brandishing his hammer, but the only enemies he found were pale and gaunt kitchen staff who cowered behind a table. The sounds of clattering metal had been ladles and pans, rather than swords and plate armour.

'Great. We're in the kitchens,' said Steiner, feeling the heat of his battle lust fade. Felgenhauer barked something in Solska, too quickly for Steiner to understand. The kitchen staff comprised a stooped man in his forties and a nervous-looking girl about Steiner's age. Her ears stuck out from beneath a crumpled white cap. Both nodded to Felgenhauer and began to prepare the table.

'What did you tell them to do?'

'We're in a kitchen,' said Felgenhauer, 'and we're famished. Sit.'

'But the Emperor!'

'Can wait a little longer. There's no point picking a fight when we're too weak to see it through.'

'But we've come all this way!'

'Exactly, past corpse spiders and the Impassable Gate and endless stairs.' She pulled a chair out. 'Sit. Eat.'

Silverdust had crossed to the great hearth of the kitchen fireplace while they argued. The cinderwraith inhaled deeply, tendrils of smoke bathing the mirror mask and slipping beneath Silverdust's hood.

'I've never seen you do that before,' said Steiner, grimacing at the unnerving sight.

I have never needed to before, but now I am fortifying myself for what comes next.

The mouse-eared girl served Steiner and Felgenhauer a hearty stew and sawed off a half-dozen slices of bread.

'You dragon rider?' she asked in heavily accented Nordspråk, her eyes wide and wary. Steiner nodded.

'You kill Emperor. Please?'

Steiner nodded and began to eat, though his stomach was a hard knot and food was the last thing on his mind.

'I wasn't sure what I was expecting,' said Steiner as they crept through the Imperial Palace, over dusty marble floors, watched over by countless portraits of long-dead Boyars. 'But it wasn't this.'

Felgenhauer and Silverdust followed him at either shoulder and surveyed the silent palace. No guards waiting at the doors, no soldiers to watch over lonely corridors, no Vigilants hurrying to and from meetings.

'No courtiers,' said Felgenhauer.

'Not much of anything.' Steiner glanced over his shoulder with an anxious look. 'Did we miss it? Are we too late?'

We must head to court. If Volkan Karlov is anywhere it will be on his throne. He's spent seventy-five years making sure no one else takes it from him; today is no different.

The finery of the palace was stunning. Varnished wood-panelled walls, high ceilings, and alcoves with painted frescos of the Emperor slaying various dragons in each of the provinces. Gold door handles shone brightly and antique sets of armour stood watch at regular intervals.

Impressive, is it not?

'All this . . .' Steiner waved his hand at the Emperor's wealth. 'It just makes me angry. There are people in the Scorched Republics barely avoiding starvation.'

I can see why you would feel like that. I have seen the poverty of which you speak. Silverdust gestured and led them down a corridor. *Come now, we are almost there.*

They came to an antechamber large enough to hold twenty people comfortably. The torches in the sconces still burned and a lone Semyonovsky guard stood at the doors, though his black cloak was ragged and Steiner could smell dried blood.

'Why don't you go home?' said Steiner. 'It's over.' The guard evidently did not understand Nordspråk or was too blinded by duty to take Steiner's advice. He raised his spear and took a step forward, only to meet a torrent of flames from Silverdust's outstretched hand. The man roared in agony and fled down the corridor, a light fading in the darkness. Steiner swore under his breath. 'Idiot.'

'Let me take the centre,' said Felgenhauer as they prepared to face the Emperor. 'If I can get him talking we might stand a chance. I don't care who wrests the Ashen Blade from him, but let's make sure we get it.'

'And then what?' said Steiner. 'He's mastered all four schools of the arcane. I imagine turning his skin to stone won't be a challenge for him.'

'Stone still shatters under the blow of a sledgehammer,' replied Felgenhauer. 'He'll want to stay in his natural form so he can move quickly. Stay close and I'll shield you from the fire.'

Steiner nodded. He didn't care much for their chances but opened the doors to the Imperial Court anyway.

'And may Frøya keep me close,' he whispered as the heavy wood swung open to reveal an empty room. The smell was overpowering, and Steiner held up a sleeve to his nose and mouth even as Felgenhauer gagged.

'What charnel Hel is this?' she muttered.

'You could fit the whole of the Smouldering Standard in here,' muttered Steiner as he stepped over the threshold. At the far end of the room was the throne and a crumpled form in black was strewn across it.

'What's a Smouldering Standard?' asked Felgenhauer.

'It's a tavern.' Steiner rolled his shoulders. 'You could fit a whole tavern in this room, and for what?'

They walked slowly if not calmly down the length of the court. The floor before the throne was littered with wizened corpses. A score of people lay dead, no doubt having succumbed to the Ashen Blade: Vigilants, soldiers and even an Envoy among their number.

'Why has he turned upon his own?' asked Steiner.

'It's easier for a man like to him to blame his shortcomings on others,' replied Felgenhauer.

Volkan Karlov sprawled on the throne. He had a high fore-head and pale eyes. He was attired in black, much like the Okhrana in his service, and his hands were splattered with blood, as if he were wearing crimson gloves.

'Another Vartiainen comes before my throne.' The Emperor's voice was hushed and whispery, hardly the booming tones of a tyrant. There was blood spattered on his brow, and dried in his hair, and a thick pool of red surrounded the base of the throne, a grim parody of moat around a castle. 'I do so enjoy killing your family.' Volkan Karlov stood up slowly. There was something sinuous and controlled in the movement, like a hunting cat stretching.

'Marek was the last of my family you'll kill.' Steiner's words were hard and quiet in the vast expanse of the Imperial Court. 'Your reign is over.'

'It will never be over!' hissed the Emperor. 'I have spent decades trying to unite this continent, decades protecting people from the arcane, and from dragons!' He took a single step closer, his eyes narrowed in fury. 'And in just half a year you have ruined everything.'

'It's hard when someone takes something you love,' replied Steiner, his voice as cold as stone. 'You took my mother, my uncle, my father, and my great-grandfather.' His grip tightened on the sledgehammer. 'But worst of all, you tried to take my sister, and that's the mistake that cost you an empire.'

'The Stormtide Prophet,' sneered the Emperor. 'Just imagine what a powerful Vigilant she would have made if she had gone to Vladibogdan as she should have.'

'But instead she is coming to kill you,' replied Felgenhauer. 'With all the powers of the goddess you chose to proscribe.'

The Emperor held the back of one hand to his mouth and laughed silently behind it.

'That was always my plan, Felgenhauer. Why go to her when I can just as easily take her brother hostage and negotiate for his life when she gets here?'

I will not permit this. Silverdust stepped forward. *My Elders warned me but I thought I knew better. Now I have come to put right that mistake.*

The Emperor locked his gaze on Silverdust and Steiner wasn't sure what happened for a moment. Volkan Karlov's eyes turned the colour of dull granite, just as Steiner had seen with his aunt and Sundra. This was the petrifying gaze of Academy Zemlya, and Steiner lunged forward to protect Silverdust; but the cinderwraith held out one hand, not turning his head from the Emperor for even a heartbeat.

'What?' was all Steiner had time to say before Volkan Karlov staggered backwards, clutching his head and uttering muffled screams. The Emperor removed his hands to reveal one side of his face had been turned to stone.

'What have you done to me?' roared the Emperor.

Did you never wonder why I chose this, Volkan? Silverdust tapped his mirror mask with one finger. *It seems you still have much to learn. Allow me to provide a lesson.* Silverdust flung his hands forward and two painfully bright motes drifted forward. The Emperor dived behind the throne to avoid the searing light.

'There is much that I have learned while you were on the island, Serebryanyy!'

Steiner looked on in horror as the corpses surrounding the throne twitched and jerked. One by one they dragged themselves to their feet. Silverdust immolated one with a fiery blast from his outstretched palm. The undead husk staggered on, until the flesh was burned away and the bones came undone and collapsed.

Steiner, be careful!

Another husk lurched forward but Steiner was already swinging. The sledgehammer removed the jaw from one husk before slamming into the shoulder of another, shattering bones. Steiner lashed out with a kick to open some space between himself and the jawless husk, before unleashing his backswing. The husk's skull caved in and was sundered from the body altogether.

'This I can do,' muttered Steiner as the husks surrounded them. The Emperor had shifted his attention to Felgenhauer, attempting to petrify her with his stony gaze, but the former

Matriarch-Commissar was far from defenceless. She reached out to the sundered body parts using the arcane, and flung them at the Emperor, breaking his concentration. The Emperor flinched with every shattered limb, and blinked as each burned appendage slammed into him.

Steiner was swinging hard. He smashed husks in the face with his elbows when his attackers drew too close, buying himself the extra moment he needed to line up his next strike with the sledgehammer. Beside him Silverdust was strangling the unlife out of the undead with hands that burned white hot.

This is not my teaching, Volkan! This is an abomination!

'Abomination!' shouted the Emperor. 'Let me show you abomination!' The doors behind the throne opened and more husks trudged forward, bony claws outstretched.

CHAPTER THIRTY-NINE

Kimi

In the end, for all of his talk about dominance, Bittervinge adopted the tactics of his enemies. He adopted the idea of taking allies.

– From the memoir of Drakina Tveit,
Lead Librarian of Midtenjord Province

The skies above Khlystburg sounded with a thunderous commotion of scaled bodies, vast wings, and scything claws. Kimi experienced a brief moment of excruciating terror as Namarii flew straight towards the father of dragons. Her every limb tensed and she hunkered low against Namarii's neck. Bittervinge approached, his wounded, partially petrified face snarling.

Ready the Ashen Blade. Namarii's voice was loud inside Kimi's head. *Now!*

Bittervinge reached out with taloned feet to grasp Namarii and rend him into pieces, but Namarii folded his wings. For a moment they dropped from the sky and Kimi's stomach lurched. She drew the enchanted blade from the sheath and stabbed upwards just as Namarii flared his wings and surged forward. The Ashen Blade opened a long and jagged scratch along Bittervinge's underside; flecks of grey ash trailed after the dagger. Kimi's arm rattled and shook as the blade scored a winding line of atrophy a dozen feet long. Bittervinge contracted around the source of his pain, coiling so hard his tail whipped past Kimi's head, nearly dismounting her.

Did you cut him?

'No more than a scratch,' shouted Kimi above Bittervinge's deafening roar. 'But it seemed to do something . . .' Her vision swam for a moment, and the city below her appeared shockingly intricate. Namarii's scales burned with all the colours of autumn, irresistible yellows and fiery reds. Even the air tasted better, intoxicating as it filled her lungs.

It was enough. Namarii performed a sharp turn and sped back towards his prey. *If we can land a telling strike, a piercing strike, we will prevail!*

'Take me closer!' bellowed Kimi, almost delirious with enthusiasm. The Ashen Blade thrummed in her hand, calling out for blood.

Tief and Stonvind collided with a young dragon with silver scales. Tief was shunted forward in the saddle, but he'd tensed his thighs and threw up an arm as the sky was filled with buffeting wings and coiling tails. Somehow he managed to hold on to his sword. Talons swiped and jaws snapped on both sides. Smears of red flicked through the sky, blood on the wind as battle was met. The silver dragon was more slender than Stonvind, but had a wiry strength all the same. The monstrous reptiles were locked together, their wings beating furiously lest they plunge to the ground. Each wrestled and strained against the other for the better position. The silver dragon huffed down a great lungful of air and the scales near her throat shimmered with a ruddy light.

'Själsstyrka?' shouted Tief, remembering the dragon that had helped Steiner escape back on Vladibogdan. 'Is that you?'

The young dragon hesitated, allowing Stonvind to grasp her by the throat and turn the full force of his arcane gaze upon the creature. Silver scales turned to grey and then fractured and split as the dragon shook violently, desperate to be free of Stonvind's grasp.

'Själsstyrka? You're on the wrong side!'

A silver tail whipped around and Tief ducked beneath it, but the sinuous appendage slapped Stonvind across one eye, breaking the dragon's concentration and his grasp.

Själsstyrka! That was what the Cinderfell boy called me! The silver dragon retreated. *But I am no man's pet.*

'I'm not asking you to be a pet!' shouted Tief. 'I'm just saying you're on the wrong side, you big idiot.'

Själsstyrka continued to put some distance between herself and Stonvind before coming about and gaining some height. It was clear the silver dragon would strike again.

'So much for diplomacy,' muttered Tief.

Big idiot? replied Stonvind. *You call that diplomacy?* He beat his wings hard to match Själsstyrka's altitude.

'Let's teach this shiny runt a lesson,' grunted Tief.

Flodvind dived to one side, avoiding the onrushing dragon that approached with bared teeth and outstretched claws. It was a dark shadow made in the image of the father of dragons. Taiga thought she saw the same maddened gleam in its pale yellow eyes.

Witless fool! Flodvind made her thoughts about serving Bittervinge clear as her opponent raked her with obsidian-coloured talons. The azure dragon shuddered in agony and Taiga held on to the saddle as hard she could. The younger, black-scaled dragon attempted to gain some altitude and escape a riposte, but Flodvind was already turning. Her head lashed forward and she caught the younger dragon's tail between her jaws.

'Steady now!' warned Taiga, clinging on to the saddle.

Flodvind shook her head from side to side like a wolfhound dragging its prey, gaining height all the while. Taiga leaned from the saddle and cut down with the sickle, missing a wing but scoring a deep cut in the younger dragon's tail. The impact of such a strike jolted the curved blade from Taiga's hand and the weapon tumbled away.

'No!' she shrieked. Flodvind snatched the weapon from the air with one of her rear feet and broke away from the young black dragon; streamers of blood filled the sky as its tail was almost ripped off entirely. Fiery breath surged after them and Flodvind rolled so the torrent of flame washed over her underside, shielding Taiga in the process.

'Oh goddess,' breathed Taiga as she looked to one side and saw the ruined city hundreds of feet below. Flodvind righted herself in the air, speeding forward with deft beats of her wings, then came about in a long graceful curve.

'Shouldn't we stay focused on that one?' shouted Taiga.

They are but distractions.

Taiga opened her mouth to object when the vast bulk of Bittervinge appeared before them, shaking and coiling in the air as if scalded or burned. Flodvind clamped on to the father of dragon's back with three taloned feet, then unleashed her fiery breath towards a ragged and infected wing. Bittervinge howled so loudly Taiga wondered if the sound might carry back to Sundra in Shanisrond.

Kimi was leaning forward in the saddle, shaking with exhilaration. She watched as Flodvind latched on to the back of the father of dragons. Her senses were alive in a way they had never been before. She saw every scale on the pair of dragons, obsidian black and stunning blue; could count every ripping talon. And the smells! Scorched flesh, the iron tang of blood, nervous sweat, and beneath everything the rotting stench of a dead city.

'I must kill Bittervinge,' she hissed.

Hold on, Your Highness! Namarii launched himself towards the larger dragon just as Flodvind breathed fire over a wounded black-scaled wing. The father of dragons snapped his great jaws at Flodvind, but he had not taken his eye from Kimi and the Ashen Blade.

'He knows we can finish him!' shouted Kimi ecstatically. Bittervinge swiped with his talons at Namarii, but it was a feint. The father of dragon's tail followed the initial strike and slapped hard against Namarii's flank. Kimi was shunted from her seat, slipping past the powerful draconic shoulders until she hanging from the front of the saddle by one hand, unwilling to let go of the Ashen Blade.

'Kimi!' shouted Taiga from no more than two dozen feet away. Kimi could only gasp as she struggled to hold on. Flodvind bit into the base of Bittervinge's skull and the father of dragons lurched away from Namarii. An awful breathless moment passed and Namarii rolled on one side so Kimi could remount the saddle. The muscles in her arms burned with the effort.

'Again!' she shouted. The elation she had felt after using the Ashen Blade against Bittervinge had faded, leaving her hungry for another chance to score a wound. 'Again!'

'Can't believe this little arsehole sided with Bittervinge,' complained Tief as Själsstyrka dived at them from above. Stonvind banked to one side, avoiding the rending claws that sliced through the air.

She is faster than I am. Stonvind gave chase all the same.

'I'm not sure that's true,' shouted Tief. 'Just more agile.' They trailed the silver dragon by a hundred feet, the ground below rising up to meet them with horrifying speed, weather vanes and the pointed rooftops of towers promising to impale the unwary.

'Use the buildings against her,' urged Tief. 'Use the stone!'

Själsstyrka pulled up out of her dive just as the side of a bell tower came apart. The silver dragon was pelted with dozens of dark grey stones at Stonvind's bidding.

'That's it!' said Tief. Stonvind had already begun to slow her descent, changing course to intercept the flailing silver dragon.

What is this? Själsstyrka's voice was an outraged scream in their minds.

This is the true power of dragons. Stonvind landed on the silver dragon from above, shredding wings and biting deep at the base of Själsstyrka's neck. The cobbles in the street below were exploding upwards, pelting Själsstyrka's soft underside mercilessly. *This is the power of the arcane.*

How? Själsstyrka was losing height, barely staying above the rooftops of Khlystburg.

Am I not called Stonvind? The dark grey dragon extended both wings and slowed quickly. Momentum carried the silver dragon onward as the shredded wings failed. A taller building shifted sideways and collapsed on Själsstyrka as she tried to pass by. Stonvind and Tief watched as a huge cloud of stone dust filled air, obscuring everything.

'You dropped an entire building on her,' said Tief, eyes wide with shock.

Själsstyrka's wings are broken but she is not dead. She will trouble us no more. Stonvind circled around and began the laborious task of gaining enough height to get back in the fighting.

Taiga was holding on to the saddle as Flodvind harassed the father of dragons. Something flickered in the corner of her vision, a dark shape approaching quickly.

'The smaller one is back!' shouted Taiga. Flodvind kicked off from Bittervinge, trying to gain some height. The younger black dragon banked slightly and came on, powering itself through the sky with wings of night, though it trailed blood as it approached. Taiga could feel Flodvind trying to respond to this new threat but the exchange with Bittervinge had cost her and she bled from a score of minor wounds.

'Flodvind, bank left!' Too late. The younger black dragon had no intention of scoring Flodvind's flesh with its talons, it simply folded its wings and slammed bodily into the azure dragon. Flodvind flipped in the air and began to plummet as Taiga slipped loose from the saddle and began her own descent. Flodvind looked at Taiga as they fell and though the dragon communicated nothing Taiga felt a strange calm. Her sickle, which until now had been grasped in Flodvind's back claw, floated to her hand, guided by Flodvind's mastery of the arcane.

'No! Wait!' Taiga cried as she spotted Stonvind and Tief, coming up fast from below. Flodvind turned her head towards the ground and flared the scorched and ragged remains of her wings. One moment Flodvind was in the air before Taiga, and the next Stonvind was beneath her. Tief grabbed her by the collar and pulled her tight to the saddle.

'Flodvind!' she screamed after the blue dragon.

'She'll be fine!' shouted Tief, but the expression on his face changed as he watched Flodvind try to pull up from the dive. The azure dragon clipped a roof top in one street, only to collide with a building in the next. Her tail coiled in the air lazily, before she crashed to the ground.

'Frøya save me, no, no, no!' whispered Taiga, even as the younger black dragon approached Stonvind.

Bittervinge was fleeing. The silver dragon, whom Kimi recognized from Vladibogdan, had crashed in the streets below, followed soon after by Flodvind.

We must go to her aid! Namarii almost turned away from his pursuit of the father of dragons, but Kimi kicked her heels against the sides of his neck, as she might do while on horseback.

'No! We almost have him.'

As you wish, Your Highness. Kimi thought she heard a little of the old Namarii arrogance in the dragon's tone, but she didn't care.

'Get above him.' Bittervinge was heading for the centre of the city and descending quickly. Namarii, who was both faster and more agile than his larger kin, followed with ease. 'Right above him!' shouted Kimi, the Ashen Blade clutched in one fist.

Kimi! You cannot be thinking to attack him in such a way. It is madness!

But she had already swung one leg over the side of Namarii's neck, riding side-saddle. A second later she had jumped clear, falling towards the father of dragons.

Stonvind was tiring, wings beating more slowly; he was finding it harder to react in time. The younger black dragon suffered no such enervation, descending like a shadow from nightmare.

'NO!' screamed Taiga, holding up the holy sickle and the knife of her goddess. A chime sounded through the air and the young black dragon flinched as if it had been struck. It turned away and Stonvind turned his petrifying gaze on their attacker's extremities.

They cannot fly with wings of stone. But the young black dragon was fast, and slipped away from Stonvind, past the range of the arcane gaze. It wasn't long before their attacker was above them, seemingly impervious to exhaustion. The young black dragon descended once more, jaws bared. Stonvind could do little but roll to one side in order to keep his human riders safe. The young black dragon clamped his cruel teeth around Stonvind's throat and Taiga screamed.

'He's killing him!'

Tief leaned out of the saddle and slashed at the young black dragon, but his sword made no impression on the glittering black scales.

Stonvind, now! The rest of you, hold on! Somehow they heard Namarii's voice in their heads above the din and panic.

Stonvind slashed upwards with both front feet, raking the soft flesh of the young black dragon's underside. Their attacker lost focus for a moment and released Stonvind as Namarii slammed into the young black dragon from above, driving him down to the ground with all of his considerable weight.

'Namarii?' Tief called out. There was no way either of the dragons would pull out of such a descent. A moment later and Namarii piled the young black dragon face first into a building, which crumpled like paper under their combined weight. Stone and dust exploded upwards in a grey cloud. Stonvind glided closer, circling the scene of the collision. Nothing moved.

'Namarii?' shouted Tief. 'Kimi?'

'Oh no, oh Frøya, please no,' mumbled Taiga, disconsolate and frantic.

Kimi had fallen through the sky like a maddened comet, the Ashen Blade held out before her. Bittervinge, the burned, petrified, gouged and bleeding father of dragons, jolted once as the blade sank between his shoulder blades. Kimi hit the black scales so hard she was certain something must have broken. She clung on with gritted teeth, her fist clenched around the hilt of the Ashen Blade.

What have you done? Bittervinge convulsed in the air. *The blade!*

Kimi had no answer; she was breathless with the arcane energies coursing through her. Bittervinge's many wounds began to worsen; his scales turned pale grey and peeled loose.

Remove the blade, else we both die.

Bittervinge was no longer beating his wings, merely gliding, momentum speeding them towards their death. Kimi realized she was smiling, tears streaming down her face as hysterical laughter escaped her. She had never felt so strong, so invincible, so alive. If Tsen could see her now!

Impetuous fool! You have doomed us both!

Bittervinge turned his head so he could see the Yamal princess who had undone him. Teeth slipped free of his black lips in a rictus grin as his eyes clouded with rheum. Kimi watched every detail of his sickening atrophy with fascination. It was all too beautiful. The sky rushed by overhead as the Imperial Palace rose up to meet them.

You fool.

Kimi grinned and twisted the hilt of Ashen Blade.

'But a fool who slays dragons,' replied Kimi as the Imperial Palace filled her vision.

CHAPTER FORTY

Steiner

To this day people still avoid the palace grounds, as if the entire place were a locus of death and suffering.
> – From the memoir of Drakina Tveit,
> Lead Librarian of Midtenjord Province

The Imperial Court, once full of the passions and life of the Empire, was now a charnel cavern, gloomy and reeking of death. Weak sunlight filtered in through a series of stained-glass windows high up at the side of the chamber above the viewing gallery. The room was bathed in sickly yellow and dirty red light, and Steiner feared they would be overwhelmed in the darkness at any moment. An undead husk raked bony fingertips across his shoulder, drawing blood and knocking him off balance. Silverdust caught him by one arm while simultaneously incinerating another husk with an outstretched hand. The arcane fire burned so hot it was glittering white, much like the flames that flickered by his feet.

'Frejna's teeth!' grunted Steiner.

I imagine Frejna is most displeased.

Steiner lashed out at his attacker, then followed up with a savage head butt that knocked the husk back a few feet.

'What are these things?'

I heard rumours that Veles could raise gholes from the corpses of the dead. The cinderwraith sidestepped a husk; then he wrapped fiery arms about its body and face from behind. There was a sickening crack as Silverdust wrenched the head off the corpse and the still burning husk collapsed. *It seems Volkan has learned the same trick.*

Not one of the dozen husks attacked Felgenhauer. The lurching undead were simply delaying Silverdust and Steiner. She had been singled out.

'You should have remained loyal, Nika!' The Emperor turned his petrifying gaze on her. She could feel herself slowing under that dire stare, her limbs stiffening.

'You sent to me to Vladibogdan!' she shouted back, flinging a corpse at him with the arcane as she did so. The corpse, which had belonged to a soldier in life, was still armoured and hit the Emperor with such force he fell to one knee. For a moment the petrifying gaze was broken. 'I had a lot of time to think about all the wrong I'd done in my life,' snarled Felgenhauer as she closed with him.

'Damn you, Nika.' Volkan lurched to his feet and unleashed a great gout of fire from his outstretched hands, but Felgenhauer was already moving, already reaching out with the arcane. One of the still-walking husks jolted sideways into her grasp. The undead horror blackened and fell apart as Felgenhauer used it as a shield, but the fire continued to roar.

'Frøya save me,' she whispered as her clothes caught fire. She would have to attempt something she had promised herself she would never do. The feeling was awful, like being buried alive or suffocated. Her mouth was filled with the taste of iron and soil. Her skin shimmered with an arcane silvery light as the fire raced over her head and shoulders. The heat was terrible, but her flesh did not crisp and burn away, made of stone as it was.

'Will you just die?' yelled the Emperor, stepping closer, arcane fire still roaring from his hands in an unrelenting torrent. A terrible sensation ran through Felgenhauer's body, starting at her stomach and coursing outwards to her extremities, a sickness worse than anything she had ever experienced.

'Not . . . now!' This was the cost, she realized. The cost of the arcane on the human body, the taint of dragons made manifest. The same cost that had claimed the life of her sister. And now she was going to perish the same way.

'Steiner!' She dropped to her knees, a statue of a woman bathed in fire. 'Steiner! I need you!'

Silverdust had never heard Nika Felgenhauer call for help. The Matriarch-Commissar had never given so much as a hint that she needed anyone else during her time on Vladibogdan. Her attitude – the self-contained way she conducted herself – was one of the reasons Silverdust had liked her. To hear her call out so desperately would have chilled Silverdust's blood if he'd still had veins to carry it.

Volkan! Silverdust floated above the husks and spirited himself behind the Emperor, his hands clutching two bright motes of light that would spell the end of anything they came into contact with. The Emperor smiled grimly; the hand he held before him continued to bathe Felgenhauer in fire, but he reached out to Silverdust with his free hand. At first nothing happened and Silverdust released his searing motes, hoping to finally end Volkan Karlov and set right his great mistake.

Wind. The Emperor had summoned wind.

The motes faltered as the breeze picked up, gaining more force with every moment. Shattered and burned body parts began to slide across the tiled floor of the Imperial Court as the arcane wind intensified.

Damn you, Volkan! Silverdust's motes were blown back towards him. The cinderwraith dodged sideways to avoid being obliterated. Behind him the throne burst into flames as the motes made contact.

Volkan! The cloak that Streig had given to Silverdust was blown free, the garments beneath providing little respite from the wind. Silverdust looked over his shoulder to see soot racing away behind him. His very essence was being dispersed.

'What good is a cinderwraith if he has no cinders?' asked the Emperor, wielding fire in one hand and the wind in the other. 'Goodbye, Serebryanyy.' He grinned victoriously. Silverdust tried to raise a wind to counter the Emperor, but he was weakening with every passing moment. His mirrored mask was torn from his face by the gale and the room spun away from him.

'Stay dead!' grunted Steiner as he caved in the head of another husk. There were just three left now, but Steiner ignored them; he was intent on reaching his aunt. The Emperor stood with his back to Steiner, one hand held out, showering Felgenhauer in flames, while the other hand was channelling a powerful wind, powerful enough to scatter Silverdust across the court.

'NO!' Steiner swung down hard, an overhead strike capable of breaking stone. The Emperor dropped to one knee and held up both hands before his face. The sledgehammer jarred against an invisible wall of force. Felgenhauer was a blackened and kneeling statue, and Steiner's eyes widened in shock when he realized she wasn't moving. Fury raged through his veins and he lined up the sledgehammer for another swing. The Emperor retreated a step and made a gesture as if he were backhanding a servant. Steiner felt the full force of the arcane strike a heartbeat later and was flung across the room. He was dimly aware of hitting the wall, but the air had already been knocked out of his lungs.

'I was expecting more,' said the Emperor with a satisfied smirk. Steiner slid down the wall, a drop of ten feet. He blinked a moment, then gasped down a lungful of air. He was still standing, though that likely had more to do with his enchanted boots than any resilience or balance on his part.

'And may Frejna's eye not find me,' he wheezed, too shocked to move.

'Your aunt is undone by the very powers she tried to use against me,' said Volkan Karlov in his whispery voice. He stroked the stony brow of Felgenhauer. 'And Silverdust is . . .' Volkan Karlov smiled at his own joke before he made it. 'Well, dust!' The Emperor took a few steps forward and the remaining three husks followed. 'And now, finally, I will capture Steiner Vartiainen and use your life to bargain with your sister.'

Steiner wheezed down another breath, rolled his shoulders and hefted his sledgehammer once more. The husks shambled towards him, creating a screen of corpses before the Emperor. Steiner prepared to charge out of sheer, bloody-minded desperation. The meagre amount of light shining into the room from above the gallery dimmed. The smile on Volkan Karlov's face faltered as he turned and whispered one word with a terrible reverence.

'Bittervinge?'

The windows above the court gallery exploded inwards in a storm of red and yellow glass, all shattered by the father of dragons. The great blunt prow of his snout and jaw sped into the room, missing teeth, scarred from petrification, scales split and broken. The muscular neck followed after, and in the blink of an eye his torso and forelegs punched through the wall below the windows. The wings, ever his most impressive asset, were shorn off altogether as the roof refused to surrender to his momentum. The father of dragons slammed down in the Imperial Court, splitting tiles, knocking Volkan Karlov from his feet and crushing the three undead husks. The mightiest reptile in all of Vinterkveld slid across the floor for a dozen feet and stopped within arms' reach of Steiner.

Nothing moved.

Light returned to the Imperial Court, though it struggled to pierce the swirling dust that had been thrown up in the dragon's wake. Steiner stepped sideways and looked Bittervinge in the eye, but the maddened gleam was gone, replaced by rheum; the lid heavy, the scales across his face translucent and ragged.

'You're dead,' whispered Steiner. 'You're really dead.' Something moved between the dragon's shoulder blades and for a terrible moment Steiner feared he was wrong. A person materialized out of the swirling dust, a darker shadow clutching a short blade.

'Steiner?' Kimi slid down the side of Bittervinge's corpse looking like an apparition from nightmare. Coated in grey dust and slick with dark red blood, she stepped forward, her gaze unusually intense.

'How did you kill him with just a dagger?' asked Steiner when he finally managed to put his thoughts in order.

'This is no dagger,' said Kimi. 'I have come for the Emperor, and I will kill him with the Ashen Blade.'

'The Emperor is mine,' snarled Steiner. 'He killed my father—'

'You think you're the only one who lost a father to the Emperor?' Kimi grabbed Steiner by the collar of his tunic and pulled him forward until his face was just inches from her own. 'He is mine,' hissed Kimi. 'Do you hear me? This is a matter of honour.' She was wide-eyed from her ordeal, over-pronouncing every word like a drunk pretending they're sober. Steiner's eye drifted to the Ashen Blade, though the weapon was covered in gore, as was the hand that wielded it. Kimi's arm was soaked to the elbow.

'Kimi. What's it doing it to you?' he asked. She released him and held up a forbidding finger.

'No! You will not persuade me to part with it. I have come to kill the Emperor and I will not be denied.'

'Let's put that to the test, shall we?' said Volkan Karlov from across the room. A patch of darkness on the floor heaved itself to its feet. Once fine dark clothes were now the colour of dust. 'I've bested a Matriarch-Commissar and an Exarch today. I'm sure one snivelling princess won't give me any problems.'

The look of rage that crossed Kimi's face made Steiner side-step on instinct, keen to be away from the murderous intent in her eyes. She began to run forward and Steiner followed a heartbeat later. Volkan Karlov simply smiled and raised up one hand, then knelt down and slammed an open palm against the tiled floor. Steiner's feet went from under him as the court quaked and the ground beneath them tore itself apart. Kimi fell into the darkness and hit the level below, lying supine in the rubble. The Ashen Blade skittered away from her limp hand. Steiner landed a moment later and stared around in shock; his sledgehammer had been jolted from his grasp during the fall.

'Kimi!' No answer came from the Yamal princess and Steiner knelt down beside her. 'Kimi?'

He heard the sound of another body hitting the bottom of the newly formed fissure. Volkan Karlov had split the court with such force the ground beneath his feet had betrayed him. Steiner, who had landed catlike amid the devastation, sprang forward, searching the debris with rising panic.

'Poor Steiner,' said the Emperor. 'To have come all this way only to fail now. Finally I will rid myself of the Vartiainen line.'

'You keep saying that,' said Steiner. 'And yet here I am.' He meant every word, but he felt the lack of a weapon keenly.

'Not for much longer,' replied Volkan Karlov.

A small cat, not much more than a kitten, hopped on to a small outcrop of debris above them and stared down at the Emperor with a curious, if affronted gaze. Another cat appeared a moment later, and then another.

'What is this?' muttered Volkan Karlov, frowning. A bright light appeared in the gloom at the lip of the fissure above them. A young soldier clutched a lantern, and from where he stood it formed a nimbus about the head of young woman attired in black.

'The Vartiainen line will not end today,' said the woman in a calm, reasonable tone.

'Kjellrunn?' asked Steiner in disbelief. His sister, the wayward, tangle-haired child of his memory, now the Stormtide Prophet, held out a hand. Her great-grandfather's sledgehammer launched from the ground and sped to her grip.

'Hello, brother.'

'Oh shit,' was all that Volkan Karlov could say before the Stormtide Prophet leapt from the edge of the fissure, sledgehammer raised above her head.

CHAPTER FORTY-ONE

Kjellrunn

Power, whether it be arcane power derived from dragons, or the political power derived from status and position, corrupts all but the purest of souls. Even enchanted artefacts are not immune to this, and the darker the enchantment the greater the corruption.

> – From the memoir of Drakina Tveit,
> Lead Librarian of Midtenjord Province

The sledgehammer sang to Kjellrunn softly in the darkness. It rose from the debris and flew to her hand like old friend. She half leapt, half fell, the weapon grasped above her head, yet she felt no rage, just the abiding calm that had settled on her since the leviathan's departure. She was Frejna's weapon now and, like death itself, she was inevitable.

The Emperor held up his arms on instinct. Perhaps he was tired. Perhaps he was injured. Perhaps he had called on the arcane once too often that day, and like a fickle mistress she refused his summons. Despite the Emperor's warding gesture the sledgehammer descended, connecting with the side of his face that had been petrified during his exchange with Silverdust. Chips of stone exploded from the man's face;

his jaw fractured. The through-swing hit the ground with such force that Kjellrunn almost lost her grip, and she landed heavily, grunting with effort, prompting a moment's hesitation. The grievously wounded Emperor stumbled backwards, hands going to his ruined face, fingers tracing the shattered geography of his jaw, shock etched in his bloodshot eyes.

'Your rule is at an end,' said Kjellrunn. 'Surrender or be destroyed.' She raised the hammer once more and stepped closer. The Emperor lurched forward and grabbed her by throat, lifting her off the ground. A terrible noise issued from his shattered face, the fear in his eyes now replaced with a furious anger.

'Get away from her!' A shadow flickered above them, followed by a flash of steel. Streig slashed downwards with the enchanted blade he had stolen from the Great Library of Arkiv. A moment later the Emperor's arm was severed and Kjellrunn fell to ground, clutching her throat.

'Nnnnnnuuuunngg!' The Emperor held out the stump. The two-handed blade had taken him just above the elbow. A silver shimmer passed over the wound before it turned to stone, an elegant way to stop himself from bleeding out. Kjellrunn admired the discipline it must have taken for him to wield the arcane in such a way when panic would have overwhelmed a lesser person.

Streig recovered from his leap into the fissure and made to strike again, but the Emperor struck him with a stone fist, before grabbing the two-handed sword by the crosspiece. The two men struggled and Kjellrunn summoned a hail of stone from the debris, pelting the wounded man. Streig stumbled away as the Emperor floated into the air, alighting a moment later on the lip of the fissure above them.

'Frejna's teeth,' cursed Streig.

'Nnnnnuuunnngg!' bellowed the Emperor from his shattered face, reaching towards the fissure with his remaining hand. The Ashen Blade scraped against stone as it was wrenched free from its hiding place in the debris, summoned to his grasp by the arcane. Steiner ran forward to snatch the weapon from the air, but Kjellrunn had other means. The Ashen Blade slowed and became still, trembling in the air as both the Stormtide Prophet and the Emperor exerted their will. For a breathless moment nothing happened, and then the Emperor turned his petrifying gaze on Kjellrunn. She looked away on instinct and her concentration faltered. The Ashen Blade slipped away, free of Kjellrunn's arcane grasp.

'No!' Steiner was already trying to climb out of the trench as the Emperor slipped the enchanted blade carefully through his belt. Now he had the pair of them, together at last. 'No!' howled Steiner.

The Emperor reached up to the roof and Kjellrunn felt a pang of despair.

'Frejna's teeth,' whispered Streig as he followed the direction of the man's grasp. 'Not again!' The ceiling was shaking; plaster dust drifted down; cracks spread in greater and greater numbers, black lines that foretold of being buried alive.

'Kjellrunn!' called out Steiner. 'Stop him.'

She knew what the Emperor was attempting, but not from any prescience; that had never been her gift. She could feel him reaching for the power of earth and the mastery of stone. She could sense him reaching up to pull down the roof of his court, risking himself in abject desperation.

'Steiner! Streig! To me.' The men obeyed without pause or question. She passed the sledgehammer to Steiner before raising both hands above her head.

'And Frøya hold me close,' said Kjellrunn as she threw up a ward with all of her concentration and every last reserve of her powers. Stone and plaster from the ceiling began to rain down, then the roof's timbers, and finally the tiles themselves. The debris clattered all around them, settling about an invisible dome of pure force, held back by sheer force of will.

'I . . . I don't know how much longer I can hold this,' said Kjellrunn, almost sobbing with the effort in the darkness.

'Kjellrunn, I'm sorry,' muttered Steiner.

'What for?'

'Everything.'

'Is there anything else you want to say to me?' she whispered.

'Volkan Karlov killed our father,' replied Steiner. The stone groaned ominously all about them. 'And now he's killed us too.'

For a moment Steiner wasn't sure if Kjellrunn had heard him. Nothing moved in the darkness and no reply sounded on the dusty air.

'Kjellrunn?' Streig's voice, quiet and low, trying to keep the rising panic he must surely feel at bay.

'I'm here,' she said at last. 'The stone is settling into place around the ward.' A heartbeat later and light lanced in from the side. The stone and timber were tumbling away, creating a ragged portal from their confinement. 'You first, Streig.' The soldier did as he was asked, and Steiner followed. The court was shrouded in swirling dust, as thick as any fog. Kjellrunn emerged from the debris of the collapsed roof and breathed out. The timber and stone that had fallen about them shuddered and collapsed into the space that Kjellrunn had protected with her ward.

'Where is he?' whispered Steiner, looking at the lip of the fissure for Volkan Karlov.

'The throne.' There was a despair in her eye that had not been there before the roof's collapse. 'Where else would he be?'

It took them a moment to drag themselves out of the fissure,

clambering up over debris and helping one another out of
the darkness. Steiner reached out for his sister, barely recognizable in her black vestments and with her hair tied back.

'Is Father really . . . ?'

'Yes,' admitted Steiner. 'I saw his shade.'

Poor Marek Vartiainen. So brave, so foolish. Volkan Karlov's
words invaded their minds, no different to the sinister whisper
the Emperor had used when he'd still been able to speak.

'And may Frøya keep you close,' said Kjellrunn before her
eyes rolled back in her head. Her knees gave out and Streig
caught her before she fell. Steiner shared a stunned look with
the former soldier.

It seems even the Prophet has her limits. The mocking tone of
Volkan Karlov's words was unbearable.

'Finish him, Steiner,' said Streig. 'Or none of us will survive.'
Steiner nodded with a grim acceptance.

'Get her out of here,' he replied before turning towards the
throne. Bittervinge's corpse formed a vast obstacle and Steiner
began scaling the monstrosity. The smell of decay was overpowering and Steiner retched as he climbed up over flaking
scales and the shattered bones where wings had once
protruded. On he went, heaving himself one-handed over
the dead dragon's ancient spine, then sliding down the other
side with the sledgehammer clutched in one scarred fist.
Volkan Karlov stood on the wide step surrounding the throne,
one Ashen Blade tucked in his belt, the other gripped in his
sole remaining hand.

*I have waited a long time to be in possession of both blades. Perhaps
in time I can even recover from the wounds I've suffered.*

Steiner eyed the dull blade, watching grey flakes fall from
the short weapon. Such a small thing, threatening to drain
his vitality should Volkan Karlov slip past his defences.

*What are you waiting for? I thought you would want to avenge
yourself for your father.*

'I do,' replied Steiner. 'And I will.' He was standing over an Imperial soldier. The man had died with his mace and shield. 'My father was a blacksmith and he always told me to use the right tool for the job.' The Emperor looked less sure of himself as Steiner stooped to pick up the shield. The Ashen Blade could only end him if it pierced his flesh.

A shield? It will do you no good.

'What was it you said earlier to Kimi?' asked Steiner. '"Let's put that to the test."' He ran forward, shield held before him, the sledgehammer clutched in a single hand. Volkan Karlov tried to evade him, but the shield slammed into the slender man, knocking him backwards into the throne, the same throne from which he had issued so many cruel decrees. The first Ashen Blade went skittering from the Emperor's numb fingers, but he sprang to his feet, eager to defend himself. Steiner put his shoulder to the shield and rammed the Emperor against the back of the throne, then followed up with a hammer strike that shattered the top of the throne and not the Emperor's skull as he had hoped.

Damn you, Vartiainen.

Volkan Karlov half slipped, half spun from the broken throne and Steiner lunged again. He slammed the shield forward and was rewarded with a dull grunt. The Emperor concentrated on keeping his footing and made no counter-attack, so Steiner dropped to one knee and swung hard. The sledgehammer glanced off the Emperor's knee and another grunt of pain issued from the petrified and shattered face. Steiner stood, using the edge of the shield to catch Volkan Karlov under the chin, but the Emperor had called on the arcane once more. His skin was now a dark granite colour, not just the stump of his severed arm, but every inch of him. Steiner grinned.

'I was hoping you'd do that.' He hefted the sledgehammer, determined to shatter the stone body of the Emperor, but his confidence was short-lived. Volkan Karlov's eyes had also changed to the colour of stone. Steiner averted his gaze, hiding behind the shield, stumbling forward in the hopes of breaking the Emperor's concentration. The sledgehammer became heavier with each passing moment and Steiner looked on with horror as the metal head and the stout wooden shaft turned to stone. Threads of arcane grey raced down the handle and Steiner dropped the weapon on instinct, afraid his hand might also become petrified.

Not so fearsome without your hammer, are you, Vartiainen?

Steiner shouted in frustration, then took the shield in both hands and raised it above his head and slammed downwards. The edge of the shield caught the Emperor in the chest and sent him stumbling sideways. He was drawing the second Ashen Blade when Steiner grappled him from behind, one hand catching Volkan Karlov's knife arm, while the other wrapped around his throat.

'This is for my Uncle Verner,' hissed Steiner into the Emperor's ear. The two men struggled, but Steiner's grip was absolute. Little by little he forced the hand holding the enchanted weapon back towards the Emperor.

You can't kill me with the Ashen Blade! My skin is as stone!

'And for my mother,' added Steiner, trembling with the effort. The Emperor's knife hand edged closer to his face.

You are a fool. You cannot defeat me!

'For my father,' added Steiner from between gritted teeth. 'And my great-grandfather.'

The tip of the Ashen Blade was just a finger's width from the Emperor's eye. Both men were locked in the fatal embrace, Steiner's body honed by hardship and toil, the Emperor's strength fuelled by the arcane. Try as he might, Steiner couldn't force Volkan Karlov's knife hand back any further.

You will not avenge yourself on me today.

'You're wrong,' said a voice from beside them. Kjellrunn

appeared from the dust like an apparition. 'We both will.' She laid the flat of her hand on the pommel.

'Do it!' shouted Steiner.

There are worse things than death!

Kjellrunn added her strength to Steiner's and the Ashen Blade sank into the Emperor's eye, until only the hilt remained, protruding from the socket. Kjellrunn snatched her hand away the moment the deed was done. Volkan Karlov convulsed violently and Steiner took a sharp intake of breath as a feeling of euphoria surged through him. For a moment it was hard to tell where the Emperor ended and Steiner began; they shook and convulsed together, life fleeing from one body to another. Kjellrunn stepped back wearing an expression of disgust as Volkan Karlov withered and died before their eyes.

'Steiner!' shouted Kjellrunn. Steiner prised his arms open and took a step back. Volkan Karlov hit the floor, a wizened corpse, the Ashen Blade still lodged in his skull. Steiner stared at his hands; his entire body was thrumming with power. Was this the arcane? Was this how Kjellrunn felt when she called on her powers?

'Steiner, what are you doing?' asked Kjellrunn, a note of panic in her voice. He knelt over the Emperor and pulled the enchanted blade free. He needed the blade, needed this feeling to never stop.

'Steiner?' Kimi emerged from the ruined court; Streig stood just behind her, sword in hand. They both stared at him with wary looks on exhausted faces. 'Steiner, I know how you're feeling.' Kimi took a step forward, her hands open to show she was unarmed. 'I felt that way too when I killed Bittervinge.'

'Such . . . power,' whispered Steiner, staring at the dull blade. The Emperor's blood had been sucked into the weapon, as if a thousand unseen mouths drank all at once.

'But it's not good for you, Steiner,' said Kimi.

'This is a power that was never meant for us,' said Kjellrunn quietly.

'No! I fought for this.' His voice was impossibly loud, his anger hot and irresistible. 'I defeated the Emperor!'

'Steiner, please?' begged Kjellrunn. 'Put the blade down.'

A faint shadow appeared beside Kjellrunn with two motes of amber light for eyes.

'Silverdust?'

It is I. Once you destroyed the Ashen Torment so the souls of the cinderwraiths on Vladibogdan could be free. Now I ask you to surrender the Ashen Blade in order to free yourself.

'But with an artefact like this' – Steiner could barely resist staring at the dark blade – 'none of my friends or family need ever die again.'

'That is not the natural way of things, Steiner,' said Kjellrunn.

There are worse things than death. An unusually long life brings its own problems. Silverdust held out an indistinct arm. *Please. Give me the blade, Steiner.*

CHAPTER FORTY-TWO

Silverdust

People speak of grief as if it is no more than a protracted bad mood, a period of low feeling that passes in time. I have always thought grief needs work and that work takes time. And yet one cannot begin the work of grief until one has moved on from the shock of loss, or the denial and bargaining that takes place to avoid it.

— From the memoir of Drakina Tveit, Lead Librarian of Midtenjord Province

It had been a long night and sleep had evaded them. The fighting had ended but their bodies remained wary and alert. One by one they had stumbled from the Imperial Court, coated in dust, silent as phantoms, hollow-eyed with all that they had seen. No one had felt much like talking. Steiner had withdrawn to a servant's common room, locking himself in with a jug of ale to still his shaking hands. Surrendering the Ashen Blade had been no easy thing and his shame had been waiting in ambush the moment he passed over the enchanted weapon.

When the sun came up, Kimi climbed to the roof, keen to catch sight of Tief, Taiga, and the dragons. Silverdust had no need of arcane senses to know the princess missed her comrades fiercely. Kjellrunn and Streig were standing before Silverdust in the antechamber outside the court. A small conclave of felines slept at Kjellrunn's feet, the sound of purring a pleasant backdrop of sound. Slivers of golden sunlight slid into the Imperial Palace through the many windows.

I believe I instructed you to return to Arkiv.

'You did.' Streig smiled. 'But I was never keen on taking orders. The decision was made for me in the end. The boat left and I was still ashore with four dozen people out for my blood.' The soldier leant on the crosspiece of the great sword, barely able to keep his eyes open.

'How did you survive?' asked Kjellrunn.

'Most of them only had knives, whereas I had this.' He patted the pommel of the sword affectionately. 'None could get close enough to kill me. They gave up after I'd given one or two of them a lesson.'

Go and rest, Streig. And a few days from now you can return home to Virolanti.

The soldier smiled and took himself away.

'What will happen now?' said Kjellrunn.

We must destroy the Ashen Blades, though magical artefacts are nigh impervious. I am at a loss how we can achieve such a thing.

'Surely Steiner's sledgehammer can break them?'

Normally, yes, but the Emperor petrified the weapon with his arcane gaze. I would not have thought such a thing was possible had I not seen it myself. I fear the sledgehammer is useless now, more likely to shatter than to damage the Ashen Blades.

The predicament, like the silence, enveloped them for a while before Kjellrunn spoke again.

'How are you? Steiner thought you'd been destroyed in the fighting.'

Silverdust held up one insubstantial limb; he had never

been so translucent. *It is kind of you to ask, though I imagine I must appear as an abomination to a prophet of Frejna. I, like the Ashen Blades, am not part of the natural order of life. Neither Frejna nor Frøya would have any affection for me.*

Kjellrunn thought on this for a moment before a tired smile crept across her face. 'I'm unorthodox. And you can't help being dead.'

No more than anyone else. Silverdust felt the woman's warmth. It gave him hope the years ahead might be brighter than the previous century.

'Why don't we go up to the roof and keep Kimi company? I'm keen to hear her side of the tale.'

Of course. I will need a few moments to attire myself. The wind is not kind to ones such as myself. The memory of the Emperor dispersing him with a summoned gale flitted through Silverdust's mind, horrifying and bleak. *Besides, I would like to find my mask again. I have owned it a very long time.*

Kjellrunn pushed open the doors to the court and picked her way across the debris, her entourage of cats following. Bittervinge's wizened corpse dwarfed everything in the room. The irony that the Imperial Court would serve as the father of dragon's tomb was not lost on Silverdust.

So much death, and yet a trace of the arcane lingers here. And of life.

'I feel it too.' Kjellrunn approached a small outcrop of scorched stone. 'This is a person,' she whispered reverently, kneeling down to see more clearly.

It is Felgenhauer. I fear she has succumbed to the taint of dragons. The price the arcane exerts on the human body is steep and when the fighting was at its most furious . . .

Kjellrunn ran her fingers over the statue's brow and spoke in a low voice. As she prayed she traced the contours of the stony face: its jaw, the hairline, the head. Stone flaked away revealing pale flesh beneath.

'Come back to us,' whispered Kjellrunn. The statue shivered and more stone flaked off. The sunlight brightened and a silver glow suffused both the former Matriarch-Commissar and the prophet, as if a writhing sigil had been burned into the floor around them. Silverdust felt an uncomfortable pressure weighing down on him. Suddenly the sensation was gone and the silver light faded with it. Felgenhauer took a shuddering breath before her eyes opened, filled with tears.

'Kjellrunn! I was trapped inside and couldn't reverse what I'd begun. How did you free me?'

'I prayed,' she replied with a smile.

I felt the most extraordinary manifestation of the arcane, at once overwhelming and subtle.

'That would be Frejna.' From anyone else the words would be boastful or delirious, but Kjellrunn said them quietly, in a matter-of-fact tone that brooked no questioning. 'However, she demanded a price.'

'What price?' asked Felgenhauer.

'She severed your connection with the arcane when she removed the taint.'

Felgenhauer looked from Kjellrunn to Silverdust as the import of what she'd heard dawned on her. She slumped forward and threw her arms around her niece's shoulders.

'Thank you.' Felgenhauer looked around the court with a wary look. Silverdust could feel her anxiety. 'Where is Steiner? Did he . . .?'

Survive. Yes. Though this has been hard on him.

'Can I see him?' asked Felgenhauer.

He has withdrawn. I suspect he is experiencing much turmoil after everything that has happened.

'Perhaps you could speak with him?' asked Kjellrunn.

Silverdust bowed and sought out Steiner Vartiainen, the dragon rider, Unbroken, slayer of Volkan Karlov.

* * *

Steiner sat at the common-room table and gently stabbed the surface with the tip of a kitchen knife. He wasn't sure why. Kjellrunn would have scolded him for marking the kitchen table they had owned back in Cinderfell, and his father would have complained about blunting the blade.

His father. The grief he had encountered in the catacombs had caught up with him. The lantern had long since burned down low, but a new light lit the room. Silverdust entered, bringing with him his usual aura.

'The Emperor said there are some things worse than death,' said Steiner, not looking up from scoring the table. 'And maybe this is one of those things.'

You speak of grief. Loss.

'Exactly. The perfect revenge. Volkan Karlov suspected we'd defeat him, and in return he's left me with an empire of loss.' Steiner felt the tears and clenched his jaw, refusing to shed them.

There are worse things than death. Silverdust drew closer. *And though I know you are in pain, you should not forget the living. Kjellrunn and Felgenhauer still live. Go to them, Steiner. Go to your family. It is what your father would want. For yourself and for them.*

'But I failed them! Don't you see? I failed him. I couldn't get my father back.'

You freed an entire continent from the tyranny of an Empire, Steiner Vartiainen. You are many things, but a failure is not one of them.

'Here they are,' said Kimi, pointing to the horizon. The sky was full of clouds promising spring rain, but the sun broke through here and there, dappling the ruined city in shafts of golden light. It was mid-morning and Steiner had emerged from his seclusion, grim-faced and silent. Silverdust had regained his mask and was attired in black once more. Felgenhauer had been put to bed and Kjellrunn watched over her aunt as she slipped in and out of sleep following the divine intervention.

I fear they bring sad news. Silverdust laid a hand on Steiner's shoulder but the blacksmith simply stared ahead, as if merely breathing were an effort.

'There're only two of them,' said Streig, giving voice to what everyone was thinking. The winged dots on the horizon came closer, travelling from the south of the city.

'Frøya save me,' said Kimi. 'Anything but that.' Silverdust could feel her growing unease as the dragons drew closer; and when they were closer still and there was no doubt that Namarii was not with them, Silverdust felt Kimi's shock.

'No, this can't be right,' whispered the princess. Stonvind and Flodvind descended and landed on the palace rooftop, though it was clear both of the dragons were in pain from scores of wounds. Tief looked at Kimi but there was no joy on his face and neither he nor Taiga raised a hand in greeting. The Spriggani climbed down from Flodvind's back.

'I can't believe how much they've grown,' said Steiner, breaking his silence at last.

Nor how much pain they have endured, added Silverdust.

'Where is Namarii?' said Kimi. Stonvind craned his neck until he was eye to eye with her.

Hello, Kimi Enkhtuya. Are you yourself again, or are you still under the influence of the Ashen Blade?

'I am myself again,' replied Kimi, her guilt a horrible sickness. 'Where is Namarii?' she asked again.

It seems you had quite an effect on him. Stonvind blinked his huge eyes and lay down. Kimi could almost feel the exhaustion emanating from the vast creature. *Namarii rescued me from the talons of a young dragon, but in doing so he sacrificed himself.*

'No. Surely he's still out there – wounded, perhaps, but not dead.'

Streig swore quietly.

You often discussed the concept of friendship with Namarii and it troubled him deeply. Dragons are not well disposed to think of others. Our very nature, all our thoughts, are bent towards domination and consumption. We live only for ourselves.

'Did you even look for him?' Kimi's tone was accusatory. Tief and Taiga's solemnity was replaced with a look of shock. Stonvind continued, unperturbed by the princess' reply.

But at the end, when Namarii came, I knew he came out of friendship. Not because he needed me to avenge himself on the Emperor, not because I was useful, but because of our friendship.

'Frøya save me. He must have thought I abandoned him.' Kimi's face contorted with yet more guilt mingled with grief.

It is miraculous to me that Namarii gave up his chance of killing Bittervinge so that he might intervene and save my life.

'We'll go out right now.' Kimi turned away and addressed Streig. 'We can find him. I need to tell him I'm sorry. The Ashen Blade . . .' But Kimi couldn't explain the awful power of the enchanted weapon, nor the intoxicating effect it had wrought on her. Tears tracked down her face and she shook with sobs.

I am sorry, Kimi. Silverdust drifted forward and laid a gloved hand gently on her shoulder. *He was a magnificent creature.* But the princess flinched away, an angry look on her face. She pointed at Flodvind.

'You! I demand you take me to Namarii.'

He is gone. The blue dragon stretched her neck until her blunt snout was a few away from Kimi.

'I demand you take me there.'

He died knowing that you would kill Bittervinge, just as he died knowing he was saving Stonvind.

'I can save him.' She pulled the Ashen Torment from beneath her tunic. 'I know it.'

You cannot save Namarii from death. The Ashen Torment does not work like that. He has been dead many hours, and even if such a thing were possible it would be deeply unnatural.

'Damn you!' shouted Kimi. 'Damn you all! I demand you take me to him!'

I will take you to his corpse. Flodvind flared her wings. *It is clear you need to see with your own eyes what you will not understand in words.*

Kimi slumped to her knees as her anger left her and the possibility of accepting Namarii's death became real. Taiga and Tief held her tight through the storm of grief that followed.

They had departed the rooftop in pairs and groups of three until Silverdust found himself alone. Hours passed by and the ancient cinderwraith decided he would watch the sun set on Khlystburg, ruined and broken as it was. The living were resting, coming to terms with the huge violence they had witnessed and partaken in, trying to find a way to justify and make peace with the swathes of death they had cut across the continent. Kjellrunn and Felgenhauer, related and yet strangers, were all but inseparable, while Tief and Taiga remained by Kimi's side, all of them grieving for Namarii. Stonvind and Flodvind slept and kept their own counsel. Streig had decided to pursue a more practical course and had taken to looting the palace of anything that looked portable.

And Volkan Karlov is finally dead. Silverdust would have wept had he been able to make tears. The stain of his hubris would forever mark Vinterkveld, but the Emperor's reign of cruelty and deceit was at an end.

'I thought you'd be up here,' said Steiner from behind him. 'Like that time on Vladibogdan, on the rooftops of the academy.'

I remember it well. I revealed my true nature to you that night.

'I never dreamed we'd find ourselves standing on this rooftop, just months later, having slain the Emperor.'

Nor I. So much has changed and I am grateful to you, Steiner. You set this in motion. Your will, your determination, your refusal to back down even in the face of overwhelming odds.

Steiner nodded but said nothing. Silverdust knew he heard the words, but his feelings were too bound up in grief for his father, his thoughts an endless roil of self-recrimination and frustration.

You are still torturing yourself for Marek's fate, yet you know that no one here blames you. You are a hero, Steiner.

'Just not to myself.' He looked away. 'I wish Kristofine were here. Everything is better when Kristofine is beside me.' He walked away, leaving Silverdust with the fading light and a great sadness. Suddenly he turned, his face caught in an expression of revelation. 'In the catacombs, we spoke to my great-grandfather and my father.'

We all did. I performed the summoning, but the ties of blood allowed you and Felgenhauer to converse with him.

'Then it follows you could summon Volkan Karlov,' said Steiner with a grim look of determination. 'We could ask him how to destroy the Ashen Blades.'

Steiner, what you are asking is no easy thing. There is no guarantee Volkan will surrender such knowledge to you.

'But there's a chance.'

There is always a chance, but everything comes at a price with Volkan.

'We have to try. We have to destroy the Ashen Blades.'

Surely there must be some other way?

'Then tell me, tell me how we destroy them?' Steiner frowned with impatience.

As you wish, but you will be hard pressed to convince the others.

CHAPTER FORTY-THREE

Steiner

All those years the rumours supposed that Veles was the ultimate authority on death magic, but Volkan Karlov had always thrived on secrecy. What came next should not have been a surprise for anyone.

– From the memoir of Drakina Tveit,
Lead Librarian of Midtenjord Province

It seemed appropriate that they try and raise the dead at night, and the Imperial Court was the perfect venue, filled with stench of death and littered with corpses as it was.

'Seeing the dead is one thing,' said Streig to the cinderwraith, unaware Steiner was within earshot, 'but conversing with them?' The soldier shook his head and grimaced.

Everyone who had fought against the Emperor had gathered for the grim ritual, though none spoke. Lanterns were held high in the gloom, illuminating weary faces and tired stares.

'Are you sure about this?' muttered Tief to Steiner.

'It might be the only way to learn how to destroy the Ashen Blades,' replied Steiner.

'I understand that but it don't seem right is all. I'm not a priestess but—' Tief fell silent under Steiner's unfriendly stare.

Taiga and Kjellrunn stepped forward. Steiner couldn't escape the feeling they were squaring up to each other, like knife fighters slowly circling their opponent.

'Sundra would not approve of this,' said Taiga in a quiet yet firm tone.

'This is our only chance to rid ourselves of the blades,' replied Kjellrunn. Their conversation was interrupted by the flutter of wings high above. As one the assembled people raised their lanterns and their glances to where the stars in the night sky stared down through the hole in the roof. The stars were not alone in witnessing the ritual to raise Volkan Karlov. Ink-black birds stared down with eyes of jet, almost invisible save for the quick, jerking motions of their heads. One of their number called out, its cry loud.

'It seems you have Frejna's attention,' said Taiga. Her gaze fell to the ground at Kjellrunn's feet, where two score cats patiently waited, eyes glittering in the lantern light. 'And Frøya's too.'

'Let's get on with it,' muttered Steiner.

'And when it's done,' said Streig, 'we can burn this whole palace down and salt the earth.'

'Agreed,' said Felgenhauer. Kjellrunn returned to her aunt's side and slipped one arm around Felgenhauer's waist, holding her steady. She was not the only one among them feeling weak after the battle. Silverdust had spent time reinvigorating himself, marshalling his powers for the morbid task ahead. Even by the standards of the arcane it was unusual.

'Doesn't seem right, using one ghost to raise another,' grumbled Tief, before Taiga shushed him with a stern look.

Let us begin, though the goddesses may not look kindly on us for doing so. The cinderwraith turned to Taiga. *You have your holy weapons, I trust?*

Taiga nodded and took the silver dagger and sickle in each hand, a look of calm resolve upon her slender face.

Silverdust held out a gloved hand and bowed his cowled head in concentration. The mirror mask reflected Volkan Karlov's maimed and aged corpse. The man was barely recognizable in death. The Ashen Blade had reaped a cruel harvest on his corpse, sapping his youth just as he in turn had sapped the youth of so many. Several minutes passed and the lanterns were lowered to the floor to spare aching arms. Steiner was ready to give up when he noticed his breath steaming on the air.

Slowly Silverdust raised his arms, gloved hands reached towards the night sky, fingers splayed. Steiner clutched the stone sledgehammer, out of habit more than anything – what use could it possibly be?

Come back to us from Frejna's realm, Volkan Karlov. We have questions for you.

The corpse at Silverdust's feet glowed with an amethyst light that shone through the cracks of Volkan Karlov's shattered face, emanating from empty sockets. The crows had been busy, it seemed.

Volkan Karlov, come back to us now, I command you.

A crow descended from the ruined roof and alighted on Silverdust's shoulder, making the already sinister form of the mirror-masked, black-clad cinderwraith more imposing still.

Volkan!

The corpse twitched and shook and the amethyst light grew brighter still.

'He is resisting us,' said Taiga. Her words stirred Silverdust's frustration, and the cinderwraith lifted the corpse from the floor with an arcane gesture.

You were formerly my student, Volkan, and I have questions.

The corpse blazed, as if an amethyst fire burned from every inch of its skin.

Gods damn you all, and you especially, Serebryanyy Pyli.

The Emperor's words sounded in Steiner's mind as if coming

from a great distance, with faint echoes chasing each word.

Was my death not enough for you?

I was damned by the Ashen Torment on Vladibogdan. As well you know. Damned to live a life without food, or drink, or friendship. Until recently.

Spare me your whining, Serebryanyy. I would rather return to the punishments Frejna has devised for me in the afterlife.

'We have questions,' said Steiner, stepping closer to the amethyst light. The spirit of Volkan Karlov turned his face, still whole, with the high forehead and piercing eyes Steiner remembered.

You have no power over me. What can you threaten me with? I am already dead and in a place of such suffering that you cannot begin to imagine.

'I will petition my goddess to release you from your torment,' said Kjellrunn, 'but only after you have told us how to destroy the Ashen Blades.'

Ah, the Stormtide Prophet. The girl who helped plunge an Ashen Blade into my very skull. What a hero you are.

He sneered. 'You can accept her offer or we can send you back this instant,' said Steiner. 'Back to your tortures.'

The spirit of Volkan Karlov bowed his head. After a moment he raised one arm and pointed at Steiner's petrified sledge-hammer.

You have everything you need.

'But it's ruined,' said Steiner. 'It will break apart with a single swing.'

'How can we trust you after decades of deceit and lies?' said Felgenhauer.

Trust? Of course you can't. But what other choice do you have, Nika?

Silverdust was tiring. Summoning the dead was no easy thing. He regarded the glowing amethyst light and marvelled that, for once, Volkan Karlov was telling the truth. Death had stripped him of his arcane defences, just as Frejna had stripped Felgenhauer of hers. The Emperor's mind, always a fortress against the mind-reading abilities of Academy Vozdukha, was now laid bare. He was desperate and afraid, yet a mote of arrogance remained, even now.

And how will this petition work? How will you wrest my soul from Frejna? Surely this task is beyond even her favoured prophet?

'I made no promises,' replied Kjellrunn. 'Only that I would pray to Frejna for your release.'

The crows on the rafters above called out, a shocking and discordant choir of outrage. Their coarse voices filled the night until one by one they became silent and brooding once more. Every bird stared with undisguised hate in their jet-black eyes. The spirit of Volkan Karlov smiled.

It was foolish to think she would release me after everything I have done to her and her precious Spriggani.

'Let's end this,' said Steiner, glowering at the apparition. 'We'll find out soon enough if he's telling the truth.'

We must take him at his word. Steiner's sledgehammer will unmake the Ashen Blades.

Silverdust tried to end the connection to Frejna's realm, desperate to cancel the summoning. The amethyst spirit knelt down and reached into the very ground with insubstantial hands and bowed his head.

'What is he doing?' shouted Taiga. 'End this. End this now!'

I am trying but he is keeping the connection open!

Volkan Karlov looked up with a smirk fixed firmly on his face.

Goodbye, Serebryanyy.

The spirit of the Emperor exploded outwards in a wave of amethyst light that passed through everyone present. The sphere of illumination became ever larger, rolling onwards until it passed, phantom-like, through the walls of the palace itself.

Tief swore in Spriggani before saying, 'I told you this wasn't right.'

Did the light harm any of you? enquired Silverdust. Everyone checked themselves over but none found evidence of physical harm.

'Perhaps it's a curse,' said Felgenhauer.

'It is a curse,' said Steiner, his voice rusty with grief. He stood up and retrieved his sledgehammer from the floor, struggling under the weight of the stone weapon. 'But it's not a curse on the living.'

Silverdust followed the direction of Steiner's gaze. The burnt bodies littering the Imperial Court were slowly climbing to their knees. Many simply tore themselves apart with the effort of standing, but some lurched to their feet.

'Gholes,' hissed Tief. 'He cursed us with gholes.' The crows flapped their wings in agitation and the entourage of cats at Kjellrunn's feet fled.

'We destroyed them in Izhoria!' Taiga held out the silver dagger and sickle of the goddess. 'And in Frøya's name we will destroy them here.'

'Form up in a circle!' shouted Kimi.

'Kjellrunn!' Felgenhauer's face was pale in the lantern light, her skin waxy. 'My powers . . .'

'Stay close to me,' replied Kjellrunn. 'Streig! Guard my aunt!' The young soldier nodded and took up position.

'There must be two dozen of the bastards,' said Tief as more of the corpses rose to their feet.

'That's around four each,' replied Kimi, 'and we've all faced worse odds than that.'

Silverdust launched a lance of arcane fire across the room, taking one of the gholes down in the blink of an eye. *Steiner, are you sure you can wield that weapon now that it has been petrified?*

The gholes came at them from all sides, bodies bent low,

arms held out wide with fingers crooked into bony claws. Steiner stepped forward and swung with a war cry containing all of his grief and all of his fury. The ghole before him simply disintegrated under the force of the blow, coming apart in a shower of bone fragments and blackened sinew.

It seems I was wrong to doubt you. Silverdust surged forward and caught a ghole by the throat as white-hot arcane fire burned around his hand. The ghole shrieked and twisted, but its head came loose in moments as flesh and bone were immolated.

'I am not dying like this,' grunted Steiner as he heaved the much heavier sledgehammer around, breaking the forearms of the nearest ghole. The creature reared back and hissed, but Steiner slammed the shaft of the hammer into the ghole's face, splitting the skull.

'I knew it was a bad idea,' muttered Taiga as the gholes charged towards her. Tief and Kimi stood either side of her, weapons drawn, faces focused for the battle to come. 'Ready?' shouted Taiga. She took a step forward and crossed the silver dagger and sickle above her head, releasing a wordless shout. The enchanted weapons chimed softly as they met and a brief aura of silver light illuminated them. The gholes, confronted by the weapons of the goddess Frøya, stumbled or hesitated. 'Now!' shouted Taiga. Kimi reached them first, hacking downward through a shoulder until her blade met the sternum and lodged fast. She planted a boot upon the creature's chest and kicked the corpse free.

'That's one!' she shouted back. Tief ducked under the slashing claws of the ghole attacking him, dropping to a crouch and slicing through the undead horror's hamstrings with a wicked-looking short blade. The ghole fell to the floor and scrambled around, using its hands to pull itself towards Tief with a single-minded fury.

'Hate these things,' said Tief, drawing a longer blade. The ghole swiped at him, but Tief met the attack with his blade and removed the claw-like hand with a deft strike. 'Hate. Hate. Hate,' he repeated, stamping on the ghole's head until it came apart on the tiled floor. The ghole stopped moving. 'That's two.'

'Three!' bellowed Kimi as she took another ghole under the chin with a powerful strike from her two-handed sword. 'And four!' The blade descended and smashed another ghole to the floor. It tried to stand but was quickly relieved of its head.

Streig, who knew of Matriarch-Commissar Felgenhauer by her steely reputation, found himself in the strange position of having to defend her. The situation was made stranger still because his opponents had been, until just moments before, corpses.

'What need for Hel with monsters like these?' he whispered, swinging his blade in a wide arc. Two gholes jumped back out of range, but a third caught the strike in the side of its head and dropped to the ground. Felgenhauer cowered behind him.

'Get back!' he shouted. Changing his grip on the two-handed sword, he thrust forward, spear-like, and ran another ghole through the throat. A twist of the blade and the creature's head came free. The last of the gholes attacking Streig came for him before he had recovered his stance. Bony claws reached out before the undead creature was flung across the court, where it crashed into the ruins of the throne. Streig looked over his shoulder. Kjellrunn smiled.

'That was close,' he whispered.

'Sorry,' replied Kjellrunn. 'This is partly my fault.' She made another gesture, striking the air with a flat hand. Another ghole was thrown into the wall, as if it had been swatted.

'Keep knocking them down,' said Streig. 'And I'll keep carving them up.' He swung again, not quite believing he was fighting shoulder to shoulder with the Stormtide Prophet.

Silence settled upon the Imperial Court once more as the gholes were bested. Steiner stalked around the room, caving in the skulls of the creatures.

'Just in case any of them entertain the notion of coming back. Again.'

'Did the Emperor really think that would pose a danger to us?' said Tief. 'Two dozen gholes are barely a threat with Kjellrunn and Silverdust here.'

'Thanks,' said Steiner, not looking up as he smashed in the head of another wizened corpse.

'No offence, Steiner, but a kid with a hammer is no match for the arcane.'

'Tell that to Vigilant Shirinov,' replied Steiner. The ceiling above them creaked and dust drifted down.

'What now?' muttered Tief. Flodvind's head peeked through the hole in the ceiling.

You may want to get to the rooftops. Something has happened, and it has affected the whole city.

'Frejna's teeth.' Steiner mashed the last of the ghole's heads with the stone hammer.

'The whole city?' said Kjellrunn, pale and worried.

The dead are walking the streets, avenging themselves on the living. Nowhere is safe.

CHAPTER FORTY-FOUR

Kimi

While the defeat of the Emperor and Bittervinge were tumultuous events, their deaths were conducted out of sight but for a few. The refugees from the city, however, saw firsthand what came next. With nowhere to go, little food, and few weapons, the tide of gholes posed a real threat to an already desperate people.
> – From the memoir of Drakina Tveit,
> Lead Librarian of Midtenjord Province

They slept badly, barricading themselves into the palace as best they could. Those who were able took watches through the small hours. The gholes did not disturb the palace through the night but no one had a good word to say come the dawn.

'We should never have summoned him,' said Kimi, fixing a saddle to Flodvind in the Imperial Gardens. 'Now things are worse.'

'No knowing how many of those things are out there,' agreed Tief.

'So you're just going to leave?' said Steiner. As ever Silverdust lingered just behind him, a looming shade. Felgenhauer and Kjellrunn were also present to see them off.

'There's an encampment to the south.' Kimi flashed an

angry look over her shoulder. 'Lots of people have fled the city, some Yamal among them. They won't stand a chance without our help.'

'They're miles away!' replied Steiner.

'And gholes hunt,' said Kimi. 'You didn't see them in Izhoria. They hunt for miles and they hunt the living. I will not let my kin die at the hands of such creatures.'

'Tief? Not you too?' said Steiner. The Spriggani was fixing a saddle to Stonvind with a pained expression on his face.

'You have Silverdust and Kjellrunn,' replied Tief. 'And Kimi has always had Taiga and myself.'

'And two dragons!' replied Steiner.

'It does sound a little uneven when you put it like that,' replied Tief. 'You have Streig too. He's a fine lad.'

'Not exactly a dragon though, is he?' replied Felgenhauer with an arch look. 'No offence, Streig.'

'None taken,' replied the soldier.

Tief shrugged with an embarrassed expression. Kimi mounted up and extended a hand to help Taiga into the saddle, but the high priestess shook her head.

'I'm sorry, Your Highness, but my brother has a point. I'll stay here with Steiner and Kjellrunn.'

Kimi looked aghast. 'What?'

'Kjellrunn is the Stormtide Prophet; our faiths have always worked hand in hand. I don't see why today should be any different.'

'Taiga, I . . .' Kimi slid down from the saddle. Flodvind flapped her wings in irritation. 'Staying here is a death sentence.'

'So you admit it!' said Steiner with a curl of his lip.

'You created this!' replied Kimi. 'No one, not one among us wanted you to bring back the spirit of Volkan Karlov, but you and your sister wouldn't listen to reason.'

'I don't have time for this horseshit,' replied Steiner. 'I have a palace to defend.' He turned away and stalked off, trailing curses as he went.

'Taiga.' Kimi took her friend's hand. 'There's no telling how many gholes are roaming the streets. They'll fetch up here soon enough.'

She has made up her mind. Flodvind dipped her head until it was close to enough for Taiga to reach out and rest a hand against the azure dragon's snout. *It was an honour to fly with you.*

'I will see you again, Your Highness,' said Taiga calmly. 'Both of you,' she added, looking at Flodvind.

'Taiga, have you finally lost your mind?' Tief frowned. 'We've always stuck together, flown together, fought together.'

'And now Namarii is gone. It's best Kimi takes Flodvind. I've always preferred to keep my feet on the ground. You know that. I'll be right here, so be sure to come back for me.'

'I will.' Tief hugged his sister and turned away, his face creased in anguish. The Spriggani's tears prompted Kimi's own and she reached inside her tunic, pulling the Ashen Torment free, lifting the chain over her head. The dragon charm glittered in muted jade green.

'You should keep this,' replied Kimi. 'Just until I return.' Taiga nodded and the two women embraced.

'Go and save your people, Your Highness. I'll look after Steiner. Not that he needs it with his sister here.' The Spriggani woman smiled and Kimi felt her heart break a little as she climbed up into the saddle once more.

Are you ready to leave? asked Flodvind, but she had never felt less ready in her life.

The flight south did nothing to reassure Kimi. Gholes dashed and scurried through the streets, hunting the living with all the hissing rage of the hateful dead. Tief was grim-faced and Stonvind remained quiet. Even the sound of the wind seemed muted as the dragons flew south.

'There!' Kimi pointed to a knot of gholes, pale skin contrasting sharply with the grasslands. The creatures ran hunched and bent low to the ground, hands reaching forward, ready to strangle the life out of whatever came close.

Stonvind dipped lower, then released a terrible sound as fire emerged from his jaws, immolating everything on the ground. A few of the creatures staggered on until the fire burned up their bodies, leaving charred bones and little else.

Tief waved from his seat at Stonvind's shoulders. The dark grey dragon returned to the skies alongside Flodvind.

'Let's hope it's always that easy!' shouted Tief above the wind. Kimi nodded and forced a smile.

Do not give up hope, Kimi. Flodvind's gentle words drifted into her mind like dandelion seeds. *This turn of events is nearly at an end.*

'But whose end?' Kimi couldn't keep a leash on her bitterness. 'We were supposed to kill Bittervinge and the Emperor. We were supposed to change things for good, but now we have hundreds of undead stalking the province. What happens if they organize themselves and start raiding other provinces?'

Flodvind declined to answer but descended gracefully. They had reached the camp. The people surged towards them, keen for news and for answers, not least for an explanation of the amethyst light that had shone from the city.

'The Emperor is dead!' shouted Tief. 'Slain by Steiner the Unbroken and the Stormtide Prophet!' The crowd called out in shock, caught between cheering the end of tyranny and mourning the end of the Empire. 'And Kimi Enkhtuya stands before you, Princess of Yamal, slayer of Veles and Bittervinge!' The crowd erupted into applause and Kimi did her best to smile, but in truth she didn't feel victorious. The rise of the gholes had soured her every waking thought. Tief told the crowd everything, while Kimi kept to herself, an imposing yet aloof presence by his side.

They had landed for perhaps two hours before the next hunting party of gholes were sighted. Stonvind and Flodvind were ready to take to the air. Kimi climbed back into the saddle, though her thoughts were far away, preoccupied with Khlystburg and the palace, fretting for friends she had turned her back on in the name of duty.

CHAPTER FORTY-FIVE

Kjellrunn

*Not even someone in command of all the facts could have fore-
seen how things would end from there. But end they did, and
in the most shocking of ways. The regrets of that day lingered
long in the minds of the living and many were left wondering
if the cost had been too high.*

— From the memoir of Drakina Tveit,
Lead Librarian of Midtenjord Province

'He's really gone,' said Steiner. Try as they might they couldn't
find his body. Marek had been erased by the Empire just as
the Vigilants had seemingly erased children with witchsign.

'I'm afraid so.' Kjellrunn held her brother close. Her heart
ached fiercely. It ached for Steiner, and for herself, but most
of all for her father. How terrible his final hours must have
been, holding out hope his children would save him, only to
be slain by Volkan Karlov.

'I'm sorry, Steiner,' said Felgenhauer.

They had retreated to an upper floor of the palace, to a
room fit for a dignitary. A portrait of a noble with a lofty
expression stared down at them, and a four-poster bed dominated the room. The furniture was exquisite and dusty in equal

measure. Silverdust and Streig had taken a room at the other end of the corridor. Both rooms were situated by staircases and it was agreed that nothing was to come up and no one was to venture down until Kimi returned.

'They could at least have taken us with them,' complained Steiner, changing the subject.

'The dragons would never have managed with all of us,' said Kjellrunn softly. 'It's a wonder they're flying at all after everything they've been through.'

'You should eat something,' said Felgenhauer, 'before the food spoils. There's no telling when we might get another chance to eat.'

'And no one wants to go back to the kitchens,' added Kjellrunn. Seven roaming gholes had awaited them the last time they had searched for food.

'I can't believe she left,' said Steiner, still nursing his grudge against Kimi.

'But we didn't,' said Kjellrunn. 'We still have each other.' She smiled at her aunt, and Felgenhauer smiled back, exhausted and wrung out as she was. A knock on the door roused them and Taiga entered a moment later.

'You should keep a better watch on the staircase,' said the high priestess of Frøya. 'Those things can move quietly when they choose to.'

'What have you seen?' asked Kjellrunn. Taiga had taken to wandering the battlements, keeping watch over the grim and restless city.

'Nothing good.' She was about to say more when sounds of fighting interrupted them. Kjellrunn rushed from the room just in time to see a flash of light at the end of the corridor. Silverdust was casting arcane fire down the stone stairwell, no doubt attacking a ghole. Kjellrunn ran on and saw Streig cut another attacker down with his two-handed sword. The ghole collapsed and fell down the stairs, a crumpled corpse to add to the pile.

'That's the second attack in two hours,' said the young soldier. 'At this rate there's no telling how long we'll hold out.'

We will endure. Silverdust immolated the corpses on the staircase with an outstretched hand.

'You'll endure, you mean,' said Streig. 'I'm fairly certain there's nothing that can kill you.'

Kjellrunn left the unlikely friends to their duty and hurried back to all that remained of her family. She would cry later, she told herself, once they were safe. Until then she needed all of her wits and all of her focus.

'I don't see how we're going to survive,' said Felgenhauer quietly. There was a resignation in her voice that chilled Kjellrunn.

'Why not?' asked Taiga. 'We've made it this far.'

'Steiner and I came through the catacombs beneath the palace when we were trying to steal one of the Ashen Blades.'

'Catacombs,' said Taiga, almost wincing.

'Catacombs containing dead war heroes from over seventy-five years ago.' Felgenhauer bowed her head and released a long sigh. 'There's no question the Emperor's parting gift was meant to bring them back. The dead city folk? They're just a convenient benefit. It's the soldiers Volkan wanted to raise, and not even death could stop him.'

The sound of naked feet slapping against stone told them the conversation was over. Steiner lunged forward, stone hammer in hand, muscles straining under the weight. Taiga took a deep breath and drew her holy weapons before following the Unbroken to the top of the stairs. Kjellrunn joined them just in time to see Steiner catch a ghole in the face with the upswing of the stone hammer. Its head came apart in a shower of dark red gore, but another two creatures were racing up the stairs behind it.

'Steiner!' shouted Kjellrunn, thrusting a flat palm outwards. The arcane responded, slamming the first ghole against the far wall. Taiga stepped forward and thrust her silver dagger into the second ghole's chest, before raking her sickle across the creature's scrawny throat. The fell corpse twitched before collapsing, clutching at its neck.

'Is that all of them?' asked Kjellrunn. Steiner leaned out over the rail and glanced down. The staircase was not quiet and Steiner's expression gave her little hope.

'We should get to the roof,' he said. 'Now.' As one they turned and ran towards Silverdust and Streig at the other end of the corridor.

What are you doing? Arcane fire reflected from Silverdust's mirror mask as he seared another pair of gholes threatening to climb the last few steps.

'There are too many!' shouted Kjellrunn above the din of fighting. Behind her a ghole broke through a window in a shower of glass. The creature hissed and flexed withered fingers, the white bone ready to rend Kjellrunn's flesh.

'No!' she bellowed. A glimmer of the old anger she had once felt rose and the ghole was ripped apart. Felgenhauer stared at her with an expression somewhere between awe and fear.

'How did you—?' But there was no time to answer such a question.

Streig was climbing a ladder that would take them to the roof. Silverdust changed one of his hands into a burning spearhead and punched through a ghole's chest as it reached the top of the stairs.

Quickly now!

Steiner was guarding the corridor they had just retreated along, where six gholes were fighting among themselves in order to reach the living first.

'The roof is safe,' shouted Streig from above them through a trapdoor. 'For now at least.' Taiga climbed the ladder next, followed by Felgenhauer.

'You go,' said Steiner, hefting the stone hammer. Kjellrunn took him by the shoulder and slipped in front of him, then made a two-handed gesture, both arms sweeping downwards. The floor in the corridor shook and the gholes stumbled and fell.

'You go,' said Kjellrunn. 'I was too late for Father; I'm not losing you too.'

'Frejna's teeth, Kjellrunn. Why are you always so stubborn?'

Kjellrunn grinned. For the briefest of moments they were just two bickering siblings, not the Stormtide Prophet, not Steiner the Unbroken, not grieving children.

Come on now! Both of you! Silverdust ascended to the roof; the cinderwraith needed no ladder to help him escape. Steiner smashed another foul creature back down the stairs and raced up the ladder as more seething gholes gave chase.

'Kjell?'

She had known there wouldn't be time to climb the ladder, but she was the Stormtide Prophet, and her ways were not the ways of mere mortals. Kjellrunn stepped through the recently broken window as the gholes closed in on all sides. She took a deep breath and focused, then levitated up to the roof. The gravel paths of the Imperial Gardens waited below her, along with a seething tide of gholes all scurrying to find a way into the palace and hunt them down. Kjellrunn smiled and levitated higher, joining the others. An idea was forming. Steiner was hammering every ghole who climbed the ladder, but they would not have long before the unholy creatures began to climb the walls and reach them.

'So this is how we go?' said Streig, forcing a smile.

Not while I remain! Silverdust's hands were two fiery blades, ready to reap a scorched harvest.

'Taiga, I need the Ashen Torment,' said Kjellrunn. 'Will you pray with me?'

'Of course,' replied the high priestess of Frøya. 'What are we praying for?'

'A cessation of all dead things,' replied Kjellrunn, dropping to her knees. Her eyes glanced towards the mirror-masked cinderwraith. 'I'm sorry, Silverdust.'

I understand. There is no other way. Promise me Streig will be safe.

Kjellrunn nodded to the cinderwraith as Taiga handed over the jade artefact and adopted a similar pose. Steiner continued to defend the trapdoor, where scrabbling claws and hissing skulls stared up from the floor below. Felgenhauer huddled close to her nephew.

'No other way?' said Streig. 'What's going on?'

Some sacrifices have to be made.

'What sacrifices?' shouted Streig, his eyes darting to the edge of the roof where a dozen gholes were pulling themselves up with a wiry strength.

'They're here,' said Felgenhauer.

'Let them come,' grunted Steiner as Silverdust cast a javelin of fire towards the nearest ghole. It fell back into the gardens three storeys below, falling like a comet.

Kjellrunn, whatever you intend to do, you must do it now!

More gholes had climbed the opposite edge of the roof, just forty feet from where they huddled.

'I can see Kimi!' shouted Streig, pointing south. 'They're coming back. The dragons are coming back!' Flodvind and Stonvind could be seen high above the city, but too far away to be of aid.

'They won't get here in time,' replied Steiner. The gholes sprinted forward and Kjellrunn drifted into the air, eyes closed, the Ashen Torment pressed between her praying hands. Her hair floated around her head as if underwater and her lips moved silently as if in a fever.

'May Frejna's eye not find you,' she said, her voice impossibly loud.

Goodbye, everyone, I will miss you. Silverdust bowed his head.

'And may Frøya keep you close,' shouted Kjellrunn, crushing the Ashen Torment between her hands.

CHAPTER FORTY-SIX

Kimi

People still speak of the day two war-weary and wounded dragons set down on the docks of Arkiv, and more than a few sincerely wish to set eyes on such noble creatures again.

> – From the memoir of Drakina Tveit,
> Lead Librarian of Midtenjord Province

The gholes' predations had stopped almost as quickly as they had begun. Even the frenzied intelligence that still lurked within the corpses feared the dragons, it seemed.

'I'm going back,' Tief had said. 'I should never have left my sister there. What was I thinking?' He was climbing into the saddle before Kimi could object. And so they had flown with all the energy and urgency Flodvind and Stonvind could muster. The gholes rushed towards the centre of the city, where the Imperial Palace stood, damaged yet beautiful in its ruination. The building was being swallowed as a swarm of undead rose up. It was as if half the city were laying siege to the place, armed with nothing more than a ravening hatred.

'Taiga!' shouted Tief, for all the good it would do him. The dragons beat their wings harder and the wind whipped past.

The gholes had climbed the palace walls and made it to the palace roof, closing in on their friends and allies.

'Oh, Frøya no. Please don't let them . . .' Kimi's words were snatched away as a column of green light raced into the air from the palace roof. A ripple of emerald brilliance followed a heartbeat later, passing through the undead hordes as it expanded in a shockwave of force. The gholes exploded apart in showers of black dust. Scores of the unholy terrors were destroyed in a moment, then hundreds. The wave of force rolled onwards over the city, cleansing all that Volkan Karlov had wrought from the realm of the dead. The gholes' ashes scattered on the wind, and motes of yellow light remained after, a vast constellation of stars in the evening light.

'Taiga?' shouted Tief again. The dragons banked around the rooftop of the palace, now silent and stained with the ashes of the gholes. Kimi was already halfway out of the saddle as Flodvind set down.

'Taiga? Steiner?' Kimi stared around in wonder as the motes of light began to rise into the evening sky. The souls of the undead were now going to their final rest, it seemed.

Streig, Felgenhauer, and Steiner were kneeling, heads bowed, while Taiga knelt too, with her hands joined in prayer. Kjellrunn was levitating in the air nearby, an aura of light emanating from her body.

'Where's Silverdust?' whispered Tief with a stricken expression.

'Steiner.' Kjellrunn's voice sounded as if she were many miles distant. 'Steiner.' Kjellrunn's brother looked up at the Stormtide Prophet.

'Not you too,' he said in a small voice burdened with despair.

'Just as Volkan Karlov's long life was unnatural, so too are my powers. I cannot remain here, but I will always be with you.'

'No, Kjell.' Steiner struggled to his feet and held out one

hand. The aura of light continued to shimmer about the prophet. 'Not after everything we've done.' His voice cracked. 'I can't lose you too.'

'These powers have no place here. The Emperor is defeated, and Bittervinge too. No one person should ever be so powerful.' She looked at the palms of her hands. 'Not like this.'

'No, Kjell.' Steiner was pleading. 'Not after father and Verner and Silverdust.'

'Look for me in the oceans. I will always be there for you.' Kjellrunn smiled with look of tender sadness before lifting her face to the darkening sky. The light emanating from her grew brighter and brighter still until Kimi averted her eyes.

'Kjell?' Steiner called out for her one more time as the light faded, but the Stormtide Prophet was gone, ascended to who knew where. All of them looked upwards, where the souls of the undead drifted higher and higher, motes of golden light, floating away from Vinterkveld and all its suffering.

'It's like that time back on Vladibogdan,' said Kimi softly. 'When you destroyed the Ashen Torment the first time.' The motes of light blinked out, one by one, until only the first stars of evening remained.

'Silverdust and Kjellrunn were still with us back then,' Steiner whispered. 'But not this time.'

Kimi looked at the wiry and scarred man who stood beside her, so different to the young boy who'd arrived in the forges months ago. He was trembling, though whether it was from exhaustion or grief she couldn't tell. Likely both.

'You did it, Steiner. You killed the Emperor.'

'Kjellrunn and I did it together, but I'm not sure it was worth it. I've lost so much to Volkan Karlov. Too much.' Steiner turned to Felgenhauer and fell into her arms, wordless and distraught.

*   *   *

The city remained as silent as a tomb, and Kimi was certain they were the only living creatures for miles in any direction. That night they slept more soundly and deeply than they ever had before, though their grief, both shared and private, waited patiently for them with the dawn.

'We should get word to the other provinces,' said Tief. 'Or the people at the encampment are going to starve to death.'

'We could fly to Arkiv,' said Kimi. 'They can spread the word via ship.'

'Good,' said Felgenhauer. She sat beside Steiner with one arm around his shoulders. 'Tell the ships to come, tell them the Emperor's rule is ended, tell them Khlystburg needs help.'

'We're not going to call it that any more.' Steiner voice was husky with grief and sleep. 'The city of whips is finished.'

'I'll come with you,' said Streig quietly. 'I'm not sure what else to do now that Silverdust has gone.' Kimi nodded and turned to Tief, expecting some complaint or other.

'Not me,' said her friend. 'I'm going to rest up here with Steiner and my sister. These old bones are good for nothing, I'd say.'

'I understand,' replied Kimi, and crushed the Spriggani in a fierce embrace.

'Always forget how strong you are,' muttered Tief. He took out his pipe but the tobacco had run out some time before and he cursed softly. Taiga kissed Kimi on each cheek and smiled. She'd barely said a word since Frøya's intervention.

'I'll see you again,' Kimi said to Tief and Taiga before approaching Steiner. He didn't look up, didn't meet her eye. The fire had gone out of him and Kimi didn't hold much hope it would return.

She stayed another day in order to rest the dragons. Tief and Taiga remained with her the whole time, reminiscing, voicing gratitude, and remembering Marozvolk in their quieter moments. When the following morning came Kimi was glad to leave. The sadness was suffocating and she had a strong desire to be in the air again.

'Are you ready?' she said to Streig.

'Time to go,' said the young soldier. 'I'll be seeing you,' he added to the others, but Kimi found it hard to believe he'd be back.

The journey across the sea did not provide any opportunity to converse with Streig, and so she had been left alone with her thoughts as the dragons stretched their wings and glided across the Ashen Gulf.

I feel your loneliness keenly. Flodvind had spoken little since their departure, but her words appeared in Kimi's mind softly.

'I've been with Tief and Taiga so long now, I barely know what to do without them.'

There is no need for you to do anything. Just sit in the saddle and enjoy the ride.

'When have you ever known me to sit patiently and do nothing?'

Do you have a choice?

'No.' Kimi smiled. 'But I'd rather be occupied with something else than these thoughts and feelings.' Her smile faded. 'I miss them. I even miss Steiner and Silverdust for that matter. And I miss Namarii too, arrogant as he was.'

You have faced many challenges, Your Highness, but the greatest challenge is how you face your grief. Will you sit with it, or merely try to escape by distracting yourself?

Flodvind's words shifted something inside Kimi, like a stubborn knot coming undone, a part of herself she had been ignoring. Kimi Enkhtuya let herself weep as the cobalt waves of the Ashen Gulf raced by below her; the wind on her face dried her tears but the sadness would remain a good deal longer.

*   *   *

Arkiv was more beautiful than Kimi had expected, and while she had no love for cities and the crowds of people they promised, she had to admit there was a majestic splendour to the island.

'How did you enjoy your first time riding a dragon?' she asked Streig. They had set down just north of the docks and caused quite a stir among the locals. The young soldier staggered down from the saddle, stiff and bow-legged, and pressed his hands to the small of his back.

'I'm not sure "enjoy" is the word I'd use.' He released a sound partway between a grunt and sigh. 'No offence, Stonvind, but I'm not made for the saddle. I'm a foot soldier at heart and a foot soldier I'll remain.'

The people of Arkiv began to gather at a distance, both intrigued and wary of the wounded dragons.

'It looks like we have some explaining to do,' said Kimi.

'Not me,' said Streig. 'The glory is all yours. Tell the story well.'

'Glory? Is that what we've earned for our troubles?'

'I scored some riches,' replied Streig, 'but only because I looted the palace.' He slung a heavy sack over his shoulder and grinned. 'So long, princess.' Streig saluted with a tired smile and headed off into the city, waving off questions from the crowd as he went. More and more of the city folk turned their attention to Kimi when it became apparent that the scruffy soldier wasn't stopping.

'What happened?' asked an older man. 'Does Khlystburg still stand?'

'Yes, but barely.' Kimi forced a smile. 'Why don't we find a tavern? I've been in the saddle for two days and I desperately need a bath, a meal and good glass of wine.'

'And your dragons will behave, will they?' shouted someone from the back of the crowd.

'Only if they're fed. Can someone provide some livestock? I'll settle up with them shortly.'

'How do we know you'll pay up?' asked an old woman with a furious look. 'We don't even know who you are.' Her words were full of scorn and Kimi's tiredness dropped away. She drew herself up to her full height and raised her voice so all present would hear her words.

'I am Kimi Enkhtuya, Princess of Yamal, slayer of Veles, slayer of Bittervinge, and champion of Frøya. These are my friends, Stonvind and Flodvind. I have crossed this continent in order to end the Solmindre Empire; I have lost friends and allies; I have fought undead gholes and Grave Wolves to stand before you.' Kimi stared down at the old woman. 'That's who I am.'

The old woman opened her mouth to speak and everyone present turned to her, curiosity burning.

'Well, in that case we should get you some food, dear.'

Kimi smiled. Tief had been right, it did sound impressive when spoken aloud.

The tavern was quickly inundated with the city folk of Arkiv. The owner arranged sittings, in which people could enter and hear Kimi talk about the Empire's downfall. Two days passed where she did little more than sleep, eat, tell stories, and beg anyone who would listen to sail supplies across the gulf to Khlystburg. She shook hands with several sea captains who promised her they would set sail as soon as they'd finished loading.

On the third day a familiar face appeared in the tavern, though Kimi hadn't seen her in months. 'Kristofine?'

'Your Highness.'

'I wasn't sure what happened to you in all the confusion.' Kimi didn't know whether to curtsey, bow, shake hands, or hug the woman. They had barely spoken during their brief time together aboard the *Watcher's Wait*. 'Sit with me.'

'I'm here with friends,' replied Kristofine. Standing just behind her were Streig and a man and woman she didn't recognize. 'This is Drakina; she was a librarian at the Great Library. This is Reka; he was a lieutenant. He helped me get to Arkiv.'

'And he wasn't the only one,' said Streig.

'I was hoping you could help me get back to Khlystburg,' said Kristofine. 'I'm desperate to see Steiner.'

'Of course.' Kimi forced a smile. 'But I'm heading south. I have to attend to my people, and I've no wish to set eyes on Khlystburg again. Not for a few months at least.'

'But with the dragons I could be with Steiner in a matter of days.'

'I'm sorry, Kristofine, but I'm not going back. Namarii died defending that wretched city. I . . .' She remembered the intoxicating effect of the Ashen Blade. 'I was not myself during that time. Scores of people died.'

Kristofine stood up so quickly the stool she had been sitting on upended and slammed to the ground.'To Hel with you then,' she muttered, and marched from the tavern.

'I did warn her you wouldn't go back,' said Streig.

'Then why did she insist on asking?' said Reka.

'Because she's in love,' replied Kimi. 'And people in love are prepared to do anything.'

'Maybe we could come to some arrangement,' said Streig.

'I said no, Streig.' Kimi frowned and looked away. 'I'm not going back.'

'Just hear me out,' said the soldier with an impish smile.

CHAPTER FORTY-SEVEN

Taiga

The Council of Midtenjord Province shepherded the former Empire through the difficult years ahead. The council members were held in such high regard that further outbreaks of war or border disputes were quickly silenced. Their fame and the sacrifice of their comrades held the fledgling union together during that first decade.

– From the memoir of Drakina Tveit, Lead Librarian of Midtenjord Province

'I am a high priestess of Frøya,' proclaimed Taiga to all that remained of their faithful crew. Tief looked up from his reminiscing and Felgenhauer favoured her with a quizzical look that might have been a frown. It was hard to tell with Felgenhauer, Taiga decided, the woman always seemed to be on the verge of frown. 'And Frøya is the goddess of love, fertility, spring, and good health.' She looked around the squalid common room they had taken over, in the squalid palace. 'And there's not much in the way of good health here.'

'Meaning?' said Tief, rising to his feet.

'Meaning we're out of food.' Taiga crossed the room to Steiner. 'This place is a tomb. It's no place for the living.'

'I need to get to Arkiv,' said Steiner. It was the first time he'd spoken all day. They had done little since Kimi's departure save recover from their wounds and an exhaustion that weighed heavy on them.

'Good. Then we're agreed!' said Taiga cheerfully. 'We'll head to the docks.'

'I didn't agree to anything,' muttered Tief.

'That's nothing new,' replied Taiga. 'Now come on.'

The city, once so full of life, was now a hollow memory. Buildings still loomed over the cobbled streets, but every row of houses had a ruin, every tower was missing its roof or bore the scorch marks of draconic fire. Taiga and Felgenhauer walked ahead of the men. Felgenhauer had picked up a spear as they left the palace, but she used it more as a walking stick than a weapon.

'How are you?' asked Taiga, surprised to discover she cared at all.

'I feel like I'm missing something,' replied Felgenhauer. 'As if one of my hands had been severed in battle. So much of who I was is now gone: the Empire, my rank, my mastery of the arcane. All gone.'

'You sound sad about it.'

'In a way.' Felgenhauer stole a cautious glance at the priestess. 'But I also feel relief. I hated what the Empire was doing. Hated that you and your kin were prisoners beneath the island. Hated that I had to keep up the pretence of a faithful Vigilant. Hated my own complicity.'

They walked together for a time and neither said anything. Taiga was acutely aware the former Matriarch-Commissar Felgenhauer had been her jailer at one time, her oppressor.

'Tief never liked Marozvolk very much,' said Taiga. 'Couldn't bring himself to trust her until close to the end. And then it was too late and she was gone. I don't want things to be like that between you and me.'

'I don't want that either.' Felgenhauer gave a guarded smile. 'I'll do everything I can in the coming months to make things right for the Spriggani.'

'If we don't starve to death first.'

'Perhaps the goddess will grant us one more miracle,' replied Felgenhauer.

The docks were strewn with debris, the houses waterlogged and smashed, but sounds of industry could be heard from two streets away.

'What is that?' asked Tief.

'Hammering,' replied Steiner. 'Someone is hammering wood.' They picked up their pace, advancing along the road until the seafront opened out before them. Tied off at the end of one pier was the *Watcher's Wait*, the dark red frigate that had appeared in Cinderfell all those months ago. Tief laughed long and loud and dirty and even Steiner cracked a smile.

'Romola,' he said quietly. 'Even in the midst of all this, Romola.'

'Hoy there,' shouted a familiar voice from the ship.

'Hoy yourself!' shouted Steiner, sounding a little bit more like himself with each passing moment. Romola marched down the boarding ramp and performed a bow with an outrageous flourish.

'And what are we calling you this week? Dragon rider? Unbroken? Hammersmith? King?' The sometime pirate, sometime storyweaver approached them with a growing expression of surprise. 'You all look terrible.'

'Thanks,' replied Tief. 'We missed you too.' Romola grabbed the Spriggani and hugged him. Then did the same to Taiga. She turned to Steiner and gave him a cautious look.

'Thanks for leaving me in Virag, halfhead,' he said with a scowl.

'Apologies, Your Highness.' Romola performed an ironic bow, then straightened up. Steiner's face broke into a smile and he caught her in hug.

'It's good to see you,' he added. 'Even if you are a terrible halfhead.'

'I am not a terrible halfhead,' replied Romola, smoothing down her jacket. 'I am in truth the very best of halfheads.' A moment passed as her eyes drifted over the people present, understanding dawning on her.

'Where are the rest?' she said quietly. Taiga spent a few moments sharing what had happened, who had been lost, and who had already left the city.

'So when are you leaving?' asked Steiner, clearly not wanting to pick at fresh wounds.

'Not for another week. Replacing the masts is a bastard of a job. My crew are fine sailors but middling shipwrights.'

'Blood and ashes,' said Tief. 'We'll starve before then.'

'We're doing the best we can,' said Romola, 'but . . .' She gestured to the frigate. 'Well, she's not been in the best of shape for a while now.'

Felgenhauer sat down on a nearby crate and sighed. Taiga wanted to do the same, but she feared if she sat down she might lose the little will that bound her together.

'We'd best get to work,' said Steiner. 'What can I do?'

'That's the Steiner I know,' said Taiga.

'This way, Your Highness,' said Romola.

'I'm not going to make myself emperor or king, Romola,' replied Steiner.

'As you wish,' replied the pirate as they walked on to the ship together and headed to the stern. The rail looked out over the sea and the endless miles of Ashen Gulf.

'What's that?' asked Taiga, pointing to the sky.

'It's a dragon,' breathed Steiner. 'And as far as I know, there're only two dragons left in these parts.'

'Kimi came back,' said Tief. 'Kimi came back!' he shouted.

'I sure hope she has some food with her, right.' Romola raised her eyebrows at Taiga. Everyone remained silent as the dragon drew closer, and the sailors downed tools one by one.

'It's Stonvind!' said Tief. The dark grey dragon descended from the cloud-blown skies, coming in low over the *Watcher's Wait*. 'But who's riding my dragon?' Stonvind circled around the dock and then settled down, wingbeats throwing up grit and debris as the creature landed. Taiga smiled, feeling the bright warmth of hope course through her.

'What is it?' asked Felgenhauer. Steiner was already moving back down the ship, almost running down the boarding ramp.

'It seems Frøya may have provided one more miracle,' said Taiga. Felgenhauer held up the blade of her hand to her eyes, squinting to make out the two riders dismounting from Stonvind.

'I see Streig. And he has a fair few saddle bags with him. I hope they're full of food.'

Steiner was running as best he could, his bruised and battered body speeding him along the pier. The second rider met him and threw her arms around him.

'Streig returned,' said Taiga. 'And he brought Kristofine.'

The first ship arrived the following day, bringing supplies from Vostochnyye Lisy. The sailors had a battalion of questions, which Taiga and Felgenhauer answered between them. Steiner was noticeably absent, though none could fault his reasons. Slowly some semblance of normality returned. Houses were resettled as work continued on the *Watcher's Wait*. Taiga led services of thanks and remembrance for those lost during the uprising. But most of all they got on with the business of living, not merely surviving, not fretting that Bittervinge might swoop down at any moment to end them with a single bite. They were living again.

'No more Vigilants,' said one sailor, barely daring to believe such a thing.

'Some will still be out there,' said Felgenhauer, 'but who knows where their loyalty lies now the Emperor is gone.'

'I think we have more immediate problems than Vigilants,' said Taiga, wincing as a score of armed men rounded the corner by the docks. 'Bandits.'

'Leave this to me,' said Felgenhauer, approaching the surly men with a confidence Taiga hadn't seen since before she'd lost her powers.

'Perhaps I should come with you.' Taiga hurried after the Matriarch-Commissar, hands straying to her holy weapons.

The armed men had not broken their stride upon reaching the docks, undeterred by the large number of sailors or the sour look Tief favoured them with from the prow of the *Watcher's Wait*. One of the men marched up to Felgenhauer. He was older than the rest and, Taiga suspected, had a hint of Spriggani blood in him.

'Felgenhauer,' said Taiga quietly, 'you do remember that your mastery of the arcane is—'

'Gone,' replied Felgenhauer as the armed man stopped before her and snapped a crisp salute.

'Matriarch-Commissar Felgenhauer.'

'No ranks today, Tomasz.' Felgenhauer's smile told Taiga everything she needed to know. 'It's over. The Empire is over and my rank along with it. I'm so glad you're alive. All of you.'

'We fell back to the edge of the city and then the gholes appeared. We've been licking our wounds since then. We picked up a few stragglers along the way.' Tomasz grinned. 'I take it you did what you set out to do?'

'Steiner did, with his sister.'

'The Stormtide Prophet,' said Tomasz reverently. 'Is she here? Can we meet her?'

'She's gone.' Felgenhauer's face twisted with grief. Taiga laid a comforting hand on Felgenhauer's forearm.

'Perhaps she has taken her place with the goddesses,' said Taiga.

Felgenhauer gave a bitter laugh. 'I would never have believed you just three months ago, but after everything I've seen, yes, perhaps she has.

'Come on now,' Taiga chided Steiner later that evening. He had holed up on the upper floor of a cottage a street away from the docks wrapped in Kristofine's arms, weaving the tale of what had happened as best he could, though the telling of it cost him greatly. Sharing the story with her, his victory and his losses, had shifted something deep within. At last he could breathe a little easier, hold his head a little higher.

'I'm ready,' replied Steiner.

'Good,' said Taiga. 'And you, Kristofine?' The tavern keeper's daughter from Cinderfell looked tired but ecstatic to be back with her man. Her hand hovered protectively near the knife wound she'd suffered, but she stood tall and firm.

'Let's go and celebrate.'

'More ships have arrived through the day,' explained Taiga, 'and they all want to meet you. Both of you.'

'I hadn't expected them to arrive so quickly,' said Steiner.

'It seems a fortuitous current favoured us.' Taiga's eyes twinkled with amusement. 'The ships have brought food and familiar faces from Arkiv.'

A festival mood had come to the docks. Sailors and captains drank to the end of an Empire that had taken sons and daughters, cousins and nephews. People supped small beer around improvised fire pits, cooking smoked fish and sharing good dark bread. Everywhere Steiner looked he saw men and women talking about the future, voicing their hopes and concerns. Steiner pressed his nose to Kristofine's head and breathed in.

'I am never letting go of you again, not for a moment.'

'That's as good a promise as any,' replied Kristofine. 'But what do you propose for the city?'

'Firstly that we should rename it Port Kjellrunn.'

Taiga nodded and smiled. 'And what else?'

'To break up the Empire.' Steiner said all this slowly, thoughtfully. 'Let the provinces rule themselves as they see fit.' Steiner's aunt joined them from the crowded docks, flanked by her cadre.

'And who will rule Midtenjord now that the Emperor is dead and you've renamed Khlystburg?' asked Felgenhauer.

'You have keen ears,' said Steiner.

'And you haven't answered my question.'

'I was going to ask you. You have the age and the experience, whereas I don't have the wit to read, and rarely do much beyond smashing things with a sledgehammer I can barely lift.'

Felgenhauer took a moment to consult with her sergeant, Tomasz, and he shook his head.

'We'll rule together,' said Felgenhauer. 'Perhaps you could form a council, so none of us get above ourselves.'

'A council. I like that idea.' Steiner smiled at the high priestess. 'Taiga, will you join us? I'm going to need someone to bring the faith back to Vinterkveld.'

Taiga considered this for a moment and smiled back. 'Of course, but I'll need access to a ship.'

'What for?' asked Felgenhauer.

'So I can visit my sister in Shanisrond, of course. She's the only other high priestess in all of Vinterkveld.'

'And Streig can head up the city guard,' added Steiner. 'With Reka and Tomasz.' More and more folk were listening in as Steiner spoke to his circle of friends.

'Fine by me,' added Tomasz, emerging from the crowd with Romola. 'Is there any more brandy?'

'We definitely need more brandy,' slurred Romola.

'And there's my minister for shipping,' said Steiner.

'I'd rather be eaten by sharks,' replied the pirate. 'I'm a captain, and my place is on my ship and out at sea.'

'I suppose you can't have everything your own way,' said Kristofine.

'You're probably right,' conceded Steiner. 'Where is the brandy?'

'It seems you've given this a great deal of consideration,' said Taiga. 'But you've not given my brother anything to do, and he'll get old and fat if left to his own devices.

'Nothing wrong with being old and fat,' replied Tief, appearing at his sister's shoulder. 'And you can bet your boots I've earned it.'

'I can't persuade you to help out?' asked Steiner.

'I'm retired,' said Tief cheerfully. 'But I'm going to need somewhere to live. Perhaps an estate and a title.'

'Anything you want,' said Steiner.

'Anything but Emperor,' added Felgenhauer. 'We're all done with emperors.'

CHAPTER FORTY-EIGHT

Kimi

Many folk in the provinces speak passionately about those times and the great upheaval in Khlystburg, but that was only a part of it. Volkan Karlov's influence extended far and wide, even to the southern reaches of Yamal.

– From the memoir of Drakina Tveit,
Lead Librarian of Midtenjord Province

It was five days after they had set out from Arkiv Island. Kimi sat by the light of a campfire in the Great Forest of Izhoria. The dark pines towered over her, barely visible against the night sky. The evening had brought clouds that bruised the sky in many shades of purple and black. Flodvind had curled herself into a crescent and Kimi rested against the dragon's flank, tired from the saddle yet content.

'Once I'd have been too scared to enter this place,' she said while cooking some of the supplies she'd brought from Arkiv. 'On account of the Grave Wolves. The first time I entered a forest in Izhoria was almost my last.'

Perhaps in time the land will heal itself. Perhaps the arcane force that animates the Grave Wolves will dissipate.

'I hope so,' said Kimi. 'There's much of Vinterkveld that needs to heal.'

Flodvind was taking the journey south from Arkiv slowly. The dragon's constitution was formidable, but the wounds she had endured were many. She was not alone in this; Kimi woke each morning to a choir of aching muscles singing a litany of pain.

This is not so much travelling as hunting in a southerly direction, admitted the azure dragon. She crossed her paws and laid her great head on them, cat-like in the darkness of the forest. The firelight danced across her scales, her horns etched in gold against black.

'A girl has to eat,' replied Kimi. 'And heal. I'm fairly exhausted after Khlystburg. I can't begin to imagine how you must feel.'

My wounds are beyond counting but mostly I feel free. Free of the Emperor, free of Vladibogdan. Kimi felt the dragon shift behind her, trying to get comfortable. *Does it not bother you that we are taking so long to return to your homeland?*

'We'll return when we're good and ready,' replied Kimi. 'For once I don't feel as if I have a world's worth of responsibility on my shoulders. I can take my time and enjoy things. Enjoy flying. Enjoy cooking this meal, this conversation.'

You have been through much. Losing Namarii . . .

'Was hard. I'm still grieving him.' The pain of the dragon's passing was still unbearably close to her skin, and many were the times tears had been her companion as they flew south. 'And there's more to come. But not tonight.'

They spent another five days in the southern skies. Slowly Izhoria gave way to the river Bestnulim, like a sliver of silver between the two countries. The memory of fleeing with Marozvolk resurfaced and Kimi took a deep breath to ward off the sadness.

There are a great many people below us and the buildings are very colourful. The dragon began descending, circling the encampment below.

'It seems the Xhantsulgarat is still here. I'd have thought Tsen would have moved on, keen to enforce his rule far and wide.'

Moved? How does a town move?

'My people live in tents for the most part.'

Flodvind circled lower. The people below ran for their homes. The shadow of the dragon raced across the encampment and Kimi's anticipation raced with it.

Are you sure you are ready to face your brother?

'I think we're about to find out.'

The appearance of a blue dragon on the southern shores of the Bestnulim River produced predictable results. The brief stampede of panicking people ceased once they realized the great reptile was content to sit patiently on its haunches beside its rider.

You are simply going to wait?

'It's better if they come to me,' replied Kimi. 'Else they think we're invading.'

There are only two of us.

'True enough, but they don't have a dragon.' Kimi looked over her shoulder at the river, where a handful of fishermen stared with unabashed horror. Kimi waved cheerfully, which only served to confuse the men more. In time a delegation arrived from among the clusters and rows of colourful tents. An older man carrying a staff walked at the centre of the officials and representatives. Kimi recognized him; he was taller than her and more gaunt than she remembered.

'Darga Bestam,' said Kimi in her mother tongue when the delegation had ventured as close as they would dare. She bowed her head and clasped her right fist in her left hand. The big man smiled.

'We're not so formal this far north, my child. You may call me Chulu-Agakh.'

'With respect, I'm not a child,' replied Kimi, remembering the first time she'd met the Darga.

'So I see,' said Chulu-Agakh with a look of amusement. His eyes wandered to Flodvind and took a moment to revel in her splendour. 'Now let me try to guess,' said the Darga of Bestam. 'Could it be you have come to join the tribe by Ereg Bestnulim? Or perhaps you have a dispute with one of my people? Or are you a long-lost relative, come back from abroad?'

'You have a good memory,' said Kimi with a smile. 'I think you know why I'm here.'

'I think I do. Come this way.' He gestured to the centre of the city of tents.

'I'm glad to see you alive,' said Kimi as she fell into step beside the old Darga. A few of the officials in the delegation raised eyebrows in surprise; others muttered to each other in shocked whispers.

'And I you, Kimi Enkhtuya,' replied Chulu-Agakh. 'It feels like a very long time since you left for Izhoria that night.' Behind them Flodvind paced through the encampment with the grace of a hunting cat. A fresh surge of panic passed through the Xhantsulgarat and the officials stumbled as they realized a dragon followed close behind. 'Your choice of companions has changed considerably,' added the Darga, doing a fine job of hiding his alarm.

'My Spriggani friends are still alive,' said Kimi. 'But not all of us survived Izhoria.'

'Please accept my condolences for those you lost, Your Highness.'

'My brother won't appreciate you using that form of address with me.' Kimi cast a wary eye on the tents ahead. Royal guards stood outside, hands on weapons, faces betraying their fear.

'Your brother doesn't have a blue dragon, Your Highness. And I think it about time we abolished the tradition that women can't be Xhan.'

'Strangely enough I was thinking the same thing.' Kimi took a breath and rolled her shoulders. 'Can I borrow your staff?' Chulu-Agakh looked confused and bowed before offering her the length of heavy wood.

'Tsen-Baina Jet!' bellowed Kimi. 'Worthless, treacherous filth! Drag your sorry carcass into the daylight where I may see you.'

I had wondered about the plan. Flodvind snorted a plume of soot. *I see you have chosen the subtle approach.*

'He exiled me the last time I was here,' replied Kimi, not taking her eyes from the entrance to the royal tent. 'The time for subtlety is over.'

The shocked silence signalled that those inside the royal tent were unsure who had arrived or what trouble they brought. One of the guards disappeared inside.

'Are you sure the staff is the right tool for the job you have in mind, Highness?' asked Chulu-Agakh.

'I'm sure,' replied Kimi. 'I've never been so sure of anything in my life.'

Finally Tsen-Baina Jet emerged from the royal tent, adopting a look of outrage, though the pretence slipped as Flodvind reared up, casting a shadow over the Xhan and the handful of royal guards surrounding him.

'How dare you insult me in the seat of my power! You are nothing but a vagabond and a—'

'Shut your mouth,' said Kimi, stepping forward. 'You poisoned our father in a deal with the Solmindre Empire. A deal that would keep our people safe and put you on the throne.'

'Lies!' spat Tsen. 'Where is your proof?'

'I have none,' admitted Kimi. 'Save for the word of a renegade Vigilant now gone to his rest.'

'Take your reptile and crawl back to the wretched town that spawned you,' replied Tsen. The rebuke, while well crafted, faltered in his mouth and Kimi knew he was struggling to compose himself.

'It is clear to me you are not fit to rule,' said Kimi. 'And so I have come to teach my little brother a lesson.'

'You are no sister of mine!' Tsen-Baina Jet gestured to his soldiers. 'Kill her immediately.' The royal guards started forward before a low growling deterred them from taking another step. The terrible sound could be felt in the soles of everyone's boots, in their bones and in their hearts. Flodvind lowered her head and yawned, revealing ranks of blade-like teeth. 'I said kill her!' shouted Tsen, his face flushed with anger. The guards turned to their Xhan with looks of fear and apology, but not one of them drew their weapon.

'I said kill her,' screamed her brother again. One of the soldiers jerked forward, training and obedience overcoming common sense. He lunged forward with sword drawn but Kimi smacked his sword hand with the staff. The weapon spun from his grasp and the soldier swore and clutched his numb fingers.

'Remember this day,' she said to the guard. 'This is the day Kimi Enkhtuya spared you.' The soldier backed away, head bowed in shame. 'Perhaps my brother can summon the courage to fight his own battles?'

'You?' Tsen sneered. 'Challenge me? Only a Darga may challenge a sitting Xhan. You of all people should know that!'

'So you admit I'm your sister then?'

Tsen-Baina Jet looked at the delegation as if he'd just been dealt a mortal wound. The officials and advisers shared knowing glances and many shook their heads with disapproval writ large across their elderly faces.

'I, Chulu-Agakh, Darga of Bestam, challenge Xhan Tsen-Baina Jet. I name Kimi Enkhtuya as my champion.'

More and more of the encampment drew close, a wordless wonder in their eyes, barely daring to believe what was unfolding.

'This is horseshit,' said Tsen. 'No one has challenged a sitting Xhan in over a hundred years. The custom is ancient, antiquated.'

'I second the challenge,' said a member of the delegation. He was a grim-faced old man in red robes and heavy-lidded eyes.

'As do I,' said a woman in vibrant blue silk robes, one of the watercleansers. Tsen-Baina Jet turned his back on them and made to enter his tent when the growling began again. The Xhan froze in his tracks.

You have been challenged according to the custom of your people. Either fight the challenge or step down. Flodvind extended her wings, and the shadow she cast grew until she eclipsed the setting sun.

'And when I win, then what?' Tsen threw up his hands. 'Surely you'll avenge your rider and murder me in a heartbeat?'

You mean if, not when. And if you win I will honour the challenge and depart.

Tsen looked from the azure dragon to Kimi, and then at the three officials who had trapped him in this predicament.

'So be it.' The Xhan shrugged off a ceremonial robe and kicked off his jewelled slippers. 'I will fight.' He drew his sword and his hand drifted towards his dagger for moment before he thought better of it. 'This won't take long.'

Kimi opened her mouth to reply but Tsen charged at a flat sprint. The delegates and officials fell over themselves in their haste to avoid the Xhan's fury. Kimi circled the staff above her head, dropped to one knee, and deftly swept the feet from under her brother. He smacked against the dust road, one side of his face and shoulder hitting the ground first. A gasp sounded from the crowd, part shock, part wincing from the force of the blow.

'I think this will take longer than you think, little brother,' replied Kimi as Tsen staggered to his feet.

CHAPTER FORTY-NINE

Steiner

Despite their differences Kimi and Steiner ruled their provinces with a deep trust and a wisdom far beyond their years. At least that's what people said. In truth the wisdom came from simply listening to those around them and not trying to do everything alone.

– From the memoir of Drakina Tveit,
Lead Librarian of Midtenjord Province

Steiner rode at the head of a column of horses. His greatcoat, which had seemed prudent when setting out from Port Kjellrunn, now stifled him in the close and sultry air of Izhoria.

'It's good to be travelling again,' he said. 'Sitting through council meetings really doesn't suit me.'

'And yet you've been attending them faithfully for ten years,' replied Kristofine with a knowing smile.

'Ten years already?' He shook his head incredulously.

'Some might even say you're good at it,' added Kristofine.

'Never say that again. Please.'

'Besides,' continued Kristofine as if she hadn't heard him. 'Felgenhauer is more than capable of running the province for a month in your absence.'

The horses continued to plod along and Steiner stared up at the sky, where Stonvind glided a few miles ahead. Ten years. Had it really been so long? Ten years since losing his father. A decade since Kjellrunn's ascension. And through it all he'd missed Silverdust's reassuring presence.

'This is going to be an emotional reunion,' said Steiner. 'The dragons have barely seen each other since the Empire fell.'

'And you?' said Kristofine. 'You and Kimi didn't always see eye to eye.'

'That's true enough.' Steiner remembered how angry she'd been with him when they'd first met on Vladibogdan, then at Virag, and finally in Khlystburg. 'But she invited me here in the spirit of reconciliation and cooperation. New trade agreements, regular contact between the temples of Frøya and Frejna, a way to keep Yamal's more militaristic ambitions under control.'

'Trade and negotiation were never your strong suit,' said Kristofine. 'Even you admit that you got where you are by hitting things.'

Steiner looked down at the stone sledgehammer hanging from the saddle. His fingertips brushed the handle affectionately. 'That's why I brought you.' He grinned. 'You were always better at talking. Remember those brigands in Karelina?'

'How could I forget?' Kristofine rolled her eyes. 'You only tell our children that story every night before they go to sleep.'

'Oh.'

'Did you think they wouldn't tell me? Children ask questions.'

'Come on.' Steiner shook the reins. 'I think I can see it.'

The town of Volknulim, as it was known, lay all around the base of a hill. It was a strange place to Steiner's eyes, a melange of wooden houses on stilts, tents pitched at the base of the rise, and the occasional stone tower. The hill itself was home to a pale building flanked by young trees.

'I can see the Temple of Frøya,' remarked Kristofine as they approached the outskirts of the quirky town. 'But where is the Temple of Frejna?'

'We'll have to ask Xhan Enkhtuya,' said Steiner, trying on Kimi's official title for the first time. Overhead Stonvind released a huge jet of fire and circled around the town. Flodvind chased him across the sky, vast blue wings beating hard.

'Those two seem pleased to see each other,' said Kristofine.

'I just hope they don't accidentally set fire to anyone in their excitement,' added Steiner frowning.

The town was equal parts meandering streams and homes. The roads, such as they were, consisted of linked wooden piers. A lot of hard work and planning had been lavished on the town despite the unfavourable location.

'It's a far cry from Port Kjellrunn,' said Kristofine.

'And yet new people are arriving all the time,' said Steinei, pointing to a caravan approaching from the west.

Kimi waited on a stone platform with a handful of retainers. A tent large enough for Steiner's entire column of horses stood behind her, rich purple fabric rippling in the breeze. Kimi herself was attired in a deep turquoise that complemented the colour of her skin and hair. Steiner dismounted and bowed in the Yamal way, right fist pressed into his left palm, eyes lowered.

'Xhan Enkhtuya, it has been much too long.' Steiner did not look up, waiting for the Xhan's response.

'Thank you for making the journey.' Kimi stepped forward. The years had been kind to her. She was still the tall, strong woman he recollected from the forges of Vladibogdan, yet there was a softness to her voice that had not been there before. 'And for bringing your gorgeous wife.'

Kristofine bowed and smiled. 'I could hardly pass up the invitation to see the rebirth of Izhoria.'

'Rebirth.' Kimi turned to her retainers with a wry smile. 'I suppose it is.' She turned to a handsome woman stood just behind her. 'Allow me to introduce my wife, Sanakh-oi.'

Steiner bowed again, noticing that Sanakh-oi bore more than a passing resemblance to Marozvolk. It seemed Xhan Enkhtuya had a preference.

'I am Chulu-Agakh,' said an elderly man clutching a tall staff. 'Please come this way for refreshments.'

Kimi looked out over the town. The lanterns resembled fireflies in the distance, and cooking smells drifted up the hill to where they stood. The cool evening breeze was welcome and Steiner was content that for once there were no landowners pushing for new laws to be passed and no dignitaries looking for trade concessions.

'This is incredible,' said Steiner. 'To have created a settlement from nothing. You should be very proud.'

'I am,' replied Kimi. 'Though I had plenty of help and goodwill. The best part of two tribes followed me up here when I first set out. We've tripled in size since then.'

'Why here? A swamp is hardly the most convenient place to found a town.' Steiner approached a long squat stone bench and made to sit down.

'Don't!' Kimi reached out to him. Steiner froze and looked anew at what he had assumed was a seat in the evening light.

'What is this?'

'Once the stones formed a shrine to Frøya on this very hillside. Taiga hoped the shrine might protect us from Veles, but in the end we had to stand and fight.'

'You fought Veles here?' Steiner looked over his shoulder. 'In this very place, on this hilltop?'

'Yes.' Kimi followed the direction of his gaze to the recently finished temple and the trees that had been planted around it. The wind moved through the branches and the sound of whispering leaves filled the evening air. 'I fought him and killed him, along with thirty-odd gholes who hunted us. I honestly doubted any of us were going to survive, but Taiga was adamant the goddess was with us. It was the remade Ashen Torment that saved us.'

Steiner glanced down at the stones. 'And the shrine?'

'The shrine is now a sarcophagus.' Kimi approached until she stood alongside him. 'Marozvolk died on this hill, fighting for me, fighting to take down the Empire. Even in the jaws of Veles himself she didn't stop fighting.'

'So you built this town to honour her. Volknulim. What does it mean?'

'An abbreviation.' Kimi gestured, searching for the words. '"Tears for the wolf" is the closest translation.'

'You lost so many people,' said Steiner. 'Your father, your brother—'

'My brother.' Kimi laughed bitterly. 'It's Taiga and Tief I miss the most, though they visit once a year, supposedly on temple business.' Her face brightened at the thought.

'I meant the people who died,' added Steiner.

'Marozvolk was a hard lesson for me. And then there was Namarii. I only knew him a matter of weeks but we shared a close bond.'

'War has a way of making everything so much more intense,' admitted Steiner. 'Though it seems like a very long time ago now.'

'People tell me that time heals all things.' Kimi tilted her head to one side thoughtfully. 'But I think of grief like a crow. Sometimes I see it at a distance and pay it no mind; other times I find it perched on my shoulder and there's no avoiding it.'

'Se and Venter,' replied Steiner. 'Watching and waiting.' They strolled around the top of the hill, away from

Marozvolk's resting place, the quiet evening peaceful and companionable.

'So, there's a question I need to ask you,' said Kimi finally.

'The Ashen Blades disappeared along with Silverdust,' replied Steiner. 'As far as I know. Or perhaps they're still in the palace. We sealed the whole building off. It's a tomb now, a monument to the Emperor's folly.'

'That's not why I asked you here,' said Kimi, 'though not entirely unrelated.'

'What is it?'

'When I killed Bittervinge I used an Ashen Blade. It conferred all of his life force to me. His mastery over the arcane was channelled through the blade.' She looked down at the palms of hands. 'I don't think I've aged a day since.'

'You're only thirty, Kimi. It's not as if you've reached your twilight years.'

'And you. You must see it. Kristofine ages normally while you are—'

'The same scarred and wiry, hard-headed blacksmith's son I always was.' Steiner grinned. 'I just have a bigger house these days.'

'Not just the same but *exactly* the same. You've not aged a day. Of course you hold yourself differently now, walk differently, but it's still you.'

'Felgenhauer had me take lessons. Said I looked like a brawler squaring up for a fight every time I entered court.'

'Chulu-Agakh had me take the same lessons,' admitted Kimi with a slightly embarrassed smile, which quickly faded. 'Steiner, I never thought I'd find myself asking this question, but when do you think we'll die?'

'And here I was thinking this would be a cheerful state visit, celebrating our prospering provinces.'

'Steiner, I'm serious. You killed the Emperor because his

unnaturally long life was an aberration, but aren't we just the same?'

'The Emperor killed to stayed alive, and he kept killing. We killed one person so that others could live.'

'You killed one person; I killed a dragon.'

'Same thing. If we were still using the Ashen Blades ten years later' – Steiner shrugged – 'then we'd be no better than Volkan Karlov.'

Kimi sighed with relief and some of the tension went out of her for the first time since Steiner had arrived. 'Thank you,' she said after a moment to reflect. 'I needed to hear that, and I needed to hear it from you specifically.'

'I can't say I'm looking forward to watching everyone grow old around me,' said Steiner. 'Well, everyone but you perhaps.'

'I'd like you to make this a habit,' replied Kimi. 'Visit once a year. I'm going to need a familiar face if I'm to keep myself safe from madness.'

'Madness.' Steiner shook his head incredulously. 'What's madness is that you never finished telling me how you defeated your brother in single combat.'

'It doesn't have the ending you're hoping for,' Kimi replied.

'Few stories do these days,' replied Steiner. 'But tell me anyway.'

CHAPTER FIFTY

Kimi

The Great Split, as it is known in Yamal, was a period of shocking change for a country and culture with such deeply held traditions. The consequences of that day will echo down the ages long after I am gone, perhaps even long after Kimi and Steiner themselves.

– From the memoir of Drakina Tveit, Lead Librarian of Midtenjord Province

'You are not my sister!' The Xhan spat blood in the dust and performed an impressive but ultimately pointless flourish with his scimitar. Kimi lunged forward, swinging hard, but Tsen ducked under her strike and lashed out, the steel flashing in the sunlight. The tip of the sword snagged against the shoulder guard of her armour but drew no blood.

'You're faster than you used to be,' she conceded through gritted teeth, already raising the staff to block his next strike.

'While you got slow.' His blade struck again, knocked aside by her staff. 'And fat.' His sword careered from the angle of her block and Kimi backed away before feinting for his knee and driving the end of the staff up towards his elbow. Tsen didn't bother to parry, just sidestepped beyond the range of the staff and grinned.

'There wasn't much food to get fat on in the forges of Vladibogdan,' said Kimi, circling him at a distance. 'Or in Khlystburg when we hunted Bittervinge.'

'Lies. You are nothing more than a summer-meet charlatan.'

Kimi swung again, her hands on the middle of the staff. She stepped forward, then changed her attack and brought the other end to bear, slamming against Tsen's parry. They leaned in close to one another, his sword biting into the stout wood of the staff.

'You should not have come back,' he whispered. Kimi lashed out with a foot and kicked his knee to one side, sending him off balance, then followed up with a strike to the back of the head. He stumbled and turned the fall into a forward roll, but dropped his sword in the process. Kimi lunged forward to finish the fight but Tsen unsheathed the dagger and threw it. Her hasty parry was not fast enough and the blade opened a cut along the side of her skull, stinging bitterly.

'Damn you, Tsen!' She pressed her palm to the stinging pain and winced bitterly. The Xhan retrieved his sword and pressed one hand to the back of his head where Kimi had struck him.

'No, Kimi, damn you. Our father never loved us, never loved me. I doubt if he even loved our mother. He sent you away to that wretched island and I had to stay here, withering under his disapproving glances. No longer! I am the Xhan now and you can take the knee or die.'

Chulu-Agakh made a tutting noise and the officials all shook their heads with expressions of disgust and despair.

'So you admit that she is your sister,' said the Darga of Bestam quietly. Tsen glowered at the old man but said nothing.

'You shouldn't have poisoned him,' replied Kimi, changing her grip on the staff.

'Poison?' Tsen's face contorted with anger. 'The old man was poison incarnate. Why do you care what method I used?'

'There's no honour in poison, Tsen.' Kimi circled him, never dropping her guard. 'That was never our way. The Yamal do not stoop to poisoning.'

'Honour?' For a moment Tsen resembled nothing so much as her little brother, close to tears after receiving yet another cruel rebuke from their father years earlier. 'There's no honour any more, Kimi. Not for the likes of us.'

'Tsen-Baina Jet, you by your own words admit you killed a sitting Xhan, not by honourable challenge, but by the low ways of poison. You are no longer fit to be Xhan and I exile you from these lands.'

'On whose authority?' Tsen broke into a mocking smile. 'Yours?'

Kimi threw the staff like a javelin and the heavy wood slammed into Tsen's forehead, knocking him off his feet. Kimi was on him before his eyes fluttered open.

'Kimi, I—' But anything else he said was knocked from his mouth by the furious fists of his sister. Blow after bloody blow.

'Shut up, Tsen. Shut up!' Kimi stood up, her knuckles stinging from the beating she had doled out. 'It's over. You're done here.'

Why did you spare him? asked Flodvind three nights later as they sat on the southern bank of the river Bestnulim. A procession of fishermen had offered portions of their catch that day, but Kimi knew the azure dragon was still hungry; the sound of her rumbling stomach was testament to that.

'Because there are worse things than death.'

How so? Surely death is the ultimate insult. A way to silence one's enemies completely.

'The spirits of the dead did not pass on at Vladibogdan.

They were bound by the Ashen Torment, forced to work in servitude for eternity. At least until Steiner released them.'

But there is no Ashen Torment to bind your brother.

'No, but being cast out from one's homeland, that's a cruel punishment. Knowing you may never see your people again, or feel the weight of familiar coins, is a torture. Missing a particular turn of phrase or hearing your mother tongue spoken all around you, that's worse. A daily grief, a sadness without end.'

Vladibogdan appears to have had a profound effect on you.

'It has.' Kimi looked north, across the river to Izhoria.

What will you do now?

'The tribal Xhans are already squabbling among themselves, deciding who will take power. Many are saying that the role of High Xhan is not for a woman.'

'But not everyone feels the same way,' said Chulu-Agakh from over her shoulder.

'You move quietly, old man.' Kimi smiled. 'You might even have killed me if your intentions were different.'

'May I remind you that you're in conversation with a dragon? Such an assassination attempt would be short-lived.' Chulu-Agakh leaned on his staff and looked out across the river.

'I'm not sure I want to rule,' said Kimi after a pause. 'Not here. There are too many painful memories.'

'And if you do not rule here?' Chulu-Agakh looked down at his feet. 'Then where?'

Kimi's mind drifted to the misty hill in Izhoria, where she had fashioned a sarcophagus for Marozvolk from the stones of an old shrine. 'I think I know the place,' she replied with a deep calmness. 'But there's no one there to rule.'

'Perhaps you should make it known you are leaving Yamal.' Chulu-Agakh turned to leave. 'You may be surprised who comes with you.'

CHAPTER FIFTY-ONE

Steiner

In time they pulled down the old Imperial Palace. Half the stone had been given to the poorer districts of the city to build new housing, though Steiner had had to argue long and hard to make it so. The other half of the stone was sent south on a series of caravans. It would provide foundations for the ever-growing city of Volknulim in Izhoria.

'You'd think I was pulling the teeth from the councillors' mouths and throwing them into the sea,' said Steiner. 'It's my own fault. I should never have asked for elected officials. Democracy is a pain in my arse.' He revealed a long-suffering smile to make it clear he was joking. 'I could have made myself Emperor and ruled without committee.'

'I've heard it said committees are where good ideas go to die,' replied Kimi with the same long-suffering smile. They sat on a stone bench that overlooked the gardens at the rear of his town house, a town house that had seen children grow up into adults and have children of their own. Cries of delight and breathless laughter could be heard from the hedge maze, which nestled among the trees beyond the long and lush lawn. The summer sun had yet to dip beneath the horizon and Port Kjellrunn was alive with the sounds of merrymaking and people taking the evening air.

'And to think, I used to hate cities.' Kimi had arrived on horseback without an entourage the day before. At some point over the many years she had simply tired of pomp and ceremony, keen to make her own way in the world. 'I am grateful for the stone.' She smiled and sipped her tea before crossing her legs neatly. 'You've helped make a ramshackle town of tents and stilt houses into something that might actually be mistaken for a city.'

Xhan Enkhtuya had always been the most serious-minded and stoic of souls, but a wry edge of humour had insisted itself upon her down the long decades. Steiner suspected it was the only way to keep one's self from despair.

'It's good to see you again,' replied Steiner. 'Though unexpected. The cynic in me is curious if all is well in Izhoria?'

'It's fine,' she replied, but the sigh that followed those words signalled anything but. Steiner waited. Once he would have pressed for an answer, but he'd learned that the truth usually emerged in good time if one has the patience to wait. Presently it did. 'I suppose I'm lonely, if you can believe such a thing. I have children and grandchildren just like you.'

'Except our children are now in their sixties and seventies,' added Steiner.

'I had forty-seven glorious years with Sanakh-oi and I treasured every one of them. She was was the most incredible, kind, patient woman I have ever met.

'She'd need to be being married to you,' said Steiner.

'Shut up.' Kimi frowned. 'Where was I? But you and I . .' Another long sigh. 'You barely look older than forty.'

'I'm not sure you've changed that much at all,' replied Steiner. 'You carry your years in your eyes.'

'I turned one hundred in the spring,' said Kimi, all trace of humour drained from her face. 'I didn't celebrate, I drank a bottle of the best wine I could find and remembered all the funerals I've been to recently. Everyone I knew from back then has gone to their rest.'

'Funerals.' Steiner sipped his tea and stared into the distance where his great-grandchildren were emerging from the hedge maze covered in grass stains and mud. They marched up the garden, giggling and bickering, barely paying attention to the statue nearby. 'I had a pang of sympathy for Volkan Karlov the other day,' he added, rising to his feet.

'What?'

'I know, hear me out.' Steiner gestured Kimi follow him down the garden. 'Walk with me.' The old Xhan did as she was asked and they began a leisurely stroll towards the statue. 'Before the Emperor died he told me that death wasn't the worst thing that could happen to a person. I assumed at the time he meant the Ashen Torment and the power it had over cinderwraiths. All those lost souls bound in eternal service. Now I've had time to think on it . . .'

'Eighty years' worth of thinking,' said Kimi.

'I realize that a long life isn't always a blessing.' Steiner felt the familiar tug of grief as Kimi took a moment to study the statue.

'Is this new?'

'It's been here thirty years, but you've not seen the garden for a while.'

'Thirty years. Has it been so long?'

'Very much so,' replied Steiner.

'It's beautiful.'

'And so was she. Inside and out.' Steiner brushed the statue of Kristofine with his fingertips.

'You'll be with her again one day,' said Kimi. Steiner wanted to smile, but he'd heard the sentiment too often.

'I know. But I keep asking myself when?'

'How about tonight?'

It was close to midnight as the old friends wended their way through the former city of Khlystburg. The roads were good and wide and mostly clean. Teams of young people hurried along the streets, lighting lanterns at the street corners.

'Hard to believe this was once the capital of the Empire,' said Kimi.

'There are people alive now that will never know of the suffering caused by Volkan Karlov,' replied Steiner. 'That's what I try and hold on to when I feel bleak. That and the treaty with the dragons.'

'And new temples in every province,' added Kimi.

'We did well, didn't we?'

'Anything was going to be better than Volkan Karlov.'

'Even so, I could never have imagined living in such a place after growing up in Cinderfell.'

The former Khlystburg had shrugged off its name and grim history and adopted the name Port Kjellrunn with a deep fervour. The city's namesake, while not officially recognized as a goddess, was revered all the same, and in some cases more vocally, especially by sailors.

'Where are you taking me, Kimi?'

'To the docks, of course.'

They walked in silence and nodded amiably to the sailors and dockers who stumbled home, cheerful with drink. No one recognized them; no one in Port Kjellrunn expected to see living legends in their midst. Finally they arrived at the pier where Romola had finally repaired her masts all those years ago.

'The shrine,' said Steiner with the hint of a smile.

'Let's pray to her.'

'What?' Steiner stared after Kimi as she walked to the end

of the pier, where a single-storey but very ornate stone building had been erected in honour of the Stormtide Prophet. 'Kimi? I'm not going to pray to my sister.'

He caught up with her a moment later, just as she was passing over the threshold of the shrine. Two statues waited inside: a young woman looking defiantly into the distance, attended by another woman kneeling at her feet.

'I don't think I saw Trine kneel once,' said Kimi, 'but I still remember the terrible language she used.'

'What happened to her?' asked Steiner.

'I don't know. Your sister ascended without telling us.'

Scenes from the Stormtide Prophet's conquest of Khlystburg had been engraved on one wall. Steiner was shown on another, locked in combat with the Emperor, while Kimi was depicted riding a dragon holding a simple knife above her head.

'I'd forgotten about all of this.' Steiner gestured around. 'All this history.'

'I think it's time I too passed into history,' said Kimi, her expression gentle, resigned but at peace.

'I'm not taking my own life,' said Steiner. 'To have fought so hard just to end up killing myself makes no sense.'

'There would be no shame in it for ones like us, but it would be difficult to explain to others.' Kimi knelt down and produced a candle, a single fish, and a hare from a small bag she'd carried. 'But I propose a different way.'

'I'm ready.' Steiner knelt down beside her.

'To Kjellrunn, goddess of the Ashen Gulf and all the seas beyond, I make this offering.' Kimi placed the fish at the foot of the statue. 'To Frøya, goddess of life and fertility and love in all of Vinterkveld, I offer this hare. And to Frejna, goddess of winter, wisdom, and death in this and all realms, I light this candle so you may in turn light our way into the world beyond.'

Steiner wasn't sure why he felt compelled to do so, but he tilted his head back until he was looking straight up. The shrine had been designed with an aperture in the roof and the stars above looked down through the opening at Kimi's improvised ceremony, her simple plea.

'We have lived long and loved long and fought long, but now we wish to take our places with those who have gone before,' continued Kimi. 'We invoke Frøya and Frejna and Kjellrunn to make this so.'

Steiner reached out and took Kimi's hand, surprised to find that his cheeks were wet with tears. Kimi caught his eye and nodded. For a moment they knelt in the shrine and Steiner imagined the candlelight somehow grew brighter and warmer.

'It's working,' whispered Kimi, looking upwards. Steiner followed her gaze. The starlight that shone through the aperture was now a column of silver, bright as any sunbeam. A figure drifted down to them, radiating light, one hand outstretched.

Steiner, Kimi, it's time to go.

'Silverdust?' Steiner could hardly believe it but there was no mistaking that voice.

'It's time to go,' repeated Kimi, smiling through her tears. The silver light grew brighter and brighter still.

In years to come many sailors and dockers would recount to anyone who would listen how they had seen Steiner, Father of the Twelve Provinces, and Kimi, Xhan of Izhoria and Dragonmother. They would say how the two friends had gone to the shrine, the very same shrine at the end of the pier in Port Kjellrunn. And though, despite speculation, no one could say for sure what happened, none could deny the pillar of silver light that had reached down from the heavens to take Steiner and Kimi to the afterlife. Nothing was found in the shrine following that holy night, but it is said the statue of Kristofine in Steiner's gardens appeared to smile more than she had before.

Acknowledgements

So here we are at the end of another trilogy. Thank you for following Steiner and Kjellrunn through the highs and lows of bringing the Solmindre Empire to its end.

Many thanks first and foremost to Vicky Leech, my editor, and to Natasha Bardon, publisher at Harper Voyager.

I'm very grateful to Julie Crisp, my agent. She has provided invaluable support over the last three-and-a-half-years.

As ever, thanks to my faithful friends and fellow authors, Jen Williams and Andrew Reid.

And last, but certainly not least, thanks to my lovely wife, and to Neville and Luna (who can't *actually* read the acknowledgements on account of being cats). While they certainly didn't speed up the process, the journey would have been a dour one without such good companions.